Short Prose
Volume One

Dumitru Tsepeneag

SHORT PROSE

VOLUME ONE

Translated from the Romanian by Alistair Ian Blyth

DALKEY ARCHIVE PRESS
McLean, IL / Dublin

Originally published by Editura Tracus Arte as *Proza scurtă* in 2014.

Copyright © by Dumitru Tsepeneag, 2019.

Translation copyright © by Alistair Ian Blyth, 2019

First Dalkey Archive edition, 2019.

CIP Data available upon request.

Dalkey Archive Press

McLean, IL / Dublin

Co-funded by the
Creative Europe Programme
of the European Union

Printed on permanent/durable acid-free paper.

www.dalkeyarchive.com

Contents

Waiting (1971)

Shorter unpublished texts

Short Prose
Volume 1

Dumitru Tsepeneag

Dumitru Tsepeneag and Oneirism
by Alistair Ian Blyth

DUMITRU TSEPENEAG'S WORK spans more than five decades and two languages, Romanian and French, and includes not only fiction written under his own name, but also a novel by one of his characters, his fictional/oneiric alter ego and anagrammatic authorial proxy, Ed Pastenague.

Tsepeneag's first short stories were "written for the desk drawer" in the late 1950s, a period when it would have been impossible for him to publish texts which, rather like the short stories and parables of Kafka, constructed their own ambiguous, oneiric world, making little direct reference to the "real world," which is to say, the social, political, historical reality of the time, and even less so the "socialist reality" as officially defined and prescribed by the Stalinist ideology of the Romanian People's Republic. In 1959, he met then-unpublished poet Leonid Dimov (1926–1987) and together they debated and developed the premises of what they called "structural oneirism," a theory and practice of writing that takes the dream as its *criterion* (Tsepeneag) or *legislation* (Dimov), and that *lucidly* creates a *reality analogous to the dream.* During a period of "clandestinity" and "theoretical gestation"[1] stretching from 1959 to 1964, Tsepeneag and Dimov theorized oneirism in opposition to the

---

[1] Dumitru Tsepeneag, "Tentativa onirică, după război" (The Post-War Oneiric Endeavour), the author's translation of an article published in *Les Lettres Nouvelles*, No. 1, February 1974. Dumitru Țepeneag, *Opere 5. Texte teoretice, interviuri, note critice, "șotroane." 1966–1989* (Bucharest: Editura Tracus Arte, 2017), 181.

automatic writing and description of extratextual dreams prac-
ticed by the surrealists. (It should be noted that Surrealism had
been one of the main Romanian avant-garde movements in the
period up to the communist takeover of Romania.) As Tsepeneag
was later jokingly to remark, "oneirism descended from the ape
of Surrealism."[2]

In 1965, after the death of hard-line Stalinist Gheorghe
Gheorghiu-Dej, Nicolae Ceaușescu became General Secretary
of the Romanian Workers' Party, retitling it the Romanian
Communist Party and renaming the country the Romanian
Socialist Republic. In this transition period prior to the full-
blown Ceaușescu personality cult and socialist-nationalist dic-
tatorship, there was a short-lived, partial, and ultimately decep-
tive cultural "thaw," which came to an abrupt end in July 1971,
when the dictator returned from a state visit to China and
North Korea and issued his so-called "July Theses," the signal
for a re-entrenchment of totalitarianism and a "mini cultural
revolution."[3] It was during this brief "thaw" that Tsepeneag
was able to publish three collections of short stories, which, as
well as new work, also included texts dating back to the 1950s:
Exercises (1966), *Cold* (1967), and *Waiting* (1971).[4] The stories
in the three collections contain dream images, narratives, and
situations which, subtly altered or grotesquely distorted, recur
obsessively, hauntingly, but also ironically, self-consciously, even
comically, throughout Tsepeneag's subsequent novels, transform-
ing his work as a whole into a single, interconnected text intri-
cately structured according to its own overarching oneiric logic:

[2] "Grupul oniric a coborît din maimuța suprarealismului," interview with Dumitru
Tsepeneag published in *Amfiteatru*, Nos. 9–10, September 1990, in Leonid Dimov,
Dumitru Țepeneag, *Momentul oniric* [The Oneiric Moment], ed. Corin Braga (Bucharest:
Cartea Românească, 1997), 246–253.

[3] The "July Theses" was the shorter, unofficial title of the more cumbersome *Proposals for
Measures to Improve the Politico-Ideological and Marxist-Leninist Educational Activity of Party
Members and All Working People*, which Ceaușescu presented to the Executive Committee
of the Romanian Communist Party on 6 July 1971.

[4] *Exerciții* (Bucharest: Editura pentru Literatură, 1966), 126, special supplement of
Luceafărul magazine, in a print run of 6,140 copies; Frig (Bucharest: Editura pentru
Literatură, 1967), 115, in a print run of 10,140 copies; *Așteptare* (Bucharest: Editura
Cartea Românească, 1971), 108, print run not stated.

anxious, bewildering journeys by streetcar; the wife who keeps growing taller and then shorter; theriomorphic images (lion, fish, bird) that recur with menacing insistence, acting as numinous symbols whose meaning, however, remains opaque, impossible to determine outside the dream logic of the text. The title story of the collection *Waiting*, one of the major texts of this period, and which will form the structural and imaginal matrix of later novels, in particular *Roman de Gare* and *La Belle Roumaine*, is oneiric not only aesthetically (the dream reality of an isolated railway station at the edge a forest swarming with indeterminate creatures, on the other side of which lies a mysterious sanatorium; a place of alternating deep snow and incessant drizzle, menaced by an eagle that grows inexorably larger and larger), but also structurally: the sequence of events (the arrival of an *anima* figure on an express delayed by the derailment of a freight train, who speaks no known language and brings with her an eagle in a cage; the death of old railway worker Manolache, haunted to the end by the dream of a lion with a human grin from his days at the circus; the disappearance of telegraph operator Lică; the station master's endless, objectless waiting) keeps shifting, doubling back on itself, repeating itself in a different order. The oneiric narrative structure of "Waiting" therefore looks forward to the dreamlike textual variations and narrative metamorphoses of *Vain Art of the Fugue*,[5] which was published in French translation as *Arpièges* (a portmanteau of *arpèges* "arpeggios" and *pièges* "traps")[6] by Flammarion in 1973, but in the original Romanian not until after the fall of the Ceauşescu regime. A shorter, earlier version of *Vain Art of the Fugue* was published in *Luceafărul*

---

[5] On *Vain Art of the Fugue*, see the articles by Laurenţiu Malomfălean and Nicolae Bârna in this issue of the *Review of Contemporary Fiction*.

[6] Although Tsepeneag had taken up residence in France by the time *Arpièges* was published, his Romanian citizenship had not yet been revoked, which meant that his exile was not yet officially irrevocable. In an interview from the early 1990s, immediately after the fall of communism, he says that he changed the title from the original *Zădarnica e arta fugii* (Vain is the Art of the Fugue) because "at the time I had a dread even of the idea of fleeing [*de-a fugi*] (the country)," Dumitru Ţepeneag, *Reîntoarcerea fiului la sînul mamei rătăcite* (The Return of the Son to the Bosom of the Errant Mother), (Colecţia Texte de Frontieră, No. 2, Jassy: Institutul European, 1993), 157.

magazine in June 1969, with the title "Fuga" ("Running" or
"Fugue").

In addition to fiction that embodied oneirist praxis, during
the "thaw" Tsepeneag was able to publish articles in the literary
press that laid out the theory of *aesthetic* or *structural oneirism*.
That such articles were published at all is indicative of the relative
relaxation of hard-line control over freedom of expression, but
notwithstanding, even before the "July Theses" and the crack-
down that was to arrive a few short years later, there were still
limits. In June 1968, Tsepeneag began to publish a series of theoretical articles in the weekly literary magazine *Luceafărul*, under
the title "In Search of a Definition." The first three articles briefly
stated the premise of oneiric literature ("in oneiric literature, as I
conceive it, the dream is not a source, nor is it an object of study;
the dream is a *criterion*. The difference is fundamental: I do not
narrate a dream (mine or anybody else's), but rather I attempt
to construct a reality *analogous* to the dream"[7]), outlined the
history of the dream in literature and art—the references range
from Homer, Virgil, and Dante to Bosch, Swedenborg, Blake,
Jean-Paul, Novalis, E. T. A. Hoffmann, G. H. von Schubert, De
Chirico, and, of course, the Surrealists—and were leading up to
a fuller exposition of Tsepeneag's own theory of structural oneirism when an anonymous voice from the wings interrupted the
text, demanding that the author cut it short and leave the stage:

> I had hoped that this series of articles (this theoretical feuil-
> leton!) might stimulate pertinent debate, wherein might be
> abandoned the preconceived ideas, the false or imaginary
> premises upon which is constructed an entire brilliant but
> pointless argumentation; I would at least have liked it to have
> been read, this theoretical patchwork, which in places is quite
> dry, because of the sallies into literary history that I deemed
> necessary, and in places perhaps not completely clear; I would
> in any case have liked it to be possible for a distinction to be
> drawn between terms employed not exactly at random, and at

---

[7] "În căutarea unei definiții," *Luceafărul*, no. 25, 22 June 1968, *Opere 5*, 46.

least for it to be understood that there is a difference between *source*, wellspring of inspiration, on the one hand, and *criterion*, a term of comparison, on the other. But the "big heat" is on and it is natural that there not be enough goodwill or patience and, ultimately, perhaps that there not be any interest. For this reason, although I had initially planned a much longer sequence of theoretical investigations, precisely in order to receive and utilize various suggestions and objections as I went along, I shall conclude with this article.[8]

The article itself concludes with a defense of oneirism against the implied official criticism of delusion, illusion, hallucination, irrationality, unreality: "Oneiric literature is a literature of infinite space and time, it is an attempt to create a parallel world, not homologous but analogous to the ordinary world. It is a perfectly rational literature in its modality and means, even if it chooses as its criterion an irrational phenomenon. And in any case, oneiric literature is not a literature of delirium or sleep, but of complete lucidity."[9]

In the first of his "In Search of a Definition" articles, Tsepeneag alludes to his forthcoming translation of a work "fundamental in oneirology,"[10] Albert Béguin's *L'Âme romantique et le rêve* (1939), which was to be published two years later in the "Studii" series issued by Editura Univers.[11] Away from the imme-

---

[8] "În căutarea unei definiții," *Luceafărul*, no. 28, 13 July 1968, *Opere 5*, 53–54.

[9] "În căutarea unei definiții," *Luceafărul*, no. 28, 13 July 1968, *Opere 5*, 58.

[10] "În căutarea unei definiții," *Luceafărul*, no. 25, 22 June 1968, *Opere 5*, 45.

[11] Editura Univers also published Tsepeneag's translations of Alain Robbe-Grillet's *Les Gommes* and *Dans le labyrinthe*. The "Studii" series included works of literary criticism, structuralism, semiotics by not only Russian and East-European thinkers (Viktor Shklovsky, Vladimir Propp, Mikhail Bakhtin, Yuri Lotman, Boris Tomashevski, Roman Ingarden, Jan Mukařovský) but also Western theorists (Gérard Genette, Marthe Robert, Tzvetan Todorov, Jean Burgos, René Girard, Jean Ricardou, Jean-Pierre Richard, Renato Barilli, William Empson, George Steiner, Wayne C. Booth, Northrop Frye, René Wellek, I. A. Richards, among many others). As late as 1988, in the darkest, terminal period of the Ceaușescu regime, a translation of Jean Ricardou's *Nouveaux problèmes du roman* was published in the series. On the other hand, the fact that such books were published does not mean they were readily available in bookstores; in the late 1980s, they were as hard to obtain as consumer goods in general and even basic foodstuffs.

diate public eye of the weekly literary press, the conclusion of Tsepeneag's preface to the translation contains perhaps one of his most incisive statements of the poetics of oneirism:

> But the dream and also poetry must be viewed otherwise than as sources of knowledge or instruments of metaphysical revelation in which aesthetic pleasure is merely an adjunctive phenomenon, resulting from the ambiguity and uncertainty of revelation.
>
> In the first place, we must take account of the fact that the nocturnal dream, being evanescent and non-recurrent, even if it brings us a revelation of a metaphysical order, is incommunicable. So, too, the poetic adventure: it is individual, it cannot be conveyed with complete coherence. Neither the dream nor the poetic state can be reconstituted. It is impossible and even pointless to achieve once more the uniqueness that like a gas disperses throughout the subconscious. For the purpose of an artist is to achieve, and to do so in complete lucidity, a *conveyable* work, relative to which the prototypical dream is nothing but a *criterion*, a distant model that provides its laws rather than accidental and far too individual images. [. . .] the modern oneiric poet seeks in the dream its structure and mechanism in order to transfer them analogically to poetry, of course employing the imaginal material provided by the surrounding reality, since none other exists. [. . .] the modern poet resorts to the dream in order to introduce into the immediate reality—which the senses perceive too chaotically, and the intellect too drily, too notionally—a new organizational and at the same time germinative power, a logic other than the Aristotelian logic of so-called common sense. It is not an evasion but an invasion, an attempt to bring into communication these strata of reality that have for so long been kept isolated from each other;[12]

---

[12] Dumitru Ţepeneag, "Sub semnul Graalului," preface to Albert Béguin, *Sufletul romantic şi visul*, trans. Dumitru Ţepeneag (Bucharest: Colecţia Studii, Editura Univers, 1970), xvi-xvii.

A shorter version of the preface, titled "Under the Sign of the Grail," was published in *România Literară* magazine,[13] omitting Tsepeneag's exposition of his own theory of oneiric literature and other passages unacceptable to the official ideology (including a reference to Jungian psychoanalysis and a quotation from Béguin's diary in which he argues that "the fundamental opposition between Spirit and History [. . .] places its seal on every act of the totalitarian states"). As Tsepeneag was later to recall, the editor of *România Literară*, novelist Nicolae Breban, invited him to write for the magazine, but on the prior condition that he avoid all mention of the *oneiric group*.[14] Similarly, according to what Tsepeneag was told by Ștefan Bănulescu, the editor of *Luceafărul*, the "In Search of a Definition" series had had to be cut short because the "comrades from the Section" were sick of studying his articles with a magnifying glass every week lest some "unseemly" idea slip through.[15]

Meanwhile, an "oneiric group" had formed around the two central figures of Tsepeneag and Dimov, which included poets Virgil Mazilescu (1942–1984), Emil Brumaru (b. 1939), Daniel Turcea (1945–1979), poet and novelist Vintilă Ivănceanu (1940–2008), and prose writers Florin Gabrea (b. 1943) and Sorin Titel (1935–1985), the last of whom was already an established author. A joint interview of group members Leonid Dimov, Dumitru Tsepeneag, and Daniel Turcea,[16] along with literary critic Laurențiu Ulici (1943–2000), who was sympathetic to oneirism, was published in student magazine *Amfiteatru*, No. 36, in November 1968. In the interview, the participants discuss oneirism in relation to Surrealism, which either draws on the dream as a source external to the text or allows authorial

---

[13] Dumitru Țepeneag, "Sub semnul Graalului," *România literară*, No. 2, 15 January 1970, in *Opere 5*, 115–120.

[14] Dumitru Țepeneag, "Despre cenzură și vis" (On Censorship and Dream), *Reîntoarcerea fiului la sînul mamei rătăcite*, 84.

[15] "Despre cenzură și vis," *Reîntoarcerea fiului la sînul mamei rătăcite*, 83.

[16] Virgil Mazilescu was also due to have taken part, but according to Tsepeneag, he got left behind in the bar where the oneirists had been drinking before the interview. "Grupul oniric a coborît din maimuța suprarealismului," *Momentul oniric*, 248.

lucidity to be obnubilated through abandonment to the dream
state of automatic writing. As Dimov puts it, "the oneirc poet
does not describe the dream, he does not allow himself to be
controlled by hallucinations, but rather, employing the laws of
the dream, he creates a lucid work of art, the more lucid and
perfect it is, the closer it approaches the dream."[17] Implicitly, of
course, oneirism was also defined in opposition to realism in
general and, given the cultural context of the time and place,
socialist realism in particular. Tsepeneag might be said to hint at
this politically subversive view when he says that dream should
not be viewed as merely "a source of poetic inspiration, but as
a second reality."[18] On the one hand, the interview brought the
oneirists greater notoriety, including attention in the West, on
the part of Radio Free Europe, for example, which viewed the
movement as a bold act of defiance against the regime's repressive
ideology and ossified cultural policy. On the other hand, even
though the interview had been "mutilated by the censors,"[19] it
was still subversive enough to provoke outrage on the part of the
communist literary establishment. There were violent attacks
against the group in the official Party newspaper, *Scînteia* [The
Spark], and by establishment literary critics. In the end, by the
early 1970s, even the word "oneiric" would be banned, along
with the works of Tsepeneag and any reference to them, in effect
erasing him as an author from Romanian literature for the next
two decades.

In the eyes of the regime, and in the words of the "investigative organ" who in 1975 opened criminal proceedings against
him for "the infraction of propaganda against the socialist order,"
Tsepeneag had since 1967 taken "a hostile stance toward the
socialist order of the Socialist Republic of Romania" and through
"the so-called 'oneiric group'" had "propagated hostile ideas, to

---

[17] "O modalitate artistică. Discuție la masa rotundă cu Leonid Dimov, Dumitru Țepeneag,
Daniel Turcea, Laurențiu Ulici" [An Artistic Modality. Round-table Talk with . . .], in
Leonid Dimov, Dumitru Țepeneag, *Momentul oniric* [The Oneiric Moment], ed. Corin
Braga (Bucharest: Cartea Românească, 1997), 71.

[18] "O modalitate artistică," *Momentul oniric*, 72.

[19] "Tentativa onirică, după război," *Opere 5*, 182.

the effect that the political regime of our country does not grant freedoms, is based on hypocrisy, aims at the complete depersonalization of the individual, that socialism is a joke, incompatible with culture and creative freedom."[20] But since Tsepeneag was by then living in France, there was little the regime could do to bring him to socialist justice. On April 3, 1975, the day after the Ministry of the Interior "investigative organ" issued the procès-verbal to begin criminal proceedings, dictator Nicolae Ceaușescu signed Decree no. 69 stripping Dumitru Tsepeneag of his Romanian citizenship, a drastic symbolic act that was not to be extended to any other Romanian dissident in exile.

In exile, Tsepeneag continued to write in Romanian, with his novels being published in the French translations made by Alain Paruit. *Les Noces nécessaires*, the French translation of *Nunțile necesare* (The Necessary Nuptials), was published by Flammarion in 1977 and is an oneiric reworking of the archaic Romanian "Miorița" myth, in which two shepherds conspire to murder a third, who is warned by a ewe lamb (*mioriță*) but fatalistically accepts his death as a cosmic ceremony in which he is wedded to Nature. Finding himself in the situation of a writer who no longer existed for readers in his native language, without any hope of ever being published in Romania again, as the country descended deeper into the totalitarian night of the Ceaușescu cult of personality, Tsepeneag reluctantly began to write in French. The transition from Romanian to French, the crossing of the border from one language to the other, is described in *Cuvîntul nisiparniță* (*The Sandglass Word*),[21] an anxiety dream in which a deserter keeps running and running, trying to escape across an imaginary frontier. The text itself mirrors the author's desertion of his native tongue, with isolated French words and then phrases seeping into the Romanian text, like grains of sand through an hourglass, until by the closing chapter of the novel,

---

[20] Procès-verbal of the Ministry of the Interior Criminal Investigations Department, dated April 2, 1975, reproduced in Dumitru Țepeneag, *Opere 3. Un român la Paris. Jurnal* (Bucharest: Editura Tracus Arte, 2016), 560.

[21] Dumitru Tsepeneag, *Le Mot sablier*, trans. Alain Paruit, Paris: Éditions P.O.L., 1984.

the whole text is in French. Railway Novel,[22] Tsepeneag's first
novel in French, is an oneiric metatext, in which a company of
actors and film crew attempt to shoot a film based on the short
story "Waiting," a film which, itself having coalesced into an
oneiric image, recurs in the later novels *Hotel Europa*, *Pont des
Arts*, and *La Belle Roumaine*. Tsepeneag's second novel in French,
Pigeon Post,[23] was published under the anagrammatic pseudonym
Ed Pastenague (the French *pastenague* is the *Dasyatis pastinaca*
or common stingray), a younger French oneiric avatar of the
author, who here asserts his independent existence as not only
a character but also an author in his own right. As Giorgio de
Chirico once remarked, "la vue en rêve d'une personne est, à certain points de vue, une preuve de sa réalité métaphysique."[24] But
neither Tsepeneag's French publisher, the late Paul Otchakovsky-
Laurens, nor his American publisher, John O'Brien, were able
to accept the metaphysical reality of Ed Pastenague as a sepa-
rate, independent author within the oneiric text of Tsepeneag's
work as a whole, and subsequent printings of the French *Pigeon
vole* have appeared under the name Dumitru Tsepeneag. Since
Pigeon vole, however, Pastenague has gone on to publish translations of Romanian poets in French and a Romanian translation
of Alexandre Kojève's *Introduction à la lecture de Hegel*, and he
appears in the guise of a failed and frustrated novelist in later
novels by Dumitru Tsepeneag.

After the fall of the communist regime in Romania, Tsepeneag
was able to return to Romanian literary life, publishing in their
original language works that had theretofore existed only in
translation (*Vain Art of the Fugue*, *The Necessary Nuptials*) and
translating into Romanian works he had written in French.[25]
He began to write fiction in Romanian once more, embarking
on a series of novels that, for the first time in his work, included

---

[22] Dumitru Tsepeneag, *Roman de gare*, Paris: Éditions P.O.L., 1985.

[23] Dumitru Tsepeneag, *Pigeon vole*, Paris: Éditions P.O.L., 1989.

[24] Giorgio de Chirico, *L'Art métaphysique*, ed. Giovanni Lista (Paris: l'Échoppe, 1994), 60.

[25] Tsepeneag translated *Roman de gare* as *Roman de citit în tren* (Novel for Reading on the
Train). Some reviewers commented on the looseness of the translation, oblivious to the fact
that it is the author's prerogative to rewrite his own work in translation.

"realist" elements reflecting the social, political, and historical changes occurring in post–Cold War Europe, in particular the issue of migration (immigration, emigration): the trilogy *Hotel Europa* (1996), *Pont des Arts* (1998), *Maramureș* (2001), and the two interrelated novels *La Belle Roumaine* (2004) and *The Bulgarian Truck* (2010), all feature journeys back and forth across Europe, between East and West.

In an interview for the *Tageblatt* newspaper (Luxembourg) after the publication of *Hotel Europa*, Tsepeneag says that in the novel he aimed to transcend both oneirism and realism by merging them within a wider space.[26] However, some critics saw the realist, documentary elements of *Hotel Europa*, Tsepeneag's first new novel in Romanian for almost two decades, as somehow in "contravention of canonical oneirism," making it the first of his books in which "oneirism no longer lays down the law."[27] But in fact, *Hotel Europa* and the four subsequent novels bring the practice and theory of oneirism to its highest level of structural complexity and aesthetic sophistication. As we have seen, in the preface to his translation of Albert Béguin's *L'Âme romantique et le rêve*, Tsepeneag argues for an oneiric textual practice that would draw not on the content of actual dreams prior and external to the text, but on "the imaginal material provided by the surrounding reality, since none other exists," applying to this material the structure and mechanism of the dream in order to produce an oneiric text.

Employing a technique first found in *Pigeon Post*, the narrators of Tsepeneag's novels published since 1996 incorporate *faits divers* into their narratives, which always unfold at the moment of writing, without the first-person authorial character having any means of telling in which direction his text might go next, the same as a dreamer has no volitional control over his unfolding

---

[26] "[M]on intention a été de dépasser en même temps l'onirisme et le réalisme, en les incluant, l'un comme l'autre, dans un espace plus large." *Le texte original existe quelque part*, Corina Mersch, entretien avec D. Tsepeneag, *Tageblatt*, Luxembourg, December 1996, quoted in Marian Victor *Buciu, Țepeneag. Între onirism, textualism, postmodernism* (Craiova: Editura Aius, 1998), 36.

[27] G. Dimisianu, "Onirismul bine temperat" (Well-tempered Oneirism), *România Literară*, No. 36, 1996, quoted in *Între onirism, textualism, postmodernism*, 37–8.

dream (although, of course, behind the authorial character can be found the author himself, with the latter lucidly structuring the dream of writing a novel in which the former finds himself hopelessly entangled). According to Tsepeneag, the Surrealists betrayed the "transcendental meaning of the dream" by setting off into the real world like reporters in search of the strange and unusual,[28] in search of oneiric *faits divers*, rather than constructing a different, parallel world analogous to the dream. In *Nadja*, for example, "the 'facts' precede the text, Breton presents them as already having happened, he narrates them."[29] But in *Hotel Europa* and the subsequent oneiric novels, rather than being an account of (real or fictional) facts that have already happened, outside the text, the narrative is always contingent, and the *faits divers* are employed structurally as a means of augmenting this sense of contingency. For example, in *Hotel Europa*, the authorial character, who has decamped to the country in the hope of finding the peace and quiet to let him get on with his novel, nonetheless finds himself unable to continue his narrative because his wife has failed to mail him a folder of the newspaper clippings he claims to rely on for inspiration; in *Pont des Arts*, while visiting Bucharest, the author character bumps into a schoolmate who went on to become a sycophantic newscaster for state television during the communist period, but was unceremoniously sacked after the fall of the regime, and this embittered old friend insists on sending the author the sundry news items he has clipped from the Romanian papers, many of which mysteriously echo the recurring oneiric images found throughout Tsepeneag's fiction (the report of an attack by a giant eagle, for example, echoes the short story "Waiting"). The texts of the novels therefore produce themselves from other texts, but in a contingent, oneiric way, the way a dream produces itself working on imaginal material from the waking world. Just as the dream digests what Freud called the *Tagesreste* of the dreamer's lived experience, the dreamwork

---

[28] "În căutarea unei definiții," *Luceafărul*, No. 5, 22 June 1968, *Opere 5*, 46.

[29] Diary entry for 11 August 1974, Dumitru Țepeneag, *Opere 3. Un român la Paris. Jurnal* (Bucharest: Editura Tracus Arte, 2016), 470.

of the oneiric novel absorbs and transforms *faits divers*, the scraps and leftover texts of the daily news.

Likewise, the characters of Tsepeneag's five novels of the post-communist period are more "realistic" than those to be found in any of his previous fiction, in that they have backgrounds that situate them within a definite social, political, historical, geographical context: a Romanian student who is involved in the post-Revolution protests against the Iliescu regime and then travels across Europe to the West, haplessly getting mixed up with shady characters from the post-communist East; an ethnic German employed by Romanian Railways, who in the communist period emigrates to Germany, where in his old age he becomes obsessed with philosophy, ecologist politics, and backgammon; a French doctor who takes humanitarian aid to Romania after the collapse of communism and later to Bosnia after the collapse of Yugoslavia; a Bulgarian truck driver who plies the route from East to West and back.

But existing within an oneiric text, the characters are dream persons and as such they are independent of the authorial character or dreamer, often acting in ways he cannot foresee and even writing him letters, as in the case of Ana, a recurring character inscrutable even to the author. In this respect, it might be argued that just as you have no control over your actions when you appear in another person's dream, so too, you have no control over the actions of other people when they appear in your own dream. Rejecting the Freudian view that dream persons are simulacra of their living selves created by the dreamer and the Jungian view that they are expressions of the dreamer's own psychic traits, in *Dream and the Underworld*, James Hillman posits that dream persons are "shadow images that fill archetypal roles; they are personae, masks, in the hollow of which is a *numen*."[30] Like the dream person, the character in an (oneiric) fiction is a shadow image, an insubstantial persona, visible only to the mind's eye, perceivable only in thought, during the act of

---

[30] James Hillman, *The Dream and the Underworld* (New York: Harper and Collins, 1979), 60–61.

writing or reading, but acting independently of the perceiving mind. One such archetypal oneiric figure haunting Tsepeneag's work is the neither living nor dead Hunter Gracchus, whose rudderless bark is driven by the wind that "in den untersten Regionen des Todes bläst,"[31] and whose recurrent appearances in *Pont des Arts* presage the death of amateur philosopher and ecologist Fuhrmann.

Similarly, in *Pont des Arts*, the late Leonid Dimov, who together with Dumitru Tsepeneag developed the theory of structural oneirism in the 1960s, asserts his metaphysical reality within the unfolding dream text by telephoning the authorial character from the beyond. The telephone itself is a recurring oneiric image in Tsepeneag's work: it first appears as a silent, menacing presence in "The Bird," a short story included in *Waiting*; in *Hotel Europa*, the telephone keeps ringing, but at the other end can be heard nothing but dissonant grating and white noise; in *Pont des Arts*, a voice finally makes itself heard, "from afar . . . from the back of beyond." Before his voice fades into a "whistling sound receding into the distance," Dimov recites stanzas of his oneirist poems, which have long since sunk to the bottom of the authorial character's memory, but whose imagery now resurfaces throughout the unfolding dream text of the novel.

At the beginning of "Weeping", the opening story of the collection *Waiting* (1971), the narrator captures the indeterminacy of things read and then half-remembered, as if in a dream:

> I read somewhere—or maybe I heard, I dreamed, or somebody else dreamed and told me the dream—that a manicurist had for a long time kept an eagle in her bedside cabinet and that a photographer reared a lion in a drawer of his desk.[32]

If a text read and then forgotten, but whose words and gist hover at the threshold of conscious recollection, is like a dream,

---

[31] "Mein Kahn ist ohne Steuer, er fährt mit dem Wind, der in den untersten Regionen des Todes bläst" (My bark is rudderless, it is driven by the wind that blows in the lowermost regions of death): the closing sentence of Kafka's short story "Der Jäger Gracchus"

[32] Dumitru Țepeneag, "Plînsul," *Așteptare* (Bucharest: Cartea Românească, 1971), 5.

indistinguishable from a dream, then the opposite might also be argued: that a dream is like a text, and that ultimately the two have more in common with each other than they do with "the real world." And this is what Tsepeneag would seem to argue in his early theoretical text "In Search of a Definition" when he says, "Interest in the dream preceded literature and I almost might venture to argue that it determined its appearance."[33] Ultimately, this is also what Tsepeneag's work as a whole tells us, with unfailing structural lucidity over the course of half a century: that the dream and the text are analogous instantiations of a second, unseen reality.

---

[33] "În căutarea unei definiții," *Luceafărul*, No. 5, 22 June 1968, *Opere 5*, 45.

Exercises

To Leonid Dimov

Memory

ALL ALONG THE PATH stood benches on stumpy lizard feet and chairs with high backs, armrests, and iron bars for legs. The slender quivering branches of the leafless trees were traced against a boundless greyish white sky. Here and there was a broad expanse of cropped, perfectly still grass, where animals arched their elongated bodies. Around the mane of droplets flowing from the basin of the fountain were birds with long legs that looked like ostriches, but also like peacocks. They had long, silky, highly colorful tails. All in the gentle, rather sad, pale gold light of an autumn Sunday afternoon. On the benches there were old ladies with stiff, spindly legs and old-fashioned, down-at-heel shoes, men with tall black hats, reading the newspaper or just sitting motionless with their eyes on the swards where those strange animals undulated like frolicsome dolphins. Consisting of red, white and green chips, the gravel of the paths crunched beneath the tiny feet of the children running to and fro. Dressed in bright colors, plump maids with chubby cheeks swayed in their midst. The stern governesses scolded with extended forefingers, they tweaked ears as pink as petals, which shortly thereafter forgot about their troubles and ran off to play. There were also, of course, funny little dogs with crooked legs: they emerged from beneath the chairs, from among the legs of the old folk, and ran tottering, mingling with the playing children; they did not dare—they came to a stop right at the edge—to venture onto the sward, so green, so luminous, where the animals with glossy pelts

3

were leaping. And everything, everything was distant and near, in a stagnant light, as if you were looking through a window.

To that park Maria used to come, holding me by the hand. She was always sleepy, her eyes were small, her face large, oily. There, by the fountain, she would meet her soldier, who waited for her resting his weight now on one boot, now on the other, twisting his cap in his large hands, plainly indifferent to the long-legged birds all around. Maria's face, chubby and good. Her hand with its rather rough fingers that squeezed mine. I would then be allowed to play and even run up to the sward. Maria would rest her weight now on one leg, now on the other, or with the blunt toe of her shoe she would poke around in the gravel. I would then know I was allowed to race as far as the corner where, with studied movements, the old man whose beard was so large and so white would be making large butterfly-like wings from colored paper. Next to him, on the bench, were piles of paper and dozens of thin laths, like kite struts. All around, the children gazed open-mouthed, their legs planted well apart in the gravel, their small hands resting on their hips or folded behind their backs. They would not have budged for anything in the world! Arms chubby or thin. Hands irritated or amused, which had a hard time tearing us away from the source of our admiration. The old man was silent, he did not even look at us, with glue or some such he stuck the struts to the wings, so many wings! of every color: white and pink, pink and green with yellow stripes, or painted dozens of colors, like peacock tails. There were only a few of us by now and the nearby benches were empty, and when the old man looked up at me and, dissatisfied, shifted his gaze to another, smaller boy, what fear and enchantment gripped us! The eyes of the old man were blue and cold, so large . . . They were like holes through which could be glimpsed the clear blue water of a mountain tarn. He stretched out his long arms, his large hands, veiny and wrinkled, he carefully turned one of the children around and set about attaching a pair of glossy green wings between his shoulder blades, wings as thin as cellophane. The green wings had a yellowish tint, the child trembled with excitement—all of us were overcome with such fear and pleasure!

We stood rigid, our arms hanging limp, and everything was still, not a leaf quivered, not a sound could be heard . . . The old man had stopped looking at us again—he had put the green wings back on top of the others, and he was slowly rubbing his gnarled hands. On the grass, the animals with feline bodies were making slow, effortless, geometric leaps.

In the distance, beyond the meadow, glinted the skeleton of a gigantic fish.

The Dragon

I ENTERED THE LIVING ROOM on tiptoes, leading my horse by the bridle. My new sword, with the red tassel, knocked against a chair. Mama jumped up from the armchair, from next to Paul, and straightening her hair, she yelled angrily:

"What are you doing, bursting in here like this, you ill-bred child!"

I told her that I was on my way to the forest, where a dragon was hiding. It was sitting coiled up in a fir tree. And I pointed at the Persian rug in front of the piano, where the Christmas tree was.

"It's over there," I said, and whipped my sword from its scabbard.

Paul laughed and crossed his legs.

Mama lit all the candles on the chandelier, smoothed her dress, and went over to the other side of the living room, next to the stove.

"It's quite hot in here," she said, and started embroidering.

After tethering the horse to a tree full of blue and pink birds, I crawled under the piano to lie in wait. The dragon was nearby, hidden away. It had slain three of my soldiers, it had stolen one of my bears, and that very day, it had broken my electric train from Santa Claus. That confounded dragon was now hiding in fear. I crawled on my knees, sword in hand, searching every nook. But Papa soon arrived and I rushed out to meet him, sword raised. He was wearing his big, black, curly sheepskin cap, his overcoat was covered in snow.

"It's snowing, it's snowing," I rejoiced, and I started hitting him on the back with my sword to shake off the snow.

Papa took no notice of me. He waved a wet, crumpled newspaper and said hoarsely:

"The king has fallen."

Mama did not budge from her chair, but Paul rose to his full height and snatched the newspaper from him.

"The king has fallen, they've toppled him," Papa repeated, and went into the vestibule to take off his coat.

Paul had large hands, sinewy arms, very strong. He could lift me by the elbows up to the ceiling, he could even toss me up like a ball and then catch me. He was holding the newspaper with both hands, right beneath the chandelier, and his face was shining. It was plain to see that he was overjoyed. Papa came back into the room, his hands in his jacket pockets. He was gnawing his moustache.

"You're both overjoyed, of course, especially you."

Paul made no reply. Mama shrugged and said that she wasn't overjoyed, why should she be? Paul still said nothing, he sat back down in the armchair and smiled at me. He winked at me. Papa was pacing up and down the room, muttering to himself. He said that things would be very bad for us now, he knew for a fact, "that lot" would run riot, and Paul was wrong to be overjoyed, as he would very soon see. Mama looked up from her embroidery and smiled, the way she did when she wanted to be beautiful and kind, but Paul looked at me and winked again.

"You think he fell just like that, without a push, out of the blue, eh?"

"No, on the contrary," replied Paul and moved over to make room for me next to him on the armchair. He was wearing a black sweater, knitted by Mama, and he smelled nice, of apples and tobacco.

I asked him in a whisper: "Why did he fall? Was he on a horse?"

Paul laughed and Papa abruptly turned his head toward us. He was gnawing his moustache. He was feeling the collar of his jacket with his short fingers, as thick as sausages. It was nice there, next to Paul, we were both talking in a whisper, "in secret."

"Did he have a big beard, the king?"

"No, he was smooth-cheeked and had a nasal voice," came the reply.

But that couldn't be, it was only princes that didn't have beards, and in the end, Paul had to explain it to me in detail. Papa glanced at us a few times from beneath knitted brows, then turned his back and started reading and rereading that crumpled newspaper. When he spoke, Paul moved his hand through the air, tracing lines and circles. He told me that the king used to hold balls in his castle all the time and didn't care about anything else in the world.

"Not even dragons?"

"Not even them."

And at the ball, everybody was happy, they laughed, and they danced, especially the ladies in their beautiful, billowing, colorful dresses, and among them moved haughty officers in uniforms dripping with braid and medals, like mosquitoes. And there were also gentlemen like Papa, in tail coats. And they all danced, and ate, and drank, and if the bugles sounded for them to go to war, not one of them went. The gentlemen in tail coats moved like beetles among the silk dresses, the officers jingled their spurs, twirled their moustaches, and explained to everybody how the enemy should be defeated. Only the men not allowed to go to the ball did any fighting.

"Were there parrots, too?"

"Where? . . . Of course, hosts of parrots, they flew around every room of the castle, lots of them." Paul's hand traced waves and circles to show how the parrots flew. "And one day, the king grew bored in his ballroom and climbed the stairs to the top of the highest tower in the castle, from where he could see the whole country."

"But what about the dragon? Did he not even fight the dragon?"

He did not even fight the dragon, he didn't even have a sword or a horse. He climbed to the top of the tower, to a room full of timepieces, which is to say, clocks large and small. He had a grandfather clock twice as big as ours, he could climb inside it, like a coffin. Up in the tower he liked to listen to the tick-tock of the clocks and to stand on the balcony looking into the distance, at the houses and fields of the land. And the clocks went tick-tock, tick-tock. At the castle gates, a crowd of onlookers gathered to stare at the gilded carriages of the guests invited to the ball.

"Weren't there any motorcars?"

"Yes, there were, the people outside gawped at them too. They were standing outside the walls, they weren't allowed inside, and they were shivering with cold. They always used to come. It was freezing cold."

"Was Gheorghiță there, too?"

"Gheorghiță was there, too, and the man with the lamp oil, and the boy who delivers the bread, and peasants, too. Some had made fires of twigs, and the servants were afraid the castle might catch fire."

We were whispering together on the armchair, and Papa could stand it no longer, he began to tap his foot, making the table and the vase of flowers shake, and that was something Mama could not abide.

"What do you keep cramming in his head? Come on! Bedtime!"

But I wanted to find out how the king had fallen, and Paul stared talking more quickly and more loudly. "Because they were so cold, they started stamping up and down, trampling the snow underfoot. And more of them came, all around the castle. They stamped up and down till the earth shook beneath them. The castle began to rock and in vain did the king cry from the balcony, 'You ought to be ashamed!' And he wagged with his finger at them because the walls were quaking, and the dancers in the ballroom were sliding all over the place, and the ladies were shrieking, and the parrots and the chandeliers were dancing to the music. Tick-tock, tick-tock went the clocks, quicker and quicker, like frightened hearts. The stamping stopped, and when the castle gave a violent shake, the king fell, poor man. From up on the tower, he fell down, bam! onto the snow."

"That's enough . . . enough!"

Mama could barely restrain her laughter and she told me to

go to bed. Father chewed his moustache, pacing up and down the living room, his hands behind his back. I took my horse and sword. Paul waved at me. I went out.

I told Lenuța how the king had gone bam! but she wasn't very interested. Although Lenuța wouldn't let me, I was dead set on putting my sword under my pillow. The next day I had to kill the dragon, and so I climbed into bed and quickly fell asleep.

Celebration

It was a blue morning, filled with cheerful little sounds. The city shone like a happy face, its every shopfront and apartment-block window beaming. The streets were abloom with tiny scurrying figures. The yellow and green buses could barely make headway. A tin policeman pointlessly spread his arms, twisting around on his heel. The trams did not dare to leave the depot. The traffic lights blinked in complicity. The people crossed from one sidewalk to another, they streamed up the street, then back down again, they gesticulated, pointing this way and that. In front of the circus, the crush was even greater. Over the squat gates the animals could be glimpsed: tame bears standing on two legs, tigers unnerved by the host of antelopes, gentle lions with almost tearful eyes, bulging grey elephants, russet foxes sniffing the bottom of the fence, fat white horses with silken manes, swans and fishes flitting back and forth. The triangular head of the giraffe gazed along the eaves. The unruly crowd thronged to stare. A flame-red fire engine came to a stop there, curious. But even so, it was not noisy, there was only a constant hum. On the other side of town, an electric train whistled. When it stopped, for a few moments, nobody alighted, and the train resumed its snaking dance.

"Give me the ladder. I have to hang up the flags."

And they inserted the flags, red flags, white flags, tricolors, and they all flickered like playful little flames.

A parrot as big as an eagle landed on the roof of the station. It gleamed every color.

"Where are the soldiers? And the planes?"

He grabbed the bugle and blew with all his might. Straight away the rat-a-tat of the drum made reply. The soldier's gait was stiff, they were shiny, determined. The planes were rather few, but what daring loops, what dizzying dives they made above the city! A tractor as yellow as wheat appeared, driven by a blue mechanic, and then two dump trucks, full of cubes with which they straight away built new, taller apartment blocks. The people gazed in admiration at the power of the crane and the dexterity of the builders.

"This will be a cinema, this a pastry shop."

The builders' hands were swift, the buildings rose as fast as the eye could see. A girl with rosy cheeks, yellow pigtails and ribbons gazed in enchantment.

"Out of the way, stand clear!"

A motorcyclist collided with a bus, they rolled over, a few soldiers fell, a boot as big as a truck skidded and broke down the circus fence, the foxes leapt back in fright, the elephants trampled backwards over the lions, the lions over the tigers, and gurgling, crystalline laughter rang out. They set about repairing the fence and calming the animals. The train stopped, nobody got off. One of them said:

"Let's begin the parade."

A space was cleared. The crowd drew back: some onto the sidewalk, some into a column. the parade began. The bugle sounded once more, too loudly. First, the lead soldiers passed by, strutting in perfect step. Behind them came the yellow and the blue truck, loaded with celluloid balls, pencils and erasers, stacks of matchboxes, little bottles with all kinds of labels, a torch that flickered on and off to the delight of all, and lots of other things besides. The girls with porcelain faces passed by, and then Pantolin the harlequin, the golden bear, the guilty motorcyclist, and behind them, all the animals of the menagerie: the tigers, deer, lions, elephants, foxes, swans, and finally, the giraffe. The parrot remained on the roof of the station, like a solitary eagle. Then came all the others, in more disorderly fashion.

There were too many of them. They had grown rather bored.

Their knees were dirty and the backs of their hands were light brown. They sat down, one next to the station, the other behind the circus. They looked at the large blue rectangles of the windows. The room was filling with light that was more and more golden, warmer and warmer. It laved their brows and their hands resting on their knees. The city had become perfectly still in the sunlight.

At the Photographer's

I WAS THE FIRST to go outside, having lost patience; I hopped up and down on the sidewalk in front of the building as I waited for the cab. Then Father came out: he was very solemn, hands behind his back, wearing his new navy-blue suit, the one with the pinstripes. He told me to behave, to stop hopping around like a little goat, but there was nothing censorious in his voice and he did not look at me. He adjusted his hat, checked his tie knot, and glanced around at the door of the building. He started pacing up and down, hands still behind his back, his head slightly bowed. Bored of waiting, I looked at the tram stop and thought about how the photographer's was quite nearby: just a few yards past the food store, in an old house that had been spared demolition, across the road from that emporium with the nice polished crates known as coffins. You could walk the distance, but anyway, the Princess balked at that. "I'll get my train dirty," she said, standing on tiptoes, and so Papa had called a cab. Gigi smiled and seemed to be constantly looking out of the window, he was even taller than usual, which annoyed me, and I didn't even wait to take the elevator downstairs. When the cab arrived, Papa wasn't outside, he had gone back upstairs to make them hurry up. The driver pulled up and asked me whether he had got the right address. "You're off to a wedding . . ." he said with a smile, shaking his head. I rushed to the bottom of the stairs, but just then, the Princess, Gigi, Papa, and Auntie Louisa climbed out of the elevator, all of them talking and laughing at once.

They took no notice of me. They didn't want to take me with them. "Never mind," I said to myself and I waited for them to set off before running on behind. I knew the way. I arrived before them. At first, I was scared that they had already had their photograph taken and then left, but that would have been impossible. But even so, I asked the photographer whether they had been already. He didn't understand, he scratched his beard with his big black fingernails—he had a pointy beard, a goatee—and looked at me like I was daft. I then described my sister to him, telling him how fat and conceited she was, how she ate cakes all day long, and how she had looked down on me ever since she went to university. "She wants to get married," I told the photographer, "and Papa wouldn't allow it at first, he told her to get some sense into her head, to finish her degree and only then, after that, and when he saw me thumb my nose at her, he banged his fist on the table and said: 'Get out, snotnose!'" And the Princess wept for days and stopped eating cakes, she ate only those small crunchy bonbons you crack between your teeth. She was fuming. I also told him about Auntie Louisa, who moved in with us after Mama died. The photographer looked at me and stroked his chin beard with his fingers, which looked like they were walnut-stained. Once I was sure I had arrived ahead of them (who knows where they had got to?), I wanted to go inside to wait, but that billy goat of a photographer wouldn't let me; he patted me on the head and pushed me back out of the door. So, I ran across the road, to the coffins, to see what was new, and a Pobeda almost ran me over, the driver braked and started swearing at me, and I stuck my tongue out half a foot and he didn't say anything after that, he restarted the engine and drove off. In the shop window there was a new coffin, a small one, very nice. I don't think even I would have been able to fit inside it. I would have to tell Dan about it at school the next day. He liked coffins and floral wreaths too, the ones with the broad black ribbons and white lettering. But unlike me, he hadn't been to the cemetery, and he was weaker than me, too. When I wrestled him, I would trip him and down he would go! But the Princess didn't believe it, she threw her head back and chortled till her goiter jiggled like a frog's. The first time Gigi came over and played backgammon with Papa, she laughed then too. I was rooting for Gigi, because he let me throw the dice for him from time to time, I rolled nothing but doubles, and Dad really blew his top, he said put the dice in a cup, and that's when she started to laugh. After Gigi left, I asked if I could have a game of backgammon with him, it wouldn't kill him, but he didn't want to, he said I should go and play my own games. What else was I supposed to do? I picked up the backgammon set and went off to play by myself, on both sides of the board, and she started laughing at me again. And there she was, climbing out of the cab on the sidewalk opposite. She was laughing as usual, and Gigi stood smiling, as stiff as a post. Dad and Auntie Louisa got out of the car, and then some fat person, apparently a woman. Another car pulled up, and then another. Everybody was cheerful. They were waving their arms as if about to take flight. They looked ridiculous. I let them go inside, all crowding into Beardy's studio together, and then I quickly crossed the street and looked through the window of the front door, which was ajar. The Princess was wearing a white dress with lots of lace and some kind of a coronet on her head. She was flushed and has stopped laughing. She was smiling, pretty. And Gigi was so tall that the photographer had to crane his neck to look at him, he danced around the two of them, his beard quivering. And the two of them grew taller as fast as the eye could see, as if somebody were pulling them upward by the hair. I slipped inside, careful lest Dad see me, hid in a corner and kept still. The photographer moved aside a red curtain, lit some large lights, which bulged like a car's headlights, and from somewhere in the back he pushed the camera toward them, which was taller than me and stood on a tripod. My sister blushed even redder, and Gigi turned as white as chalk. Auntie Louisa took out a handkerchief to wipe the tears from her eyes. The others were making a terrible racket, they were talking, laughing their heads off, and then Beardy said: "Quiet, please! We're filming now!" I stood on tiptoes to get a better view, although there was no need, since the bride and groom had risen about two feet off the floor and kept on rising as if drawn upward on strings.

Nobody said anything. Auntie Louisa was muffling her sobs. The photographer crawled inside a box behind the camera. All you could see now were his hands. Silence fell. Some of them lowered their heads, as if in guilt. Or in embarrassment. They stood stock-still. The couple were rising higher and higher. You could now see their shoes: his were like big black boats, pointed at the prow, hers were smaller, half covered by the hem of her dress. Fat as she was, that confounded Princess was now rising into the air like a balloon! I cast a furtive glance at Dad: his eyes were moist. Auntie Louisa had burst out sobbing. Another lady was crying too, but more softly. Gigi's head was now just an inch from the ceiling. The photographer tore himself from the belly of the camera and waved his arms, shouting: "What are you doing, comrades? You're perched too high up. I can't photograph just your lower half. This is too much!" His shouts jerked the others out of their lassitude. I leapt from my hiding place and I was the first who tried to jump up and catch them by the legs, but I couldn't manage it. "Lend a helping hand," shouted the photographer, "Don't just stand there like statues! Do something!" Everybody started jostling, like in a crowded tram. People were clinging to the legs of the bride and groom and tugging, gently at first, just giving them a shake, "Get down, that's enough!" and then with all their might, but without result. Auntie Louisa was screeching, "It's shameful! What will people say!" And poor Dad was completely at a loss, he kept turning around and around and trying to tell everybody that in his opinion, she should have finished her degree first and only then should she have . . . I clambered on top of a chair and shouted at the top of my lungs, like at a soccer match: "Go Princess, keep it up!" By now all of them were all trying with all their might, it was no longer a laughing matter, the couple's heads had gone through the ceiling: chunks of whitewashed plaster were falling down onto the heads of those below. Having tried in vain to position his camera so that he could at least photograph their legs, he didn't know what to do, he kept tugging his beard in desperation, never in his life had he witnessed such bloody-mindedness, such shamelessness . . . My sister was kicking her legs, for them to leave her alone, since she knew what she was doing. Gigi had lost one shoe, and a hulk of a man was hanging from the other, but in the end, he gave up. They were rising faster and faster, they broke through the ceiling, they went up through the attic, through the roof. We all ran out into the street to see how far they were minded to go. "It's shameless! Indecent! Call the fire brigade!" somebody shouted. And I felt like laughing, I had crossed the street the better to see them and, leaning against the coffin display window, I watched in delight. They kept rising, holding each other's hand, all by themselves, and they were beautifully dressed and the sky was blue.

The Pigeon

WE SAT DOWN on the curb of the sidewalk and none of us said a word. Radu gazed blankly at the State Food Store, although he knew very well that he wouldn't be coming from that direction. Having wetted his finger in his mouth, Tudor was busily rubbing his scraped knees; he seemed uninterested in anything except the reddish scab above his kneecap. The same as the rest of us, his knees were green from the grass we had been crawling through before, because we were Indians looking for chestnuts. He'd cleaned one of his knees a little, all that was left was a reddish eyebrow and a bit of green below it. I kicked a small, puny chestnut, which had been hiding among the leaves in the gutter. I couldn't understand what was going on . . . We'd been waiting for more than an hour, we'd collected hundreds of chestnuts, a mound of chestnuts, which we'd covered with leaves in a corner of the park. We'd scraped our knees and knuckles picking them up. Oh, how furiously, how elatedly had we shaken them out of the trees, their thorny shells sometimes falling right on our heads! Oh, the pain of extracting the kernel from those small green hedgehogs that prickled our hands! And he was late!

"Cut it out with that leg of yours, do you hear!"

Aha! So it annoyed Dan, too. He stood up and kicked the leaves, incensed.

"We're waiting here like idiots! He's not coming, can't you see?"

We'd made an arrangement with the Pigeon, after all! Hadn't

it been clear, what the hell! He needed chestnuts, we needed penknives, the kind with lots of blades, we needed soda siphon nozzles, and he'd also promised us an airplane compass, a big one.

The sun, more and more swollen, redder and redder, slowly
sank among the branches. In the distance, a few roofs caught fire.
When I saw him for the first time, he'd been wearing a checked
shirt and was strutting along, his mouth slightly open. It was
a habit of his: to hold his head raised and cocked to one side,
his mouth half open, as if he were always gazing up at a balcony. The soda-siphon cart jolted over the cobbles and we'd said
to ourselves, "What the hell is that clown doing around here?
Good God!" And what long, bandy legs he had. Dan took out
his catapult and shot at the soda siphons from behind a fence.
He hit a pink one, the stone ricocheted and hit the Pigeon on
the arm. He looked around him, puzzled, scared, but continued
on his way. But when he reached the corner he turned his head
and seemed to smile. After that, he came down our street every
day. He rounded the corner by the tailor's and came into sight,
his chin raised, his face as big and round as a ship's compass, his
brow slick with sweat. He would appear suddenly, while we were
kicking a ball or playing horses and jockeys, never thinking he
would come. Until we realized that he was going to come every
day, that is, until we got used to him. From afar we would hear
his cart jolting over the cobbles.

"Listen! The Pigeon's coming! Look, he's coming!"

He would loom from the direction of the Co-Operative, cast
a glance at the store window, and you wouldn't be able to tell
whether he was looking at the people inside the tailor's, or at
the dummies, or at the reflection of his large body as it pushed
the handles of the cart. Then he would raise his chin, and his
brow would glisten in the sunlight. We'd become used to him
being like that, with his checked shirt, hulking, awkward, we
liked that he stuttered and when he was angry he could never
find the words, he would roll them like pebbles; we liked that we
couldn't understand a word he said. Sometimes he would stop,
rest the cart handles firmly on the ledge of some wall or on the
stone parapet in which the park railings were embedded, and he

would look at us. He would fold his arms across his chest and gawp at our game. At first, he kept silent, he didn't come any closer; if we were in the park playing redskins, he would lean against the railings and stand there staring for who knows how long. One day, he pulled from his pocket a slightly rusted penknife, but with three blades, as well as a nail file, and handed it to Radu. "It's nice," he said, "you have it." Radu took it, and the rest of us were miffed. Another day, the Pigeon brought another penknife, with mother-of-pearl inlays, and gave it to me. That's how we made friends with each other: he brought us penknives and siphon nozzles, and we let him play countries, although he wasn't very good at it and didn't take any notice of the rules. But he was good with a catapult, he could aim better than any of us. Especially with the sling. He left us speechless with amazement one day when with a single shot he shattered a light bulb placed on a fence as a target. But he refused to shoot at birds and used to lecture us about it. He became furious if we aimed at sparrows, he turned red in the face and stammered all kinds of threats. He said it was a sin to strike anything that flew. And he would wave his arms like a madman.

We liked the Pigeon and I think he cared about us. Once, he brought us a ship carved from wood, as big as a shoe brush, with a mast and sails, which could float on a lake, he said. But we didn't have a lake and there was nothing we could give him for it in exchange. He then came up with the idea of our collecting chestnuts, because he needed them, he said he could powder them and make us all rich. And now here we were, and he hadn't come! Might he have gone down a different street? Might he have fallen ill?

The sun sank lower and lower, the shadows of the trees lengthened from one sidewalk to the other. Maybe he'd tricked us, said Dan, who, hiding behind a fence or a tree, sometimes liked to have fun aiming at the soda siphons with his catapult. "They're not birds, are they?" Dan would say, giving us a wink. But why didn't he come? He wanted to take revenge, that was it, but I for one still couldn't believe it.

We were sitting on the curb of the sidewalk, our backs to the

park, getting bored . . . Emil suggested a chestnut fight, as we'd
have to throw them away anyway, but we weren't in the mood.
We couldn't be bothered even to talk. Dan slapped his catapult
elastic over his thigh. Tudor tended his wounded knee. Still no
sign of the Pigeon. Two or three of us went home. We others sat
in silence and a mist enveloped us all, we saw each other as if
through joined eyelashes . . . From afar could be heard the rumble of a tram. But not only that. We listened tensely. We could
now hear the noise of pushcart wheels over cobbles. It was him!
We all jumped to our feet. Dan wrinkled his brow, his nose, and
gave a shrill cry: "To the chestnuts!" We looked at each other
and came to a silent agreement: we'd teach him a lesson, we'd
show him! Like Red Indians on the attack, we leapt the railings
of the park. We raced across the grass, the flowerbeds. Behind
benches, behind trees, we waited for him. Nobody moved a muscle. We held our breath. From behind the corner, past the tailor's,
loomed his bulky frame, lit by the last rays of the sun. He was
pushing the two-wheeled cart with ease. It was he, the Pigeon,
but even so, we had difficulty recognizing him. The chestnuts
dropped from Dan's hands, he emerged from behind the trunk
of the tree where he had been hiding, and moved forward a few
steps. We followed him. We could not believe our eyes. We went
outside the park, to the sidewalk. We watched, leaning on the
park railings: the Pigeon was wearing a frock coat. He strutted
along, not at all discommoded by his new clothes, the comically
tall top hat worn at a backward slant. As usual, he was peering
up at some unseen balloon. He was gazing fixedly, almost staring, a rigidity somehow in keeping with the frock coat. He now
resembled our headmaster at the end of school year festivities,
although the headmaster didn't wear a frock coat.

   One of us called out in a whisper: "Pigeon!" And then the
Pigeon's pushcart pulled level with us and we saw that it was
packed with brightly colored soda siphons of every hue: green,
pink, yellow, violet. And those marvelous soda siphons were both
soda siphons and something else altogether. For example, some
of them elongated like craning necks, the lever became a bird's
beak, and the others, beneath our very eyes, turned into flowers.

There were white soda siphons, grey ones, that puffed out their feathers like doves, their craws quivering. And there were violet soda siphons, red ones with levers like a cockscomb, glass cockerels and peacocks spreading their fans.

"Pigeon . . ." whispered Dan once more.

The Pigeon did not stop, he did not look back. He walked solemnly, his chin raised, his top hat at a backward slant. He was looking at something up in the treetops.

"Pigeon! Wait, Pigeon!"

From the pushcart, as if at a signal, the white and grey doves took flight. The peacocks took off too, and then the long-necked birds. The Pigeon did not stop. He did a circuit of the park, once, twice, countless times. And we followed him, like fools . . .

Astronomy

I AWOKE BECAUSE of the light. I hadn't drawn the blinds, and the light that morning was pouring into the room like lukewarm water, more and more of it, brighter and brighter, it had gilded the walls, the bookcase, the chair, the table, it had flooded the bed, I could feel its cunning caress on my cheeks, my eyelids. Drowning, choking on the light, I writhed, kicked off the blanket, awoke. Small birds, hummingbirds of every color, were dancing in the blue rectangle of the window, grass and flowers had sprouted from the rug, long orange and red fishes sliced through the room in every direction. Then Șerban came in. "Come on," he said, "everybody's up on the roof," and he ran back out, calling to everybody in the building, "Everybody's up on the roof!"

I got dressed. The birds and fishes had dissolved into the light; now there were only golden arcs and leaves spinning up toward the ceiling.

From our apartment it's just a few steps up to the attic, to the laundry room, and from there you come out onto the flat roof that covers the whole of the top of the building. Chaises longues and chairs had been placed among the television aerials, and almost all the tenants were there, in groups, seated or standing, talking, gesticulating, pointing at the horizon: a huge red sun was lumbering upward above the gardens and houses. Those who arrived earlier were saying that first of all a red cockscomb had risen, about this big, no sooner had it attained roundness than comrade Năstase saw the yellow, crinkly globe of the moon alongside it; but that was impossible, the moon was somewhere on the other side of the sky, Șerban had spotted it on school mornings, he'd seen it from the tram: pale, frozen, and it had been winter and there hadn't been as much light as today. It must have been another sun, a smaller one, which was trying to rise for the first time. And we kept talking, arguing heatedly, sweeping our arms in circles to point at the sky, and auntie Louisa traced the sun with her finger and seemed very angry at comrade Năstase. We crooked our arms, traced the moon and the sun, in the light that was growing stronger and stronger, our bodies were elongating, growing taller among the television aerials, and it was as if we were dancing. Not even Madam Popescu was so fat any more; like a sailor perched on a mast, she stretched out her arm and cried: "Look, another sun is rising!" We looked in that direction, shading our eyes with our hands, and the superintendent alone muttered something surly about how that way was north. It was a blue sun, very far away, beyond the town. "A whale's black," said auntie Louisa, "slowly rising from the water." Șerban gave a cry of delight. He'd brought his bicycle and the parrot cage; perched on the saddle, he couldn't get enough of gazing at the blue sun.

"It's no longer any hallucination," said comrade Năstase, turning to the rest of us. "It's a blue sun . . ."

Auntie Louisa seemed slightly embarrassed; she had forgotten to lower her arm. We all stood motionless beneath the blaze of all those suns, and small, multicolored birds once more began to dance in front of me, gamboling hummingbirds and long blue and orange fish. The superintendent mopped his brow with a large red handkerchief, like a headscarf. "It's going to be too hot," he kept saying, "it's going to be too hot . . ."

Mama arrived, she hadn't taken off her apron, and that blonde girl also arrived, the one I always bumped into in the elevator, lots of them, they all arrived. We were on the deck of a sailing ship, lying on deckchairs, some were smoking, the conversations died down, some got undressed to sunbathe, the blonde girl stripped down to her chemise. Șerban was going wild on his bicycle, riding with no hands, with his feet on the handlebars, doing figures of eight, shouting all the while: "Everybody's up on the roof!" Lathered in cream, the blonde shouted from her deckchair for him to cool it. And then we all fell silent, we patiently waited for the cockerels, the whales and the peacocks from the ends of the earth to lift their cockscombs, backs, tails, we patiently waited for yet more sunrises. But the superintendent kept muttering at intervals: "It's going to be too hot, you'll see . . . Too hot."

Dead Fish

I was there too, in front of the restaurant, among the crush of onlookers crowding around the fish on the sidewalk. Jostled and trampled though I was, I could not bear to leave. Something was dragging down the satchel on my back. A lady was leaning on it and she was fat and she had a shrill, indignant voice.

"What nosy people! What nosy people!"

It was early. The restaurant was closed. In the passageway leading to the kitchen lay three blocks of ice piled on top of another and some strewn flowers. Next to them was the fish.

"A dead fish, that's all it is," said the woman, who was now beside me and had grasped my hand protectively.

She had a hot, sweaty palm. Her shrill voice rasped against my eardrums.

The glassy eye of the fish gazed past us fixedly. The scales were like green fingernails, bluish at the edges. It was sprawled half in the passageway, where the ice was, half on the wet asphalt of the sidewalk, its head pointing toward the gutter.

"A fish on the sidewalk?"

"They must have brought it for the restaurant . . ."

"And such a big one too!"

A tall man, as wizened as a smoked herring, holding a yellow briefcase under his arm, pushed his way through the crowd before walking away. He gave me a suspicious look and wagged a minatory finger. Others walked away too.

"A fish . . ."

They shrugged. The woman next to me was still none the wiser. How could they leave it there, as if on display? She shook her head in reproach. Then she brightened up.

"Put it on a spit, just like that, as big as a calf . . . You'd feed a whole wedding party!"

"It's plump, plump," said a man, who started to pat me on the head. "Good for a carp broth too!"

They were joking, chatting. Some were smacking their lips hungrily. It was a workaday morning. The sun was barely up. I couldn't bring myself to leave. Dead, it seemed bigger, longer. As big as a person. The whitish belly was slowly turning livid. The scales no longer gleamed. Only the eye was still shiny. The people were walking away. The lady with the bugle-like voice me to task:

"What are you gawping at? Haven't you got anything better to do? Haven't you got school to go to? It's a dead fish. What do you keep staring at it for?"

Everybody agreed with her. They were moving their heads up and down, nodding in approval. Likewise their arms. I left. But at the corner I stopped, I looked to see whether the woman was still there, and I went back. A few people still remained. A stooped old man holding a brat by the hand, two or three others. Folk were in a hurry to get to work, but the odd person still stopped. They were content to look from a distance, in passing. I leaned against the restaurant window and looked into its eye, which said nothing to me. All fish eyes are the same. I didn't dare to touch it. And I didn't know whether it was him, I wanted it not to be him, the fish who used to come to my window in the evening when I was alone. Then his scales would glitter like beads of amethyst. He would press his muzzle to the window, his thick lips, and stay with me until the moon rose over the house across the road. When I was sad he used to dance in front of the window in the yellowish light of the street lamp. It was a comical dance, he was cumbersome, he sometimes used to lose his balance and flip belly-up, he would whack the lamppost with his tail, he would almost tumble snout-first onto the sidewalk, but then right himself just in time, and he was very dear to me, and I used to laugh my head off at his antics. I don't know whether he

was the dead fish. With my parents, I moved to another neighborhood not long after that, into a tall block of flats, where I
had a balcony. And I used to go out onto the balcony to look at
the lights of the city, those little golden fishes.

After that I started high school.

The Doctor's Visit

IT WAS THE TURN of the seventh grade. The older children came out, raucous, their shirts open, fastening their belts, hopping up and down impatiently, making signs at the others. It was stuffy, sweaty.

"Quiet!" shouted the nurse from the doorway, stepping aside to let some out and others in. "One at a time, come on, and keep it quiet!"

She had large breasts and her uniform was damp at the armpits. The children from the eighth grade had all come out, and the seventh grade were taking off their sweaty shirts, elbowing each other, skylarking. The doctor looked up from the register and in a calm voice demanded silence. When he spoke, his grey moustache moved up and down. His perspiring bald patch gleamed. But he had a gentle, even voice, and the commotion subsided somewhat. The nurse went over to the table, her short uniform bared her knees, she shouted, "Quiet!" and then the names of the first boys in the register.

"Abagian, Antonescu, Arghir."

Abagian had grown, he was almost as tall as the nurse; he positioned his large, cropped bonce beneath the horizontal rod of the measuring scale and smiled dopily.

"Why didn't you take off your sandals, eh?" asked the nurse and slapped him across his fat white back.

"He's got dirty feet," a voice insinuated, eliciting laughter, and the boy crossed his arms over his chest and looked away.

Through the window could be seen the other wing of the school, its washed windows glinting in the sunlight. And the sidewalk on the other side of the road.

"Take off your sandals," ordered the nurse.

And she signaled the next boy to climb onto the scales. Suddenly angry, Abagian took off his sandals without using his hands, shaking them off like slippers to reveal feet that were indeed dirty before climbing back onto the measuring scale. The heat, but also an inexplicable excitement, which he could in no wise suppress, caused to him to sweat copiously: down his ribs, under his armpits, there trickled threads of sweat, which he furtively tried to wipe away with the palms of his hands, but in vain. He looked at Arghir, who was small, scrawny, with long underpants that came down almost to his pointy knees, and he thought him more ridiculous than himself. And that calmed him. He then plucked up the courage to cast a glance at the line of other boys, amused and implacable spectators. Near the back of the line he spotted Varlam, who had not even taken off his shirt, but merely unbuttoned it, and who looked scared.

"Come, get down now," said the nurse, brushing his shoulder with her large, bulging chest. "Step in front of the doctor."

Before the doctor, who gazed at him through his glasses benevolently, Abagian felt safe. He had his back to the other boys, to the nurse, the doctor had a large, bony hand, he pressed his temple to his chest and back, gently, protectively. The strong, firm hand tapped him, skillfully palpated him, without tickling him. The boy was brave enough to lower his underpants a little and, in reply to the doctor's whispered question, to admit the truth. When he walked back down the line to get dressed, he glimpsed the blue, friendly sky through the window. He got dressed slowly and did not miss the opportunity to laugh along with the others when Botez Constantin, also known as the Spelk, tripped over the scales and the nurse picked him up and put him back.

"He gets dizzy spells," called out a high-pitched voice, and the doctor raised his hand to ask for silence.

Abagian laughed along with the others, but more indulgently, since he had finished and was free to go. He groped inside his pocket for his cinema money and even felt a little proud. Next to him, Varlam maintained a pensive silence; it was as if he were trying to hide behind the others. He had his shirt on, even though it was terribly hot and he would have to take it off eventually. Abagian winked at him, for no particular reason, and Varlam turned red, lowered his eyes. Varlam had always been withdrawn. Abagian knew that, but Varlam was now downright terrified, perspiring and extremely fat. Abagian was fat too, but Varlam was fatter. Abagian gave him an encouraging smile and, tucking his shirt into his trousers, winked at him again. The doctor's voice then made itself heard, inviting those who were dressed to leave. Abagian shrugged and headed for the door with the others. Varlam went over to the window, looked at the sky, the roofs of the houses, the sidewalk where a few kids were playing hopscotch. They couldn't toss the pebble properly and didn't make it past square five. They didn't even try to hop different patterns, to avoid this or that square, to make stork's leaps—the whole algebra of hopscotch! A little girl tripped and fell. She was wearing blue hair ribbons. A fly landed on the windowpane; it buzzed, perhaps wishing to go through the glass, to get out. On the other side of the window, everything was so blue, so shiny . . .

The doctor was in a hurry, he had had enough for one day. There were still some of the younger grades to do, but he would leave them till tomorrow.

"Breathe in! Out! Hold your breath! Come on, don't be shy . . ."

The doctor's hands, large and skillful, moved agilely over the boys' backs and arms. Realizing that she had to hurry, the nurse picked up her pace too. She slapped the boys with her chubby, sweating hand, urging them to get a move on. The boys were happy to get away faster too, they no longer elbowed each other, they no longer giggled at every stupid little thing; in disciplined fashion, they let themselves be measured, weighed, slapped, palpated, they breathed in, they breathed out, they showed their bellies without making a whole production out of it, they heaved a sigh of relief, and left. There were only a few to go now.

"Udrescu, Varlam, Voinescu. Why don't you take your shirt off, Varlam?"

The nurse's voice made him start. There were only a few of them now. Some were still getting dressed. Two or three, the tail end of the register, were waiting their turn. Varlam sat down heavily on a bench to take off his shoes, moving sluggishly, in deliberate slow motion, looking all around him and at the door. The nurse looked at him.

"Udrescu: one metre sixty-eight. Sixty-four kilos."

"Bravo, Udrescu," the doctor congratulated him, peering at him over the top of his glasses.

Udrescu puffed out his chest. Taller than the nurse, muscular, he went over to the doctor, with a swaying gait.

"Swimmer?"

Udrescu nodded solemnly. The doctor was obliged to stand up in order to listen to his chest. The nurse gazed at him in admiration. Voinescu said in a squeaky voice:

"He's champion at swimming!"

And he puffed out his own puny chest, displaying his ribs. On the bench at the back, Varlam continued to take his shoes off. He took his socks off too.

"I'm very glad, I'm very glad," said the doctor. "You're well-developed all over," he added, with an imperceptible smile at the nurse.

The nurse sat down on a chair and cooled her face by flapping a cardboard file. The damp patches around her armpits had spread.

"There are still four grades to do," she said. "We'll finish them tomorrow." she stretched out her legs, her thick, hairy calves.

"I say . . ." The doctor lifted his glasses onto his forehead. "This . . . this Varlam, didn't he show up?"

"Ah, Varlam!" exclaimed the nurse, remembering. She twisted her chair around to face the back of the room where, on the bench by the medicine cabinet, the fat boy, barefoot, sweating, in his underpants, but still wearing his shirt, heard his name and, pressing up against the wall, was almost trembling.

"Come on, Varlam! What's wrong with you? Are you ill?"

The nurse stood up. In the doctor's surgery, there were now only two other boys left, whispering in a corner. She went over to Varlam, who stood up and mumbled something unintelligible. His legs bare, in underpants that barely fit him, with his shirt he covered his flabby white chest, like a girl's. The nurse took him by the shoulders, stroked his sweat-beaded forehead and burning cheeks.

"You've got a fever, you're ill," she said, slowly leading him to the doctor. "Varlam Eugen is ill, doctor. He's got a temperature."

On his feet, his stethoscope hanging over his chest like a necklace, the doctor regarded him with concern.

"Let's have a look," he said, and tried to take off the boy's sweat-soaked shirt.

The boy resisted even now, although something told him that in the end it would be better not to. With maternal solicitude, the nurse hugged him from behind. Thrusting her arms up beneath his shirt, she lifted it up, half covering his head. The boy gave up resistance and raised his arms. He had a white, puffy body. His underpants were hitched up over his stomach, to where his fat chest drooped down. The doctor clasped him by the shoulders and turned him to face the nurse. Covering his obese bust, at the same time the boy took care to hold up his underpants as high as possible.

"Deep breath. Another. Don't breathe out. Now go and lie down on the couch."

The boy shuffled over to the couch. He stood there without sitting down. But the sister held him by the shoulders and pushed him back, forcing him to sit down.

"Come on, lie down," she said gently.

The boy leaned back on the hard couch, trying to cover his chest and belly with his arms.

"Lie down already!"

The nurse placed her hands on him and gave him a shove. The boy felt her nails poking in his flesh and sank back, giving himself up to her will; with one hand he still clutched the elastic of his underpants, with the other he covered his face. He was trying not to cry. The fingernails retracted and the hands became soft and caressing once more. The doctor then approached, frowning terribly, he moved the nurse to one side, gently but firmly, and his large, bony, confident hand palpated the boy's stomach.

"Does it hurt?"

"No," whimpered the boy.

The doctor's hand moved down to the boy's belly, moved aside the hand that was still trying to keep the underpants hitched up, and with a quick movement pulled them down.

"Does it hurt here?"

The boy groaned, no longer putting up any resistance, but his fat body quivered like a gelatinous mass. From the child's belly button grew a white rose. The doctor raised his spectacles onto his forehead, cast a brief glance at the nurse, and then, without a word, pulled up the boy's underpants, but with care, covering his belly.

The nurse went to the window, leaning her elbows on the sill. She pressed her forehead to the pane. On the pavement, the children were playing hopscotch.

For an Album

SHE WAS SITTING with her legs pressed together, pointing the toes of her shoes upward, resting on the thin heels, since it was quite cold, autumn. The boy next to her had propped his chin on his fists, his elbows on his knees, and was looking at the lake. The sun was slowly sinking, turning the water red. A falling leaf landed between them. I was sitting on a bench a short way away, on the other side of the path. In my pocket, I had a pair of pruning scissors, slightly rusty, but still sharp. I stroked them with my fingertips; they were cold. A falling leaf landed between the two of them and the girl picked it up, twirled it between her fingers, let it go. The boy was looking at the lake.

"Let me teach you a game," he said.

The girl leaned forward, picked up the leaf again, crushed it. All that remained in the palm of her hand was the stem and a little yellow dust.

"What game?"

The boy turned to her and smiled. He leaned against the backrest of the bench.

"A game of . . . numbers. Instead of 'a', you say 'one', instead of 'b', 'two', and so on."

"You invented it just now." The girl gazed at the pointed toes of her shoes. "Just now."

"Yes," admitted the boy. "But it's nice. We'll be the only ones who know it."

She remained silent.

"Look . . . twelve, one, eleven, five."

"What's that?"

"Think about it. The twelfth letter of the alphabet, the first, the eleventh, the fifth."

"Lake," said the girl, clapping her hands.

A tall man with a moustache walked past, turned his head to look at them, shrugged, and strode away. A flock of seagulls was whirling around the sun. The willows, their tops slightly reddened, bowed low. I took the pruning scissors from my pocket and snipped off a twig above my head.

The boy said, "Nine, twelve, fifteen, twenty-two, five, twenty-five, fifteen, twenty-one."

She looked up at the yellow leaves, softly moving her lips. Finally, she understood. "It's easier with numbers," thought the girl and smiled at the lake.

From the bushes appeared a little old man, hopping on short, crooked legs. He was wearing a tatty coat and a round hunter's cap. He came to a stop behind the couple and looked at them curiously, craning his neck.

Now it was easy.

"Nine, twelve, fifteen, twenty-two, five, twenty-five, fifteen, twenty-one."

"Nine, twelve . . ." whispered the girl, finally looking at the boy.

The little old man was enchanted, he took two steps back. He was holding a small bow. A tiny crossbow, to be exact.

"I'm cold."

Sitting next to the boy, the girl shivered, the sun had sunk beneath the waters of the lake. The park slowly turned blue. The boy put his arm around her shoulders and clasped her to him as if under a wing.

"Nine, twelve . . ."

The little old man laughed softly and then, making soft steps, vanished into the bushes. It was then that the idea came to me. I stood up, walked over to them, produced my pruning scissors, and quickly, but carefully, cut around them. I cut them out of the landscape along with the bench and some of the foliage behind them. A leaf of darkness was left behind, into which I did not have the courage to look.

Wings and Wheels

WHAT AM I SUPPOSED to do now? I loaf around the workshop, getting under the others' feet. Mister Vasile is right: lately I've been aimless. He's noticed that I've been out of sorts, but the old man doesn't know what it is that's weighing on my mind. I feel like sticking my finger in a vise and tightening it till it really hurts, so that I'll be able to scream and maybe that way get it off my chest.

You're a wimp, a milksop, that's what you are!

And maybe Costică is right, but all he knows is that I was going to take a girl from our factory to the cinema, I'd even bought tickets, but in the end, I gave them to him. My mouth tastes bitter from so many cigarettes. I'm not used to tobacco. I smoke from anxiety, like Costică says. And I've noticed that others are laughing at me too, winking at each other, making innuendos.

"He's a dope," they say.

Some of them think I'm crazy or suffering from some kind of infirmity, although they have to admit I'm a good locksmith, there aren't many who are better.

Let's say I go to Costică and confess, unburden myself, like I would to a brother, but how can I tell him so that'll understand, so that he won't make fun of me, like he usually does? How to begin?

He'll think I'm making it all up just to impress him. Costică isn't a bad guy, but he always has to make light of everything and he also likes to boast, to talk about himself, he doesn't have the patience to listen to other people.

And another thing, he treats the girls, I don't know, he treats them roughly, too roughly, maybe that's the right way, but this time it's different, it's not just any other girl we're talking about here. He even has his own theory: they're all the same and the only thing you need is a pair of trousers and a motorbike . . . Two wheels are enough . . . Straight away . . . bang! they fall into your clutches.

Obviously, if you've got four wheels, all the better . . . and he smiles with those big white teeth of his.

He's not a bad guy, and he does care about me a little. Maybe we ought to go for a drink, he likes plumb brandy, and then I'll seize my moment. I'll tell him she's an orphan, she has an aunt who's an invalid, she's been looking after her since she was a child.

When he drinks plum brandy, he becomes maudlin and sings ballads.

But he'll hardly go out for a drink with me, a greenhorn, and even if he does, let's say tomorrow, after the soccer match, how will I tell him, how to begin?

The first time I saw her, she was wearing quite a short skirt, which bared her knees and a little thigh. Then I looked up and saw how beautiful she was, how different she was from the others, even though she was surrounded by a whole gaggle of pretty girls.

"She was like . . . like an angel."

"Get out of here, you're tipsy already. Look who I'm drinking with . . . a milksop."

How will I explain it to him, how will I make him understand that my heart was thudding like at school when the teacher called me in front of the blackboard? He'll laugh at me, he'll knock back his drink and start singing:

I'm in love with two blue eyes,
Fond something-or-other eyes . . .

Except I won't really get drunk (I'll pour my drink out under the table), so that I'll be able to tell him everything . . . And in the end, even if I do get drunk, so what, it'll give me more courage!

"Look, Costică, I'm going to tell you everything, and you'll understand. Sing away, I don't mind, but I want you to understand . . ."

I'm in love with two blue eyes . . .

"That's right, she's got blue eyes, but that's not important. Just a second while I finish this drink and then I'll explain it to you. When I saw her for the first time, I stopped in my tracks, like a bullock in front of a new gate. See, I'm being honest with you! It was exactly like that. I was staring like a bullock. And the girls saw me and they started to titter and nudge each other: Look at that bullock, girls, look how he's stopped in the middle of the road! He'll get run over."

They were laughing their heads off. And still I couldn't budge from the spot. It was as if I was nailed down. Those floozies were laughing, I was blushing in shame and embarrassment. She was the only one who wasn't laughing. She looked at me for a long moment, she said goodbye to the girls, and then all of a sudden, she rose from the ground, effortlessly, and started to fly. Don't laugh, Costică, she was flying, I swear! She had flimsy wings, like a butterfly's, which she beat slowly, effortlessly. She kept her legs pressed together and her arms folded across her chest, and it was as if she'd grown longer, slenderer. She rose higher and higher, keeping the same motionless posture she'd had when she was talking to the other girls. She rose as high as the top of the poplar tree.

You'll laugh, Costică, obviously, you'll laugh. But calm down, otherwise you'll burst a blood vessel from all that laughing.

"Hey, waiter, a glass of water, please!"

How am I supposed to tell him all that? I'll tell him I was joking, obviously, I was joking. She didn't have wings, she was just like the others, only more beautiful, more beautiful and taller, how can I put it? It was as if somebody were pulling her upward by the top of her head. I'll order a bottle of plum brandy and sausages and pickles. And I'll tell him the whole story, even if he laughs and mocks.

After that, I saw her every day. I stood waiting for her when she arrived for work, when she left, I looked for her in the lunch break. Sometimes, Vasile would send me to the shop where they worked. One day, the rotor of a loom seized up and I was lucky enough for him to send me to repair it. She was standing right by her machine, occasionally looking at me from the corner of her eye, because the spanner was trembling in my hand.

And in Costică's slightly hoarse voice, in his drawling song, there'll obviously be more and more mockery.

I'm in love with two blue eyes . . .

And as she walked among the machines, like a peahen, with her wings folded, she trod softly, barely touching the floor! And her deft, skillful hands like lizards among the cotton weft . . .

After two weeks of moony looks, bashfully walking past her, I plucked up courage and went to buy tickets for the cinema, although something told me I was daft and that she wouldn't go out with me.

"Sing, Costică, sing away, but listen to me too, because I feel like smashing this glass, shattering it between my fingers, when I think about what happened."

I knew she wouldn't go with me, but still I went and bought the tickets.

And I walked home slowly, the heel plates of my boots tapping on the cobbles. I didn't know how I was going to put it to her, we'd never exchanged so much as a single word, and there I was, about to invite her to the cinema, out of the blue? I dragged my heavy legs, street after street, and the evening was blue, thicker and thicker, and I had no idea where I was. I do know that there were few people around and all of them were in a hurry. After a while, I saw her floating lightly by the roof of a house. And I ventured to call out to her, but my voice was drowned out by the growl of a motorcycle. I came to a stop, as I always do when I see her: my legs grow limp and no matter how hard I try, I can't budge from the spot. Rooted there, standing pressed up against the wall, I saw the motorcyclist pull up by the sidewalk and without turning off the engine, he called out to her in a strong, commanding voice. She descended and, motionless, her hands drooping down beside her body, she looked at him from a distance. He called out her name once more and signaled for her to climb on the back of his motorcycle, but she shook her head, and how I rejoiced!

I'm certain she hadn't seen me, I was standing across the road, leaning against the wall of a garden, it was getting darker and darker, and I don't think she recognized me. She declined and the motorcyclist lost his temper, his voice grew hoarser and then, you know, something terrible happened . . .

"Hey, waiter! A glass of water! I'm thirsty, Costică, I've never been so thirsty. Can you feel my hand burning, can you feel it, do you understand?"

"Get on with the story, you milksop! Cut out all the . . . you know."

He grabbed her arm, she snatched it away and tried to take flight, to get away from him, and I was standing there like a bullock, I didn't do anything to save her. I was trembling. Just as she was about to escape, he jumped up and caught her by one wing and yanked it like a savage. With a single wing, she kept trying to rise, but he caught hold of it and ripped it off. She didn't cry out, I don't even know if she was crying. It was completely dark by now; the streetlamp was some distance away. She stood tall and straight before him, and he bent down, picked up the wings from the sidewalk and I don't know what he was saying as he pointed at the motorcycle, at the wings, and even at me, because in the end she obeyed, she straddled the motorcycle and before I knew what was happening, they both vanished amid the growling and backfiring of the engine.

And now what am I supposed to do? How can I tell you that the motorcyclist was you? I recognized your hoarse voice and your leather jacket.

The next day, she was pale, but calm. She avoided my eyes and walked just like all the other girls, her heels tapping on the asphalt.

(*Gazeta Literară*, no. 44, October 1964)

The Bird Tower

Viewed from behind, from a certain distance, they did not seem so far away from each other. They were slowly descending that sloping street at the edge of town, for a few minutes they held each other by the hand once more, but that was because she was wearing high heels, there was no point in him imagining any other reason, now of all times. Neither of them tried to break the long-woven silence. With high heels it's hard to walk on that bumpy paving, she took his hand without giving any explanation, the way you would grab onto the bannister of a stair. She was looking at the ground, she held her other hand away from her body, she was moving her lips. Damned street! Old crooked. It had all been a stupid mistake. He remained stubbornly silent. He could feel her hand, her long fingernails, the way she tightened her grip at intervals. That potholed street was torture on her slender ankles and high-heeled shoes. From the corner of his eye he could see her moving her lips, knitting her brows. He helped her hop over a pothole, her red nails dug into his hand for a few moments. He gave a clench-jawed smile. The street wound ever downward. The tower stood at its end.

On our bicycles we hurtled downhill, whooping, and at the bottom, at the end of the street, the tower loomed high, beyond it might have been the sea. We liked to think that beyond it the sea began, in which case, the tower was obviously a lighthouse. At dusk, the sun slowly set, swallowed by the void behind the tower, we would whoop, our hands gripping our handlebars, we hurtled down, at an insane speed, and we shouted the lighthouse has been lit, listen to the

*sea waves, the dull roar of the waves. And as they took frightened
flight, the birds from the tower had pointy, slightly bloodied wings,
we sensed real carnage, there were so many of them, their shadows
flitted crazily over the paving of the street, beneath the wheels of our
bicycles, and we yelled wildly, in fear and delight.*

It was all a stupid mistake, even he admitted that. Her stiletto
heels pecked the crooked cobblestones like beaks. It wasn't his
fault and, in the end, he didn't blame her. They could have sepa-
rated without them taking this walk, she was probably thinking,
but he wasn't to blame if she thought they had to make a clean
break, the way you snap a thread or a lace that's tied too tightly,
you don't waste time trying to unknot it. See, she's not even
holding his hand now, she doesn't need the bannister any more,
she's got the hang of walking down that potholed street without
sidewalks that isn't even a street.

*We were redskins, we were cowboys and Indians standing up
in our stirrups, we fired our pistols and rifles without mercy, some
of us were mown down, but that was the whole charm of it, like
at the cinema. The sun above the tower was a bowler hat, and the
birds were gushing in every direction, with reddened feathers, an
explosion of feathers, beaks, claws. The bicycles hurtled downhill,
the tower kept growing, it was a giant that had blotted out the birds
and the sun, but we were there too, Indian braves, come to free them.
The birds soared up, heralding victory, one behind the other we
surrounded the vanquished tower. Then we climbed the hill again,
that was less fun, before launching a fresh assault, because we were
Indians and sometimes cowboys, we were fearless, riding our bicycles
to wonderful adventures ever new.*

He needed to say something, anything. For example, he
should have pointed at the tower and told her: Look, this tower
has been here on this street for years . . . But there was no point,
it was something that belonged to him, both the street and the
tower, which was in fact a lowly ruin, where the birds made their
nests in summer. They were his memories; she didn't deserve
them. It was a mistake, obviously, but she couldn't let it pass,
and she had become a stranger once more, a girl like any other,
a girl you had taken to the cinema.

They had almost reached the tower. It looked like the trunk of an old tree, peeling, worm-eaten, leaning slightly. From a distance, from the end of the street, they looked like two lovers in search of an out-of-the-way spot. He walked with his hands in his pockets, shivering. They will walk around the tower, then they will go back, they will climb that hill, the stony road with its sparse, pale grass. And her hand will lean on his arm again, like on a bannister. He was cold. Beyond the tower, where once had been a waste ground covered in weeds and thistles, there was now a kind of park, there were even benches. But they will go back. She is leaving town. He wasn't angry at anybody; even without that letter, he would have known. The walls of the tower were blank. But at the top, on the other side, there was there a small window, so he remembered.

We surrounded the tower, the gigantic, armless cyclops, vanquished, but never budging, and beyond, the sea had dried up, it was now a plain of green and black stone, yellow in places. We dismounted, weary, disappointed, we stood motionless for a long time, resting one hand on our bicycle saddles, until the black wings fluttered into the distance, toward the horizon. And we turned our gaze to the single eye of the tower, the yellow, glassy eye of the tower, where we knew the watchman sat. We had never seen him, some said he was a cricket, that he was tall and more powerful than we, that he had long arms and wore a top hat. And it was nice to be afraid, we had our pistols at the ready, but it was late, and now, on the way back, with the tower behind us, pushing our bicycles by their horns, we were no longer Indian braves, we were no longer in high spirits.

On the way back uphill, her high heels helped her, she didn't need to lean on his arm. She realized that he wasn't going to say anything, he wasn't going to demand any explanation. What would have been the point of sitting in the park? They went back. Maybe it was better that way. She turned her head to look at the tower. She did so for his sake more than anything else, but he didn't notice or pretended not to. The sky was cloudy, it had bulged slightly and turned red, mostly around the tower. They climbed slowly, their feet pressing down on the stone as if on a shovel blade, they were leaning forward, one arm stretched behind them, fist clenched.

At the top, at the end of the street, a group of children on bicycles appeared. They were whooping, whistling, clicking their tongues, standing on their pedals, riding with grim determination. The tower soared, it grew higher and higher, they were Indians, and beyond, beyond the tower, might very well have been the sea.

Aria for Trumpet

His lips stung, his throat felt dry, his legs heavy, stiff. He quickened his pace. He clutched the trumpet case beneath his arm more tightly. It had been raining, the bulbs of the streetlamps shone on the wet pavement now in front of him, now behind; his staggering shadow swept the puddles. He had played well that evening, but cussedly. He'd played hoarsely, sometimes even stridently, on purpose. Cornel had lost his temper at one point; he'd looked over at him. But even so, he'd played well, better than if he'd played right. And Cornel hadn't had the guts to upbraid him, there weren't many people there, a redheaded woman at a table on the left, she'd been looking at him all the while, but not even she had had the guts. He'd played hoarsely, but he'd played well. Hoarsely and furiously. He stepped in a puddle, lost his balance, steadied himself on a lamppost. The trumpet case slipped and he caught it just as it was about to hit the ground at the bottom of the iron post. He got angry and then laughed. Even if they had invited him, he still wouldn't have gone, and Cornel knew it. But that was up to them. He deliberately stepped in another puddle, a small one—two handfuls of rainwater: the bulb of the streetlamp shattered into dozens of dirty yellow shards. He stepped in it with his other foot, he started to hop, to slap at the water with his feet, utterly smashing the lightbulb. He had a headache. He wouldn't have gone. His shoes were now wet on the inside too. Mihaela could hardly even be upset about it. There had been a time when she always got annoyed when he came in with dirty shoes. She cared about

48

her carpets, the luster of her parquet, which she rubbed herself, she polished it with wax, she liked it to shine, but he teased her, called her Parquetina, and she would get even more annoyed, at which he would change it to Serpentina! That was what he'd meant: Serpentina, a wee serpent with golden scales, a nasty serpent . . . He shattered the lightbulb of another puddle—so many puddles! And he felt cold and afraid. Mihaela was all alone in her room, which smelled more and more of medicaments. Doctor, tell me the truth, tell me, please. The standard, pathetic words. The doctor gave him a slightly ironic look, knitted his brows, a little smile at the corner of his lips. Those stupid words . . .

He started to walk more quickly. He felt glad to be going home early, proud even. He clutched the case beneath his arm. Again a puddle, the lightbulb showing its yellow grin, and the anger and fear, and in his ears the sad, hoarse melody he'd played that evening, the melody Mihaela liked so much: blue-grey bird in the garden, as big as a bustard, big and alone, except for the curly-haired boy who brings it food, a nasty bird, blue-grey, among the flowers and the fruit trees in bloom, nobody loves it, only the child, since he doesn't know it is ugly and nasty (how could he know that?) and old. A sad melody, seemingly without any rhythm, there was only a single passage that is happy, or rather, that is livelier, and Mihaela would tap the faucet of the sink with a fork, nor did she know, or maybe she pretended not to. And then to the rhythm of the fork he would begin to improvise happy, lively melodies, twists, cha-chas, and they both whirled around the kitchen, stamping up and down, the trumpet wailed, croaked, squealed, and Mihaela would laugh fit to burst. A whirlwind of sounds and colors, the fork tapping red and blue enameled pans, the greenish-white cupboard that Mihaela herself had painted in a beautiful, childlike way: birds with crooked wings and long beaks, red fish with lacy fins, leaves as big as trees, hands. The stamped around like wild things, until the neighbors made a scene, even though they were fond of them, they knew them and put up with a lot.

A dark street with a single lopsided lamppost. When he was little he thought that lampposts spring up in the places where people die, or some such thing, and he was afraid of them, of their pale light, particularly the crooked lampposts on the out-lying lanes where he grew up. He broke into a run, the trumpet case tucked under his arm, from time to time he looked behind him and he was afraid, the same as in childhood, of the claw-and-muzzle shadows cast by the yellow light of the lampposts. In the distance, covered by a frozen blue-black sky, he saw the bridge. He stopped running only when he reached the housing blocks: there was more light there, surer light—neon lampposts.

He went inside and would have liked to find her sleeping, although he knew that the pain kept her awake till late. The parquet creaked, the door groaned softly, the bedside lamp was lit. In the room it smelled of medicaments, of ether, and there was also another, piercing smell. The bedside table was piled with little boxes, bottles, phials. From an overturned bottle a white oily liquid was draining drop by drop. He cast a furtive glance at the bed: she was asleep. He could see only her head, her sharp nose, her hollow cheeks. She had fallen asleep with the light on. She looked as if she had sunk down into the bedsprings, with only her head poking out. He didn't have the courage to go any closer, to touch her hand. The quilt, scarlet, dried blood, did not move in time with her breathing. He sank into the armchair, cradling the trumpet, without taking off his raincoat. If the doctor had lied, if . . . He closed his eyes, angrily clenched his eyelids, his fists, and to calm himself, in his mind he began to play the sad mel-ody, Mihaela's melody: the bird motionless among the flowers, the blue-grey, almost purple bird, with small raspberry-like eyes. He played it for a long time, clutching the trumpet case to his chest. Finally he heaved himself to his feet and, without looking at Mihaela (her nose is so pointed, like a carrot!) he extinguished the lamp. He bit his lips and clenched his fists, clutching the trumpet case to his chest. He didn't have the courage to kneel beside the bed and take her hand, feel her pulse, or to slip his hand under the quilt and place it on her thin chest. He sank into the armchair again. The blinds hadn't been drawn properly and through them seeped the cold, now unsettling neon. Again he tried to play the melody, but other tunes kept sounding in his ears: syncopated rhythms, twists, bossa novas, a furious hammering in his head, which deafened him. I'm afraid, that's what! Now he was alone again, with the blue-grey bird from childhood, and he knew, now he knew that the bird was bad.

He had to calm himself. He started counting, he stretched his legs, he put the trumpet down beside him, he rested his head on the cold, slightly rugose backrest of the armchair. A corpse beneath every lamppost. Some people die on the street, they lift their hands to their hearts or their foreheads and they die, they fall, firstly to their knees, then they lean on their arms, their elbows, and they stretch out on the pavement, on their backs or on their sides, or they tumble forward on their faces, it's as if they are sleeping, as if they are crying.

He was awakened by the groan of the door, the creak of the parquet in the vestibule. He lifted one arm, he let it fall back, his body felt heavy, sluggish, sleepy, he was surprised it was dark, that it was not morning, that there was no sun, only the cold, hypocritical light of the neon seeping through the blinds. The door to the apartment and then silence. He tore himself from the armchair and rushed to the bed, groping. He felt the quilt, the sheet, which smelled of ether. Mihaela was not there. She had left. He lurched to the door, tripped over the trumpet case, picked it up, took it with him, pressed the door handle, the door banged against the wall, he ran downstairs two steps at a time, reached the main entrance. It was locked. He paused for a few moments, his forehead resting on the thick pane. He understood: she was now light, so light! He rummaged in his pockets and found the key. The strongly lit street, a fine mist, violet around the neon tubes, and in the distance, above the buildings, the bridge. He began to run: even strides, not too close together, he had a long way to go, he breathed steadily. The streets around the building were brighter than usual, the bulbs of the streetlamps grinned a yellow, congested light—miniature, bloated suns. Countless streetlamps, he ran and he ran, his shadow now behind him, now in front of him, now falling to one side, now monstrously elongated before him. He ran to the bridge, he felt no tiredness, the pavement was becoming springier and springier. The whistle of a locomotive and the cadenced clack of the wheels over the rails. He was amazed at how quickly he had arrived. Unexpectedly, the bridge loomed before him, its rusting metal skeleton shivering as if from the cold. From a distance you couldn't tell: it was trembling, its metalwork was chattering, a few electric lightbulbs jerked back and forth, cast madly dancing shadows over the pavement. A moment's hesitation, then he began to climb the steps, which shuddered beneath his feet. When he reached the top, he found himself jostled by a crowd of young people in raincoats, they were coming home from a party, or maybe they were just vagrants. He stopped, braced himself, clutching the case to his chest. He wasn't afraid, but he was in a hurry, he still hoped to reach her, to persuade her to come back home, she had probably left wearing only her nightshirt, and it was quite cold outside. The raised collars of the raincoats, the caps pulled down over the eyes, the hands stuffed in pockets. There were also two girls, one of them looked a little like Mihaela. He wasn't afraid, but there was no point wasting any time trying to explain to them, to reason with them, and Mihaela was wearing only her nightshirt. He jumped to his left, holding the case under his arm, and he rushed forward among the struts of the bridge, which shook from every joint. But he didn't even reach the halfway point of the bridge: they were in better shape, more fleet of foot, one of them dived at his legs, another grabbed his collar and pulled him to the ground. Beneath the bridge a locomotive passed whistling, and a puff of warm steam, smelling of coal, enveloped them all. When he came to his senses, he looked up, faces, not threatening but mocking, appeared and disappeared in the mist. There was a smell of coal and rust. The bridge shivered softly, like a paralytic old man. One of the girls knelt down beside him and felt his brow, his face, he could feel her slightly rough hand on his lips, smelling of tar, then on his throat, his chest, her nails dug into his flesh and he shuddered. What have you got there in the box? A child's voice. And the others laughed. One of them kicked the case. It opened. The trumpet was revealed, calm shiny. He hadn't hurt himself as he fell, he felt no pain anywhere. He leaned on his elbow and slowly but determinedly pushing the girl aside, he rose to a sitting position. One of the boys, with a swarthy face and a large, hooked nose, picked up the trumpet and blew it at the top of his lungs: the trumpet lowed, the boy took fright, dropped it. The others burst out laughing. The girl was choking with laughter, hiccoughing. You're a trumpeter then, are you? Go on, give us a tune! Let's hear you . . . He got to his feet and tried to explain to them. I'm in a hurry, he said in a weak whisper. He felt a hand on his shoulder and then the girl's head resting on the hand. I'm in a hurry, you know, she left, got out of bed . . . she's wearing only her nightshirt. I have to bring her back . . . A wee lad with thick lips and jug lugs grabbed his collar abruptly, it made him blink, but he managed to control himself. It's pointless your crossing the bridge! And the lad made a scornful gesture, which the others understood. Are you going to play or not? The girl pressed her body to him, protectively. Lucky you've got that trumpet. Go on, play!

He had no choice. He grasped the trumpet, the boys moved to one side, one of them yelled shrilly, Twist! and he began to play a syncopated melody, silently tapping his foot. The lad with the hooked nose clapped his hands, so too did the girl, and they started to dance. They swayed their hips, they jerked their legs, they lowered their shoulders, but keeping them rigid, they span around on their knees or backs. They'd throw off their raincoats and clapping their hands, panting, grunting, they were dancing like the devil. The trumpeter had become inflamed too, carried away by the tune he started to move to the rhythm of the dance. Rock 'n' roll! shouted the lad with the hooked nose. Then they demanded a bossa nova. Frenetic shadows beneath the trembling lights of the bridge, the continuous drone of the ironwork and the grunts of pleasure, the panting and the whoops of the danc-ers. When they tired and let him go, he couldn't find the case: it must have fallen down between the railroad tracks . . . What are you looking for? Better leave it . . . It's dark down there, the trumpet will cheer you up, see how it shines! They walked with him to the end of the bridge, where the steps down to the other side began. Down below it was pitch black. Here and there a faint light, a crooked, humpbacked lamppost. He grew afraid.

How good it would be if he could keep their company, those high-spirited guttersnipes! He looked at them from the corner of his eye: they were standing a couple of paces away, with their hands in their pockets, their heads bowed, not speaking a word. He raised the trumpet and started to play a devilish twist, stamping his heel on the first step of the bridge, causing it to shake even harder. He descended another step, still playing, and looked over his shoulder: none of them moved. He said: Aren't you coming? The lad with the hooked nose took a step forward and yelled: Get out of here, go on! He then turned on his heel. Come on, lads, he's shitting his pants. A slicker! The young people went away with their hands in their pockets, without haste, without looking back. He stopped playing. He descended the steps and reaching the bottom of the bridge, he realized that there was no point in his going any farther. Well, yes, he was afraid, he could feel the hairs standing up on his skin. It was pointless, it was stupid what he was doing, better he went home . . . But to walk past the young people again, the dancing guardians of the bridge, and then to go all the way home, in the cold, to the empty house . . . He would go by one of the dark side streets that led down from the bridge. The trumpet shone in the darkness, he held it up in front of him with both hands, like a torch, as if he were about to play it. He began to feel small bodies brushing against his ankles, rats or maybe moles were swarming along the street, which went endlessly downhill. He paused to listen to the short grunts, the ceaseless dry rustling, and, at intervals, the squealing. He did not dare to make any sudden move with his feet, to kick them, to squat down and catch one in his hand. He set off again, taking short, fearful steps. The whole street was swarming with rats. At the end of the street there was a crooked lamppost—there couldn't have been a better sight! As he approached the yellowish light, he saw hideous shadows with claws and snouts in the yards on either side, creatures larger than rats, more and more of them, chittering, going in and out of the yards, the houses, climbing the walls, the fences, and even the lamppost, squealing in pain, burnt, blinded by the lightbulb. Clotted blood at the bottom of the lamppost, blood streaming down the stem, rats mad with pain, the eyes of beasts of prey peering from every direction. He couldn't go back. The next street was even darker. Small purple flames flickered in the distance. He turned down a street at random. There seemed to be fewer rats, the lampposts were more frequent, they were squatter, they smoldered. In the gateway of a house was a cherry-red bell, resting on a fence pale, and on the other side of the fence, beds of luminous flowers and fruit trees in blossom. He decided to enter. He grasped his trumpet tightly. The gate was ajar, the rats slipped inside too, they ran among the first flower beds. In the whitish light of the dwarf lilies, the rats seemed frightened, fear gleamed in the red pinpricks of their eyes. They ventured no farther. The garden seemed limitless, the fruit trees in blossom, the vegetables, the apricots seemed to grow thicker and thicker, more and more luminous. A strong, milky white light, streaked with iridescent blue, a fragrant, mysterious orchard. His heart shrank, in both fear and delight. He then raised the trumpet mouthpiece to his lips and almost without realizing it, he began to play, timidly at first, that same sad melody, then more and more boldly, more and more loudly; he raised the funnel of the trumpet and filled his lungs. He played and he did not take fright when the blue-grey bird appeared from the bottom of the garden among the flowering apricot trees; he had never seen it walk, it looked like a big turkey, without wattle or crest, it approached slowly, with a rocking motion, and the flowers shone more brightly. The rats fled from its path, squealing in fright or maybe in token of respect, the light of the flowers grew ever bluer, he played, he was not afraid, he looked at the bird the same as in his childhood dreams, in slight astonishment and even pity, since it had spread its ridiculously short wings and did not rise up; astonishment, but not fear, although now he knew. He also played the livelier, more syncopated passage, the bird took shorter and shorter steps, the garden gradually turned blue, the bird's plumage grew broader, bluer, which is to say, they turned first violet and then blue, they fluttered before his eyes, then arranged themselves in a fading, bluish weave, which grew thinner and thinner, the translucent silky lacework touched his eyelids; he felt happy, as if after some triumph and opened his eyes: dawn seeped through the blinds. In bed, Mihaela was breathing evenly, the redness of the quilt had died away.

He stretched his numb arms, his bones cracked pleasantly, it was morning. He got up from the armchair, opened the blinds, he also half-opened the window. Outside: the street, a bicycle, a few hurried passers-by, a truck. He took a deep breath of fresh air. In the distance, over the houses, loomed the bridge and the golden-blue sky. He picked up the trumpet from next to his feet and, suddenly unable to keep still, he all but ran into the kitchen. He raised the trumpet and began to play the melody that obsessed him, he whirled around, hopped up and down, and all the red and blue enameled pots jumped up and down too, and so did the greenish-white cupboard, the fish with their lacy fins, the birds with their comical claws and beaks, and the hands, the orange palms by Mihaela, who had come back, she had come back, but he, madman that he was, stupid as he was, twist, twist—his wonderful trumpet, his trusty, shining trumpet . . .

Confidences

WE HAPPENED TO BUMP into each other on the street. I hadn't seen him for ages, it was raining, and as he was walking with his head bowed, I could have just walked past him. After he got married to Olga, he moved to Onești and I didn't see him again. He was walking with his hands in his pockets, looking at the ground, I thought he must be depressed, otherwise why the hell make a show of it? He no longer had that spring in his step, when he used to roll along on the whole length of his soles, like a high jumper; he was shuffling his shoes over the pavement, and his shoulders sagged a little. He had had big plans when he left and Olga, clinging to his arm, happy, would have gone anywhere with him, she loved him. It was drizzling now the same as it had been then, but he kept his head bowed, the cold rain was falling on the back of his neck. I was sure he hadn't seen me, I could have walked straight past. But nonetheless, I caught him by the sleeve of his raincoat, stopped him. He looked at me docilely, it was as if he didn't recognize me. His hand was limp, sticky, like dough.

"How are you, old chum?" I said, forcing myself to appear as friendly and ebullient as I could. His listlessness, his impassivity irked me. The rain kept falling, cold, relentless. "I haven't seen you for ages!" His raincoat hung from him, baggy, rumpled, the cuffs were frayed, he wasn't wearing a tie, the collar of his shirt was black with grime. Unshaven, with bags under his eyes, he looked old. His eyes, too—they were tired, sunken in their sockets. "What's the matter? Are you ill?" He shrugged, irritated by my questions. He then dragged me into a tavern.

57

I don't like drinking, and there are certain drinks that make me ill. I shouldn't have gone in. It reeked of booze, of dregs, of something sour. Mingled with a smell of crushed cigarette butts, ash, sweat. It made me feel nauseous, I would have liked to get out of there. Or at least to sit down by the window and look out at the drizzle, which was becoming finer and finer, purer and purer.

"I'm not sitting there, it's too far to the back," I said, and although he muttered something, he turned around and we both sat down by the window. He ordered vodka for both of us, even though I'd told him from the outset that I didn't drink. After which he sat without saying a word, his eyes glued to the jug of vodka. Maybe he was waiting for me to drink first and was upset at me being so finicky. "Aren't you drinking?" I made an effort to say it in a gentle, friendly sort of way, but my voice sounded curt, almost hostile. "Aren't you drinking?" I repeated, this time in a wheedling, almost embarrassingly shrill sort of voice. Annoyed at his silence, I added: "Didn't we come in here to have a drink? Why are you sitting like a tailor's dummy? Why don't you say something? Aren't you drinking?" And I knocked back a shot of vodka. He started laughing like a madman, banging his hand on the table, until he upset the bottle. He was laughing at me, obviously, at my grimaces and choking cough. "Bugger you!" I hoarsely whispered to myself. The vodka had scorched my gullet, I could feel it as it reached my stomach, burning everything in its path. He called the waiter and order another quarter liter of vodka. There was no longer any doubt about it: he was taking the piss. I stood up and made to leave.

"Stay a bit longer! Please! There's something I want to tell you."

His voice was wheezing, faint. I sat back down, although I wasn't at all curious. I did so out of politeness, or out of cowardice, call it what you will. Through the window, the street gleamed in the rain, it was a river growing brighter and brighter, and the people were tramping through the water, hunching their backs.

"Listen," he began, "I think you met my wife, Olga . . ." I nodded. I think I met her before I met him, the idiot! He poured some vodka in his glass, a large one, and drank it in one gulp.

He then looked at me fixedly, while I tried to avoid his gaze. The waiter went from one table to another, with his slightly bandy-legged gait. He was bald. There weren't many people in the tavern. Someone had come with his dog, which sat next to him, by his chair. What did I care about his wife! I knocked back my vodka and it didn't scorch so much this time.

"This big, this is how big . . . she shrunk to the size of a doll! The size of a doll!" he said, breathing heavily, he leaned across the table and spreading his hands, he showed me: "This big!" I didn't want him to continue, we clinked glasses, and the waiter with the duck's walk refilled the jug. Through the window, the street was brighter and brighter, although it hadn't stopped raining. The people were no longer hunched up, some children were running through the water flapping their arms. I didn't want to hear any more, I wasn't interested, I was also a little frightened. But how to stop him? With the palm of his hand he smoothed the tablecloth, which was stained with wine and grease, and looked me straight in the eye, while I tried to avoid his gaze. Maybe I was tipsy. The waiter looked at us inanely, picking his nose. There were only a few customers, each seated at a table by himself. Apart from the old man, who had his dog with him.

"I'm not lying to you, really I'm not. This big!"

He told me some convoluted story, constantly getting muddled up, stopping at every sentence to take a drink. He had grasped my hand and I didn't have any choice, I had to listen, even though I didn't want to and I couldn't make head nor tail of it. His eyes were shining. The waiter brought another jug. God, it was awful!

He buried his face in his hands, as if he were about to burst into tears. But I knew, I understood that he wouldn't have been able to cry. I dragged my hand away, put it in my pocket. With my other hand I was holding my glass of vodka. I felt revulsion by now.

"A year ago, she shrank to the size of a little girl, understand?"

"Understand what?"

The waiter was probably bored, what with not having any customers. He kept looking at us, straightening the tables next to ours, and without us asking him to, he brought us a plate of pickles. I refused to understand. The words came out of his mouth all sticky.

"You know, she kept dwindling, I could see her dwindling. But she didn't even realize. She would laugh when I told her, say I was joking. That was a year ago."

I looked out of the window as I listened to him, it was raining, and the children were running through the rain with their arms spread wide. He told me that he couldn't understand it either. Above all he couldn't make her see that it was now ridiculous for them to go out together, to a restaurant, to the theatre, as she would have liked. She played the piano all day long, she grew sadder and sadder, but she didn't realize a thing. What was he supposed to do? At the factory, he was surly, everybody got on his nerves.

"After a time, certain things, you know, became out of the question. Understand? I'm still young . . . You're a man, you know what I'm talking about. And she kept getting nastier and nastier . . . and smaller. She was nasty, all right . . ."

It had stopped raining. A truck came to a stop in front of the tavern. The driver barged inside, slamming the door behind him, the way he would the door of his truck. He was tall, burly, he wore his hair in a fringe, and in his grey quilted jacket he looked like a bear. The waiter swayed his way over to him.

She was nasty, she was always moaning, she complained about him leaving her on her own, the nights were torture. He pitied her, but what could he do?

"Put yourself in my shoes. Tell me, what could I do?"

He started coming home later and later, sometimes he didn't come home at all. He'd hooked up with a woman from work, an engineer, like he was, she was cheerful, clever. Olga would get bored at home all alone, but what could he do? She wanted to go out, to restaurants, to the cinema, she wanted to have a good time . . . But he would have made himself a laughingstock. She was too small . . . He broke off what he was saying. He called the waiter and paid the tab.

"Let's go."

"Where?" My head was throbbing, I was revolted at that whole story of his. "Go where?"

"We've moved back here. There was a kerfuffle and we left. What right did they have to interfere? Tell me, what right did they have?

It had stopped raining, but the eaves of the buildings were dripping. The street was glistening, like a wet back. Light was coming from every direction, the clouds had thinned out, and it was if the people were floating.

"Where are we going?"

"To my house . . . you'll see."

He lit a cigarette and quickened his steps. I could barely keep up with him. I would have liked to roam the streets on my own; my head felt like a boulder. Why was he telling me all this? Was he trying to torment me? He knew I loved her once and wanted to torment me. He was taking the piss . . . I grabbed him by the sleeve and yanked it.

"Stop. I'm not going."

"You can't not come. You've got to come. I'm begging you!" He held his face close to mine as if he were about to kiss me. He hissed in my ear: "You've got to come!"

I couldn't take any more. I raised my fist and belted him in the face. Then I shoved him and ran off. I was staggering, my head was spinning. I came to a stop by a wall and threw up. It was a relief. When I lifted my head, he was standing next to me. He was looking at me imploringly, humbly, even.

"You've got to come. Believe me. You've got to. It's not my fault. Come on. Let's go."

And he started to run, down the middle of the road, corners of his raincoat fluttering. I ran after him. I caught up with him. He was panting, his eyes were shining. He whispered to me hoarsely: "Believe me. I didn't love that other woman. She had a big mouth, dyed her hair, thought she was clever."

He took out another cigarette. His fingers were trembling. I had to light it for him, with my lighter. One day, Olga left home and he didn't know where she was, she was gone for almost a month.

"When she came back, she was taller. God! She was more

beautiful, too. As beautiful as she was in the beginning . . . You won't believe me, nobody will believe me."

I could see he was trying to cry, but all he could do was emit pitiful yelps.

"Come on, come and see her! She's the Olga she was in the beginning now, my darling Olga."

I couldn't understand a thing, and I felt like throwing up again. He fearfully took me by the arm, gently propped me up. And we set off in the direction of the railroad station, where he said he lived. The clouds were dissolving, more and more patches of blue sky were appearing. The street gleamed less now, and the light had risen to spread evenly over the whole city. At the door he hesitated, before inviting me to go inside first.

"Yesterday, she grew even bigger."

"Who?" I asked in bewilderment.

"She grew. Understand? She's taller than me now. And she doesn't love me any more, she doesn't love me. She told me so yesterday, in no uncertain terms."

In the mirror in the hall, we saw ourselves: pale, weary. We were hideous. He started to call her, he went from room to room, still in his outdoor clothes, his shoes sopping wet, he went to the kitchen. There was nobody at home. It smelled bad. I would have liked to open the window. In the bedroom, the doors of the wardrobe gaped open, the bed was unmade, on a chair there was a crumpled-up dress, its sleeves hanging to the floor. And it smelled bad . . .

He grasped me by the lapel of my coat. His face was contorted, and it was then that I knew he really was suffering and it touched me. I took his arm, to guide him to the door.

"She's gone for good! It's the end!"

He rushed to the next room and then came back. He knelt down to look under the bed, he climbed on top of a chair, but the suitcase wasn't on top of the wardrobe. His broad, soft hands were covered in dust, helpless. I felt pity, I felt repugnance . . . I took him by the shoulders and guided him to the front door. We went out into the street. The sky was blue. The people were treading softly, they floated around us, tall people.

Icarus

HE HAD FALLEN ASLEEP, leaving the light on. His face was half buried in the pillow; one arm dangled over the edge of the bed, the other was twisted underneath him, palm-upward. This ever since he was a child: he tucked one knee under his belly and looked like a swimmer in some liquid that had suddenly turned colloidal. The coverlet had slid off, the sheet was rumpled from his tossing and turning. From time to time he moved his arms and his head, turning his hot face onto the other side, with fluid movements which, if you ignored the pauses between them, made it look as if he were swimming. There were also intervals when he turned onto his back, one leg still flexed, his mouth slightly open, emitting a thin snore like the buzz of a bumble-bee. But he didn't remain in that position very long, probably the light bothered him, he would twist back around onto his belly with an abrupt movement, and the buzzing would cease, so that only the deep, regular breathing that slightly moistened the pillow could then be heard in the room.

He had sent the blanket flying with a kick and it lay in a heap at the end of the bed. The buttons of his pajamas had come undone, exposing his fat, white body, which was covered in long sparse hairs. Seeking the coolness of the wall, he abandoned the overheated pillow, finally tipping it, with a sweep of his arm, into the coal scuttle. The poker that was leaning against it fell against the door of the stove and the noise dragged him from the depths of sleep, he raised his arm, clutched the wall hanging, three quarters of which came loose. He twisted around to

63

the edge of the bed once more, groggily got up, and went to the table. He drank from the water jug, not bothering to pour himself a glass. He looked around him and, as if remembering something important, went into the bathroom, whence he returned cradling an ironing board. He tested it on his shoulders, then tried a little lower, over his shoulder blades, standing hunched over. The image in the wardrobe mirror was slightly ridiculous, but he didn't care about that. He unfastened the suspenders from the trousers hanging over the back of a chair, and a smile briefly flickered over his lips. But he was in a hurry. Using the suspenders and some ribbons that had once adorned a chocolate egg, he managed to attach the ironing board more or less over his shoulder blades. He looked in the mirror again. The striped pajamas, like a prisoner's uniform, and the wooden wings . . . There was nothing funny about it, nothing at all. Feeling embarrassed nonetheless, he went to the window—the board jiggled slightly on his back—and opened it determinedly. With some difficulty he climbed onto the ledge and peered out.

The lights of the city floated doubtfully, not at all invitingly. The rumble of a tram gave him an unpleasant surprise. For an instant, he was gripped by a kind of fear. He hesitated. But only for an instant. He felt the rough stone beneath the soles of his feet, beneath his clenched toes. Then the fall. Falling and then rising and again a gliding descent . . . He held his head up high, as high as he could, and his arms outspread. The board weighed down on the points of his shoulder blades. He twisted his whole body to the right, jerking his legs like a tail, to avoid flying into the building at the end of the street. He gave his legs another flap, like a dolphin, and started to rise. The back of his neck was aching, and the light of a star was boring into his eye. He flew for a long time. He had left the city below, with its noise and its lights. The air was ever colder, ever purer. He reached a strip of sky that was less dark, he stretched out his arms, saw that they were blue, elongated. Alongside him, the flutter of huge silken wings: a butterfly as big as an eagle was flying around him, zigzagging ever closer, ever closer, brushing his face with cool draughts of air . . .

With an abrupt sweep of his arm, he tipped the pillow on top of the coal scuttle. The poker fell onto the door of the stove, a star exploded up above, on the left, and wave upon wave of sound thrust him up from the depths of sleep. He raised his arm, clutched the flowery wall hanging, which came loose and fell on him. He twisted toward the edge of the bed and groggily got up, went to the table. He drank from the water jug, not bothering to pour himself a glass. He was thirsty. He looked around him and, remembering, quickly went into the bathroom, whence he returned with the ironing board. He tested it on his shoulders, then tried a little lower, over his shoulder blades, hunching over. The reflection in the mirror was slightly ridiculous, but what could he do? He removed the suspenders from the trousers hanging over the back of the chair and gave a weary smile.

(*Ateneu*, no. 10, 1966)

Tall and Distinguished

HE FINISHED SHARPENING the indelible pencil—he always left it till last, the wood was hard, the lead atrocious, crumbly—he looked at the clock and smiled. Wretched sharpener! He tapped it on the serrated edge of the ashtray, to empty the shavings. It was in the form of an ice skate: that was why he had bought it. He also had a globe, a whale, a nice white elephant and—no reason not to admit it—a ballerina. But they were all broken, the blades were blunted, and as for the ballerina . . . better not say. He looked at the clock and smiled. He neatly laid the files in their drawers, he put the stapler back in its place, the sharpeners, the box of paperclips; the only things he kept out were the green marble pen tray, the inkwell, and a ream of paper, so that the desk wouldn't be bare. Then he locked it.

It was hot, too hot even. He laid his hand on the edges of the scorching radiator fins. Outside it was sub-zero. This difference in temperature wasn't good, obviously. Horşia was reading *The Century*. He kept the magazine in the half-open drawer while he read avidly, hunching his head between his shoulders so that all you could see from behind was a tuft of hair. What if the boss came in! He rested his shoulders on the glass top of his desk, as if on a lectern, and stroked his moustache with a crooked forefinger. He liked to look distinguished. He drummed his fingernails, immaculate as ever, and wondered what the boss would say if he saw Horşia with his head stuck inside the drawer like an ostrich. What would he say? But nothing came to mind, and probably he wouldn't even notice. He took the ice skate from his pocket and guiding it with two fingers let it glide over the rink of the desktop; it foundered in a mound of snow: the ream of paper. Whence it sped away and managed two superb pirouettes. A moment's hesitation, then he bent down, unlocked the drawer, and took the other sharpeners from the back of the drawer. He placed them on the ice. But now Horşia stood up and jingled his bunch of keys, as if to say: time to go home. He quickly stuffed the fish, the ballerina and the others in his pocket. Horşia looked at him with slightly narrowed eyes. That was up to him! He stood up, looked at the open drawer, took his hat from the hook of the stand, put on his overcoat (it was new!) and went out the door in front of Horşia. He wasn't in a hurry, but the thing was, that Horşia sometimes liked to joke around and, not to put too fine a point on it, to make fun of him.

It had stopped snowing. Trampled by so many tires, by so many soles, the snow had turned the color of halva. On the tram-lines it had turned to mud and probably in the center of town there wasn't any snow at all: it had been carted away in trucks. Maybe it would snow that evening . . . Coming out of the can-teen, he headed home, by force of habit, but then he changed his mind. The sky was indigo and at the edges, in the distance, among the trolleybuses and overhead wires, it took on a gloomy dark violet color. Stray yellow-green sparks flew above the trams. The streetlamps would soon light up. It got dark so quickly! He held his hands behind his back, like bear paws in their fur gloves. His hat was crammed down over his ears. He didn't feel the cold. On the rooftops the snow was in shadow, turning greyer and greyer. He wasn't cold. He had no reason to enter the tavern on the other side of the street, but he crossed the road nonethe-less. Out of the tavern came two tall men and a woman with a birdlike face. She was pale and there were dark rings around her round eyes. After a few steps—by now the woman had walked away—he felt the need to take another look at her. She bore a striking resemblance to Luci and, look! the streetlamps lit up all at the same time, like that time in the living room, after the departure of the old man with the long white beard, his empty sack slung over his red silk shoulder. All the lights had come on—both the chandelier and the wall lamps—and there were the presents heaped under the tree. Luci, in her frilly dress, had first handed him the box with the ice skates. She knew what she was doing! He had stood there dumbstruck, clinging to the arm of the armchair: he was overawed . . . And the ice skates were not the only thing. Why was he standing there just holding the box? Luci insisted he open it. The metal of the skates was cold, as keen as ice.

He chewed a corner of his moustache, grimacing. It seemed to have grown colder: he felt a prickling behind his eyelids, as if he were about to burst into tears. Although covered by the brim of his hat, his ears had turned numb. A tram passed with an infernal rumble. He quickened his steps.

He still had the ice skates. For a long time, he had not even put them on his feet. Luci had made fun of his "idyllic love" for them, he didn't know what she meant, but he did like the ice skates very much: the gleam of them, the coolness, the sharpness of the chromed metal excited him terribly, and also daunted him. The truth was that he didn't want to break them, as Mr. Tassopol said (Tasso was Luci's term of endearment for him), albeit not maliciously, although he was older than Ştefan. He stuck his hands inside the skates and, on all fours, sliced the flowers and grass of the carpet. "You're niggardly," said Ştefan, "like your ma, you inherited your tightfistedness from Luci." That evening, Luci quarreled with Ştefan, who didn't come back after that. Only Tasso came. Obviously, other people came too, but more seldom, and they weren't like Tasso, who let him clamber on his knees and tickle his bald patch. Luci was very amused when she saw him do that and said that the bald patch was like a maid's mirror, in which you look on New Year's Eve to see who'll marry. In fact, they were all light-hearted and brought him candies, chocolate, toys. But sometimes Luci would sit with her head in her hands, staring into space. At which times her eyes would become perfectly round, they would shrink to two malicious blue beads set in the shadow of dark rings and fear. One day, he got it into his head that Luci was a bird. The voluminous sleeves of her kimono hung like lifeless wings.

He flicked the light switch. The room was in a terrible mess: the unmade bed, the quilt hanging to the floor, the teapot, salami peel and crusts of bread on the table, a crumpled-up newspaper under a chair, a necktie, the radio blaring. He smiled. He had been in a hurry in the morning, he had even signed the register two minutes late. He tidied up the table, picked the necktie and the newspaper off the carpet: "The Liberation Day Skating Rink is open daily between ten a.m. and ten p.m." He quickly got undressed and climbed into bed without turning the light out. He didn't want to read, his eyes ached, but lately he had fallen into the habit of sleeping with the light on. The lamp didn't have a shade, it was nothing but a metal cup with a socket for the bulb. And the bulb was brutal: its long talons bored into his brain. If you looked straight at it, the light hit you, struck you right in the forehead, whereupon rings of molten gold would start to spin, growing more and more numerous, faster and faster. He turned on one side, his cheek on the pillow, and waited for sleep. Which is to say, first of all the steps, steeper than the stairs of his building, which he ascended and descended every day (so many stairs!), which led to where everything was shining and still, in dream. Then he remembered the skates. He saw Luci watching him like a tired bird and he remembered the skates. Using a key, you could lengthen them as much as you needed. You clamped them to the sole of your boot, tightened the screws, and then, "Keep your balance, you're a big boy now," but in vain, he still couldn't learn how to do it. He would suddenly get the urge, even in the middle of the night, he would get out of bed, take the skates out of the box, stroke them, test the sharpness of the blades, run his hand over the cold metal, smile. He put them on his feet and, in front of the mirror, struggling to keep his balance, never tired of looking at himself. His legs would bend and start to tremble from the tension, but sooner or later he would have to learn to keep his balance, even to glide across the ice of the skating rink, making elegant curves, about-turns, and even pirouettes, with one leg slightly raised and arms forming a graceful circle above the head. He would wear that black suit of fine cloth, a white silk bowtie, and a top hat. He would descend the steps into the arena of ice, the night sky would be slightly red, velvety, with a little mist. On the mirrored surface surrounded by thousands of people, what artistry he would display, how tall and distinguished he would be, thousands of eyes would watch him, moist with admiration or envy, as he flew over the ice.

(*Gazeta literară*, No. 2, January 1966)

One Morning

THE SUN HAD only just risen and Auntie Luiza opened the window that gave onto the park. Faintly gilded, the tops of the trees were trembling. Birdsong flooded the room. She smiled, standing on tiptoes to gaze along the deserted street. In a few minutes, she would get washed, dressed, comb her hair, and go to the park, the same as she did every morning. She smiled once more. The sound of Vasile's snoring could be heard. She went away from the window, her bare soles slapping the parquet. Sinbad was asleep, the lazy thing, in his bed by the stove. He was snorting softly, his muzzle resting in the crook of one foreleg. His light brown body, with its fur as glossy as leather, moved in time with his breathing. His ears hung limp. Auntie Luiza relented and let him sleep some more. On the sideboard, her old-fashioned and slightly fraying straw hat looked like a sunflower. Next to it were her white mesh gloves. She groped for her slippers under the bed, stooping with a certain amount of difficulty. For the last few days, she had been getting a stabbing pain below her ribs. She had even told Elena about it, who had tried without success to convince her of the benefit of suction cups. She straightened her back and took a deep breath. She avoided looking in the mirror and, quite noisily, pressed the handle of the door to the bathroom. Ever since she could remember, she had washed with cold water in the morning, wrestling with sponge and soap. She emerged from the bathroom invigorated and content beneath her robe. She no longer felt the stabbing pain. She had rubbed herself with the towel till her skin turned red. She bent down to touch the floor with her fingertips, she raised her arms, leaned back a little, bent to the side, first on one hip, then on the other. After repeating this a few times, she began to get dressed. She put on a long dress of green taffeta with yellow stripes, a dress from her youth. She looked in the mirror only when she combed her hair. She had had black, glossy hair, but even now it was still black . . . And her eyes—her eyes had always been young and lively.

She adjusted the straw hat on her head and spryly turned to the window. A beam of sunrays, as if from a spotlight, lit up the green canopy of the park. Sinbad now woke up. He yawned sleepily, then leapt onto the carpet, his crooked paws scrabbling in their haste to reach Auntie Luiza. He rubbed up against her legs. She forgave him his laziness this time, too. She stroked him with one shoe and then called him to the sideboard. From a drawer full of lace, ribbons, fans and beads, she took his collar. Sinbad made no protest. In the other room, Vasile had probably woken up by now and would be in a hurry lest he be late for work. With Sinbad on his leash, Auntie Luiza went down the hall, which had a fusty air, and carefully opened the front door. Sinbad lumbered down the stairs. They came to a stop by the gate. The ice truck was passing, rattling over the broken cobbles. The park was just a few steps away. Auntie Luiza hurried to get there, as if she were late. She crossed the street, tugging on the leash in slight annoyance. A breath of wind brought an unfamiliar smell to her nostrils. She recognized it as a sea breeze and experienced a pleasurable thrill of remembrance: Those tranquil and so blue mornings, when she stretched out on a deck chair, gazing with half-closed eyes at the sea, which stretched all the way up into the sky. She gave another annoyed tug on the leash. It was as if Sinbad had to stop at every single railing! Those mornings scented by saltwater and seaweed . . .

In the park, she found her bench and sat down, stretching her arms out on the backrest. The clouds looked like sailing ships blown along on the wind. Enjoying his freedom, Sinbad was wreaking havoc in the flowerbed. The wind blew more strongly, bringing strange scents, tossing the leaves, making them rustle. Thrashed by the leaves and trees, the air was making a low rumble, like the sound of waves. The air rose like the tide and washed over the park. To his amazement, at the end of the street Sinbad discovered a sailing ship gently borne along on the wind. Among the flowers, the dog froze to the spot. The ship slowly approached, old, elegant, its sails raised in greeting. On deck, the sailors were getting ready to weigh anchor. The enormous, rusty anchor lodged next to a chestnut tree. Sinbad took fright and gave a shrill bark. It was only then that Auntie Luiza saw it. Her hat hanging to one side, she gazed in bewilderment. The sailors were young and blond. They came from far away, from the north. Barefoot, nimble, the climbed the rigging, lowering sails and hoisting multicolored flags. Auntie Luiza half-stood up, unsure, then, overwhelmed by emotion, she sank back down onto the bench. The wind had died down. So too had the light. Sinbad approached the ship, circling, barking. The sailors did not keep still for a single moment. In their short-sleeved shirts, tight over their muscular torsos, they looked like acrobats. And how old the ship looked, with its timbers blackened by countless fires! Its hull was green with seaweed, its prow as sharp as an arrow-head. Auntie Luiza straightened the hat on her head, opened her purse and, with unusual care, started to powder her face. In the mirror, despite her wrinkles, her face looked quite young, and her eyes were dark, lively. The sailors started to scrub the deck. Their bodies moved so rhythmically and with such ease that it all looked more like a gymnastic workout than a chore. Her voice slightly altered, Auntie Luiza called Sinbad, who had succumbed to ecstasy by the park railings as he watched the strange monster. Auntie Luiza now moved closer to the ship, on unsteady steps, treading over grass and flowers. Her gloved hands anxiously kneaded each other. She sat down on another bench. The sailors had finished scrubbing the deck. Lined up on the upper deck, they were all gazing out over the park. How closely they resembled each other, tall, strong, blue-eyed, their sunburnt faces impassive! Their brawny arms were tattooed with dark blue curlicues. Auntie Luiza looked away and again called Sinbad. Her voice was shriller, stiffer. She half-turned her back on the ship. She was sitting up straight, rigidly, with her hands in her lap. A thin mist gradually enveloped the park. After a time, when she looked out of the corner of her eye, the sailors were hoisting the sails. The wind was ripe for them to cast off. The multicolored flags fluttered in farewell. Again the rumble of the waves, the rustle of leaves and water in her ears. The sky abruptly paled. The anchor slowly rose, with a grinding of chains. Luiza gave a start. She got up from the bench, called to Sinbad, who was yelping with his head and paws poking through the railings. The ship lumbered into motion, swaying as it went. Luiza took a few steps backward, then, without thinking what she was doing, she climbed up on the bench and with her arm outstretched helplessly after the ship, she watched till it vanished from sight. Called once more, Sinbad came to her, his ears hanging limp, his crooked legs hesitant. Wearily, without looking at the dog rubbing up against her legs, Auntie Luiza put her gloves back on.

In Our Yard

AT THE CRACK OF DAWN, Mrs. Ignătescu would hang the rugs over the frame and then Ion would whack them now with a carpet beater, now with a walking stick. The dust would rise, spreading like a fog throughout the yard. The rabbits would scatter in fright, the outraged hens would retreat to the coops at the back. Mrs. Ignătescu's dog would bark. The commotion used to wake all the tenants. Mrs. Năstase would bring out her rugs too. A window would open, and from within a squeaky voice would declare that a pregnant woman needs peace and quiet. This always sent Mrs. Ignătescu into a rage: Not only did Berta not have a husband, but she was impertinent to boot. Ion would grimly whack the rugs and laugh, his face sticky with dust and sweat. The housewives would bicker, breath in the dust and sneeze. Mrs. Ignătescu would place her hands on her hips. It was then that the milkwoman would arrive, protectively cradling her canister like a baby. What dust! Old man Căpriță would emerge from his poky room with an empty bottle for some milk. He would cough (demonstratively) till he choked. Other tenants used to come outside to buy milk too. Ion always couldn't care less; he would only whack the harder. Mrs. Ignătescu's bugle-like voice used to rise above everybody else's. Sometimes, it was then that the trashman also used to arrive, with his clanging cowbell. The crates of trash would be dragged across the yard, making a deafening noise. Another quarrel would start: Did they expect Mrs. Ignătescu to be the only one to give him a tip? Finally, Mrs.

Ignătescu would lug her rugs back inside. Mrs. Năstase only had two rugs, and Ion, exhausted by then, would give them only a perfunctory shake. Gradually, the commotion would die down. The hens would go back to their coops, warily, taking short steps. The rabbits would go back to gnawing the rather rotten wood of the carpet beater. A mother hen would hurriedly gather together her chicks, beating a path for them by jabbing left and right with her beak. Silence would return to the yard: the only sound would be the clucking of the hens and the sizzling of pots and pans in the kitchens. One day, Mrs. Năstase bought a cock. The cock would enjoy Mrs. Ignătescu's hens, but what could Mrs. Năstase do about that? A magnificent cock! When they saw its big, flame-red crest, when they heard its cock-a-doodle-do for the first time, the hens shivered in pleasure. As for the rabbits, they seemed downright servile in the welcome they gave it. It was a tall, rather strangely dressed boy who brought it. After releasing the cock in the yard, instead of leaving, he timidly went up to the carpet-beating frame and began to examine it. His black trousers, which clung to him like leggings, and his skintight black t-shirt lent him the appearance of a gymnast. He was blond, with a long, swarthy face. His raised his arm and touched the cross-bar of the carpet-beating frame. He seemed dissatisfied with it. One of the bolder rabbits brushed his bare foot with its moist, sticky muzzle. The lad flinched, but looking down, he smiled. He stroked the grey back with the sole of his foot. Then he stood on tiptoes to see whether he could touch the crossbar with his head. His movement was too sudden and he hit his forehead. He shook his head and taking a step back, his heel trod on the rabbit, which fled in fright under the walnut tree by the fence. Mrs. Ignătescu's voice made itself heard somewhere and the lad walked away, went out the gate, into the street. But I saw him hanging around the next day. He was trying to peer through the fence pales. Maybe he missed the cock. Late in the evening, with another two lads, who were dressed the same, he determinedly entered the yard. They sidled up to the carpet-beating frame and, after standing motionless, looking at each other, for a few moments, made some hand signals. One hoisted himself up on the crossbar, as straight as a candle. Another coiled around it like a snake to hang upside down. The third stood lookout. They took turns romping on the moon-bathed crossbar of the carpet-beating frame. I couldn't get enough of looking at them. The agility, the strength, the skill! Their game ended badly: straining under the weight, the crossbar started to creak, to crackle, and finally snapped. They weren't hurt, they all landed on their feet, like cats. After which they made a run for it.

When Mrs. Ignătescu discovered the deed, she made a huge scene, questioning everybody in the building. She was outraged and at the same time puzzled. Who could have snapped the crossbar? It was hardly a thread! She moaned to everybody. Where was she meant to beat her rugs now? Damn this life! As for me, although I was questioned, I said nothing. I looked her in her bulging eyes, full of sympathy, but I could have danced for joy. I would be able to sleep longer in the morning. Ion was summoned too. Mrs. Ignătescu poured out all her ire on him. But how was Ion supposed to know? Let his hand fall off, whoever did it! He picked his nose with a stumpy finger, not at all bothered. Why was she so het up about it, it was no big deal . . . He wasn't a carpenter himself, but any carpenter would know what to do in a jiffy. The cock tried to climb onto the snapped crossbar, which now hung almost to the ground. It lost its balance and suffered an embarrassing fall, right in the middle of the hens.

I had peace and quiet for a few days. And not only me. The hens clucked merrily around the carpet-beating frame, hunting worms in the rotten wood; the rabbits ran hither and thither, chased by the cock; Mrs. Ignătescu's mutt got into the habit of wetting one of the poles.

One morning, the gymnasts showed up again. On their shoulders they carried stout new planks, freshly planed, hatchets, hammers, pliers, and a box of nails. You'd have thought they were going to build a gallows rather than repair a humble carpet-beating frame. They had clear blue eyes, they made swaying confident movements. They cheerfully, eagerly started work. The whole yard rang to the sound of hammers. Their solemn labor was more like a dance. From time to time, they gave each other meaningful smiles, but they never spoke. We quickly got used to them. Nobody interfered in their work, not even Mrs. Ignătescu. The rabbits gamboled fearlessly among their bare feet; the hens jumped up on their shoulders and pecked the gymnasts' food when they sat down in the shade of the walnut tree. The days passed, but the work did not make much progress. Nobody criticized them for it, although they ought to have done. For example, why had they moved the poles of the frame closer together and made it more than meter taller? How would Mrs. Ignătescu's Persian rug fit on it now? And once the crossbar had been fitted, you would need a ladder to reach it. What intrigued me was that Mrs. Ignătescu did not rush them. When she came back from the market with her basket laden, she would stop, watch them for a few moments, and then go inside without saying a word to them. Sometimes, Berta, with her big belly, would come outside into the yard to watch the carpenters. And, so far as I could tell, she liked what she saw. You might even say that not only had everybody become used to them, but also, they had fallen in love with them. Or at least that's how it seemed to me. It wouldn't be the first time that I've been wrong. The work went slowly. For some time, they had been mostly horsing around. They did somersaults, made death-defying leaps, walked on their hands, leapfrogged each other. Or else they had fun with the cock. They would lift it on top of one of the poles of the frame and tease it. Proud as it was, the cock was nothing but puffed-up display. It could barely keep its balance, spreading its wings and not daring to jump down. Nobody said anything to them. I saw Mrs. Năstase walk past them, stifling a laugh with her hand over her mouth. Once, when they weren't there, I went over to the frame and saw what they had been doing all that time: they had hammered hundreds of nails into the poor poles, emptying the crate they had brought the first day. But a fresh crate soon arrived and the hammering recommenced, at a brisker rate. They studded the poles of the frame from top to bottom. With what skill they hammered the nails in! I was forced to alter my opinion: the lads knew their trade. The heads of the nails were colored; hammering nail next to nail, they created all kinds of multicolored arabesques.

Autumn arrived. Mrs. Ignătescu, assisted by Ion, lugged home provisions for the winter. Mrs. Năstase boiled tomatoes at the bottom of the yard to make broth. The rabbits multiplied and swarmed all over the yard. One evening, Berta was taken to the maternity hospital. The carpenters continued their work, with the same slowness and thoroughness, but somewhat more determined to complete it. One day, they laid the crossbar at last: a thick, beautifully polished pole, in which they had of course embedded nails, in such a way as to make it look as if it was painted with black and red stripes. Gathered around it, the acrobats were hammering in the final nails. They reinforced the corners with slantwise slats. It was then, for the first time, that the astounding thought struck me: our carpet-beating frame had become a gallows. It was still rectangular, but much taller, and ultimately, it was beautiful. I for one liked it; I didn't need any carpet-beating frame. But why did Madam Ignătescu and Madam Năstase make no complaint whatever? For the life of me, I couldn't understand it. Where were they going to beat their carpets now? For one thing was obvious: only if you had a stepladder or only if you were an acrobat would you be able to reach the crossbar and hang your carpet over it. And even if you did, how would you beat it after that? One day, when the woman arrived with the milk, I asked her what she thought about the transformation: it's not a carpet-beating frame any more, it's a gallows! The milk woman gave an indulgent laugh, poured the milk in my jug, and left. Should I tell Madam Ignătescu that those rascals had hoodwinked us? True, she didn't know that they were the ones who had broken the carpet-beating frame in the first place. So, I kept mum, besides, I was the one who . . . But even so, it was too much, in our own yard . . . Madam Ignătescu, I thought, not without satisfaction, would kick up a fuss . . . And then woe betide those lads! She would set the whole neighborhood on them.

The acrobats had just finished decking the frame with flowers and multicolored streamers. One of them had a roll of thin rope on his arm. A kind of silk rope. He wound it around his arm, closing now one eye, now the other. A rabbit nibbled at his heel.

I'm not going to tell Madam Ignătescu. I'm not going to tell her anything. She can see for herself. Besides, wasn't she the one who hired them? It's too late now. She even might not believe me and start berating me. It's happened to me before. I opened the window to let in a little cool air. The sun was setting. the lads took off their short-sleeved shirts and went to wash themselves at the pump. They were merry, merrier than ever. They splashed each other, skylarked. They were laughing their heads off. Their wet bodies gleamed red in the setting sun. None other than Madam Ignătescu brought them some towels. They frolicked around her, chased each other, splashing her with water. Infected by their merriment, she started tittering, as if someone were tickling her, and slapped them on the backs with her broad, chubby hand. She moved her wide hips nimbly. Madam Năstase and her husband, comrade Năstase, came outside. Ion was picking his nose and grinning his big, crooked grin. They were all laughing, they couldn't have been happier.

All of a sudden, the lads ceased their skylarking. All too abruptly did they become serious! Wielding a stick, Madam Năstase sent the brood of hens off to roost. The rabbits went by themselves, lured by the cabbage leaves thrown next to their hutch. Only the cock remained. Making signs, the lads asked Madam Ignătescu something. Of course they could, since they'd finished the job! They thanked her, making lithe bows. Nimbly, Madam Ignătescu went inside, taking Ion with her, and then both returned, dragging the large Persian rug. The lads looked at her gratefully. No, it's no trouble at all! The lads rushed to help her; with a few deft, strong movements, they laid the rug at the feet of the frame. They looked at each other, smiled, and began the performance. First, to warm up, they did a few graceful pirouettes, a few somersaults. Then, making an amazing leap, two of them caught hold of the crossbeam of the frame and, as if on a trapeze, performed a few numbers worthy of the greatest acrobats. They span around, flapping like wings, they threw themselves into the air and then caught hold of the bar with a single hand, they lifted themselves, feet upwards, they let go, head downwards and just as everybody breathlessly froze in fear, they caught themselves and hung by their feet, like bats. After standing frozen for a few moments, comrade Năstase began to clap his large hands. Bravo! Bravo! Madam Ignătescu dabbed her sweating brows and forehead with her handkerchief. Oh, the excitement! The lads descended, tireless. They turned to look at me. It was then that old man Căpriță made his appearance, thin, his back hunched. He was ill, coughing. The acrobats looked at me. I felt awkward, I didn't really know what they wanted. The others looked at me too, and Madam Ignătescu gave a disdainful snort. It was a good job the lads were there—she had a great liking for them! The lads set in motion once more. This time they danced. The sun sank lower and lower, bathing their faces in russet light. and how their eyes gleamed! At first, their dance had something stiff and solemn about it. Their faces were grave, their eyes focused. Undulating slowly, they went around the carpet-beating frame; silent and supple, they coiled around the posts. It was a serpent's dance. Everybody watched them in excitement, perhaps even a little frightened. Gradually, their movements became jerkier, their pirouettes speeded up, their faces shed their solemnity. Their eyes gleamed more and more brightly. Their arms moved almost in a fury, their bodies convulsed, the dance became frenetic. More and more quickly, more and more quickly. Their faces, colored by the last flickers of the sun, had something devilish about them. All that could be heard was a protracted, serpent's hiss. They abruptly stopped. Right in front of me, very close to the window from where I was watching them. They made a deep bow. Their arms hanging next to their bodies, exhausted, but happy, they gazed at me steadily. I gave a childlike, sincere smile. Boundless joy blossomed in their eyes. They were so tall, it was as if they had trickled down from somewhere. They stood there, tall and straight, in front of me, until I was no longer able to suppress the smile of complicity they were waiting for.

Balancing Act

THE PERFORMANCE WAS to take place in the town square. The square was quite small: less than forty meters in diameter. Not that the town itself was big, or the houses, or the people. The people strolled with pleasure around their little square and admired the feeble spurts of the fountain at its very center.

That morning, they all got up earlier than usual, the town's brass band went up and down the main streets playing merry marches. The jaunty trumpets made a strident sound, causing all the dogs to bark. Just as they entered the square, a mutt crawled under a fence and rushed at the plucky drummer, ripping his trousers. This incident made them lose their time, and trumpets, French horns, tubas mingled their notes in a protracted and finally a panting roar, which all but terrified the peaceful townsfolk. Immediately after lunch, long before the performance began, almost all the townsfolk crowded around the fountain. They were merry, loud, they jostled each other, argued and joked, in order to pass the time. Above their heads stretched the tarred high wire on which the great acrobat was going to cross the square, at a height of more than ten meters. The wire was connected to two stout posts, taller than any house around the square. The houses were so small in that town!

The acrobat kept them waiting rather a long time. The impatient children began to whistle. The other spectators clapped their hands. Others still, tired after so much waiting, sat down on the rim of the fountain, whose jets of water had been turned off for that afternoon only. Everybody was looking in the direction of the town hall, the tallest building in the square. In front of it, soaring above the clock tower, stood the first pole. The other was on the opposite side of the square, in front of the club house. Finally, the acrobat made his appearance. From the slate roof of the town hall, the acrobat bowed to the public. Shouts and applause erupted; they put their fingers in their mouths and whistled or gave piercing whoops. Many stretched their arms in his direction, pointing him out to the people next to them. They were all merry, abuzz. The acrobat agilely sprang from the roof onto the pole. He clambered with ease up onto the platform at the top of the pole, from which stretched the wire. He bowed once more. Further applause. Hesitantly at first, then with greater and greater confidence, he set off along the wire. There was no net beneath him, he held no bar to balance himself. He walked the wire with his hands in his pockets. Unbelievable! The crowd was dumbstruck. Their mouths agape, their necks craning, none of them moved. Tensely, they watched every movement of the high-wire artiste. The acrobat had reached the middle of the wire. He stopped. He spread his long thin arms and let out a brief, piercing yelp. Then, with the greatest of ease, he turned a somersault; he landed on the wire, swayed a little, and continued his calm walk, with his hands in his pockets. The people down below were panting, sweating, their mouths were dry with excitement. Before he reached the end of the wire, the acrobat performed some more numbers, each more dangerous than the last. He pulled all of them off wonderfully, with an elegance such as the townsfolk had never seen. Reaching the opposite pole, he stopped, looked down for the first time, and allowed himself a little smile. After a moment's hesitation, the crowd burst into applause and cries of admiration. He did not pause for long. He set off back along the wire, still with his hands in his pockets, his head held high, sure of himself. The people no longer stood still; they watched him, walking in the same direction as he. They were no longer so excited. In their eyes, there was no longer fear, but only admiration. The acrobat repeated exactly the same numbers: he turned somersaults, he knelt down, he walked backwards, he did pirouettes. Reaching the pole in front of the

town hall, he gave a deep bow and, smiling, acknowledged the
applause. He then set out again. Down below, the crowd was
talking about his skill. Everybody was enchanted, everybody was
happy. They had spent a pleasant afternoon, one they would long
remember. They gave each other friendly smiles, full of good
will. From time to time they glanced up at the acrobat, who was
diligently repeating his numbers. The children chased each other
around the square, skylarking. Their anxious mothers called to
them by name and complained to each other about their bois-
terous progeny. In small groups, the crowd began to disperse.
Some of them made the effort to cheer and call out another
bravo as they left. The sky gradually clouded over, and the sun
sank without reddening the horizon. The acrobat turned another
somersault and all but fell. The few spectators still remaining
breathed a sigh of relief when he regained his balance. They then
applauded and left, shouting: Bravo! Bravo! The acrobat had
reached one of the poles once more. He bowed. In the square
there was nobody but a little old woman, who was watching
the spurting water in delight, and two or three boys, who were
trying to climb the poles. The acrobat gave a weary smile. The
performance had lasted a long time. Far too long. He looked
above him. The sky, a glossy grey, awaited the dusk. There was
something stern, unforgiving, in that glow . . . The acrobat gave
an inane smile and shrugged. The little old woman tottered away.
The children were playing with a dog: they were tormenting
it, they tied a tin can to its tail. The dog yelped, struggled. It
managed to escape and ran away. They children left too. What
a quiet town! The acrobat stretched out his arms and took a few
steps along the wire. A pirouette, two pirouettes, another pirouette, dozens of pirouettes. He grew dizzy. He looked up at the
sky again and pricked up his ears. He felt like laughing, for no
reason, and then he froze. From somewhere far away came the
sound of a trumpet. He gave a start. The sound became louder.
Trumpets were booming from on high, commandingly. Down
below, he thought to see the movement of people once more.
But it was only the dog, which had returned and was sitting
there with its ears pricked up. The acrobat tiredly rubbed his

brow. The trumpets sounded louder and louder, more and more commandingly. He raised his long, thin arms, he stood on tip-toes—how tall he was!—and jumped. His supple body sprang upward, but only a little way, before plummeting to the ground. The dog took fright, yelped, ran away. After which it returned, cautiously circled, gave a brief bark, came closer, and started to lick the powder from the cheek of the acrobat, whose face was now visible beneath his make-up.

Cold (1967)

Cold

The Chairs

FIRST OF ALL, there appeared a man dragging a chair behind him. He was barely able to drag it over the knobbly asphalt of the square. It was a huge chair of solid ebony, carved with all kinds of ornaments. A real throne. The man carefully placed this heavy, old-fashioned throne in the very middle of the square. Then he went away.

A few minutes later, he reappeared with another two smaller and lighter chairs, which he placed upside down on top of the first. He pulled out a handkerchief and mopped his sweating brow. Then he went away again.

Before long he returned with another man of the same height and similar appearance. Panting, each carried a load of chairs on his back. It was obvious from a mile off that they were in a hurry. They heaped the chairs higgledy-piggledy on top of the others. Then they rushed away. When they returned, they were pushing a kind of handcart, a wheeled platform, upon which were piled dozens of chairs. In great haste, they unloaded the handcart and went away again.

They repeated the same action for the next few hours. Finally, a host of chairs had accumulated in the square, of every shape and size: large chairs as solemn as church pews, comical stools with long spindly legs, squat tabourets with bulging velvet cushions, tall, rigid thrones, expensive chairs carved from rare essences of wood, chairs made of rough boards painted green, long benches, low banquettes of scuffed wood, cumbersome kitchen chairs, armchairs with gilded arms and legs . . . A sea of chairs.

Evening had fallen. But in the distance, low on the horizon, there was still a patch of blue sky. It was colder now, colder and colder.

The two men looked very weary. They were panting, covered in dust, their faces smeared with a mixture of grime and sweat. Their clothes were torn, revealing their knotted muscles. They allowed themselves not a moment's respite. They had rolled up their sleeves and were toiling with a will. First, they lined up the heavy benches with iron backrests into a square that served as a foundation, and on top of them they hoisted the biggest thrones and armchairs. With astonishing agility, one of them perched on the other's shoulders and clambered up the backs of the chairs as if up a ladder. One by one, the man on the ground tossed more chairs up. It was obvious they were working to a well-thought-out plan, arranging the chairs in an order fixed in advance: on top of the thrones came the upholstered tabourets, on top of them, a layer of high-backed chairs, further up, banquettes placed on their ends in perfect balance, and so on. When the man below no longer had the strength to toss the chairs up to the height the other man had reached, they resorted to a method as simple as it was ingenious: using a rope looped around the arms of a chair, they fashioned a kind of mobile pulley. In this way, the other chairs rose into the sky. From time to time, the man below asked:

"Can you see it yet?"

Each time the answer was no.

At which the two men carried on their toil, doggedly determined.

Once the final chair had been tied to the rope and hoisted aloft, it was barely possible to see the man perched on the pinnacle of that huge pyramid. The man left down below cupped his hands to his mouth and shouted:

"Hey! Can you see it now?"

There was no reply. He repeated the question, bawling at the top of his voice:

"Answer me, did you see it?"

There was still no reply. In a rage, he began to kick and punch the chairs, to rattle the carved backs of the thrones like the bars of a cell.

He shouted up at the man on the peak once more.

Then, weary, he sank down on the cold pavement of the square and hiding his face in his hands he burst into tears.

1959

He

HE WAS AS TALL and handsome as smoke. He sat on the edge of the bed, motionless, his hands pressed between his knees. His smile had frozen on his lips. He was dear to me. I wanted to cheer him up and I crawled around the room on all fours oinking softly. And I knew he wasn't looking at me. I crouched under the piano waiting. Around him the air quivered, blurring his rigid, delicate outline. His face had something simultaneously stony and waxy about it. How tall and handsome he was!

From under the couch there appeared first one snake then another. Hesitantly, coyly, they slithered over the flowery carpet to his feet. Then slowly, slowly, they crawled up his boots, up his calves, his thighs, his hips . . . They clasped his body in their cold, strangulating rings.

I could control myself no longer. I started to weep, there under the piano, muffling my sobs, since I was ashamed for him to see my weakness.

The Umbrella Shop

I LEFT THE HOUSE under a dreary, grey-blue sky. The procession of clouds had halted. There was an oppressive stillness, a heavy, nagging sense of expectation. I felt like breaking into a run, falling down, hitting myself, crawling on all fours, senselessly. But I controlled myself. I was walking in no particular direction, scraping up against walls, shuffling my feet on the asphalt sidewalk. And I was gritting my teeth. Then it started to rain. A drizzle of silky raindrops that pattered on my face gently, caressingly. The rain soothed me. In my shirt-sleeves, with my hands in my pockets, I now walked with a spring in my step, my mind empty, I walked in the rain. The sky was unchanged: grey-blue, livid, stony. The rain grew heavier, the raindrops more violent, and by now I was cold. I thought about taking shelter somewhere. I arranged my wet hair, wiped the water from my face, and I would even have taken off my shirt, but I felt a chill.

From a corner of the passageway, a little creature hopped toward me, bleating softly. I took two steps back, but even so, I wasn't frightened. It was a strange creature: the body of a woman and the head of a goat; its hair was long, blond. Baa! It came even closer, rubbed up against me. And it bleated all the while. Not knowing how to react, I kept moving backward, until I found myself back outside the passageway, in the rain. I made a run for it. I tripped over a dog that burst from under a gate right in front of me. I picked myself up and carried on running.

It was getting dark. The sky was an unbearable dark grey.

My eyes alighted on the sign of the shop I had just reached: an umbrella shop. I stopped and without the slightest hesitation went inside. A strange room, bathed in a dim, scarlet light that shone from somewhere to the side. There was nobody behind the counter. I coughed, to signal my presence. Nobody came. I looked at the umbrellas lined up on the shelves like birds with folded wings. I sat down on one of the plush chairs next to the wall and tapped the heels of my shoes in the hope of being heard. Finally, the velvet curtain at the back of the shop moved to one side. A fat, almost obese, woman appeared, her wads of flesh wrapped in a yellow dressing gown with a print of large, bright red flowers. I stood up and made a deep, respectful bow.

"What do you want?"

A reedy voice, like a child's.

"As you can see, I was caught out in the rain in only my shirt-sleeves."

She gave an understanding nod.

"I would like an umbrella."

"But of course, with pleasure."

She rubbed her chubby, ring-bedizened hands together and smiled. She had a large, round face, black wavy hair, and glossy, unnaturally glossy skin. Red, enameled cheekbones. The rest of her face was a shiny, yellowish white. She looked like she was made of porcelain. And she had the round, bulging eyes of a fish.

"I would like an umbrella . . ."

"But of course, with pleasure."

And she continued to smile at me. Time elapsed. She smiled at me, rubbing her fleshy hands, while I, shoulders hunched, took little steps backward and forward, bowing ceremoniously. She then slowly turned around, rotating her large, pillow-like haunches, took down an umbrella from a shelf, and handed it to me over her shoulder. I opened it and lifted it above my head. What a beautiful umbrella! It really was a beautiful umbrella, with an ivory handle depicting a dragon's head and with yellow silk tassels attached to it. Then why was I overcome by such sudden sadness? I felt weary, I felt as if I were about to burst into tears and weep with my forehead resting in the lap of that obese, yellow, glossy woman . . .

"It's too small . . ."

It was as if she had been expecting this answer, for she immediately handed me another, larger, umbrella. She stood holding the folded umbrella and I knew my eyes were moist. Before me, the fat woman showed the same glossy, smiling face.

"This is also too small . . ."

Calmly, she handed me another, which likewise I rejected, then another and another: dozens of umbrellas, each more beautiful than the last. I was ashamed and I felt like crying, I wanted the earth to swallow me up, but what could I do?"

"Then, what do you want?"

"A large umbrella . . . a large one . . . so that lots of people can stand under it, lots and lots of people . . . These are too small . . ."

"All right, but are you sure . . ."

"Yes . . . I'm sure . . ."

On the counter I placed the last umbrella I had tested.

"I would still like a larger umbrella."

The shopkeeper started putting them back on the shelves. She swayed her large hips. I was trying to smile at her; trying to find an excuse, I respectfully lowered my head almost to the wood countertop. I was feeling more and more embarrassed about not being able to buy any of the umbrellas. Making another low bow, I tiptoed outside.

It was no longer raining. But the sky was still just as grey. I shuffled my feet over the wet asphalt, heedless of the puddles that had formed here and there. I walked slowly, my mind empty. I hugged the walls—the eaves were still dripping—always hugging the walls. Aimlessly. The street lamps were lighting up one by one, although night didn't seem to have fallen yet. They cast a sad, pallid light. Up above, the grey sky had descended even lower, was even more oppressive. A faint but cold wind glided over my forehead. I walked hesitantly, unsteadily, my arms dangling heavily to either side. I saw her huddled up next to a fence. When she saw me, she quickly got up and threw herself at me. She was swaying her thin, bony hips provocatively. Baa! She hopped joyfully around me, now on one leg, now on the other; she jerked her head in every direction, she bent backwards, she waggled her hips and bleated softly. She was dancing! Touched, I stopped and nodded my head encouragingly. Then, plucking up courage, she took me by the hand, she had cold, rough fingers, and pulled me after her.

1960
(*Ateneu*, no. 6, June 1967)

On the Tram

I HAD BEEN WAITING for the tram for more than a quarter of an hour. Here it was at last! With my fists, with my elbows, striking left and right, I was able to plant one foot on the step and a get a firm hold on the handrail. In front of me, a lady as big as a wardrobe was resting her whole weight on me. With a struggle, I managed to push her inside the tramcar and then clamber in after her. The tram set underway. The ticker collector looked at everybody in suspicion, asking whether they had tickets. I gave her an ironic smile and showed her my season ticket. I will admit that I also had a little luck that day: shielded behind the fat lady, within a short time I reached the middle of the tramcar and at the first opportunity, I settled comfortably into a seat. I didn't even look at the other people. I was looking out of the window at the swarming city. After which, I got bored of it, closed my eyes, and joggled by the rather jerky motion of the tram, I dozed off with the hum of people talking in my ears. Or maybe I fell fast asleep.

When I opened my eyes once more, I noticed to my amazement that there were no more houses or streets to be seen. We had left the city. In the light of dusk, an amazingly glossy blue plain stretched away. The setting sun cast red, violet streaks. At the grey base of the sky I could pick out birds wheeling ever lower. From somewhere on the horizon a white horse with a flaming mane appeared. The birds swooped on it with their powerful curved beaks. I looked around me. The tramcar was empty. Even the ticket collector was gone. Through the window opposite was visible the same glossy plain, like a motionless lake. Other horses with flaming manes leaped fearfully up close to the tram, only to be left behind. Up in the sky lurked the huge birds. I opened the door at the front of the car to speak to the tram driver, but he was gone too. What a farce! A tram without a ticker collector, in the middle of a plain! Before long, night would fall and I was all alone in that tram, which had gone off the rails . . . I missed the fat lady. I would have felt safe if she had been there. I sat down on a different seat and watched the birds pecking at the half-burnt corpses of the horses, which were arriving in larger and larger numbers, fleeing desperately from over the horizon, their manes flaming. A shrill, happy grunt made me turn my head. I took fright at first, like an idiot. It was a chubby pink piglet, which had crawled from under a seat. Why should I be afraid? I picked up the piglet and sat down with it by the window. It was growing dark. The horses were galloping alongside the tramlines, their manes flaming, assiduously pursued by the birds with beaks of steel. I stroked the piglet, my heart quailing. What soft, delicate ears it had! It grunted shrilly, nestling in my lap.

Ultimately, there was one hope: maybe the tramlines would come to an end . . . and then the tram would set off back to the city.

1959

Cold

THE TRAM WAS RACING along faster than usual. I was smiling. The high speed stretched out the outlines of the houses and people. Other trams glided in the opposite direction: red, yellow, green. Because of the high speed, all I could make out was the colors. The image was elongated, distorted, and so maybe they weren't even trams. Then it started to snow. Just like that, out of the blue. Large fluffy flakes were falling with unnatural slowness. You'd have thought the window had been splashed with whitewash. The city was slowly, slowly left behind. The buildings grew lower and lower, sparser and sparser. From the last building stretched an iron fence, not very high, which was endless. Behind it was a fog massed together in the form of monstrous clouds. I had to get off the tram. Look, the outlines of a few people at a stop! The tram slowed. It halted. In those long, faded blue overalls of theirs, they looked like shop boys. But nonetheless, they had wings: small, comical, barely visible wings. Their long, gleaming faces gave me a welcoming smile. They bowed each in turn, fluttering their little wings. I was cold; I felt embarrassed. I stuffed my hands in my pockets and walked on, annoyed. What was with all that bowing! I walked faster and faster and without looking back, even though I didn't know the way. But not only because of the cold. I was genuinely in a hurry. Instead of night, a dense, grey-white smoke was descending. I broke into a run alongside the fence. I was cold. For an instant I thought of turning back, maybe they were going in the same direction too, but behind me nothing was visible. Because of the fog, obviously, because the asphalted road down which I was going was illuminated: a whitish, soothing light, which, unfortunately, soon took on a yellowish cast. When I bumped into the first post, I understood. I had entered a forest of streetlamps. The smoke had grown thicker. The posts of the streetlamps were invisible, I had to grope with my hands to find their cold, wet iron. I had become weary. I huddled up at the base of a streetlamp. I hugged my body, trying to stay warm; then I stood up and started hopping up and down, slapping my arms, my hips. The mist enveloped me in a shirt of ice, and the cold cruelly, gradually permeated me. I breathed on my hands like a lunatic. I couldn't run, because I risked colliding with all the posts. Like a rat caught in a trap . . . A rat! I shouted. How faint was my voice . . . Somebody was dumping mounds of cotton wool on top of me, burying me, suffocating me. And the cold! I could feel my muscles being rent beneath my skin. I was stiff. Wisps of fog entered my lungs. And in spite of it all, I could not forget that I had come here from somewhere else.

1959
(*Ateneu*, no. 10, 1966)

Insomnia

THE WINDOW FRAME is creaking in the wind. I had just dozed off. With a mechanical gesture, I run my hand over the wall to my left. It feels cold, rough. The clatter of boots can be heard from the street more and more loudly. The steps are determined, the steps of somebody who has to carry out an order. I lift myself on my elbows. The clattering suddenly stops. I strain my ears: a faint sound of scraping metal and muffled lapping, then silence. The dirty bulb of the streetlamp on the pavement opposite casts a yellowish, dirty light. It has stopped raining. Across the street is a two-story building, with no balcony. At one of the windows, during the day, a fat man appears, wearing a policeman's cap, but without a tunic, only in a shirt and suspenders. He smiles. Behind the roof can be glimpsed the spire of a church. From where I am looking, in the building on the right can be seen only one window, illumined with a blood-red light, a little above the level of my window. Again I hear the clattering: hurried steps, now moving into the distance. Sometimes, the policeman's daughter appears, or maybe it is his wife. I'm not sure whether she is beautiful; sometimes I think she is. The clattering can no longer be heard. To the right of the bed, I usually place a chair to serve as a nightstand. I stretch out my hand and grope for my cigarettes. My fingers end up in the ashtray. I get up and go to the window. A rather large fish whose scales glint violet is circling the streetlamp. It is tethered to the post by a string or some wire and keeps going around and around, always keeping the same distance, of around a meter, and the same speed, like a record on a gramophone. In the morning, music can be heard from the house across the street. It is now dark everywhere, apart from the window on the right, where someone is probably developing photographs and needs a red light. It has stopped raining, but the street is still wet; the asphalt gleams slyly beneath the streetlamps.

"You're never going to be a good engineer."

What could I answer to that?

The fish keeps going around and around at the same speed. The scales have taken on a reddish tint. The sky is still cloudy. It's going to start raining again. A soldier runs toward the entrance to the park. He stops. He looks behind him. He breaks into a run again. I'm cold. I climb into bed and pull the blanket over my head. My left knee is aching. I shiver under the blanket, with my knees crooked, my face to the wall. On the other side of the wall, Tante Luiza is walking barefoot around the room. The window is creaking again.

Is it the wind that make the fish go around and around the lamppost or is it a concealed mechanism that . . .

The policeman's daughter must be very tall; she has long, thin arms. She never comes to the window with her father. And I've never seen her leave the house. True, I haven't sat keeping a look-out for hours on end. Sometimes I see her in the morning: she opens the window, takes a deep breath, strokes her shoulder-length hair, she might glance at my window, she might not, after which she closes her window and vanishes. It is then that the policeman appears, he is always wearing his cap, he is fat, and he smiles.

In the next room, Tante Luiza's feet slap across the floor. She would be better off reading her fortune in the cards. The window creaks, rattled by the wind. The streetlamp casts its yellowish, dirty light. The fish is probably still going around and around. I try to press my knees to my chest. Is the blood-red window still visible? There must be a mechanism, no matter how small, no matter how basic . . . I stretch out my hand and run it over the rough, cold wall; lower down, by the floor, it is covered in mold.

(*Ateneu*, no. 6 June 1967)

On the Curb of the Sidewalk

I HAD BEEN INTENDING to go to a friend's house when I left home, but I lost my way. The sky was grey, like the cobblestones of the roads, and like that empty plaza in particular, which was as smooth as the round bottom of a stone jar, which I reached after much wandering; had it not been for the walls of the houses, I would have broken into a run, I would have run to the edge of the plaza, somewhere on the horizon, obviously, I would have ascended the slope of the sky and run madly, wheeling faster and faster, till there was no more up or down, till I grew dizzy. But there were walls and buildings that prevented me, and there were people: a few had left their houses, they were taking a walk or hurrying to wherever they had business, there weren't many, but they wouldn't have let me do it, out of compassion, naturally. And so I quietly walked along the curb of the sidewalk, my knees slightly bent and my head bowed, so as not to see the sky that was as grey as the pavement on which I trod. I did a circuit of the plaza, once, twice . . . Even so, there was a difference between the sky and the pavement: the leaves and the footwear of the people treading on them. The asphalt of the sky was smoother, cleaner, unless it was some illusion due to the distance. I was holding my arms outspread like wing pinions to keep my balance, because I was so alone and I liked to walk along the curb. And when I have to cross the street, which is seldom, I break into a run, not because I'm afraid of the cars—I like it when they whistle past me—but to reach the curb of the other sidewalk more quickly.

The grey of the curb—since I'm walking with my head bowed, my arms outspread—is exactly the same shade as the grey of the sky, which is to say, rather whitish, slightly bluish in places, when you look very carefully, and sometimes it pales the same as when, without wishing to, you think, only for an instant, about how you are going to die. For an instant, from below a leaf, a merry eye gleams, and so I stop, my arms still outspread, and I wait, but it lasted only an instant and perhaps I imagined it. And there is another difference between sky and sidewalk: sometimes the sky strikes you as bluish, friendly, and you gaze at it as you would at a tall, good-natured gentleman, you wait, you finally lower your eyes, you wait for him to pat you on the head. And then, for an instant, no longer, you believe that what is known as the sky is not the familiar underside of a stone slab, but perhaps a bottomless lake or perhaps the breath of somebody on the other side.

Looking up, I noticed that somebody was mimicking my gestures. A man, not very tall, with large, jug ears, so far as I could see, and arms outspread like wings; like me, he was wearing a rather large, unbuttoned green loden cape and he was walking only along the curb. A few meters ahead. I stopped. He stopped too. I lifted one arm in the direction of a treetop—there was a little break in the clouds there. He did likewise. Then I squatted and he did likewise, I held my arms in front of me, then to the side, and I rotated them, as if exercising, we both lost our balance, one foot slipped into the gutter, I fell on one knee and, after we picked ourselves up, we started running and no matter how hard I tried, I couldn't catch up with him, the distance between us was always the same. I stopped. He stopped too. We mopped our brows with our handkerchiefs, I could see him panting, his head slightly bowed, his shoulders moving up and down to the rhythm of his breathing. He was tired. I was tired too. I felt sorry for him: why was I chasing him like that? People were walking past us, we were on quite a busy street, they were all looking at me in amazement or scorn, some even stopped for a few moments, shaking their heads in disapproval. From underneath a leaf in the gutter, the mocking gleam of an eye. I felt afraid, guilty. Ever in front of me, only a few meters away, his head bowed in fear or shame, he was motionless, he did not walk away: stubborn man! We were both looking down at the grey stone of the curb. Up above, I sensed the slab of the sky descending ever lower to crush us. I squatted again, I huddled, I lowered my head till all I could see was the asphalt and the eye gleaming in the gutter, mockingly. Then I looked up to see him and I got to my feet and I saw him taking off his trouser belt, drawing it with a sweeping gesture as if it were a sword, I saw him draw one end through the buckle to make a noose, O, God! and then rush to the tall black railings of a gate. What was he doing? Was he insane? I ran after him, but then I stopped to cry for help as a policeman's uniform had appeared from around the corner. Help! He's going to commit suicide, don't let him, it's all my fault . . . The policeman came up at a run, his rubber truncheon bouncing against his hip; an arm cased in blue cloth grabbed me by the collar, the arm ended in a big, strong hand, I could feel it pressing down on the veins in my neck. Help!

He yanked the belt from my hand, shouting at me: You drunkard! And my neck hurt from his big, rough fist. Then he let me go. He was holding the belt, looking at it as if it were a snake, his fury and bewilderment had abated; I was standing with my head bowed and only from time to time did I cast a furtive glance to see how confused he was: he was trying to compose a protective smile on his face or at least to find some word of consolation and he could not, he kept angrily twisting the belt in his hands, and I didn't want to help him. I stepped to the side and broke into a run. My running away was so unexpected that once I was about a hundred meters away, I turned my head and saw that he was still there, next to the gate with the tall iron railings, painted black, he was standing dumbly, holding the belt twisted around his hand like a snake, he couldn't make head or tail of it. I thumbed my nose at him, then turned on my heel and with a spring in my step continued walking along the curb. From time to time I had to pull up my trousers, which kept falling down my waist, one arm served as a suspender, the other as a wing, but I was free and the curbstones gave off a slightly bluish mist, and the sky was far away again, and it gleamed, a bottomless lake or perhaps the breath of somebody from the other side.

1965
(*Cronica*, no. 31, September 1967)

Prayer

WITHOUT MY REALIZING IT, I had come very close to the forest at the edge of town. I was holding a rolled-up newspaper, which I was using as a riding crop, whipping my imaginary boots or flicking the bushes in my way. It was quite cool, maybe even cold, but I felt fine, much better than on the streets of the town. I lovingly trod the rich black soil scattered with brushwood and leaves, I joyfully snagged the fabric of my trousers on the thorn bushes. And I was whistling. It was a copse, a remnant of the legendary forest of yore. I had no reason to be afraid of losing my way. A little tired, I sank down on the stunted, prickly grass and, lying on my back, with my hands underneath my head, I tried to see the sky through the foliage of the trees. The rustle of the leaves, the hum of the insects hiding in the grass, finally started to irritate me. Calm and bold, a tiny light-brown beetle was scaling my arm. I grasped it between finger and thumb and crushed it. Something greenish, sticky spurted from its little abdomen, as big as the head of a pin. It was disgusting. In revulsion I wiped myself on a burdock leaf. My previous good mood was gone. If all those insects started climbing over me and I felt thousands of tiny legs crawling over me and minuscule mandibles nipping my flesh . . . It would take them only a day to devour me. I jumped to my feet in terror. I went up to a tree and hugged it. We were the only vertical beings in the whole wood. My hands barely touched when I put my arms around it. I pressed my cheek to its knobbly bark. It was cracked, rough, it scratched

109

me, comforted me. But all the while, the ants were climbing up me, swiftly slipping beneath my shirt, where the skin was soft and warm. I thrust my hand through the collar of my shirt to pick them off one by one, like bits of hair after a haircut. But there were too many. I took my shirt off. I wiped my chest, my back, rubbed myself thoroughly. And because I now felt cold, I started running among the trees in a zigzag. Coming to a stop, I took a long piss against the trunk of a birch tree. It was then, through the branches, that I saw in the distance a procession of white figures advancing solemnly. I couldn't make out their faces, but I was struck by their stiff, rhythmic gait. And by their clothes: it was as if they were swathed in majestic togas, which fell to their ankles. Their foreheads held haughtily aloft, their gaze fixed in front of them, they took slow, rhythmic steps. For a time I lost sight of them. They reappeared a little farther away, in a clearing. There they stopped, in a compact, motionless group. I tiptoed through the trees, my eyes always fixed on them. They were standing motionless in front of the trunk of a huge, felled oak tree. When I moved even closer, I noticed that what had previously looked like togas were merely large hospital gowns of ordinary cloth. As if at a signal, they all kneeled down. Their heads were large, shaven, completely shaven, their faces were brutish, sunburnt. They were clasping their hands as if in prayer and muttering something I couldn't make out. I was just a few meters away from them, hiding behind a tree. Ugh! What insane, repulsive mugs they had! In the middle, a fat man with scarlet skin and sagging, oily cheeks knelt with his mouth agape, his lips quivering; another had a lump as big as an egg at the back of his head, and the gangling, lanky man beside him was rocking his pointy head back and forth in a ridiculous manner. In all, there were six of them, each more hideous and deformed than the next. The murmur of their voices gradually became a crystalline song chanted as if by a children's choir. I scrabbled with my fingers for something solid I could throw at them. It didn't occur to me that they outnumbered me and could give me a severe beating. But I couldn't find anything: only leaves, dry twigs, grass . . . I took a coin from my pocket and aimed it at the fattest of them. I hit him right on the bonce. Ha, ha! What a good shot! But look at that, he didn't so much as blink . . . Their shrill song, the song of eunuchs or angels, was driving me out of my mind. I emerged from my hiding place and sneaked up behind them. They were barefoot; their soles of their feet were grimy, cracked. I crossed my mind that I should tickle their feet, but I quickly thought better of it. It would have been pointless; they wouldn't have felt anything. Then what should I do? To be honest, I couldn't help but feel a certain admiration for their self-control. Or else they were too caught up in their stupid, meaningless ceremony, so absorbed in their prayer that quite simply they failed to register my existence. That egged me on all the more. I lifted my newspaper and furiously whacked one of them across the back of the head with it. It wasn't a strong blow—the cudgel was made of paper—but he ought to have felt it. Throwing caution to the wind, I ran around and around them, hitting them on the head with the newspaper. Whack! Whack! Whack! Whack! Their song rose even higher. Their sweat-beaded faces gleamed in ecstasy. Then I thought of another idea. I scooped up some ants from an anthill and as they continued their harmoniously squealing hymn, I sprinkled them over their tanned necks and narrow brows. Then I ran to hide behind a thicket. A pointless precaution, since they didn't seem to feel anything. I had gone beyond amazement; I was now weary and somewhat uneasy. Maybe they were dead . . . but that immediately made me burst out laughing. I would have liked to leave. What did I care, in the end! But that song, so strange, so pure, rooted me to the spot. A ray of sunlight pierced through the web of branches and leaves and lit up their faces. Why had I tormented them? What had they done to me, those peaceful, gentle creatures praying in front of a tree trunk? I should have set off back home, what was I waiting for . . . I went up to them again, without fear, without wanting to do anything this time. Their childish voices soared up, pellucid in the silence of the forest. I listened for a while, with my arms folded. Then I stood in line with them and, almost without wanting to, knelt down. The earth was soft beneath my knees. I crooked my arms, joined my hands together. I lump rose in my throat and I felt like weeping. And then, to hold back my tears, I started to sing with them. Hesitantly at first, softly, then more and more confidently, more shrilly, more loudly.

1959
(*Povestea vorbii*, no. 9, 1966)

The Intruder

THE TRAM THAT TOOK ME there was very nice. Freshly painted, in yellow and green stripes, it looked like a huge caterpillar, gleaming in the sun. I thought I had reached the end of the line, which is why I alighted. But the tram lazily went on its way, the rumble of its wheels accompanied the tinkle of its bell. Shading my eyes with my hand, I watched it recede into the distance until it disappeared. Then I set off down the lane that opened up right in front of me. A lane like you find at the very edge of town, overrun with greenery. The squat houses, painted various bright colors, were surrounded by little vegetable and flower plots, and there were pots of geraniums on the porches. The fence pales and the trunks of the fruit trees were whitewashed. It was a street like the ones I'd seen at the edges of countless other towns, but nonetheless, there was something different about it. Was it just that there were no sidewalks? From between the cobblestones sprouted tufts of grass that were a rusty green. From the trees along the edge of the road hung strange, scarlet fruits, larger than apples, or else pink, oval fruits, like rosy eggs. In a gateway, a barefoot, naked child, his head shaven and glossy as an ivory ball, was playing knucklebones. I went up to him and patted his nacreous head. He did not flinch away. He looked up at me with limpid green eyes. He smiled.

At first, I walked slowly, slightly disoriented, then intimidated, I don't know why, I kept looking back, in the direction of the tramline, which after a while fell out of sight. It wasn't disquiet, but rather a pleasant, enveloping fear. I started to walk faster and faster, trying to descry through the increasingly dense vegetation where that so peaceful street might lead. Behind the windows of the houses, you could detect no movement. Nobody went in or out of the low crooked doors. In the garden of a building somewhat larger, a few children were walking, holding each other by the hand, their round, glossy heads bobbing up and down to the same rhythm. In another garden, among the flowers, I saw an egg. Never had I seen such a large egg. It looked like it was made of stone. Three children, taller and slenderer than the others, were walking around and around the egg, barefoot, solemnly bowing from time to time. I went up to the fence to get a better look. Between their long, pale fingers coiled slippery snakes, winding their way up their arms and chests and around their necks. I liked their ceremonious game, but even so, I did not dare open the gate. And besides, there was something that urged me to keep going. Maybe the most sensible thing would have been to try to find a tramline. I really did think I had reached the end of the line. That's why I got off! For an instant I thought about going back, but finally, I kept going, quickening my pace. The lane was always the same, I thought it would never end . . .

I started to run, flapping my arms. I felt so light! A long, slender snake slithered from under a fence. I bent down to pick it up and it coiled around my neck. Through the leaves of the trees a greenish-white light was now filtering. The snake caressed my cheek coolingly. I was running, taking long, springing steps and I wouldn't have been surprised if I had taken flight. And the lane was no longer a street but a path through a forest. Birds with long tails and shining feathers of every color accompanied me, gliding among the branches. From the trees fell red and green fruits as big as watermelons. They struck the stone path soundlessly, rolling past my feet. Two children appeared from a garden and after a moment's indecision, they broke into a run, as nimble as deer. And after them came others and yet others, until they formed a procession behind me. The only sound was a continuous rustling. I don't know how long that wonderful run lasted. After a time, the lane became broader and broader, the trees thinned out, the birds were left behind, the children slowed their steps, and before me opened a plaza as wide as a plain. The snake began to struggle, strangling me. I uncoiled it from my nape and let it go. It crawled hurriedly back. The children came to a stop. They bowed their ivory heads and went back, in sensible single file. All on my own, I kept going. Near the middle of the plaza rose a stone egg, grandiose, domineering. Without fear, I headed toward it and taking short steps, I began to walk around it. The broad plaza was paved with asphalt, as smooth as a tray. There was not a blade of grass to be seen. But the sky was green. It was like a glass cupola.

1960
(*Cronica*, no. 31, September 1967)

The Specialist

The Specialist

I LIVE IN A QUIET NEIGHBORHOOD, near the edge of town, in a traditional house, not very poky, but very old. The house belongs to a distant relative who rents me a small room next to the kitchen; it used to be the maid's room, after which, more recently, it served as a second larder. It's small, moldy, and full of spiders. But I like it. Maybe because the only window looks out on the garden, a long, shady garden. True, the part you can see from my room is more of a walnut orchard, since the flowerbeds are visible only from the windows of the other rooms. I forgot to say that the rooms are all in a row, like the carriages of a train, and that makes the house look very long. Likewise the garden, which, viewed from the street, is a corridor of greenery, with flowers in the middle and a real forest at the back. The walls and also the stone fence that separates our garden from the neighbors' yard are covered in ivy. Naturally, that's why it's so damp in the room! There is only one thing that's hard to tolerate: the smell of roux that comes from the kitchen. In the morning, which is when it's cooked, I always go out; but the smell lingers throughout the afternoon, especially in winter, when you can't keep the window open very long. A week ago, major preparations for the wedding feast of the landlady's daughter got underway. A cook was brought in from a restaurant and the fire burned in the stove for two days straight. The banging of the chopper, the squeaking of the meat grinder, the pounding of the pestle, the sizzling of the steaks—what a din; not to mention the smells. It wouldn't have been so bad if I'd been able to leave the house, like in the past; but unfortunately, my shoes were being repaired and, despite my pleas, the cobbler couldn't finish the job in less than two days. I lay in bed with the window wide open, with a quilt, a blanket, and two pillows over my ears. I was suffocating, I was boiling. Toward evening, I sneaked into the garden and picked an armload of roses and lilies. I was hoping their perfume would overpower the other smells. I sprinkled flowers everywhere: the bed, the floor, the table. I don't know how, but I tripped over the suitcase in which I keep my clothes. I lost my balance; only by grabbing at the wall did I manage to stop myself falling. A quite large chunk of plaster came loose and broke in pieces on the floor. The missing plaster left a dark patch, which wasn't very noticeable, because a broad swath of the mold-eaten wall looked like a map of unexplored continents. That evening, I didn't pay much attention to it. I swept up the broken plaster and went to bed.

The next day, preparations for the feast were in full swing again. The mistress of the house was berating the maid. Annoyed by the commotion, the specialist in the culinary art declared he was unable to work in such conditions. The time had come to make the cake and he had to concentrate. As he spoke with the authority of a true specialist, the women were cowed into silence. My eyes were drawn to the spot where the bare patch in the plaster had appeared. It was somewhat higher than the bedstead (what an old-fashioned, ridiculous bed I have!) and appeared to have grown bigger. In fact, that wasn't what attracted my attention, but something else, difficult to explain. I couldn't remember how it had looked the previous evening, but that morning, it had acquired a dark violet hue that was visible only at certain moments. The rest of the time it was black and, which was all the stranger, it was round, perfectly round. Despite the lilies, a smell of garlic permeated the room. On the other side of the wall, voices had been raised once more; the lady of the house was not at all satisfied with the serving woman. I would have loved to have seen what the chef looked like! I like those fat, oily, cheerful people; comforting people, in a word. I heaved myself up onto one elbow to open the window. In the garden, a light breeze was swaying the leaves of the walnut trees. Obviously, the skinless sausages and steaks are fried right there and then, during the meal. You know, madam, explained the chef, with the skinless sausages, it all depends on how much of each ingredient you combine . . . To be honest, I like skinless sausages too. The rich, sticky voice of the chef was making me salivate. I buried my nose in the chalice of a rose and swallowed. Finally, I came to a decision. I opened the door to the kitchen and signaled the serving woman. It was plain that I looked ill. The lady gave me a sympathetic look and in a kindly voice asked me whether I had eaten. Yes, I've eaten. I just wanted to ask the servant to go and tell the cobbler to get a move on: how much longer can I wait like this, in my stockinged feet! I slammed the door in annoyance. To be honest, I'd opened it mainly because I wanted to see what the specialist in the culinary art looked like and in the vague hope that the mistress of the house wouldn't be there. But the chef had just left. I set eyes on the patch once more. It now had green tinges and was shinier. I ran my fingertip over it. Then, in puzzlement, I shrugged and climbed into bed. I couldn't fall asleep no matter how hard I tried. I was just dozing off when the servant came in. She'd brought me food, I couldn't berate her for waking me up. I turned over in bed to face her and asked her what the cobbler had said. Naturally, the cobbler hadn't even started repairing my shoes.

"He told me to tell you to be patient till tomorrow."

The servant smelled of sweat. She looked dull-wittedly at the unmade bed, the greasy bedclothes, the flowers wilting on the floor. She didn't see the patch. Or maybe she saw it and didn't pay it any mind. In any event, why was she smiling at me inanely?

"Where did the chef go?" I asked.

"He left and came back."

She didn't know.

"Does he have a moustache?"

She looked at me and burst out laughing. I think the girl liked me. She'd brought me a piece of steak and a pickled bell pepper. But she got on my nerves. I was sitting there in front of her, in my stockinged feet, and I didn't know what to say. I breathed a sigh of relief when she left. And I looked at the patch again. I began to examine it in detail. Its perfect roundness frightened me. And it was no larger than the lens of a telescope. A spider sailed down next to it and then quickly rode back up to its web, which hung from a corner.

By evening, the commotion in the kitchen had died down. The only sound was the specialist sharpening his knives. The wedding was the next day. I felt a little better, I had thrown out the flowers and managed to sleep for two or three hours. My head was clearer. From outside wafted a cool, perfumed breeze. I jumped out of bed and started to look for my shoes.

It was then that the specialist entered.

The door opened slowly, with a creak. Into the room stepped a short, thin, red-headed man wearing clothes too large for him. He looked at me solemnly and, since it was too dim to see, turned on the light switch; it was as if he knew it was there, to the right of the door. Although something told me it was none other than the specialist, I hastened to ask him.

"What do you want? Who are you?"

His bulbous nose gleamed in the glow of the lightbulb. He had a long, bony, haggard face, small eyes, hidden beneath slitted lids. He turned his gaze toward the wall. He pointed a finger at the patch and asked in a professional-sounding voice: "Has that been there long?"

I said that it had been there since the day before, when a chunk of plaster fell off. He glanced around the room. I was slightly ashamed of the mess: the remains of the steak tossed on the table. Annoyed, I asked him once more who he was. He gave a bored shrug and sat down on the bed. His legs didn't reach the floor.

"This room has quite a lot of mold . . ."

"Yes, it does."

"What's over there?"

I thought he meant the garden.

"Not outside. Over there, on the other side of that wall."

"Ah! The laundry room . . . That's why there's mold.

He smiled, baring his toothless gums. He swung his legs back and forth: now one, now the other, now both at the same time.

I had never imagined that a specialist could look like that . . . I now understood the scorn in the servant's voice.

"Are you really a specialist?"

He made no reply. He cocked his head to one side and then, suddenly, he said: "Let's begin!"

There was something domineering in his voice. He leapt from the bed, stamping his little shoes. From his pocket he took a knife and a scraper. He solemnly showed them to me, then began to examine the patch carefully. It was beautiful. It had the violet tints once more. He cast me a glance and, murmuring to himself, started work. First of all, using the knife, he scored the wall all around the patch. Then, holding the scraper in both hands, he set about grating the patch. He worked slowly, his jaws clenched. Sitting on the bed, I admired the steady rhythm of his movements. From time to time he paused, took a deep breath, peered at the wall, moving his eye close, as if he were short-sighted, and then recommenced his grating.

More than an hour elapsed and still no result. Not that I knew what to expect. As for him, he said not a word. The sweat poured off his brow, the veins on his temples bulged to bursting point. I grew bored and sleepy. Finally, just as I was looking elsewhere, he gave a little cry of triumph. A goodly portion of the patch now had a reddish hue. The specialist ran his hand through his hair and wiped his sweating brow with a handkerchief. Looking up at me, he gave a start, as if seeing me for the first time.

"Lend a hand with the scraping!" he said imperiously.

I took the scraper from him and set to work with a will. My movements were faster than his, but probably I didn't know how to grate properly; in my grasp, the scraper squeaked and whined. It was as if I was scraping a piece of glass.

"Keep going, keep going!" he encouraged. "That's what it's like at first. Hold it straighter. That's the way!"

I toiled with all my might. The raw-meat red of the patch

bored into my eyes. Another hour later, the patch had faded to a pale pink.

"Now let me take over," he said.

He handled the scraper with the same precision and rhythmic motion. As the patch faded, the little man became livelier and livelier. He scraped away merrily and even began to whistle. A change came over me, too. I was no longer at all sleepy. What is more, I even felt excited. I stooped over him, watching, my cheek brushing his ginger hair. The patch had turned white. It looked like whitewashed glass. The specialist turned his head toward me; his eyes gleamed. My heart was beating heavily. I couldn't imagine what would happen next. Ah! the scraping of the knife over glass, that screeching noise that used to make me shudder . . . Gradually, the patch became transparent. The weary hand of the specialist, its veins bulging, nonetheless maintained its rhythmic motion. A final screech of the knife and then the specialist's cry of joy! He stepped aside and shouted: "Place your eye to it and . . . look!"

Trembling, groping my way across the wall like a blind man, I pressed my cheek, then my forehead, and finally my eye to it. I was too close, too excited. I turned around in confusion. On the bed, the specialist was covering his face with his stumpy red hands. Maybe he was crying. When he looked at me, his face was scarlet, his gaze steady.

"Did you see it?"

He did not wait for my reply. His voice abruptly grew faint. Almost in a whisper, he said: "I'm not allowed to. I find out where it appears, I scrape, I grate, I clarify. But I'm not allowed to."

He ran his hand through his hair, wearily. I couldn't understand any of it.

"Are you the specialist?"

He nodded, looking at me bitterly. He was so small and sad, sitting there on the edge of the bed . . .

"But now . . . I have to go."

His steps were hesitant. He gathered up his tools, stuffed them in his pocket. He slowly pressed the door handle, gave the wall one last look, then abruptly went out, closing the door behind him.

After he left, I strained to push the bed into such a position that its head would be right beneath the enchanted eyeglass.

1961

Engraving

A GREY MORNING. Dim sun swathed in mist. Numerous large tents on the plain. From a tent emerged a knight in shining chainmail, he mounted the chestnut horse tethered by the tent and galloped off diagonally across the plain before vanishing over the horizon.

Time flowed slowly. From the tents appeared cumbersome hideous monsters with contorted arms, deformed legs, splayed fingers, they were bald or had a muscle that sprouted like a crest on their flattened heads. A savage battle broke out among them: they clutched at each other, bit each other with grinning mouths, scratched, slashed, blood spurted everywhere. Until they were all dead.

After a while, the knight returned hurriedly driving a herd of frightened oxen with blows of the whip. He saw the corpses half covered with large, silver vultures. He dismounted his horse and leaning his elbow on the saddle, stood there alone amid the lowing of the frightened oxen and the fluttering of the birds. For a long time he stood there motionless, looking in a daze.

The Dyke Watchman

THE CHEST-HIGH DYKE of rough stone blocks stretched for as far as my eyes could see. On the other side floated thick mists perhaps concealing from the gaze dizzying chasms. It was a grey day with a sun as glassy as a bird's eye. And it was silent. I walked slowly alongside the dyke letting my hand brush over the rough stone; I walked with weary, unsteady steps, although the ground I trod was smooth and soft. The place looked deserted. Here and there a stunted shrub with small pink flowers like pearls or a tuft of scrubby vegetation beneath the endless wall. When I saw it, motionless on top of the dyke, I came to a stop. It was standing on its hind legs and had the look of a hedgehog; but its fur was a glossy blue, as fluffy and soft as an Angora cat's. I took a few more steps and came to a stop once more. Right in front of it. It did not budge. Even its small eyes, sunken in its sockets, were rigid.

On the other, the mists had begun to advance in waves: like a sea of vapor and froth that threatened to overflow, to breach every barrier, to flood everything. The sun shone ever more glassily and faraway.

A Little Town

THE HOUSES HAVE no doors. They have only a window and even that is rather narrow. Houses as if for midgets, with tiled roofs and dazzlingly red pantiles. Across the lanes, or rather the spaces between houses, on lines stretched from one eave to another, laundry of every color and variety. And in the square, large white sheets. On the ground, yellow sandy soil. The mornings are blue and chilly. The wind blows most of the day, ballooning the sheets in the square like sails.

All the houses look the same, are built the same. So too the inhabitants: small and cheerful. Living among the laundry, constantly forced to stoop, with each generation their stature has been gradually shrinking. Very little has remained of their old appearance. They rest their oval heads on their chests, they no longer have necks, their legs are bandy. Nonetheless, their sartorial elegance has been preserved and—hard to believe—their wings. Small wings at the ankles.

Landscape with Horses

It's EASIER THAN it looks. The main thing is to keep going straight ahead. You don't even have to hurry. First you turn the corner of your street, you cross the road, the tram line, then another road. The secret is not to stop. You can look back, you can look right, left, you can regret it. Please believe me, it's not all that far to go. A few streets that all look stupidly alike, a few houses that gradually shrink till they vanish, a few crossroads, a few days. And after a while, your gait will be smoother and smoother, suppler.

I will arrive one clear morning. I will then notice for the first time that the light comes not from above, from one side or another, but from everywhere, it will be within all the things around me, I will perceive it simultaneously with the lines and colors of the landscape.

One clear, round morning. Maybe the road will go gently downhill, then climb a slope planted with rare trees, leafless violet and orange trees with shiny black berries as big as walnuts. Eye-like berries. Long thin horses will smoothly gallop among the branches without budging them. Perfectly arching jumps. Tails glittering every color.

The sky will be grey-white, mild. And there will be so much silence and so much motionlessness that I will stop. Alert, calm, I will wait. That wait will have something retributory, something predatory about it. In vain will I scour the depths of the landscape. In the distance, among the purple and orange branches, herd after herd of green horses slowly floating like cumbersome birds. Until my eyes tire. A huge horse, as white as ivory, will move ever closer toward me. Ever closer . . .

And that endless morning, there will be so much silence.

Gurru

He lives at a great height above the earth on a gnarled, crooked branch. He has a pointed, bristly snout and grinning fangs. Covered with harsh, smoky fur, the body ends in a long hairless tail, as thin as a rat's. The forepaws are of a whitish gray, so too the belly, thick with ticks as big as fingernails. Gripping his large claws, hunched, he can sit motionless for days and nights at a time. Sometimes, on autumn mornings, solemn white birds—the only ones that reach him—envelop him in lazy, undulating swoops.

Nonetheless he is alone.

When it rains, he seems humble and wretched, crouched up there on a branch, but really, he is happy. The rainbow dazzlingly paints his wet fur.

He is cowardly and nasty. The twinkling of the stars annoys him, and their tinkling makes him cower fearfully. On moonlit nights, his hitherto inert tail lifts its tip like a viper and swishing angrily it bats against the taut rays of light. A queerly sweet music comes into being. And he takes fright and trembles, his snout slobbering.

He is so alone, so old . . . Who knows how long his eye, its glass slightly chipped, has been gazing fatuously from up there.

The City of Peacocks

I WAS HEADING in that direction, toward the edge of the plain whence came that cold green light. It was as if the sun had descended into frozen chasms, thereby losing its heat and color. Gradually, the faint reddish or orange glints vanished and there remained only that transparent green, without doubt gushing from somewhere very far below. Behind me, grey, gloomy dusk was falling. The few sparse leafless trees scattered across the plain were my landmarks. And I noticed that the ground I was crossing was sloping more and more steeply. At first, the slope was barely perceptible, but later I found a veritable mountainside behind me. In the sky, thick, dense clouds were lowering menacingly; I was afraid of a storm and my only hope lay in the strip of green light, which grew broader and broader, closer and closer. In fact, very soon I was no longer able to call it a strip, because it formed a reverberation that filled the whole horizon. Denser in the direction in which I was going, paler toward the margins, the cold, glassy, green light drew me with irresistible force. I began to run. The smooth, sloping ground accelerated my flight. Faster and faster and faster. I felt no weariness. Nevertheless, after a time, I stopped. I looked back; it was as if I had descended from the sky. I was proud rather than surprised. The colossus behind could no longer even be named a mountain: it was an endless slope descending from the sky. I set off once more. The soft ground I trod, brighter and brighter, more and more elastic, was covered in stunted grass of a translucent green. I bounded joyfully and only with difficulty did I resist the temptation to roll around on the grass. Strangely, the same smooth, boundless plain still stretched before me. I was overcome with sudden merriment. I ran and shouted at the top of my voice. And it was not long before I began to descry the outline of a city in the distance. In the glare of the green light that was growing stronger and stronger, spreading somehow circularly, I could discern the faint shapes of crenelated walls and, set farther back, a tall tower. I ran faster, waving my arms and shouting even more loudly: for joy, obviously. No, it was not a mediaeval castle, it was a city, rather a strange one, true, surrounded, as far as my eyes could see, by tall, indented walls and with a tall tower in the middle, which gleamed orange and green in the intensifying light, as did the other, lower and more shaded, roofs.

I ran for a long time; I thought I would never reach it. The lightening sky was an inverted, bottomless lake. The shore was far behind, rocky and dark, stretching downward to the earth, with which it merged in an arc. And the city, bathed in curtains of light. I was moving toward it through the gleaming grass and I was sure that I was treading the bottom of a sea. And the greenish, glassy light, which rounded and united everything . . . A sphere!

When I had only a little way to go before I reached the huge gates of thick, matte green glass, I descried above the city the slow, circular flight of birds. I was to discover they were peacocks. I stopped to follow them with my eyes and I was enveloped by sweet lassitude. Finally reaching the glass gates, which were painted with the heads and fans of peacocks, I did not dare to knock. I walked around the walls, which turned out to be made of glass or some similar material, and I was all but terrified by the silence within the city. On my way there, the absolute silence, shattered at intervals only by my shouts, had not frightened me, I had thought it natural; but so large a city to be so silent! Even so, I wanted to enter within whatever the cost. I put aside all fear, released from my throat a cry very much like that of a peacock (an excellent idea!) and rushed to bang on the gate with my fists. Although I pounded with all my might, the noise was ridiculously faint. I gave another cry and only then did the two leaves of the door slowly open. I hesitated. I saw a long, deserted street of not very tall red and yellow houses, but all of this through a greenish mist that distorted every color, lending it a wearying gleam. I took a few timid steps forward, the doors were already closing behind me, then I gave another cry. That shrill, strident cry made me feel better, it emboldened me, reassured me. I slowly walked down the amber pavement of the street. I had to be careful, because it was slippery and, because of the chaotic reflections of the houses to either side and the all-pervading green that laved its surface, it deceived the eye and misled the foot. The flock of peacocks was no longer hovering above the city, but from a courtyard now appeared a peacock, pacing gracefully and solemnly to greet me. I came to a stop in front of it and, not knowing what to do, how to comport myself, I stood motionless, my arms pressed against my body, my knees slightly bent, and my head thrust forward. The peacock unfurled its radiant fan and gave a slight bow. To that greeting I replied with a deep, respectful bow. The peacock then walked around me with measured steps and went down a side street.

I was left alone in the middle of the road, undecided, awkward. As I stood looking in every direction, I noticed a small, ferocious-looking animal creeping alongside the wall of a house. It had a head as big as a rat's, protruding teeth, with two fangs on either side of the whiskered snout, a long neck, and a body much larger than the head, covered in greenish-tinted fur. It rested on sharp claws that scratched the amber pavement, making an unbearable sound. I crossed to the other side of the street—there were no sidewalks—and decided to enter a house, any house, to rest for a little. I entered the courtyard whence the peacock had emerged shortly before. I cautiously looked all around me. The door of the house was ajar. Stooping, I slipped inside a low room dimly lit from outside. From the very first, my attention was drawn to a strange form placed in the middle of the room: a form made of a stone unfamiliar to me, glinting like emerald, greatly elongated in the upper part and squashed at the base. As I was tired, I curled up around it and from this hitherto unimagined position of recumbence, I examined the rest of the room.

There was not much to see: a vaulted ceiling—a true cupola—and small rectangular windows, barred and without panes. The light came not through the windows but through the walls themselves, which were made of semi-transparent glass. Next to a wall, I espied something red, fleshy, but nonetheless gleaming. At first it did not move. It looked like a snake or an eel. From a corner, another, larger one crawled to the center of the room. I could make out its bulging eye, positioned at its more swollen end, and what looked like long, thin strands, like whiskers. It undulated slowly over the floor, aiming at the stone pear around which I was curled. Why should I be afraid? I gently stretched out my hand to it. Another, quicker one reached my hand; it paused cautiously, raised its snout of scarlet flesh and touched me with its feelers. It tickled and by reflex I jerked back my hand. Probably this startled it, for I saw it move its whiskers in every direction and then retreat. A pity. The other one watched it without being curious enough to see the danger from closer up. The pear on which I was perched was obviously their nest. It was there that they waited for their master, the peacock, to come back. I uncurled myself from around it and, to repair my mistake, crawled after them on all fours. I caught one of them, the longest, in a corner of the room just as it was about to crawl up the wall. I held it in my hand, it writhed in fright, just like an eel, and I gently laid it around the pear. Sitting on the floor, I pressed my cheek to its silky skin. Then I fell asleep.

Probably from the sky (otherwise, from where else?) oranges were falling. Actually, it was hard to tell whether they were really oranges. Round, elastic, they were bouncing onto the slippery pavement, rolling downhill along other streets, toward the plaza. Thus began the festival of the peacocks.

I was in the garden, where I very much liked to walk, although it demanded a certain amount of effort: the clayey soil was covered with the creeping tendrils of an extraordinary plant and you had to be careful not to trip up on those rubbery, coiling, red and purple intestines. When the orange balls started to fall, I was savoring the perfume of a huge flower in the form of a bell with a flaring lip. I ran to the fence to watch the sight, which promised to be wonderful. From courtyards hurriedly came peacocks and peahens, dragging their fans, and they headed in the direction of the town's main plaza. I could wait in the garden no longer. At the crossroads, ring dances were being struck up. Dozens of peacocks wheeled around, carefully avoiding the oranges. The dance, sedate at first, gradually grew faster, wilder. They stamped, releasing cries that no longer seemed strident to me, as I was accustomed to them. In the plaza, a large ring dance was in progress: hundreds of peacocks wildly span round and round, trampling each other's tails and shrieking. I picked up an orange and saw that it was more like a ball of polished wood, but this impression did not last, since another was certainly made of plastic, and a third was a pleasantly aromatic fruit. After a time, the peacocks' dance became downright furious. From the sky spheres were now falling, which burst on contact with the pavement and stained the amber with their juice. It started to smell nasty. I hurried back so that I could go to sleep again. I had befriended one of the eels, which now slept wrapped around me.

I walked around the tower, wracking my brain to find a means of entry. It was more than mere curiosity. I had the impression that the peacocks expected it of me. When they saw me by the tower, they all moved away, some even rose into the air with encouraging shrieks and flew around me in concentric circles. The tower was in fact a conical cylinder—at least that was how it looked from a distance—made of a gleaming green stone with tints that were now orange, now reddish white. It had an uneven, scaly glitter to it, and the pinnacle, which could be seen only from a great distance, sometimes suddenly gave off a strange, intense glint, like an eye. All were afraid of that piercing glitter. The peacocks fled hopping on crooked legs, stumbling in fear, sweeping the pavement with their fans. It was then that those fearsome mammals emerged from their secret hiding places and ran around madly, their muzzles snarling, slobbering, leaving repulsive streaks in their wake. And the rosy eels would try desperately to get out of the houses through the barred windows, they swayed their fleshy, whiskered bulbs in the air and then fell into the street with a muffled thud.

The base of the tower was lighter in color. On closer inspection, scratches left by claws and fangs could be seen. After a while, high up, toward the tip, I glimpsed an oval window or rather an aperture. There was therefore a chance, but how could I reach it? I stubbornly tried to scale that colossus, which was as smooth as glass, and greatly regretted not having wings. But could the peacocks reach it? No, obviously not, there was not a single foothold, not even the tiniest crack. How hard I tried! I often fell asleep there, exhausted, propped against the cold stone of the tower. In my sleep I could feel the clammy snouts of the furry rats, but I was too exhausted to care. In any event, knowing they were harmless, I had long since ceased to fear them; I felt only disgust. I did not succeed in getting inside (but perhaps there wasn't even an inside . . .) and after a time I even came to the conclusion that my attempts were stupid, pointless. I went away disappointed, I roamed the streets at random, without replying to the peacocks' bows, and did not stop till I reached the main plaza of the city. And for the first time I thought of leaving the city of peacocks. I closed my eyes and maybe I had even fallen asleep, when a swishing of feathers and tapping of beaks on the pavement roused me from my torpor. I was surrounded by peacocks; I would never have imagined there could be so many. They were treading on each other's glittering fans, they were puffing out their feathers in impatience, striking the amber pavement with their beaks. I rose to my feet in confusion, bowing to every side . . . The peacocks regarded me with hostile solemnity, some opened their fans. Something had happened. I looked up; at first, I could not make it out: a whitish mist was descending ever more swiftly, a fog that had enveloped the upper part of the tower and was coming lower and lower. Hundreds of peacocks were staring at me, hundreds of fans were growing ever more radiant in the milky light that threatened to engulf all. The fog came lower and lower, half of the tower had vanished in the smoke. I let out a cry and started clear a path for myself, shoving, panting, so that I could flee that city, so that I could get as far away as possible. But would I ever be able to forget their steady gaze as they stood around me, their beaks lifted in despair?

I fled like a coward from the city of the peacocks. The horizon had shed its greenish light. A pale, dreary morning was beginning.

1961
(*Povestea vorbii*, no. 7, 1966)

Down Below

Down Below

IT WASN'T TOO COMPLICATED and anyway, after so long a time, always the same movements, the same movements, it becomes a reflex: he pressed a few buttons, turned this or that handle, flicked a switch, pulled a lever, pushed, pulled, turned, always the same buttons, handles, dials, levers—it was no big deal. He could do it even in the dark, the way you know where your mouth, nose, ears are in the dark, always in the dark, they were part of his very being and had been for a long time. There was only one light on the whole control panel, a limpid, greenish eye, above the serrated dial that he had to turn only very seldom; and then a short twist, the tinkle of a little bell and a chirring like a camera, for a few seconds. And over there, the dense, all-enveloping, and lately rather damp darkness. First of all (if there can be a first of all in a circle, in a cycle of actions), he took three steps to the right and pressed a smooth, almost velvety button, he pressed it with his middle finger, lately it had been getting stuck and he had to jab it hard, sometimes he used he used his ring finger too, he pressed the button, another two steps to the right, where he twisted a dial two or three times (it was impossible to say when or why he would have to do so twice or when he had to do so three times), then another dial slightly higher up, at the height of his forehead, he would grasp it between thumb and forefinger, and he had to lift his arm level with his ear, to flex it more than he had to for the other dials, because he had to apply greater torsion, it was higher up, and he felt short and increasingly weak—then he turned a handle: right, left, up, down, right, left, down, and waited. He didn't know for how long exactly, but he could sense when he suddenly had to crouch down and press three keys with three fingers, making a longer pause between the first and the second (a triolet!), and then standing up again, two steps to the left, pause, he pressed a button, another two steps to the left, another button, he stooped slightly, pulled a lever that was terribly cold—his hand froze to it—and then, sometimes, very seldom, he would briefly twist the serrated dial at the other end, he couldn't see the green light overhead, but he could feel it on the back of his neck, like a piercing gaze, perhaps even an ironic gaze, perhaps even a mocking gaze, although sometimes it was merely scornful or, extremely seldom, compassionate. He turned on his heel, took a few stealthy steps—the last of which made a sloshing sound because of the puddle that had formed there—and before pressing the button, he took a deep breath. Click! And the melodious chirring would last for a few moments.

He didn't work at the control panel the whole time; he was able to take quite lengthy breaks, during which, apart from the unpleasant duty of turning a huge wheel from which probably hung a long, heavy chain that creaked dreadfully, making him have to throw all his bodyweight at the wheel and endure the screech, the now piercing, now hoarse whine of the chain (it was horrible!), but apart from that he had nothing to do. A button to press or a switch to flick here and there. He walked with slow steps through the darkness taking care not to move too far away from the green eye so that he could return in time when he sensed that the moment had come to resume work, that is, to press, pull, turn the same buttons, dials, handles, levers, making the same reflex movements over and over again; to go back to the place from which, taking three precisely calculated steps, he would then arrive in front of the smooth button, as velvety as the back of your wrist, another two steps to twist the dials below and above, for which he had to lift his arm as high as his ear, and then the handle and a pause and a crouch: the three keys pressed with his forefinger, a pause, and almost simultaneously, the other two, the middle finger and ring finger, like playing a piano. And again the pressing, the twisting, up, down, right, left, countless buttons, handles, dials, keys, and, from time to time, the switch beneath the ironic green eye. He had plenty of time to walk around: taking long, slow steps, his knees slightly bent, avoiding the puddles that had formed here and there, after he heaved the wheel, he would walk around and think about how lately it was much easier. That wasn't quite what he thought, because that lately was immeasurably long, but at any rate, it was clear that the work was easier. Back in the old days, there hadn't been a control panel with velvety buttons, handles, convenient dials, but rather thick ropes, pulleys and wheels like ship's tillers, heavy chains reeking of rust—you had to hang on them with all your weight, to pull steel levers or thrust at them with your chest, and just a palm's breadth above his head or even lower there were endless scorching pipes, twisting like snakes, and the air was now too dry and stifling, now hot and damp. There hadn't even been the green eye back then, but only oppressive, eternal darkness, hot and evil-smelling.

True, he hadn't worked alone back then.

Gradually, the pulleys, the wheels, the pipes were replaced with that control panel, the green eye had lit up, and finally, all that remained was the large wheel, and even then, he wasn't sure he was required to struggle with it any more. His work had become easier, but now he was alone, deprived of the pleasure he discovered one day, after climbing an endless flight of rough stone steps, the pleasure of peering through a hole the size of an ear, or perhaps smaller, the pleasure of peering at light, at colors and snatches of dancing bodies, for a faint music was audible, coming from very far away, but music nonetheless. As there were two of them, one of them had been able, when the work didn't require more than one pair of arms, obviously, to climb the flight of stairs on his hands and knees, since the steps were narrow, making them almost vertical—he could feel the harsh, cold stone against his knuckles—to clamber up to the crack through which stole a pale ray of light. It was a whitish-grey light, as faded as the colors that flickered for a few instants to the rhythm of a distant music just as faded: a flecked, etiolated grass green and a pale, grated-lemon yellow and a pink as whitish as the skin behind your wrist; and at intervals, strips of sky blue, for a measly second, flashes of clear blue, and then once more the grey and whitish pink and the far-off, slow music, and snatches of dancing bodies. He couldn't stay long, he quickly climbed back down the steps, still on his hands and knees, moving backwards, he was needed to set in motion the huge wheel connected to the hidden chains, an invisible system of pulleys and, among the chains—he could hear them clanking against them—enormous snakes of scorching cast iron, who knows how high above. For not even by the height of the steps was he able to calculate how high above. The crack had appeared in a kind of tube descending vertically past the steps, which continued to rise just as steeply, and he had never dared to climb higher, crawling under that huge tube, so large he wouldn't have been able to put his arms around it. It had been better when there were two of them, although the other man's body was covered in harsh fur and he had sharp incisors which he sometimes sank in his shoulder or thigh. His long, knotty, clawed arms would grasp him ferociously, but there was no time for such games: the pulleys, the wheels, the levers, all that scorching ironwork, reeking of steam and verdigris, had to be kept in motion. After a time, the chains that formed the pulleys vanished one by one and those that remained were increasingly difficult to work, it required greater and greater force, the strength of both their bodies. They would hang from the end of the chain and pull with all their might. And so they had become shorter and shorter, the pauses when he could clamber up the rough stone steps to look through the crack: faded colors, but also blue flashes, strips of sky, and distant sounds and outlines, music and the bodies he wanted to glimpse dancing.

It was a torturous time. Now that he was alone, he often walked around thinking of that time and was unable to say how much time had elapsed since then; it was somewhere in the past, and that was all. The puddles, ever more numerous and noisier, that is, ever deeper, slow, calculated steps, the care he had to take not to move too far away from the green eye, the same movements: press, pull, turn, buttons, levers, dial, a simple twist of the fingers or arms, but he was alone. Along with the final chain, which they had both used to pull, hanging as if from a huge bell, the other man had vanished too. Quite simply, he had been pulled aloft by a mysterious, implacable force, and in vain had he tried to hang onto to the ascending body, in vain had he resisted with all his might; he felt that he too was being pulled up by the chain along with the other man who had to vanish, and he would remain alone in the darkness, in front of a control panel with countless buttons, handles, dials and levers, with the ironic green eye boring into the back of his neck, the green eye, which was sometimes scornful and sometimes, very seldom, extremely seldom, compassionate. He could feel himself being pulled upward and he wouldn't have unclenched his hands had he not banged his head against one of the scorching pipes. The powerful blow—the chain had been yanked away in that instant—stunned him and he fell; he lay dazed, almost unconscious, for a long time. When he came around, all the chains had vanished, all the wheels as big as ship's tillers—only the well wheel remained, and at the back of his mind continued to flicker the hope that the unseen chain which he heard banging against the walls of the concrete cistern would bring back the other man—and in their place, the splendid control panel with dozens of buttons, dials and handles, easy to work making simple movements, always the same, and behind him, the green eye.

He had remained alone.

He no longer dared to climb the steep steps, to look through the crack. But how he longed for another glimpse of the strips of sky and the patches of whitish-pink skin, how he longed to hear the soft, far-off music and to glimpse the outlines of the dancers through the mist.

The green eye blinked imperiously. It was time. He bounded up to it, then he counted three steps to the right and pressed the smooth, almost velvety button, he pressed with his middle finger, assisted by his ring finger, because the button had grown stiff lately, another two steps to the right and he twisted the dial twice only, then the dial above, lifting his arm level with his ear, then he pulled a handle, right, left, up, down, right, left, down, he crouched and pressed the three keys, he stood back up, two steps to the left, pause, pushed a button, another two steps to the left, another button, he stooped slightly and pulled the dreadfully cold lever, a dial, a button, another button, a handle, the same reflex movements over and over again, he pushed, pulled, twisted, and behind him the green light, the mocking or merely ironic, but seldom compassionate, green light.

1964
(*Luceafărul*, October 1967)

That Circus

That Circus

THE TOWN LAY at the foot of some rather high hills that rose by stages to become mountains. Before the circus set up there—quite a long time ago—some had even built houses on the sides of the hill, clearing the forest. They didn't venture very high, although Grandfather boasted that one of our forebears had built some kind of cabin right at the top, on the crest, heedless of the disapproval of the other townsfolk and the mayor in particular, who found his authority diminished: to live at such a height, up there, above the town, above your more or less timorous peers—that was going too far!

He was an upstanding man, Grandfather boasted, and Mother would smile, indulgently. Grandfather had large, horny hands and when he talked, his eyes would light up, his hands would leap back and forth like nimble, gamboling animals. I was knee-high at the time and didn't understand much; I knew that the circus was up on the hill, with its acrobats, its conjurers, its huge, wonderful, frightening beasts, which had escaped from their cages or come down from the mountains, nobody was brave enough to climb the hill and it had been a long time since the circus people had descended to the town to give performances, as they used to do in the old days. Once in a blue moon, a scrawny acrobat, wearing a patched, greasy sailor's shirt, would come and do a few modest routines, which impressed not even the children, or an old conjurer, wearing a shabby green frock coat, would produce some tatty ribbons from his ear or mouth, a snake, a rabbit—nothing spectacular.

Only the old folk still remembered the circus of yore, the astounding shows that had lasted for days at a time. The whole town used to light up with pleasure and awe. There was even a special place, an arena, where people had used to gather to watch the wonders. There were flying acrobats with bodies like fishes who floated in mid-air like falcons; rubber gymnasts who climbed endless ladders, vanishing from sight; ballerinas and conjurers; and above all the great, the unsurpassed animal tamer, of whom I dreamed so many times in childhood, although I was sure he was dead and that the animals had escaped their cages and become wild again, and nobody dared climbed the hill any more, and the houses on the side of the hill were long abandoned, the forest had spread everywhere.

When the great tamer came down from the mountains, to the shrill notes of trumpets, at intervals drowned out by the roars of the beasts and the joyful whoops of the crowd waiting at the edge of town, breathless with impatient excitement, everybody stopped work, the bells tolled till the spires and roofs quaked, it was a true holiday, all the people felt it, and even the mayor himself, with his white beard spread over his broad chest, would come out onto the balcony of the town hall and raise his right arm in salute. Then came the trumpeters on their white and black horses, blowing at the top of their lungs, then the elephant with the yellow tusks, carrying the baldachin, richly adorned with gold and gems, of the great tamer, who gazed absently over the heads of the crowd, and his smile, always the same, was ever more faded, ever wearier on his withered lips. Behind him came the beasts, in cages or roaming free, magnificent, never before seen animals: white giraffes with violet spots, tigers with red and yellow stripes, bears of every color, huge, fearsome animals, scornful of the swarming, heaving crowd of curious, frightened people, who were determined not to miss a single detail of the show that had now commenced and which enchanted them all: they never knew when it would begin, there was no gong, no spotlight, just two or three orange or pink suns that rose as if by command specially for that day. The tamer was as motionless as ever, his eyes, said Grandfather, shone, rolling in their sockets, and a murmur rose from the crowd as they awaited the marvels with baited breath.

And they were marvels indeed! cried Grandfather, who was old, but even so, he had not forgotten the tamer's exploits. I would listen to him mouth agape as he told his stories about the tamer, it was if I could see before my very eyes the long whip cleaving the air like a lightning bolt, the tigers flying over the arena, the elephants rearing up as if in prayer, the white bear climbing up a rope so high that nobody could see it any more, he would vanish into the orange of the sun that hung like a balloon right above the audience. The women and children would scream in fright when one of the ballerinas thrust her curly head into the maw of a lion, then her shoulders, her arms, till all that could be seen were her hips and her long legs waving up and down as if she were swimming, and then her arms, shoulders, neck, head would emerge safely, the audience would fall silent, and then they would roar, they would give a standing ovation. Grandfather's weather-beaten but nimble hands were tigers and ballerinas, bears, dancers and kangaroos hopping after the colored balloons that Plato, the public's favorite conjurer at the time and the only one allowed in the ring during the tamer's routine, blew up using a long pipe like an alphorn, and there were so many colors, so much jubilation, Grandfather's hands leaped joyfully over the dining room table, and we would listen to him wide-eyed. Then the hands would abruptly tire, the light in Grandfather's eyes would fade; it was so long ago. Grandfather was deaf, he couldn't hear our questions, he would sit silent, not even looking at us, his hands would lie limp, like two animals exhausted by vain flight, motionless, dead.

Grandfather was the only one old enough to have seen the circus shows back in the day, when he was a child, but Mother said that it wasn't true, that he was recounting what he had heard or perhaps read about them. Luckily, Grandfather didn't hear her. Mother used to get annoyed about anything to do with the circus and I remember how she once chased away the tall lad in gymnast's costume, shouting "beggar!" at him and turning red with fury. Most people were like her, although some used to talk about the circus from time to time, albeit as if it was something so long ago that it was now just a legend. In any event, such talk was mainly to be heard in the taverns, after one too many glasses, the tone was slightly mocking and bored, and only after every other subject had been exhausted. Grandfather was among the last enthusiasts, perhaps the only one I ever met. After he died, my interest in the circus faded, probably because it was drawn mostly from the anecdotal. I didn't forget Grandfather's stories, but I didn't think about them any more: they remained at the back of my mind and only seldom did I recall the tamer.

More or less the same thing happens to all of us: in childhood there is a grandfather seating in an armchair, aged, but with hands as nimble as the ballerinas and tigers, sometimes the hand clenched into a fist and imperiously pounded the table, it was the tamer and our souls thrilled to his harshness and dexterity, sometimes, moving four fingers like paws, it was a ravening beast, but cowed by the tamer's whip, or balanced gracefully on the tip of the ring finger, it was the fearless ballerina dancing among the beasts. Grandfather was full of enthusiasm, all these things he had seen in his childhood, with his own eyes he had seen them, he didn't even notice Mother's smile. The children believed him, they played at circuses, we all wanted to be the tamer, even the girls, although they were more suited to being ballerinas.

Whenever I had the chance, I ran to the edge of town, where they had begun to build the wall, and I gazed up at the green hills, the yellow, red, green blotches that I suspected were circus wagons abandoned by the acrobats and beasts after the death of the tamer.

Few were those who ventured beyond the town wall and none brought back any explanation. Some claimed to have seen nothing but ordinary forest animals typical of those parts (and there were many of them), others kept a downcast silence. A few never returned; they vanished, ascending into the mountains.

We would ride our bicycles to the wall and look up at the hill. We would strain to see the wagons and the trapeze artistes and ballerinas and animals and, atop his white elephant adorned with gold and gems, the tamer, the famous, legendary tamer:

Grandfather's large, brawny fist would pound the table, making the glasses, knives, forks rattle, and we would give a start, close our gaping mouths and gulp; our throats were dry with excitement.

Then I grew up and Grandfather became more and more elderly, his fist paler and paler, more and more wrinkled, I became interested in other things, I would ask him only about the ballerinas, but as a joke, making an innuendo, and the old man would get annoyed, shake his feeble, translucent fist at me.

When he died, when he was laid out on the bed, with his fists clenched over his chest, with his white face set in a frown, I remembered all his stories about the circus and as I looked at him, slightly amazed at the annoyance visible on his face—it was neither fear nor surprise, it was quite simply frozen annoyance, bitterness even—I realized, and it struck me as a brief, but powerful thought, that Grandfather had lied. Mother was right: he hadn't seen any of it. Nevertheless, he had told us the stories with such passion, particularly the ones about the tamer, about the huge elephant with the yellow tusks, the baldachin adorned with gold and gems, the tamer's weary smile and that whole horde of beautiful, frightening beasts.

Stretched out on the bed, the annoyance was frozen on his face. He would have liked to carry on lying, although we no longer had either the time or the inclination to listen to him, what was for certain is that he would have liked to carry on lying . . .

1964
(*Cronica*, no. 8, February 1967)

The Fence

I was coming back by another, more roundabout road, but now, around noon, it was nicer around there. A strip of shadow still remained by the wall of those old houses, with their mysterious passageways whence wafted coolness and the smell of mold. I carefully calculated how many houses, how many meters were left before I would arrive. In the mornings, I didn't go that way, because I was in a hurry.

I had just one more street to walk down and I now thought I could see the fence. I was always afraid I might miss it, that I might not reach it.

On the corner, the yellow roadworks sign had stopped the traffic again. They'd probably started digging that morning, the ditch was deep, all you could see were their brawny sunburnt necks and sweating brows. I was forced to make a detour; I hadn't been anticipating that. I broke into a run. On my back, the satchel bumped up and down noisily, I ought to have taken it off. The passers-by looked at me askance, some waved scolding fingers. And how long the ditch was! Within were colossal serpents of cast iron struck by blinding swords of flame. I found a place to traverse, a bridge, the flames of the welders dazzled me. A green mist descended for a few moments. On the sidewalk, I regained my senses. The fence gleamed in the sun, tall, as black as pitch. I quickened my steps. The crack was further on. What bother I had finding it! If I stop to think, I don't know what it was that attracted me to that huge fence, its laths that soared up to the sky, rigid, black, like mustached soldiers standing to attention, shoulder to shoulder. Once I saw a leaf floating like a kite above the fence: slightly yellowed, it rode with its petiole downward, it didn't allow the wind to blow it at random. And after it stretched thin arms that could not reach it. The fence was twice, thrice my height, gleaming like glass, I couldn't climb it. And it wasn't easy for me to discover that nonetheless it had a crack, which was no wider than a stick of chewing gum, but round, just right for use as an eyehole.

An expanse of grass, without flowers. Nothing but grass and large fleshy leaves, sprouting straight from the ground. The air shimmered like the surface of a lake or else it was my eyelid quivering in fear and pleasure . . . The leaves spurted from the ground, they were elongated, their veins were as pronounced as a fish's skeleton, and among them glided thin women, who were all arms, and fishes with scales glinting like chainmail.

The fence now seemed to me hostile, stony, taller and more massive than ever before. To the right of the hole was pasted a brightly colored poster for the circus.

A Stage Production

Maria from the Middle School
A Stage Production

I WAS VERY CURIOUS to see what trick Iosif had got up to. He'd been all puffed up when he left, confident of success, he'd put on his new suit, carefully combed his hair, smoothed his moustache, straightened his tie. His trousers were rather tight. In the end, he might just pull it off. Brown-haired, slim, with broad, strong shoulders and a cocky gleam in his lively eyes, he had everything he needed to woo and win a girl. You couldn't help but admire the sheer elegance of the way he straddled his motorcycle. A true knight of the present day! But that wasn't enough (and I think he knew it) to make Maria fall in love with him, to sigh for him at night in her schoolgirl's bed, to inscribe his name in fancy letters on all her exercise books. His mission was all the more difficult, damn it all! and even though our plan was brilliant, even though his skill and experience were beyond all doubt, I was still nervous. True, I was also counting on the young girl's taste for adventure, on the mirage of a new, unfamiliar life outside the walls of the boarding school. No matter how fearful of the consequences, no matter how much of a mother's girl she was (which was exactly how I wanted her to be), she might just let herself be beguiled . . .

So, I got down to business. I wasn't confident, but I didn't sit around and beat my brains about it. First, I lugged what furniture there was out into the hall. I'd been thinking of leaving the bed in the care of Magda—she'd been moaning about

how hers was rickety—but I found the door locked. After that,
I hammered a few nails in the wall, for hanging clothes on,
naturally, I wiped the dust and, changing my mind, I pushed
one of the chairs back inside the room; there would be need
of at least one. Now a little tired, I sat down, cross-legged, and
waited. The idea of emptying the room had come to me that
very afternoon; I hadn't even had time to tell Iosif about it yet.
Why should I tell him anyway? As if Iosif understood the whole
story I'd got myself mixed up in! He was a character in his own
right; a complicated character, but a character still. I was sitting
on a chair and looking out of the window at the tiles of the
house opposite. He wouldn't agree with it. He would think it
was stupid. Ever since the time when he was a two-bit actor, he
had been accustomed to there being, if not a curtain, then at
least some pasteboard scenery, a bit of cloth, something; there
had to be something! And then there's the matter of where she'll
sleep . . . He'll toss his head or shrug his shoulders in embarrassment. What are we, horses? He'll lose his temper, start shouting
and waving his arms about, shaking his long hair. I'll patiently
explain that having a set limits the audience's imagination and
that he's backward-looking, that he lacks boldness, and besides,
he has no conception that a work of art (yes, a work of art,
Iosif!) requires every sacrifice. Even though he won't understand,
he'll gradually calm down. It will be a performance that Maria
will watch in astonished, slightly fearful, silence. Then Iosif will
whisper to her in a honeyed voice—what he whispers is up to
him—and I will tiptoe out the door.

I heard footfalls on the stairs. I gave a start. The footfalls
ascended to a higher floor. The heavy footfalls of a strong, weary
man. It must have been the Wrestler. I didn't need him; he
wouldn't make his entrance until near the end. When I met Iosif
at the tavern on the corner, I was with Magda and the Wrestler.
We were starving, and Magda had got hold of some money. We
were wolfing down beans and sausages, looking in gratitude at
her red hair, her large garishly rouged mouth, her gold teeth—
her rather vulgar smile. And she wasn't at all ugly; on that score
we were both agreed. We were both admiring her, munching our

beans with a hearty appetite, when she made a sign to me and whispered something in my ear. That was up to her, I had nothing against it! Iosif came up to our table, bearing a jug. I replied to his greeting, none too politely, with my mouth full. But the Wrestler stood up and, after wiping the grease from his mouth, gave him a hearty handshake. All of us were very drunk! It was Magda who paid the tab, overjoyed that Iosif had recognized her. She'd known him for a long time, since when he was still an actor. For which reason I couldn't help but conceitedly mention that no matter how down at heel I might look, I was nonetheless a writer; I was writing an amazing play and it would be great if we could work together. We looked at each other, highly touched, almost bursting into tears. Iosif was drunker than any of us. He stood up to recite to us from *Hamlet*; he kept stumbling over the words and finally the tirade degenerated into a howl. But he had talent, sir, that he did; Magda could vouch for that. He had talent by the cartload! Within a few years, he would ended up in a leading rôle! Yes! that was what he was cut out for: the leading rôle! Obviously, he had a whole story behind him, a story of greater or lesser success, which he told amid interruptions and hiccoughs.

"But you're still young . . ." I was stumbling over my words, too, but my mind was still limpid, as proven by the fact that even then I knew how useful to me Iosif could be.

"I'm a failure, sir, a failure, that's what . . ."

I thought: here's the right man for a melodrama. All I needed now was the female character, the incarnation of innocence. I knocked back another glass. All of a sudden, I became cheerful.

"You're still young, my friend, on my word. Hey, Magda . . . if mister Iosif here agreed to work with me . . ."

The four of us set off home and because Iosif no longer had any fixed abode, he slept in Magda's room. It wasn't till two weeks later that Magda came and asked me to let him sleep in my room. My bed was sturdier and bigger. Iosif soon became very dear to me. The big toenail of one of his feet was crooked, scaly, black; a motorcycle had run over it. It was as if all the other toes were scrunched up against the big one, sheltering under its hoof-like nail. (A devil's hoof.) A nice guy, that Iosif! When he had money, he was very free-handed. There would be drinking bouts one after the other. We also used to invite the Wrestler and Vasile, and sometimes Magda would come, too. Lately, she'd been wearing expensive dresses, a gold bracelet (real gold, I swear!), and she no longer had a single tooth missing. But she was very busy. A fat man with a ruddy, chubby face used to visit her. Almost every day. He trod heavily, but he looked all around, especially when he left. He was very elegant. Magda would show him to the door and thumb her nose at his back. One afternoon, he bumped into Iosif at the top of the stairs. Iosif was drunk. He was also furious, for some unknown reason. They ended up having a fist fight. Iosif punched him in the face and made his nose bleed. Magda shut her door and pretended not to hear. After which the fat man never set foot there again. There were also other scandals. "But what business is it of ours?" said the Wrestler. "We're just fellow tenants." "Come on, it's not quite like that. Magda pays for our drinks, sometimes she even gives us a few coins." Iosif frequently lectured us about his theory of comradeship. "We're all on our uppers," he would say. I would listen to him (we were in our cups, obviously) and didn't even attempt to suppress an ironical smile. The Wrestler unloaded sacks at the railroad station and sometimes put on bourgeois airs. Iosif used to tease him for having a book of savings stamps. "It's none of our business," the Wrestler would say. Magda even used to bring back pupils from the lycée. That was going too far. We might all end up in the lurch, if we got involved. But the Wrestler didn't say a word when Magda was around. Iosif used to claim (when it was just the two of us, over a drink) that the Wrestler was in love with Magda. I thought about that idea of his seriously and finally agreed with it. It's a good idea and I'm going to take it into account. But for the time being, it's something else that's important. We needed a girl, what with one thing and another . . . he knew that, it wasn't the first time I'd talked to him about it. Without her we wouldn't get anywhere. Iosif nodded his head, firmly convinced, and he looked so ridiculous (since he didn't actually understand anything) that I almost burst out laughing.

"Off you go, Iosif, and don't come back without her!"

Maria, as Iosif had described her, was indeed perfect for the part. She was blonde, she had a round face and blue eyes. She was innocent, she was an orphan, she was at boarding school, a prize-winning pupil, sir! At their very first meeting, she recited to him some poems by Eminescu; Iosif recited to her from *Hamlet*. Their eyes were bathed in tears. "My word of honor, sir!" I was going to meet with them both one day so that he could introduce me to her. For some reason or other, I was late, and they left before I got there. Iosif was annoyed. He said it wouldn't be his fault if I pulled faces about her later.

"I have perfect faith in you, Iosif."

Nobody else knew about our project. And Iosif appreciated that. Actually, I have no idea what went on in his head. I told him, "Look, Iosif, you absolutely must entice a lycée girl called Maria and bring her here."

He winked at me and patted me on the shoulder. Which annoyed me.

"You've got a filthy mind. Get it into your head that I simply need a female character, nothing more."

"Right you are, sir!" And off he went to borrow a motorcycle.

Footfalls on the stairs once again. Iosif's heavy, shuffling footfalls, followed by lighter, more hesitant footfalls. I was excited, I must admit. I straightened my hair and stood up.

Maria was exactly what I was looking for. The flaxen hair in pigtails, the round, rosy, porcelain face, the blue, expressionless eyes. She was incapable of laughter; when she smiled, her face lit up and her eyes gleamed, bulging slightly. She was perhaps a little fat; her breasts were overly developed. Her skin was soft, velvety, completely hairless. She always looked you straight in the eye, but only when you spoke to her; when she said something, which was very seldom, she lowered her gaze. She had a reedy little voice, but it was even and pleasant. She would answer questions monosyllabically, drop by drop, barely moving her lips or face. And what astounded you was her utter indifference to what was going on around her. (At least so it seemed, and in any event, I was none too happy about that.) The first evening, at my invitation she sat on the only chair in the room, pressing her shoes, her thighs, her knees closely together. She sat perfectly still. She looked fixedly now at Iosif, now at me. As I had predicted, Iosif, was furious.

"What the hell are you playing at, sir, moving all the furniture out of the room!"

My explanations only made him all the more furious. He was yelling, flailing his arms, and didn't want to know about any of it. Maria watched us calmly, placidly, even. She raised not so much as an eyebrow; she twitched not so much as the corner of her mouth. I finally managed to calm Iosif. He took the money and went to the tavern. Perhaps he thought his mission was completed; but what is for sure is that he felt slighted. It had been no easy task to fetch Maria and I hadn't evinced the slightest admiration; I'd taken the feat for granted. He went off to the tavern without so much as a word; he didn't give the poor girl so much as an encouraging glance. Ultimately, that too was part of his rôle, although—and you can't say I'm wrong about this—the transformation was too abrupt, he made his exit too quickly. But Maria's serene calm was incomprehensible; it was as if she had come there not for him but for me. She was wearing a plain blue dress, similar to a lycée uniform; her flat-heeled shoes were more than proper, and her stockings were made of cotton. For that reason, the diamond-studded gold watch didn't look as if it was hers, and it lent an irritating, discordant note (in the end, I sold it, obviously). She was sitting on that chair as calm and impassive as a cat. I walked up and down in front of her with my hands behind my back, with my head bowed, pretending to be preoccupied, because I couldn't find anything to say to her. Without the others, I feel not only alone, but also pointless. I was straining to hear footsteps on the stairs, the Wrestler's, Magda's, or even Vasile's. All of a sudden, I turned to face her and curtly asked her what she was doing there, what she expected of me. I for one couldn't help her at all, absolutely at all. If she wanted to sit on the chair and wait for him, then she could go ahead. I was trying to be abrupt, to provoke a reaction, to see some kind of expression on her face or in her eyes, to make her cry, instead of her looking at me like that, with her glassy blue eyes. She made no reply, no move. She looked at me fixedly, or not even that much: her blue eyes were simply pointed at me and somehow it was as if she wasn't even looking at me. She sat stock-still on the chair and it was only then that I understood (or else I suspected and it was later that I understood) that Iosif had brought me a doll, a big doll with flaxen hair, a rosy face, and blue eyes. But even if that was the way of it, there was still nothing that could be done. And I left the room as if exiting a stage.

Magda immediately agreed. She gave Maria one of her dresses, altered it for her (Magda was good at sewing), took her to her room, where she also slept for a few nights, and must have told her something, because Maria would smile rather strangely. I asked Magda, but she refused to tell me. Iosif also behaved oddly. He returned sooner than I had been expecting, without saying a word, gave me a friendly pat on the shoulder, and went to Magda's room.

What the hell! When an author notices that he's been deceived in regard to his characters, that they're no longer under his control and are acting on their own volition, it's not exactly pleasant. The writer is deflated like a pricked balloon and might even evince despair, which is to say, he might tear up everything he's written. Especially if he's been harboring numerous illusions as to his authority. One protagonist makes his entrance too quickly, another dies too soon or acts more despairingly than is permissible. What is the poor author supposed to do then? Should you mercilessly punish your own creation, destroy it precisely because it has taken on life?

I told Magda simply this: "You know, Magda, Iosif has got involved with a young girl and I don't know what to do about it. He says he wants to marry her or that he's promised her he'll marry her, one or the other. If word of it gets out, it will be a problem, you do realize. She's underage, you do understand."

Magda understood straight away. She was even enthusiastic about it. She clapped her hands merrily and gave me a wink. Then she took Maria to his room.

"Iosif must keep his promise," she said, almost laughing. "He must."

Without even asking me, Iosif moved the furniture back inside the room, he tidied up, scrubbed the floor. He whistled cheerfully and rather than answering my questions, he gave me a friendly but also ironical look. I felt slighted, ignored, kept backstage. Such is the fate of the playwright, you'll say, to remain backstage. Fair enough, you're right, but at any rate, my intentions should also be taken into consideration. I should at least be able to know what my characters are thinking.

"Listen, Iosif, I want you to give me an honest answer, I'm begging you." (Listen to that, now I'm begging him!) "Tell me straight, tell me, do you love Maria?"

Iosif was busy polishing the furniture, which was so shabby that it was hardly worth it. He looked at me in slight astonishment.

"What do you expect?"

I could sense he was being ironic.

"Iosif, what's wrong with you? You don't care about me any more. You don't show the slightest respect. Listen, am I or am I not the author?"

It had only been a few days since Maria arrived, since the beginning of the play proper, I mean, and there I was, being gradually pushed out. In other words, after going to so much trouble to find myself the characters, after gathering them all together in the same place, after breathing life into them, damn it! after telling them what they have to do, how they should carry on, well, after all that, I found myself thrown out into the street.

"Iosif, don't forget that I'm in charge."

I'd lost my temper and I didn't realize that he might interpret my outburst in a completely different way. True, the blockhead felt slighted, he thought he'd been thrown out of the house; no matter how much I begged him to forgive me after that, no matter how much I tried to explain what I'd actually meant to say, I couldn't do it. He still wouldn't have understood! In vain did I try to turn my characters into my accomplices or even my friends. I felt more and more alone, and ridiculous to boot. The Wrestler brought a bottle of rum and the three of us drank it together; Iosif was still acting all offended. I got drunk and tried to tell the Wrestler all my misfortunes as an author, an author hoodwinked

by his characters. The Wrestler is so good and so stupid. Then
Magda and Vasile arrived. We were together again and ultimately, I loved them. We were bound to one another, the devil
knows why. I thanked Magda for being nice to Maria and smiled
at Maria, who, pressing her knees very, very firmly together,
was looking at us, silent, trusting. Magda then announced that
Iosif and Maria had decided to get married, but they still had to
obtain an official dispensation, what with Maria being underage.
And they all looked at me and I don't know whether it was the
rum or my foolish vanity, but I had the illusion that their eyes
expressed a certain respect.

Let's say I went to try and obtain the official dispensation.
But that's of no importance. From that evening, I had to sleep
in Magda's room and give up my room to the young couple.
(And please believe me, I hadn't slept in that room for a long
time.) A few peaceful days passed. The Wrestler would leave at
the crack of dawn and I would go to his room to write. Iosif
was looking for a job. (How I had to beg him to do that!) And
Maria was radiant, as if gilded. She sat on the bed or a chair,
with her chubby hands in her lap, quietly, and lately she regarded
me with a kind of gratitude, in her own way. It was then that
the sparrow appeared on the window ledge. It was a blue, fresh
morning, somehow glossy. A morning that had returned from
who knows when. I sat and looked at Maria as if for the first time,
without astonishment, even admiringly, because I had discovered
the mother in her doll-likeness, in the radiance of her cheeks,
which at first had struck me as too ruddy. The bird on the window ledge chirped joyfully at us and, as if from a spotlight, a
broad swath of light poured into the room, illumining Maria's
face even more brightly.

"Look, a sparrow at the window," said Maria in a reedy voice.
And we both looked at the sparrow hopping around with a certain solemnity. It was then that the idea came to me. One of
those seemingly insignificant ideas that the audience doesn't really
notice. I ran out of the room and returned all in one breath,
bringing a motorcycle pump. The sparrow had flown away; the
light had subsided. I murmured something in Maria's ear and she

looked at me, trustful, motionless. And slowly, slowly, Maria's belly began to swell. Iosif was a little worried; he was now looking for a job in earnest. For a time, he naïvely thought they would take him back at the theatre. When he saw that Maria was pregnant and came to tell me, as if imparting a secret, his expression betokened what you might call responsibility. Iosif was going to be a father. When she found out, Magda was deeply touched, and I felt like an author once more. Every morning, I would sneak into Maria's room with the motorcycle pump and carefully counted the days.

I already said that the Wrestler put on bourgeois airs. (Or Iosif said it—it doesn't matter which!) He even had certain principles. For example, he wouldn't tolerate lycée boys visiting Magda or our throwing bottles at passersby when we had a drinking bout. He liked to work hard, to get up early in the morning, to come home exhausted, and to have money put aside. But he was the most generous man in the world, he helped everybody when they were in need, and I think he was secretly in love with Magda. Toward me he behaved protectively more than respectfully; true, he felt much stronger than I. When he flexed his muscles in the mirror (in the end, I'd moved into his room, what else could I do . . .), only then did his face betray his pride. For he knew very well that he was strong and it helped him. I told him that Maria was pregnant; I deliberately said so in a joking tone of voice. He gave me a stern look (I was expecting it) and asked whether I had obtained the official dispensation for the marriage. I lied to him, obviously, saying that everything was almost ready. Why did Maria's fate touch him so deeply? With his thick fingers he buttoned up his shirt. He had a large face, with a jutting chin and a fleshy nose.

"The landlord found out from Maria," he told me. "He's none too happy about it."

I'd predicted that, and when that terrible argument erupted in Magda's room, and Mr. Popescu threatened to call the police, I was overjoyed, because everything was going like clockwork. Exactly the way I wanted it. Magda came out into the hall in only her nightie, screaming for help, and as luck would have it, the Wrestler was just climbing the stairs. The man in Magda's room was probably quite burly, because otherwise the Wrestler would have finished with him more quickly, there wouldn't have been such a hullaballoo, the landlord wouldn't have threatened us with the police. They fought each other with chairs, Magda was screaming, and Maria came out and started crying softly, clutching her dressing gown over her swollen belly. By the time the blue uniform of the policeman appeared at the bottom of the stairs, the Wrestler was panting victoriously, his opponent was lying on the floor with a broken head, unconscious, obviously.

"I'll kick you out, you lowdown whore!"

Mr. Popescu, who ought to have known she wasn't all that lowdown and had himself climbed the stairs to her door many a time, was out of his mind with rage. I was the one who summoned the policeman; I was even afraid he might not get there in time. The policeman took a statement and if he went away in the end, it was thanks solely to Mr. Popescu. That was the first time the police had ever come. The landlord had proven to us all that he was a vigorous man and quite capable of keeping the peace in his own house. On that occasion, I found out that Iosif's papers weren't in order. When he heard about the commotion, he was deeply shaken. For the next few days, he looked hungover, I was afraid he might start drinking heavily again, that he might beat Maria or humiliate her in some way; obviously, her distended belly no longer held any attraction for him. It would mess up all my calculations. But it turned out differently. He quarreled with Maria, whom he held guilty for everything that had happened. They had a terrible row, they threatened each other, and by the end, I think they even came to blows. The more Maria's belly swelled, the more irritable, the more irascible we all became. Even the Wrestler, who was usually so calm and conciliatory. Then, one fine day, Iosif disappeared. Maria came to tell me that he hadn't come home, that she'd been waiting for him for days.

"What a cad! What a cad!" said the Wrestler, thumping the table with his fist in indignation. Magda was drunk most of the time; nobody could get on with her any more. So, we decided to call for Madam Ana and, if necessary, the doctor too.

And Maria gave birth. All by herself, in the night, without calling for help; she gave birth without either the doctor or the midwife. In the morning, I found her all smiles, full of the importance of the event, gazing steadily, serenely. I wanted to see the baby and it was true, nestled beside her was a rigid little thing, a rubber doll, one of the ones that makes a squeaky little cry when you squash its belly. I smiled in satisfaction and gratitude. I took Maria's chubby hand and planted a kiss on it. Just then, footfalls came from the hall and I took fright somewhat, thinking it was Iosif; but when I opened the door I was confronted with the solemn faces of three respectable gentlemen in top hats, carrying umbrellas and armfuls of gifts. They entered one by one, without looking at me, and made low bows in front of Maria. They had brought with them parrots, ribbons, celluloid balls of every color, a host of spinning tops, little rubber lizards and rabbits, and many other toys besides . . . They were tall and respectful, and they held their bared heads slightly bowed. The setting sun lent a sheen to their bald pates. They were obviously her uncles and they loved her; I felt like a spare part, I mumbled something, but I don't think they heard me. They left as haughtily and solemnly as they had arrived, without looking at me. Magda was climbing the stairs, downcast, no doubt after some dissolute drinking bout. She kissed their hands and I was amazed that they paid attention to her. For a long while, I stood at the top of the stairs, watching them descend.

That night there was another hullaballoo. Magda sent Vasile out to buy booze, she sent the Wrestler, she sent me, and (can you believe it!) she sent Mr. Popescu. Oh, how I implored her; for even after the first bottle, Mr. Popescu declared that it was a doll, not a flesh-and-blood baby and that we shouldn't think we could pull the wool over his eyes. That he knew what went on in cases like that, where girls gave birth in secret. And why hadn't we called the doctor? And where had that Iosif disappeared to? And so on, a shower of questions. Obviously, I tried to mollify him, I made a sign to Magda for her to shut up, but after another few glasses, the Wrestler lost his temper; from that moment on, I lost hold of the reins, as they say. And a hullaballoo ensued.

In terror, Maria fled to her room with the doll and the Wrestler gave the landlord a drubbing. Probably drunk from beforehand, Magda was screeching like a madwoman, rolling around on the floor, and she made such an uproar that the whole house was up in arms.

"Call the police!" Mr. Popescu was shouting. He had escaped from the Wrestler's grasp and, shielded by two tenants, he was shouting at the top of his voice that murder had been done in his house.

"She killed her baby, the criminal, the whore!"

I went out into the hall, not knowing what to do; I wanted to go to Maria's room, to reassure her, to protect her. On the stairs, women with children in their nightshirts, woken from their sleep, still groggy, were crying. A little old woman was shaking her fist at me. But I wasn't afraid for myself, please believe me, I was thinking only of Maria and her baby. I had to go to her and soothe her, ask her whether I could call on the help of her uncles, those tall, haughty gentlemen. But the screams from the stairs had grown louder, the Wrestler was fighting who knows how many people at once, punching them and then hitting them with a chair that happened to be handy.

"Help, the murderers are going to kill us!" the women were wailing, and then the police arrived. Four policemen came, headed by a lieutenant holding a revolver, his face tense, his eyes fierce. "Over there! Over there!" screamed the children, the press of people around the Wrestler dispersed, and maybe by accident, I don't know, but a bullet flew from the barrel of the revolver, shattering the only light bulb on the landing. In the pitch blackness, the panic was even greater, a lot of the women fainted, a child fell down the stairs and broke his arm. The policemen's torches revealed bodies piled on top of each other and blood and the Wrestler, who had retreated to the stair below the attic, exhausted, sick of the fray.

Order was gradually restored, and the doughty policemen began their inquiry. In the first place, where was Maria? Sweating, bloodied, appearing and disappearing in the uncertain light of the torches, the landlord insistently demanded she be arrested.

Not only the Wrestler, but also the whore, the murderess, and all the lowlifes from the mansard. Only then did I intervene. Let me tell you, when I brought out Maria, who was as white as a sheet, clutching to her breast the rubber doll, and when all the people assembled there, in front of the door, eager for scandal, shouted, grunted like a herd of pigs, I realized that there could be no other denouement. And short as I am, I pushed my way through their midst to the lieutenant and just as I was about to tell him, somebody shoved me and I wasn't able to shout in his face that I was the author and I was going to be famous. They jostled me, they shoved me, nobody took what I said seriously. And it was pride, not fear, in my voice, damn it!

Bucharest, July 1964

Waiting (1971)

Weeping

HE WAS SITTING in the cupboard covering his eyes and forehead. He was probably crying.

I read somewhere—or maybe I heard, I dreamed or somebody else dreamed it and told me the dream—that a manicurist had for a long time kept an eagle on her nightstand, and a photographer had reared a lion cub in one of the drawers of his desk. But he was neither an eagle nor a lion, since he was crying. Nor was he a man, although his dreadfully thin, gaunt body looked like a man's. He had two emaciated legs, blue with cold, but the toenails were like powerful, hooked eagle's talons: the more they grew, the deeper they sank into the old, almost rotten, wood of the cupboard. He was almost completely hairless, apart from a tuft above his blue, shriveled sex and a few strands on his hollow chest. He was so thin that you could see all his ribs. Between two of the ribs there was an enormous scar, on the side by the heart, a scar left by a knife or spear or maybe by a skewer of the kind on which they used to roast a lamb or game or an entire bullock over the fire.

He covered his eyes with his hands, all you could see was his chin, from which sprouted a few long strands of ginger hair, and his yellowish, slightly swollen lower lip. His arms were thin, fleshless, the back of his hands corrugated, each with a round black mark, as big as a coin, whether scars or birthmarks I do not know. I did not dare touch him, feel him, move aside the hands beneath which he hid his eyes, pull him out of the cupboard, invite him to sit on a chair or the bed that he might rest.

If he was crying it meant that he existed, that he was not dead, although he stood motionless, always in the same position, his chest did not move up and down, or else it moved so faintly that it was imperceptible, but he cried, that was for sure (or was he pretending?), I had spotted two or three teardrops trickling down his chin.

I haven't the slightest idea how the manicurist dealt with the eagle and more to the point, I don't know how she managed to keep it a secret from the other people who lived there—or maybe she lived alone and the eagle was her only comfort in the world—I don't know, but as for myself, I confess that I was both afraid and repulsed (or maybe I even felt pity . . .), I couldn't stand the sight of that naked, tear-streaked body, and therefore I closed the door of the cupboard, which creaked, and I went back to bed.

The bed is right in front of the cupboard, two steps and you're right next to it, and it's quite rickety, I can feel its springs poking me in the ribs, it takes me quite a long time to find the right position and, with the blanket pulled up over my eyes, to fall asleep.

In my sleep I could hear his muffled weeping and his sighs, I could see the gnarled backs of his hands, with the two scars, the two round, light-brown coins, I could see him covering his eyes; for he didn't want to see me, and therefore I had to dream him (a great deal of effort!) in order to see his face in my dream, his sad, occasionally cheerful, eyes, to see him differently than he had revealed himself to me inside the wardrobe, frozen as if in a mirror, to make him stop crying, even if only in my dream.

There he was sitting under a tree in blossom, wearing a top had, but the rest of him is completely bare (that's my fault, obviously!) and still scrawny; but his skin was whiter, healthier, without the gooseflesh you get when you're cold or repulsed. At his feet lolled a lion, then two beautiful, shapely women arrived, wearing flimsy silk dresses. They had long hair and coy, sometimes cunning, eyes. They pressed their cheeks to his tall, pointy shoulders, sitting to either side of him, and up above the sky was shiny, it was probably very hot, the lion gave a bored yawn.

They sat like that for a long time, as if posing for a photograph, all three were very sad, it was as if they were waiting for something. But they weren't crying, I rejoiced, they were sad, but they weren't crying!

Another time I saw him on a bicycle, whose back wheel was bigger than the front one, and the spokes were golden, they shone. Instead of a bell, to the handlebars he had attached a kind of pump, a long funnel, a kind of horn, but which he didn't use. He was wearing a sailor's shirt, with blue and white stripes, with long johns of the same material, which made it look more like a prisoner's uniform. He was riding the bicycle over a sandy beach, although the sea was nowhere in sight. It was deserted all around, he was in a hurry, his top hat rocked back and forth on his head as he pedaled, and barely did he make any headway. His face was grave, not gloomy, but preoccupied, his brows were knitted, his forehead furrowed: he needed to go somewhere, he had a very precise task to perform. And indeed, I saw him again another night, or maybe the same night—what difference does it make!—in a town, above which solemnly wheeled an eagle, a town with white, sunlit walls, and a crowd of people had gathered there, to whom he talked at length. This time he was wearing a kind of gown, which came down to his ankles, so voluminous that it flapped against his body, and the sleeves, his arms, looked like wings as he spoke. His eyes shone, they were no longer sad at all, and from time to time he pressed his lips together in an ironic smile. And how they admired him! The people followed him around, they followed his bicycle with the golden spokes, they drank up his words, they listened open-mouthed, and he spoke and he spoke . . . I don't even know what held us so spellbound, much of what he said I'd heard from others before him, at least so it seemed to me, but the way in which he spoke, that arm of his which poked from the sleeve of his gown like a bird's neck, the fingers of his tensed and then suddenly comforting, protective hand, and his voice, the timbre of his voice, that was indeed something I'd never heard before: it was a voice that somehow came from elsewhere and passed through him as if through a megaphone, he merely moved his lips and his arm, a bird's neck

and conductor's baton, or to be more precise, given the extraordinary agility with which he moved his fingers, he was a puppet
master, and we moved, we jerked, we trembled at every word or,
contrariwise, we froze, holding our breath, tensing our necks,
our mouths dry, we sweated, we were tortured and happy, and
up above our heads, the eagle wheeled in lower and lower circles.

Now here he was by a water pump, in a garden full of flowers, on the outskirts of town, holding a large red pot, stooping
toward the silvery stream, and in the background, hidden among
the flowers, a man was looking at him, trying not to be seen. In
the doorway of the house, on the porch, a tall, blond woman
appeared, smiling sleepily. It was very early, a spring morning.
After he filled the pot, he straightened up and met the woman's
gaze. I had never seen him so happy. He was wearing the same
overalls, those of a shop boy or rather a medical orderly, because
they were of a pure, dazzling white. Then down from the sky
an eagle descended, landed on his shoulder, and he lifted the
pot so that the bird might drink. It was a large, silver-grey eagle,
with powerful, curved talons, which, the more they grew, sank
ever deeper into the rotten wood of the wardrobe. No, I shut, I
slammed the doors of the wardrobe, I couldn't bear that muffled,
endless crying any longer. I collapsed on the bed, face down, and
tried to get back to sleep, or to carry on sleeping. Let me go back
to that garden on the outskirts of town and let it be morning, and
let him be cheerful, happy. From there, at the back, hiding among
flowers taller than ever seen before, a forest of flowers, I gazed at
him, happy and at the same time envious: his movements were
so precise, so self-confident, so necessary. A gentle light settled
over the garden, over all things, and everything became perfectly
still for an indeterminate time.

I can hear his muffled weeping again or maybe I'm still
dreaming. A plaza, a throng assembled in front of an enormous
building (a town hall? a ministry?) angry voices, clenched fists,
his pale, bewildered face, he is taken into a room, where he stands
before an officer seated at a desk. The officer speaks to him calmly
at first, even gently, he remains standing, at the door there is a
tall man dressed in grey civilian clothes, the officer has delicate

features and his speech is quite subdued, but gradually I see him lose his temper, he keeps asking the same questions and seemed dissatisfied with the answers, what does he want? he says, confess! I confess, no reason why I shouldn't, my legs are aching, he's red in the face, the veins on his neck are bulging, talk! I talk, he yells, bangs his fist on the solid oak desk and the inkpot spills, the pen falls, the nib pierces the floor like an arrow.

And once again the crowd outside, grunting, then screaming, the soldiers make a wall with their lances, but they won't hold out much longer.

The scenes merge, blend together. I want to escape. And I also want to escape this unbearable crying, I feel my face with my hands, my cheeks are wet and so I bury my face in the pillow so that I might cry or carry on dreaming.

How beautiful the garden, up there on the hill, at the edge of the town. He was surrounded by lots of friends or admirers who stood around him, while he sat on a bench, which is why I couldn't see him very well, I could see only a part of him, half his face, the red beard, or only his brow, the hem of his gown, his hand, raised as he spoke. The bicycle was leaning against a tree a short distance away. Some children were gazing at him insatiably, without daring to come closer and touch him. Next to him, on the bench, there were two men and a woman with reddish-blond hair, who held her head bowed, burying her face in his white gown. As ever, he spoke with a gentle, even voice, pointing at the treetops. Through the garden gate came a band of soldiers led by a young officer who looked at me and winked. My legs are aching, my kneecaps, I ought to stand up.

Then he is alone again, with his head in his hands, he is thinking or weeping. Next to him, a very elegant man pops up as if out of the ground, holding a small doctor's bag. He shakes hands with two old acquaintances, the elegant man is highly talkative, he talks a lot and probably too loudly, since from time to time he asks him to lower his voice: he raises his finger to his lips and the man nods and laughs, he shrugs, there is nobody else around, only a peacock unfolding its fan on a path a short distance away. But he probably knows that I am here too, hidden behind a bush, he looks in my direction and smiles—he is no longer wearing the gown, he is naked and thin once more, with the top hat resting in his lap to conceal his sex—then he raises his finger to his lips again and the other man agrees to lower his voice, he moves his lips close to his ear. He stretches his head toward his lips, he gives a smile that is slightly ironic and then obviously amused, he gives a short laugh, raising the top hat. They look like two accomplices planning some rather dodgy business, or maybe they are talking about women. The elegant man places a hand on his shoulder and stoops slightly, then he abruptly turns his head, allowing himself to touch his back with his ear. Then he laughs again. The doctor takes from his bag a pair of black gloves, he carefully pulls them over his fingers and stops laughing.

Now he is seated at a long table, it looks like a banquet, and he is the center of attention, the meal is in his honor. But he is always the center of attention. This is neither the first nor the last time. He is wearing the white gown again, but it is no longer so white. On his left shoulder, there are a few red stains, and here are others on one side of his chest, but it doesn't stop him speaking self-importantly. After a while, he even stands up, he looks at us all and says something, giving a slightly ironic smile, yes, the smile that has always annoyed me, although I can hardly claim that as an excuse . . . They are all most puzzled and they point at each other, they point at themselves, there is such astonishment in their eyes that you'd think he'd told them who knows what, and he becomes abashed, he falls silent for a few moments, letting the others marvel, he gives a satisfied smile, as if after telling a joke, and he looks in my direction, he seeks my eyes, but I deliberately look in a different direction, at the back of the room, where the blonde woman has appeared, the one they say is a manicurist, others disparage her, she lives in an attic, but it's not true, she has a cottage on the outskirts of town, stupid gossip, and anyway, I for one like her. Finally, he sits down and begins to eat with good appetite, he cuts off big pieces of steak and stuffs his mouth, heedless of the questions they ask him. Then he pours blood-red wine in his glass and fills mine too. He looks in my eyes and I

don't have time to avert my gaze, it's amazing how much alike
we look, it's as if I were looking in a mirror. During dessert, the
photographer appears and immortalizes us all.

A lot of the time the scenes repeat each other, old scenes crop
up that I barely recognize any more. I don't even know if they're
anything to do with me, although I'm always there, as is only
natural. Take this winter scene for example: people rushing along
a street, as if being pursued, or alarmed at something terrible that
is about to happen. Clanking metal, swords, screams could be
heard. Somebody told me not to stand at the window, and I was
a toddler, a woman held me crying in her arms, and the man
next to her kept casting terrified looks, rushing now to the window, now to the bed where they had laid me. In the sky could be
seen a blinding red light, as if from a fire. Rays of light scorched
the sky. The next day, we set out by car, we went somewhere
far away, all I can remember are the loft and the ringdoves with
large silver wings, like an eagle's, and the dog with a lion's mane,
chained behind the house. At night when the moon rose, the
beast roared and groaned, trying to break the chain or to rip up
by the roots the tree to which it was tied.

The scenes welter. In one, here we are, the two of us: he is
shut inside an old cupboard, hiding his face in his hands, and I
open the cupboard and find him there, I take fright, then I realize it's a practical joke, come out of there! I tell him and he cries,
he is stark naked, his body blue with cold, he has a large, nasty
scar under his ribs, and he cries ceaselessly, I hear him crying in
my sleep and I toss and turn in the sheets trying to escape the
image of his naked, tear-streaked body.

I used to see him sometimes, when he passed by on his bicycle, we were both very young at the time, he was a shop boy
and always wore a gown that looked like a medical orderly's or a
doctor's, it was so clean, and I was a photographer's assistant, I
had learned to develop photographs and even to airbrush them.
I often waited to capture him, to photograph him as he haughtily pedaled his bicycle or when he thought he was all alone
and summoned a silver-grey eagle, which sat on his shoulder or
knees, digging its powerful claws into his flesh. Truth be told, he

even liked to have his photograph taken: after a while, he went around with a whole gaggle of people following him, he wanted to open a new theatre, something the likes of which had never been seen, they didn't have a venue or enough money, it was more of an itinerant troupe, and I tagged along with them, I liked being around them, especially at parties, the shindigs they had, when women came, oho! what a time . . .

After that, so many things happened, maybe some of them weren't even real, maybe I only dreamed them, or I'm dreaming them now, or I've heard other people talking about them. I can't remember all of them, a lot of them have been lost or they have faded like photographs kept out in the sun for a long time; but others are imprinted so strongly that all I have to do is close my eyes . . .

That autumn afternoon, or that spring afternoon, but a dull spring, as dreary as autumn, I was sitting on a bench in the park, it was silent, all that could be heard were the cries and whispers of the children playing on a distant path. I sit on the bench and daydream or maybe I'm even asleep. For an instant I think to glimpse two women under a flowering tree, to the right and the left of him, resting their cheeks on his thin shoulder, and this time, too, he is completely naked, but on his head, he has a rather shabby top hat, and by his feet lolls a lion that yawns so widely it almost dislocates its jaws. The children carry on playing, but when they see the tall man with the top hat who is awkwardly standing next to a tree—the women have left and maybe I'm mixing up the scenes and there is no lion—they rush over noisily, joyfully, they surround him, cling to him, shake him like a tree, and then with their small impatient hands they push him to a thicker tree, a chestnut—how the crowd would be rooted to the spot, drinking up his words, but now he is silent and smiles gently, as if giving his blessing—and tie him to the trunk with ribbons, with bows of every color, and his top hat falls off, rolls over the grass.

The children start stabbing him with their little wooden swords and their spears made from twigs, and he laughs, it probably tickles him, and the children laugh too, more and more people come, they jostle around him as happy as can be. Then the children's relatives appear or the people looking after them, who till now have been sitting on benches, reading the paper or knitting, feigning uninterest, they all come to stab the body crucified against the tree with whatever they have: hairpins, thumbtacks, paperclips, pens, a penknife, even a small picnic fork. An old woman timidly approaches, from her old, scuffed handbag she takes a pair of knitting needles and pokes them in his belly. He no longer laughs, he merely smiles approvingly or even encouragingly. I go up to him too. I don't know what to do, I awkwardly walk this way and that, I twist and I turn, from his eyes I can tell that he hasn't seen me or that he hasn't recognized me. The people have begun to leave, but now others arrive, the coming and going is utter chaos. The children had grown bored, they had found a new game to play elsewhere in the park: they were digging a grave. The eagle had landed on a branch above his head, which now hangs to one side. I rummaged in my pockets, all I had was a fountain pen with a gold nib and I was thinking about how I would spoil the nib and I felt sorry. That's why I hesitated, I kept walking around the tree, thinking about stabbing the fountain pen in his ear or his eye, and then, once everybody had left, retrieving it. I let myself be buffeted by the people arriving, who were stabbing him with all those very different objects, people who were in more and more of a hurry, obviously they were afraid because it was getting dark, the sun had already sunk behind the park, its last rays were long and russet.

In the gloaming, his body began to resemble a bird with iron plumage or a scaly prehistoric animal. There were fewer and fewer people, nobody was laughing any more, the merriment and spontaneity of the beginning had turned into a ritual of mechanical and increasingly hurried gestures. Each person came, stabbed him with objects that were more or less the same: needles, penknives, hairclips, pens—one person alone was more inventive, he had poked a key in his mouth and quickly walked away without looking back. Before I could make my mind up, he saw me and recognized me, the smile faded from his lips, tears welled in his eyes. I took the fountain pen from my breast pocket, I carefully

unscrewed the cap, I looked at the gold nib, which shone in the
last rays of the sun, and still I couldn't make my mind up. Tears
were rolling down his cheeks, which were studded with dozens
of needles and thumbtacks, so many that they formed an iron
mask. His eyes were the only place left, the eyes that wept—from
pain? from pity?—since they had stabbed two rods in his ears,
like antennas, I couldn't tell what they were exactly.

All the people had left, satisfied at having done their duty and
nobody else came. I was now alone with him.

Why are you crying? Answer me, why, what for, who for?
And again I closed the doors of the cupboard, which creaked
on their hinges, and I went to lie down, I threw myself onto the
bed as if into warm, soothing water, since I could no longer bear
his ceaseless, systematic crying, even if here, in the cupboard, he
kept his eyes covered and I could see neither the pain nor the pity
in them. Let me go to sleep again and let me do so in such a way
that I won't see anything but pleasant scenes, scenes in which he
looks happy, in which he is even giving a slightly ironic smile,
surrounded by women, who always loved him, surrounded by
women and by children. Riding his bicycle in his white robe,
with his top hat pushed slightly back, it's warm, it's silent, the
houses are white, the women are beautiful, tall, shapely, they
smile at him, some of the more daring ones wave at him; or
else seated on a bench, surrounded by other men, to whom he
speaks gently and they listen to him respectfully, with my camera
I crouch hidden in a nearby bush and I am joyful and envious,
or in that garden at the edge of town, with the flowers and the
water pump, where I witnessed him so happy.

The scenes repeat each other, they merge, a lot of the time he
appears naked, wearing only the top hat, and the eagle strikes his
thin chest with its beak, the women around him smile, looking
from the corners of their eyes, a few soldiers trample over the
flowers in the garden, they have swords and spears and they run,
they go from garden to garden, the images welter and I have to
make an effort to wake up. But do I really wake up? For I cannot hear his crying, I lift myself up on my elbows, I strain my
ears, I wait, but that muffled weeping can be heard only at long

intervals, and then I don't know whether I am awake or dreaming. I haven't opened the cupboard for a long time, I hang my clothes on the backs of chairs, I spread my overcoat on the floor, so that he'll have room and I won't bother him by opening and closing the door all the time.

I have readied everything. For maybe one day, intrigued by my lack of curiosity, or rather my self-control (or fear?), maybe one day he himself will open the door, he will look in slight bewilderment at the mess in the room, and to cover his nakedness he will take the dazzling white shirt I have specially laid on a chair in front of the wardrobe, then he will see the smoking jacket, brushed and ironed, the top hat, the cane with its small ivory knob, he will get dressed, slowly, carefully, he will take a chrysanthemum from the vase and put it in his buttonhole, and, his eyes still red from weeping, he will open the door to my room, he will cast a final glance over his shoulder, I will pretend to be asleep, and he will be gone.

I will be alone and I will try to be as happy as I can.

(*România Liberă*, no. 3, January 1969)

Abortive Journey

I WAS IN A HURRY that morning. I had dreamed of weddings all night long, yes, sailors' weddings and big ships with colored streamers and cockerels, and I woke up a little dazed. I knew that I had to leave as quickly as I could, somebody or something was waiting for me, and I might be late. Outside the light was whitish, dense, opaque. I hurriedly got dressed, I draped my raincoat over my arm and stepped into the street. It was quite cold; it had probably rained overnight. I ran to the tram stop. I was the only person there, with no trams in sight. The light had thinned, the sky had gained a faint blue tint, and high above a long silvery fish was passing. I bowed my head as if I were guilty of something. The previous night, in my dream, the bride had caressed my brow with thin, cool fingers, and everything was shaking gently around me: I had grown tipsy on the champagne and even now my mind felt foggy. The tram arrived unexpectedly. I didn't hear it and I barely had time to board before it set off. Straightaway, the door closed behind me hostilely, catching my raincoat. What was I supposed to do? The carriage was almost empty, apart from a dozing sailor. I crouched down by the door, holding what was left of my raincoat, and waited, casting imploring looks at the ticket taker. I murmured a few words, I knew I was guilty and I would have liked to apologize, but she didn't look in my direction. She had eyes only for the tired sailor, who was sleeping with his forehead propped against his arms, which rested on the back of the chair in front. One ear was visible, enormous, scarlet, like a chunk of raw meat glued beneath the beret with its blue ribbon. The ticket taker was very beautiful; in her reddish-blond hair sat a parrot. I beg your pardon, I said, but the door closed too quickly. She didn't look at me, she took no notice of me, she smiled at the sailor, who had begun to snore. Even so, I still had to purchase a ticket; I couldn't travel without one. I'd liked a ticket please, I said, somewhat more loudly. Maybe she's deaf, maybe the one who gives out the tickets is actually the parrot. Please, miss, I can't move, open the door for a moment, my raincoat is caught in the door. She had a pale, white face, her thin lips spread in a smile that looked forced, I couldn't see both her eyes, only one of them, and even then, only from the side.

The sailor was snoring loudly by now and to top it all he had begun to let off farts. The ticket taker smiled even more broadly. I plucked up courage: Miss, I very much like to travel by tram. When I have the money, I'm going to buy a tram all of my own. I'll decorate it with pennants and parrots, I'll attach wings to it . . . But look at me, I have the right, or at least I will once you give me a ticket. She didn't look. She remained just as motionless as before. And it struck me that perhaps she wasn't looking at the sailor either. Perhaps she wasn't alive . . .

The tram glided so smoothly that all that could be heard was a continuous swishing sound. From where I was squatting, all I could see was the sky, which had turned white once more, almost a milky white, and the tops of some very tall buildings. I espied a cockerel on the top of a building and I rejoiced, for no reason at all. It must have been a very large cockerel for me to be able to see it from the tram. My legs were aching. The ticket taker continued to ignore me. The soldier was snoring and at intervals let off farts. I could bear it no longer, I felt as if I were suffocating. What about the stop? Did that tram ever make its stops? I called out: The door, please, I'm suffocating! I stood up, still holding the raincoat with one hand, one sleeve had fallen onto the floor, and it was very dirty inside the tram: dust, cigarette butts, tinsel, wedding rosettes, orange and banana peels, confetti. The air was getting fustier and fustier. If only they could open a window . . . Outside, the sky was covered in immense flags, which were rosy, violet, even scarlet, like the sailor's ear. The buildings had changed their appearance, they now looked completely different: colorful, gleaming, decked as if for a celebration. I'd like a ticket, please! It was obvious I would arrive too late; the wedding was probably almost over. The sailor seemed to choke, he gave a croak, snorted, whistled; he had shifted position, he was now leaning back, with his temple propped against the windowpane, and that was why he was snoring more loudly. The ticket taker gazed tenderly at the sunburnt face, the ginger moustache, the thick, shiny nose. His beret had slipped down to his eyebrows. In the woman's hair, the parrot was beginning to show signs of restlessness. I plucked up courage: I'm very understanding, but this is a complete mockery . . . Open the door, I want to get off. I've had enough!

The ticket taker then suddenly turned her head and looked at me. I want to get off! I'll never forget the look on her face: a combination of horror and pity, of scorn and desperation. I can't take any more: he keeps farting. And the stop never seems to arrive. I want to get off! I heard the door at the front open, the door by the driver, and the soldier woke up and looked all around him in a daze, the ticket taker covered her mouth with her hand in a gesture of horror and powerlessness. I had let the other sleeve of my raincoat fall to the floor and I was gesticulating in indignation: This can't go on. Why don't you make the stops? We ought to have arrived by now, given how long we've been traveling! I couldn't see the tram driver, but it was obvious that the door at the front had opened. Open the door at the back, I told the ticket taker, who continued to look at me, with her hand over her mouth. I want to get off! Obviously, I could have alighted at the front, which was the regulation anyway, but to be honest, I was slightly afraid to go there. And my raincoat . . . I didn't want to leave it behind. I would get off by the same door by which I'd got on and that was that. Open up! I started pounding on the door with my fist, I kicked it, the soldier's mouth was still lolling open, the ticket taker had frozen to the spot, and the parrot had disentangled itself from her hair and was flying up and down the carriage. I pounded on the door in a fury, even though for me it was anyway too late, the banners were no longer visible, the sky was blue and at its very center the sun looked like a bloodstain.

The Bird

I SAW FIRST the wall and that rather dark painting: a landscape, a garden, or simply a vase of flowers; then, in the middle of the room, the top of a long dining table, with a fruit bowl, sometimes empty, but sometimes full of oranges or very red apples, Jonathans, and finally, in one corner, on a tall, narrow table, the telephone: a large, unusually large, black telephone. It was like an animal crouching ready to pounce, although that isn't the best comparison: it didn't look anything like an animal, except for its bridled aggression, so black and cold and mineral was it. Be that as it may, the sensation of its crouching ready to pounce, of its waiting and watching, was a sensation that was obvious, to me at least, since I had seen it (studied it!) so many times. There wasn't much to see in the rest of the room: the backs of two or three chairs, the arm of an armchair, part of a cupboard and a sideboard. That was all.

And then I shifted my gaze to the floor below, where the girl was seated at her little desk, her knees propped against its edge, leaning back in her chair, shielding her face from my eyes with a book wrapped in blue paper, which she was holding in both hands, her thighs were completely bared, and the book was too close to her nose and eyebrows to fool me; from time to time her eyes peeped out, as if she were adjusting a vizor, and then she would cover part of her thigh with one hand, while with the other hand she lowered the book, I would move my hand to attract her attention, she would drop the book on the table, resume a normal sitting position, rest her elbows on the desktop, hold her head between her hands, concentrating on the book, or else she would pick up her fountain pen or pencil and write a sentence or two in her exercise book. I would turn my back, take off my pajamas, in any event only the upper half of my body was visible, and then suddenly turn around and go to the window. As I spread my arms and took deep breaths or raised them above my head, standing on tiptoes, I would catch her peering at my window, craning her neck like a bird, her forehead almost touching the windowpane, and I would give a malicious smile, wave my arm with my fingers spread. She would cover her face with the book, maybe she blushed, I couldn't tell, she was pretty, tall, her legs were white, quite plump, as were her breasts. I would draw the curtain and lie down on the bed. In the other room, Matilda would be sighing.

From the bathroom I could see the boy with the violin: thin, gangly, he scraped away all day long (practicing!), wearing only his pajamas, for hours at a time, with the window open, probably the tenants were used to it by now, the way you get used to the noise of the street, the cars, the trams, you finally stop hearing it. The boy's mother often walked around wearing only a chemise, although, granted, she was thinner than Matilda and not so young; she would sit on a chair in front of the window, lost in thought, unless, like me, she was curious about what was going on in the building opposite. She had broad hips which she swayed when she passed from one room to another, and large, rather sagging breasts. Her husband appeared more seldom, he had a moustache and large, heavy hands, I would have liked to see those abattoir worker's or woodcutter's hands caressing those hips, but unfortunately, the bedroom was on the opposite side of the house, with the window overlooking the street.

Matilda had a visitor again. I pulled the pillow over my ears so that I could sleep.

The schoolgirl's father is a captain or even a colonel, I don't know much about ranks; sometimes he enters, stands in the middle of her room, she takes no notice of him, concentrating on her homework, he plucks up courage, tiptoes up to the chair where she is sitting with her temple resting on one hand and with

the end of a pencil clamped between her teeth, and he timidly
strokes her hair, satisfied at always finding her with her nose in
a book; only then does she deign to twist around and cast him
a glance, perhaps a smile, and then he goes out, still on tiptoes.
A large black car comes to collect him every day. I've never seen
the mother.

I tossed and turned in the sheets, adjusted the pillow under
my head, pulled it out from under me, put it back again, put
another pillow over my ear, hitched the plaid blanket to beneath
my chin, but I was hot, I threw it to the end of the bed and lay
on my belly, with one knee flexed, crushing my stomach against
the hard mattress with its rigid springs. I'd never seen her leave
the house, to go to school or elsewhere. Not that I'd ever tried
to do so, I'd never lurked in front of the building, hiding behind
a tree on the opposite sidewalk or under an archway, in the passageway of that old building near the corner of the street, I'd never
waited for her at the gate of the lycée at which I assumed she was
a pupil, I didn't even know her name; only once did I see her
getting ready to go out, she had put on her uniform and gathered
her books from the desk, hurriedly stuffing them in a satchel, I
quickly got dressed, ran down the wooden stairs, which creaked
and groaned underfoot, went out into the street, walked up and
down in front of my building for a few minutes, with my hands
behind my back, whistling, I probably looked more ridiculous
than suspicious, but even so, an individual I'd not noticed thith-
erto looked at me a few times, amused at first, then intrigued,
and finally stern, and he gave a wink, twisting his mouth slightly,
but probably I only imagined it, ultimately, he was ridiculous
too, more ridiculous than suspicious, with his hooked nose—
an aquiline nose as he will have called it, consoling himself in
front of the mirror—I spat and walked away, and since then I
haven't repeated the whole routine; I found it humiliating. I
have to admit that I would have liked her to come to see me, to
climb the narrow, creaking stair, to stand before my front door,
flushing, then to give two, short rings of the bell. Matilda, in her
pink chemise, in her slippers with the yellow pompons, would
rush to open the door—she never lets me open it—and in a little

voice, but not too shrill, she would ask whether I lived there: I beg your pardon, madam, but does a man who wears green pajamas live here, a man with the body of—how can I put it? the body of an athlete, he exercises every morning in front of the window, although actually, I can only see his chest after he gets undressed . . . Matilda is short of breath and when she speaks to somebody, no matter whom, she is always flustered, she covers one breast with the palm of her hand and, Yes, of course, miss, he's at home, this room over here.

The bed was squeaking dreadfully beneath Matilda and her gentleman caller of that night. I was sweating under the plaid blanket, with the pillow over my ear, so as not to hear them—I was tossing and turning—Matilda's groans and the squeaking of the bed, the creaking of the springs, the man's furious panting, her grunts of pleasure, all those noises coming through the door between the two rooms, I'm going to move, I can't stand it any more. I pressed the pillow over my ear even harder, I have to think of something else, something completely different, I bury my face in the pillow: a number of people carrying a stretcher on their shoulders (or is it a coffin?) are heading toward a river, the sky is blue, but a fine mist envelops the procession. The mist grows thicker and thicker, I can't see anything, and all of a sudden a door bangs, I lift the pillow from my ear and listen, a little frightened, to the slapping of bare soles down the hall, in fact it's ridiculous, I cover the side of my head with the pillow once more and smile, I feel my irritation pass, I am filled with a sweet torpor and look, there's the bird that Irina bought at the fair, that garishly colored bird, it has all the colors of the rainbow, but even so, it's not at all garish, sooner it's strange: perhaps because of the very long neck and the eyes that bore straight through you, small, yellow eyes. I could no longer hear any noises. Thick, scarlet, velvet curtains had come down all around me. I opened one eye: a reddish light was seeping from somewhere, I could hear the door handle moving, and I was in my childhood once more, frightened by the cracking of the furniture, by the little creatures scurrying in the corners, the creaking of the parquet floor, footfalls as soft as felt, no, rather the patter of tiny paws, or rather claws, a muffled snap, then padded footfalls, the footfalls of a bird, perhaps a peacock. A hurried exhalation right next to my ear, then the warm arms of Mother or Irina.

Whom are you looking for? She had disturbed her at that late hour, I ought to have gone to open the door, but I was afraid it would be one of her gentleman callers, nobody ever comes to see me. Whom are you looking for? Her voice sounded slightly annoyed, she was probably barefoot. If he didn't answer her, why didn't she shut the door in his face? Because he couldn't answer her, it was obvious, the bird couldn't speak, it was a bird bought at the fair, a porcelain bird, and it had that horribly long neck, of course, Matilda would be looking it up and down, because the bird had grown, so much time had passed since then. Or maybe it was the girl from the building opposite or better still Irina, I would have liked to see her, to see her again if only for a few seconds, and I couldn't do it, it wasn't the first time I'd tried and hadn't been able to do it, no matter how hard I tried to picture her face again. And I had hardly forgotten her, sometimes I even missed her, but I couldn't picture her: I saw her only fragmen-tarily, I saw only an isolated anatomical detail here and there, as if she had been chopped up and the pieces had been hidden away in every nook and cranny of my memory; and I could still see her long blond hair falling to her shoulders, but this was sooner the image of an idea, a conventional image, there are so many young women with long blond hair, yes, a conventional image of my admiration for her beautiful hair.

The red curtain slowly moved aside and the bird appeared, tall, svelte, with a neck longer than an ostrich's, perhaps longer even than a giraffe's, and perched up there, the small head with those yellow, glassy eyes. Matilda, in a very sheer, lowcut nightdress was standing with her arms folded over her pillowy breasts and gazing in slight puzzlement at that unexpected visitor; she looked now at the bird, now at me, but she was no longer angry or even upset, her puzzlement gradually acquired a hint of admiration, and after a few minutes of silence, I started to feel rather awk-ward, Matilda thrust her head between the curtains and called out a man's name: Costache or Mihalache. The man appeared, short, bandy-legged, wearing only long johns, he barely came up to the bird's chest, and he went to stand next to Matilda, raising his hand to his mouth in amazement, or perhaps he was yawning, he was sleepy; he too folded his arms across his chest, then he looked at the shapely woman beside him as if asking her opinion or blessing for what he had a mind to do. Matilda put her arm around his shoulders and pressed him against her, protectively, maternally. We stood like that for a long time, motionless, without saying a word, the scarlet light was becoming more and more tiring, I closed my eyes. With a swan-like motion, the bird lowered its head toward my bed, I saw it through my half-closed eyes, its small yellow eyes bored into me, and I decided to clench my eyelids tightly shut, so as not to see it. A little way away, the river had turned blood-red and the stretcher bearers did not halt, I looked at their shaved heads in terror, at their beak-like noses, the white togas in which they were garbed. I fell asleep.

The telephone was in its place, its motionlessness was alive, hostile. It looked as if it were crouching about to pounce on something or sooner to demand satisfaction; it was like the eye of a being from beyond our world, cold but attentive, immobile but unsparing, all-seeing, keeping a tally of everything, to demand satisfaction one fine day . . .

In the fruit bowl there was a single orange. There was still too little light for me to be able to make out the painting on the wall. For the time being, all that could be seen was a rectangular patch, somewhat to the right of the telephone.

Down below, the girl was studying hard. She was wearing a blue dressing gown and had turned on the lamp with the long flexible neck. I tried to attract her attention by waving, I fluttered my necktie, a newspaper, a shirt, I took off my pajamas with slow, sweeping movements, I lit the lamp, all in vain. Then, going up to the window, I took a better look and noticed that she was smiling, still looking down. It had begun to rain outside. A grey curtain came down between her and myself. I looked elsewhere. The boy with the violin had not started practicing yet.

On the other side of the door I could hear Matilda's thin snoring. I didn't feel like doing anything. I took one more look at the girl and climbed into bed. The ceiling was slightly cracked and dirty; in one corner, there was a spider's web, the spider was nowhere to be seen, probably it was crouching ready to pounce in some fissure; but there were no flies, I couldn't see a single one. I closed my eyes and once more the procession moved toward the river that could be glimpsed in the distance, black and oily. Ten paces away, I espied the bird: it was standing motionless, its small yellow eyes gazing at the river . . .

I had never seen anybody talking on the telephone. You would have thought the apartment wasn't lived in, had it not been for the fact that, through the window of the next room, which was obviously part of the same apartment, there appeared at intervals, and particularly at night, the outline of a tall woman combing her hair or simply looking in the mirror on the wall or only passing through, vanishing through the door into another room or into the bathroom. All that could be seen was her outline, thick curtains hung in the window and were never opened. In the room with the telephone, which seemed to be the dining room, there were no curtains, only wooden blinds that were never lowered, or at least I had never seen them lowered. And why would they be? And who would lower them if nobody ever entered that room? Maybe it was because it was never used that the telephone struck me as so terrible in its menacing wait. True, I never spied for more than two hours at a time: I would lie down on my bed, pick up a book, or simply fall asleep. Therefore I couldn't be sure that nobody actually entered to speak on the telephone or to use the room, for example to bring the apples and oranges I saw in the fruit bowl, sometimes more, sometimes fewer, sometimes none at all. They probably ate them in a different room, or in the small kitchen, or maybe they went out to eat at a restaurant, who knows? There are all kinds of people . . .

My right eye was twitching. I forget whether it is a sign of good luck or bad. Matilda claimed it was bad luck (or good?). Whichever it may have been, it was the opposite of what Irina claimed. That I know for certain.

It was no longer raining. The girl had gone to school, obviously, because she was a schoolgirl, she had to go to school, she couldn't sit around all day gawping at me . . . Matilda wasn't at home either. I was alone. I was standing at the window, in my green pajamas, and I couldn't tear my eyes away from that telephone. As usual, there was little light in the room where the telephone was, the painting was visible as nothing but a blotch on the now grey wall. The sky was obscured by thick clouds, descending ever lower over the roof of the building opposite. In a room to the side, a light came on. A fat man in a khaki, military shirt leaned out to looked down into the yard. Silence. It was the silence that lured me, because of the silence I rented this little room.

I didn't know what to do . . . I picked up a book, stretched out on the bed, and tried to read. I couldn't take in any of it. I can't explain it, but I felt oppressed, overwhelmed by the heaviness of the increasingly dense, stifling air. The ceiling had descended a little lower, because of which the room seemed even smaller. I ought to get up, open the window, I'm suffocating. Obviously, I live in an attic room, so what can I expect? As for Matilda, she treats me wonderfully, I have nothing to complain about. Every morning, she brings me coffee in my room, entering without knocking; she thinks it's more affectionate that way. First, I heard a soft pop, then a creak, I saw the door handle move as it was very slowly depressed by a deft hand, the door opened a crack and there it was: the white, puffy arm of Matilda bearing a green plastic tray on which was placed a steaming cup of coffee. Thank you, you're very kind! She made no reply, I divined a smile on the fat round face daubed in cream. Because of the cream, she remained behind the door, only her arm entered the room, elongating preternaturally, and deposited the tray with the cup of coffee on the table.

The girl hadn't come back from school, I couldn't see even the boy with the violin. The military man had turned out the light. It started to rain again, a dense drizzle. I sat down at the table, facing the window. As usual. The telephone was in its place, never budging, never anywhere else; it is always there, in the corner on the left. It's as if it's bigger and more menacing in its ceaseless crouching ready to pounce, almost ferocious. I didn't know what to do. I was bored, I didn't feel like doing anything. The girl wasn't at home, the violinist was nowhere to be seen, nor was his mother, the officer was probably out too. I went and tapped on Matilda's door. No answer. I opened it. There was nobody in the room, neither she nor Mihalache. They weren't in the kitchen either. I was alone. I went over to the window again. Somebody had entered the room with the telephone. I couldn't see who it was yet, but I sensed there was somebody in the room. I strained my eyes. On the right, where only part of a sideboard was visible, I espied a small creature dressed in colors so garish that they were bright even in the semi-darkness at the back of the room. Particularly the red and the yellow. Then I saw that above the little creature extended a long neck which terminated in a very small head. It vanished into the part of the room that I couldn't see from my window. Maybe I could see it only from the bathroom. I waited. For a few minutes, my heart thudded fit to burst. It was the bird from the fair! I no longer had any doubt. Look! It was moving there, next to the sideboard; it was very unclear, the light was getting dimmer and dimmer. The rain continued to fall with the same doggedness. Up in the sky, the clouds were gathering, blacker and blacker.

I started to get changed, I took off my pajamas and mechanically did a few exercises. I was no longer afraid, merely excited. I now knew. I had to be calm, unafraid, I had to be patient. I now knew. It is lurking, getting closer. One day it will come. Now I was alone. I sat down on the bed with my head between my hands. There was no point in my leaving. Or moving out of Matilda's. I lay down on the bed, on my back, with my legs stretched out, pressed against each other, my arms stiff by my sides. The stretcher was being carried smoothly, as if it were gliding. They were moving somewhat faster, but carefully choosing where they stepped. The river was glittering, black and silver, in the sun.

(*România literară*, no. 17, April 1970)

Failure

WHEN I LOOKED BEHIND, there was a plain, a lake, I had been running a long time; not a single tree could be glimpsed, nothing but the sky, a grey, upside-down lake; sometimes it looked like it was greenish glass, but only sections of it, like windows, and behind them, thin birds, frozen in flight. I ran a long time or, more accurately, I slid, since everything was slippery, or maybe it seemed that way to me, now that I was looking back. In the distance, that is, back the way I had come, the horizon had shriveled like aged skin, it was puckered, drooping. In that direction, obviously, there were cities, people, those I had abandoned. It was growing dark. I climbed the steps of the first wagon and hunching up I went inside. There was no point to it, it was no act of bravery, I did it almost without thinking. I had been running for so long over the empty plain and now it was growing dark, it was perhaps a residual habit: to seek shelter for the night. After that, when I thought about it more, I realized that it was no accident; how wide was the plain, how wide the sky! and to come across these derelict wagons, like broken toys, right in my path, to cease my wonderful flight and just like that, without hesitation, to enter one of them like any other traveler rushing to catch the train, not to be left all alone beneath the eyes of the sky, the night, drowned in darkness. A stupid fear that I had not rid myself of, I needed walls, pent up, suffocated between walls for so long that I was afraid now I was free. The silence of the plain and the shine, not one tree, not one rabbit, not one hummock and always the fear that in fact I was dreaming and about to wake up . . .

And then they loomed into view, green, with flowery curtains at their windows, the wooden wagons of a traveling circus, with their large rubber wheels. That is what I thought they were and instead of going around them, here I was standing on the steps of one of them, glancing over my shoulder and, almost overjoyed, pressing the rust-speckled and all too solid yellow handle. It was not till later that I realized it was nothing but a trap.

I stand at the dirty window of the wagon and look out over the shiny plain across which I once slid free. The sky no longer has windows with thin birds frozen in flight, or else I can no longer see them because of the increasingly dirty window. And the only windows are these, pointed in the direction of the city whence I fled. On the other side, there is a thick wall covered in mirrors.

Homesickness

I WOKE UP ALL ALONE in that creaking bed (do you remember it?), that hard bed, which is to say, in places the mattress had lumps of wool in it, if wool it really was, there was probably also kelp, wool that had become bunched up from all the bodies that had slept on top of it, but that night, or to be more exact, what remained of that night and then till late that morning, I slept heavily, like a log, and you left me there in that lousy, bedbug-ridden hotel— during the night I hadn't felt anything—you left and probably you ran your hand over my hair before leaving, nothing more, you went, I remained, it couldn't have been otherwise, the night before we had both seen him coming out of a tall old house near the port, creeping close to the walls of the houses, along the narrow winding streets that lead to the seafront, you grasped my hand, squeezed it, I put my arm around your shoulders, there's no reason to be afraid, no, I'm not afraid, but he's terrible, why is he so timid, why does he walk hugging the walls, what could I say to you? He was wearing his usual garb, a kind of smoking jacket with silk collars, and he probably had a chrysanthemum in his buttonhole. He was shuffling his feet over the cobbles, he wore shoes with long, pointed toes, he walked in a trance, without looking left or right, it was as if he had a specific goal and was afraid he might be late. We followed him for a few dozen meters and then gave up. Nevertheless, you left, you had recovered quite quickly after the shock you had had, you had forgotten him.

There was still nothing we could have done to help him.

Yes, you're right, we couldn't have helped him. Best that we pretend we never saw him in the first place.

Never?

Yes, never. Except that after you left, I saw him again; although I did everything I could not to; I didn't think about him, I tried to forget he existed. If you had been here, it would have been easier. But I woke up all alone, in that squalid hotel room. A newspaper had been thrown on the floor in one corner, with an announcement that the circus was leaving town. You should have taken the newspaper with you . . .

You'll call me ridiculously sentimental, but what did you want me to do? Don't think I don't realize, even though I'm not sentimental, that's not the right word for it. I don't know how to explain it to you.

It doesn't matter, skip that part.

Anyway, the item in the newspaper was dated a few days before they left. They knew they were going to leave, they'd known for a long time. Ever since they arrived. That day, on the ship. People were waiting excitedly on the quay, it was autumn, a crisp morning, ruffled by a strong breeze. I was waiting for them to disembark, with my heart in my mouth. It seems so long ago that I'm almost unsure whether it really happened. The buzz of the crowd, that childlike gaiety, the excitement that filled us all! The animal cages made the strongest impression on the people of the town, the cages with gilded bars from which all kinds of magnificent animals gazed calm and composed, even with a trace of irony, at the photographers that were rushing everywhere, waving their cameras. Do you remember?

Well, anyway, they knew even then that they would leave, they probably even knew when, the exact date; the boss, that burly man dressed always in blue, he will have known for sure. Don't you think?

There, you see, I don't like that, how can I put it . . . I know in advance what you're going to answer, I don't even need to see you. I know all your comebacks. Maybe it was because of that that you left . . . For you left, and that's why I'm all alone. The light falls on the newspaper tossed over there by the armchair.

Never mind that!

At first, I didn't believe it, I imagined that you would be coming back, that you had gone to watch the sunrise, revolted by the drunkard lying on the bed, probably I was snoring, and I know how it annoys you. I always snore when I'm drunk. I thought you would be coming back, that's why I didn't get out of bed. I was looking at the newspaper on the floor by the armchair and thinking about pretending to be still asleep, to see how you would get annoyed. Do you know that you forgot your shoes? In your haste, you left them on a chair. I saw them and it was then that I realized the suitcase was gone. But still I didn't get out of bed.

And then what?

Then I . . . It'll pass, I said to myself as I got dressed. Outside it was very hot. I went back inside the room and picked up the newspaper.

You'd have done better to leave it there!

You're right. I told myself the same thing, afterward. But why didn't you take it with you? You did it deliberately, the same as you did with the shoes. I imagined you'd gone out to watch the sunrise. And I went back to sleep . . .

In the end, you still woke up. Better you tell me what happened next . . .

How easy it is to be right! I woke up, obviously. But I thought that you had gone out to watch the sunrise. You'd been wanting to see it for a long time and I hadn't let you, I held you tightly in my arms and if you tried to release yourself from my embrace, I woke up and didn't let you go. Why do you want to see the sunrise? And so, you took advantage of the fact that I was sleeping the heavy sleep of a drunk, besides which I was snoring intolerably, and you left. I would have gone back to sleep . . .

But didn't you wake up all the same?

I know that's what you're going to say, that's what you might say, that's what you might have said. But you left me in that squalid bed, which creaked at the slightest movement (do you remember?) full of hard lumps of wool, or maybe kelp, the mattress, I mean, what with the countless bodies that had lain contorted on it . . . You left me sleeping like a log. When I awoke,

I went out of the room, I came back, I read the newspaper and I went out again, because I felt as if I were suffocating. I didn't want to think about him, it would have been pointless. I tried to forget and I also got drunk the days that followed. When I woke up, I saw your shoes and the newspaper tossed on the floor by the armchair, and I started all over again.

Tell me, did you really see him?

I can guess that question from your eyes, even though I can't see you, your feigned amazement, because if you stopped to think (but you don't stop, you go!), if you wanted to be completely honest, you would realize that you don't even care. Isn't that wonderful! Given that you yourself don't care, you might have helped me to forget. We would have made love on that disgusting bed, lumpy with clumps of wool or kelp, swarming with bedbugs, we would have thrown the newspaper in the bin and, if need be, we wouldn't have gone outside till he deigned to fly away. But you left. You gave my hair a motherly stroke and you left. You'd known for a long time that you were going to leave, ever since you arrived. It couldn't have been otherwise. The evening before, we both saw him, and you seemed more disturbed than I. Maybe you really were . . .

What can I tell you? There's nothing to tell. You forgot to take your shoes, or maybe you left them deliberately, the same as the newspaper. And I went outside the hotel to wander around at random. I always came back drunk. At night. That way I avoided the bed bugs, or rather I didn't feel them. I slept soundly. Although, as you say, in the end I still woke up. In the same room. The light gaily rushed over the walls, I set eyes on the shoes, the newspaper, I tried to go back to sleep—maybe you left to see the sunrise or simply to go for a walk—I wouldn't be able to, and so I would have to get up and go out. To tell the truth, I didn't miss you as such. But together, if we had stayed together, I mean, it would have been easier. Maybe in the end I would have forgotten. You would have been troubled from time to time, I would have held you in my arms, protectively, and time would have passed more quickly.

Yes, of course, in the end I would have still woken up all alone, but later, a little later . . .

A few days after you left, the sea was no longer so rough, it abruptly grew calm, as if by magic. Probably that's what gave him cause to hope, I don't know . . . although it wasn't the waves that hindered him. It was toward evening and I was walking along the seafront. All alone. I was walking and looking at the waves growing smaller and smaller, as if they were retreating, and as the sun sank on the other side, the sea paled and a fine mist, growing more and more visible, descended from the horizon over the liquid expanse, whiter and whiter; it was like steam, like the panting breath of the sea . . .

Skip this part, please! Better you tell me whether you saw him. Are you sure you saw him?

I'm sure I saw him, although he was standing with his back to me, with one hand lightly resting on the parapet—but then there was his top hat, although he's not the only person who wears a top hat . . .

Spare me the wisecracks! What top hat?

No, seriously. I mean that it wasn't because of the top hat that I was sure I saw him. The top hat! I admit that it's a little arrogant—that ostentatious elegance! . . . But there's also some-thing else. A distinguishing mark. I'm not from around here! I'm not from around here! You understand? That top hat of his is a cry—like his wings—a cry of pride and desperation, both of them ridiculous, pointless, in other words. It's hard for me to explain to you why . . .

Tell me: did you see him? Are you sure you saw him?

Let's take it methodically. Why don't you let me speak? You keep interrupting me, even if you're not here next to me, even if you left me in that hotel room full of bedbugs . . .

Never mind that!

So, the sea was calm. The waves had retreated as if at the flick of a switch. Then the mist started to come down. It was wonderful! . . . I was walking along the seafront, my shoulders stooped, my hands behind my back, and from time to time I went up to the parapet and ran the palm of my hands over the rough stone. Fascinated by the view, I wasn't looking around me. In any event, the seafront was almost deserted, more and more deserted. I was standing stock-still, looking at that wispy steam that blended sea and sky in a single greyish white, and I didn't notice when he came or where he came from.

And was it he?

I told you, it wasn't the top hat, maybe he wasn't even wearing it, I was quite a distance away, fifty or sixty meters, or even farther. A lion was lying at his feet.

A lion?

Yes. Like that painting that we both saw in a book. You were the one who pointed it out to me.

As I stood leaning against the parapet, busily stroking the warm, rough stone, I sensed that I was no longer all alone. I turned my head and I saw him. His wings were quivering. It was plain that he was excited. Wearing his worn black suit, with a jaunty flower in the buttonhole, he was standing, gazing into the distance. He saw nothing around him. He was gazing intently at the sea and the sky, the mist . . .

He wanted to fly!

Yes. He sometimes rose on tiptoes, ready to take flight, and then the lion would growl, I could make out its snarling maw, as if it were laughing. As for him, he didn't turn around. He stood motionless. He had been abandoned here, in some room of that bedbug-infested hotel, he had nothing else to do, every morning he looked at his wings, which were grubbier and grubbier, at his top hat, at the newspaper tossed on the floor by the armchair, at the shoes . . . And even if he had attempted to fly, even if he had decided to climb up onto the parapet, with one hand keeping tight hold of his top hat, with the other trying to maintain his balance, and then stood on tiptoes, jerked, suddenly taken flight, soaring up into the sky, desperately beating his wings, higher and higher, dwindling to the size of a seagull or a swallow or a gnat, even then, after flying in a circle, then another, this one slightly lower, flying in lower and lower circles, I'm sure he would have come back, perhaps without the top hat, which would have made him, if not more ridiculous, than in any event more insignificant; the top hat served a purpose. Or else I've grown accustomed to it . . .

And didn't he try to fly?
No, he didn't try. But his wings were quivering.

The Accident

AN AIRPLANE COULD BE HEARD droning and old man Leu said, Sorry, just a second, and went to the window, with one hand holding the razor, the other covered in foam. He couldn't see the airplane, he drew the rather grubby curtain in annoyance, but the droning noise persisted, Where can it be coming from? asked old man Leu and, Do forgive me, I'll be right back. Mihalache stopped work too, raised his scissors level with his ear, twisted them back and forth, as if to say, He's crazy, the others laughed at the joke, the droning moved into the distance, it could be heard more and more faintly, and old man Leu turned back to the rest of the barber's shop, panting, red in the face, I saw it, it was very high up . . .

Saw what, old man Leu?

I saw it, and using a towel he wiped the foam off his hand, then started sharpening his razor on the leather strap hanging from the wall. His customer, with one cheek shaven, the other covered in foam, muttered something, you couldn't make out what, and old man Leu apologized yet again and re-soaped him, after which he took two steps back to admire him.

Lică started talking about airplanes: the French had built a very big one, terrifyingly fast, a thousand kilometers per hour, I swear to you on my life . . . It wasn't the French, Mihalache contradicted him, it was the Americans, wasn't it, old man Leu? But old man Leu wasn't in the mood for talking, his mind was elsewhere. He scratched his head with the nail of his little finger, his hair was greying at the temples, as were two locks on the top of his head, he had no way of hiding them. He looked in the mirror, his moustache was still white, glistening with brilliantine, and it wasn't dyed, no matter what they thought . . .

Have you flown this month, old man Leu?

He didn't answer, he had to be careful when he was busy with the razor at somebody's throat. And why did they have to bother him all the time? They asked him just because they imagined he liked talking about it, but they knew very well, the whole barber's shop knew that every two months old man Leu took some time off work or had days deducted from his annual paid vacation, and flew to a city as far away as possible; one summer, he had gone all the way to Budapest on an airplane so big that you couldn't even tell you were flying. And each time he would tell them all about what had happened during the flight, whether there had been turbulence or some problem with the engine and all kinds of other details, but it was hardly the case that he chattered about it all day long. He washed the face of the customer leaning over the sink. Cologne? Aftershave? He wafted him with the towel, carefully, even somehow tenderly, combed his hair, how young he is! how he resembles that other young man, the likeness is amazing . . . Now, on seeing him shaved, he was able to tell more easily. The young man stood up to leave and old man Leu felt himself turn red as he slipped the tip inside his pocket.

Mihalache was the only one he talked to at any length, when they played backgammon. He confided in him that it was best to fly on a small airplane, on the big ones you didn't feel like you were flying, you sit in an armchair like in the theatre and through the porthole you see motionless clouds like shaving-foam sheep, or the sky, and if you couldn't hear the rumble of the engines, you'd think it was all a trick, that the airplane was standing still, what do you mean, standing still? then hanging from a cable, or something like that . . .

You've got some funny ideas . . . said Mihalache shaking the dice in his cupped hand like a crapshooter.

They didn't play in the shop, Mihalache came to his house, he was younger than he and a bachelor, you've got some luck, it's as if . . . and old man Leu chuckled, then he poured raki in the glasses, drank, wiped his mouth with the back of his hand, and smacked his lips in satisfaction. Released from Mihalache's cupped palm, the dice tumbled endlessly, you really know how to throw 'em! And Mihalache gave a smile, as if to say, tough luck, and on your home turf too, you might as well sit and read a newspaper, old man Leu, otherwise you'll get bored. Old man Leu slapped his thigh, poured himself another tot and knocked it back.

Haven't you ever got dizzy? Haven't you felt like throwing up? Old man Leu smiled, shaking the dice in his big red hand. Why don't you try it for yourself? The other man knew that it gave old man Leu pleasure if he feigned amazement, and maybe he really was amazed. He leaned over the board, one arm raised, his fist clenched lest he drop the dice: Try what, man? You wouldn't catch me in one of them contraptions, and the dice tumbled merrily. Old man Leu gave a rather supercilious smile. You're afraid! No, I'm not afraid, I just don't want to. What, can't I go by train? Why wouldn't I go by train, I can look out of the window: plains, mountains, rivers . . . What's the hurry?

Mishu was lying on the sofa, with its floral coverlet; as he was used to the rattling of the dice, he was sleeping peacefully. The smile remained on old man Leu's lips and he carried on playing, not paying much attention. A car raced by outside, a dog started barking, followed by yet more dogs, a real uproar. In the yard, the ducks could be heard quacking in fright. Old man Leu went to the window and back. What, aren't you playing? He took the dice and cast them on the polished wood of the box. He made a bad move. He slapped his thigh, but it was obvious he didn't really care. What are you up to, old man Leu? Mihalache planted his hands on his hips and looked Leu up and down: a button had fallen off his shirt and the collar was dirty. His smock at the barber's shop was none too clean either.

Old man Leu whetted his razor, his mind elsewhere. He had been whetting it for five minutes, his gestures mechanical, repeated hundreds of thousands of times before. There was a single customer in the barber's shop, whom Mihalache was attending to. It was hot. The driver hadn't stopped, it was past

midnight, outside only two streetlamps were lit, the bulbs of the
others had been smashed by catapults. He couldn't stop himself
shouting a curse, even though the car had vanished from sight.
It was quiet, an unusual, unnatural silence, with not so much as
a dog barking. A customer entered the shop and went up to his
chair. This one free? Yes, take a seat, then he tested the razor's
edge on the tip of his thumb, he needed to sharpen the other
side too. You've gone berserk with that razor! called out Lică and
laughed like an idiot. He didn't answer. The customer sat down
on the chair and stretched out his legs, he was tired. He looked
in the mirror for a few moments: he had a big head, thin, slightly
ginger hair, a round face, his face looked quite young, although
it was covered with a few days' growth of bristly, ginger beard.
Finally, he leaned back his neck on the leather headrest.

He closed his eyes, giving a soft groan. What'll it be? The
beard? The young man nodded, lowering his chin to his chest
a few times, folded his hands over his belly . . . the dogs hadn't
barked, there wasn't a single soul on the street outside. He hadn't
seen the car.

Poor old man Leu! Mihalache thought to himself, pitying
him, and glimpsed a small round bloodstain just under the
grubby collar of his shirt. He said nothing and cast the dice, a
double six, That's some luck you've got, murmured Leu dreamily
and lost yet another game. The coverlet on the bed was tatty, in
ribbons because of Mișu's claws; he was asleep now, purring softly.
It's your turn, said Mihalache and Leu took the dice, tossed them
up and down in his palm, flung them: one die rolled onto the rug,
Mihalache bent down to pick it up and accidentally banged his
head against the box on which they were playing, upsetting the
checkers which got all mixed up. Mihalache was red in the face
from bending down and from chagrin, and no wonder: he had
been winning. I'm not playing any more if you're not careful, I'm
not playing! But Leu remained calm, just as distrait as before.
They carried on. It was hot, and they were slightly drunk from
the raki. They were now both making all kinds of mistakes. The
car had gone past at great speed, it had vanished around the corner, or else there hadn't been any car, he was damned if he knew

. . . What could he do? He looked at Mihalache, at his rather bulbous nose, what would he have done in his place? The car sped past at an insane speed, all the windows rattled, the head-lights lit up the room like it was day. They were car headlights, of that he was certain.

He had finished shaving one cheek when he heard the air-plane. Damn it to hell! But the rattling was getting louder and louder and he couldn't restrain himself, he said, I beg your par-don! just a second, leaning toward the ear of the customer, who seemed to have fallen asleep, and he rushed to the window hold-ing the razor, his other hand covered in foam—there was no airplane to be seen. He hesitated a moment, then he pressed the door handle, descended the three steps, crossed the yard at a run, almost losing his slippers, there was nobody on the street, the car had turned down a side street—it was no longer to be seen. In the middle of the road lay a motionless body. Leu took a few steps in the direction that he suspected the car had taken, he had seen the headlights flashing across the room, and he left fly with a curse. What would Mihalache have done in his place?

What are you looking at me for, play! Come on, you can bear off that point! Old man Leu wasn't himself. Lately, he'd been worse than usual. Mihalache stopped work, raised his scissors level with his ear and swiveled them a few times, shook them. He's nuts! Lică laughed, the others laughed, as if it were a joke, the rumble of the airplane was growing ever fainter and old man Leu came back, out of breath, with his razor in one hand, his other hand covered in foam, they all fell silent and looked at him. Did you see it, old man Leu? Lică asked, as the silence was becoming embarrassing. I saw it, and he wiped his hand on a towel, then he tried to whet the razor on the leather strap. They all knew how much old man Leu liked airplanes, but even so! What's up, aren't you playing? And Mihalache rattled the dice in his cupped palm.

Old man Leu lived somewhere near the edge of town, in a long, squat house; he had two rooms and a kitchen, other tenants occupied the rest. The yard was unsurfaced, and when his wife was alive, he used to plant flowers. At the bottom of the yard there was a pump, next to an old apricot tree that had started to wither. It was also there that the ducks waddled around quacking, or where a few geese gaggled, which weren't his, maybe they belonged to the other tenants, maybe to the neighbors, they went back and forth between the two yards at will, slipping through a gap in the fence. On Sundays, especially in summer, Mihalache used to come over to play backgammon. Mihalache was younger than he and had incredible luck with the dice, you load them, that's what! Like hell do I load them! pay more attention, what, do you think that luck is all that counts? Old man Leu took another swig, straight from the bottle, Mihalache pretended not to notice and cast the dice, which rolled the length of the board, with a rumble like that of an airplane up in the sky, way up, where it's blue and silent, with the snow- and ice-capped mountains below, more beautiful than real mountains, or the huge sheep, as white as foam, or perhaps the hair and beard of an old man, hanging between heaven and earth . . . And you've never felt dizzy? He shook his head and regarded Mihalache with a gentle smile. Why don't you try it? It's so good to fly, to know that beneath you are countless little creatures, as small as ants, and you're up there, you close your eyes and you have wings . . .

But I thought you said that in an airplane you can't really feel . . .

That's right, but in small airplanes you can feel you're flying. Not in those big . . .

And then Mihalache lost his temper and declared that for the life of him he couldn't understand what was the point of taking the risk when you could travel by train, which was cheaper and more comfortable, you could look out of the window, admire the view, the mountains, the plains . . . Why should I be in a rush?

He soaped the cheek of the customer again, who seemed to be asleep: motionless, his face in the air, his hands folded across his belly, he looked like a dead man. He approached, making small hesitant steps, shuffling his slippers. He saw that he was young, almost a child, and he had wings. Large, white wings. He bent over and saw that there was no blood, not a single drop. Maybe they had thrown him out of the car after beating him to death, or maybe there hadn't been any car, he had simply grown tired and fallen there from up above, onto the dark cobbles of the street. Have you flown this month, old man Leu? He made no reply. Why do they tease him so? What do they want? Below the chin, around the Adam's apple, the beard was harsher, sprouting in every direction. He had to be careful. What would Mihalache have done in his place? Probably he wouldn't have gone outside in just his long johns and his slippers, after midnight; he would have turned over and gone back to sleep. But he couldn't sleep, he couldn't sleep and that was that, he'd played backgammon all afternoon with Mihalache and the bastard had kept shaking those dice in his ears. He kept tossing and turning in the sheets, accidentally kicking Mishu, who mewled and found himself another place to curl up. He couldn't get to sleep, and he tried everything: he thought of the day when he'd flown for the first time, the night before the flight, his fear that they wouldn't let him board the airplane, what's an old man like you doing here? it was a small, recreational plane; best of all is to fly on a small airplane, on the big ones you can't tell you're flying, you sit in an armchair, all buckled up with a safety belt, and you look out of the window at the clouds, as motionless as snow- and mist-covered mountains, and if it weren't that you heard the muffled roar of the engines . . . And you've never thrown up? No, never, I've never felt dizzy and I've never felt sick. He was born to fly! He smiled. Then Mihalache lost his temper even more, his forehead turned red: There's no point to it, it's stupid!

Silence. Nothing but the steady snoring of Mishu, who was purring away under the blanket, curled up at his feet. And all of a sudden, the rumble of an engine and the wheels racing over the cobbles at an insane speed. He couldn't restrain himself, the headlights of the car—you'd have thought it was an airplane taking off—illuminated the room, and he then tossed off the blanket, Mishu gave a frightened meow, and he put on his slippers and rushed to the door, pressed the handle and within seconds he was outside, in the road, swearing. The car was no longer to be seen. Murderers! Animals! He took a few steps in the direction in which he thought the big black car had vanished, that is, to the left, then he turned around and saw the white body lying on the cobbles. The wings were long, longer than arms. He touched them: down as soft and white as a goose's or swan's. He looked around him. Nobody to be seen. Then he picked up the boy, holding him by his armpits, and began to drag him, the limp wings jiggled. Maybe he wasn't dead, maybe he would come round. On the street there was not a soul to be seen, and there was silence, it smelled of lilies and carnations. An unnatural silence. The only sound was the shuffling of his slippers on the road, then on the earth covered with little tufts of grass, then on the steps, the three steps, the clack of the door handle: the wings were too big to fit, they caught on the doorframe. He was forced to twist the body on one side, it wasn't very heavy and it was warm, he could feel its warmth through the thin silk shirt with its large lacy collar, and all of a sudden, he grew afraid, he started to push and jerk the body of that winged being, which he was lugging inside the houses without even knowing why: maybe he'd live, maybe he was just unconscious . . .

Mihalache crossed his arms and looked old man Leu up and down. It wasn't scorn, it was sooner concern and obviously curiosity. The dirty collar, that bloodstain, the shirt flapping open: he had a button missing. Poor old man Leu! But he didn't say anything and rolled the dice once more. Old man Leu then cast, but so clumsily that the dice tumbled onto the floor, one rolled under the sofa, the other who knows where, under the rug or under a chair. Mihalache bent down to look for them. Leave them, said old man Leu, to hell with them! Let's stop playing . . . And he got down on all fours next to Mihalache, who was lying flat on his belly and had thrust one arm under the sofa. Leave them! yelled Leu, and the other man turned his head to look at him in fright and at the same time bewilderment, beneath the sofa his fingers had encountered something soft and downy. Was that a goose under the sofa? Leu grabbed his other arm and started to yank it: Leave them, leave them there! Mihalache extracted his arm from under the sofa and, without saying another word, stood up, holding onto a chair. He banged his hip against the backgammon board, which sat precariously on a stool from the kitchen, and upset the board, the checkers scattered all across the room.

The young man had a big head and slightly ginger hair, a round, pale face. He was handsome, with wings longer than arms, the wings with which he flew above the city, all alone in the thin, blue air of the upper reaches. What could he do? He went to the window. The street was just as deserted. For an instance he thought about calling the police, but was he dead, and who would believe him . . . They would torture him with all kinds of questions, they might even beat him. He lifted the corpse in his arms and put it on the sofa. He stroked the blue velvet trousers and patent-leather shoes with long, pointed toes. Maybe he would open his eyes . . . He pulled a chair up to the sofa and sat pensive for a long while. Something had to be done, so much was clear, but what? The young man had thin lips and a pale face, probably when he crashed down on the cobbles he had broken something inside, like a clock falling onto the concrete, and then it's goodbye! There was no point calling the police . . . He turned him over on his belly, the wings were too big for the sofa bed.

He entered the barber's shop, out of breath, red in the face, disheveled, he'd probably been running. They all looked at him interrogatively, Mihalache stopped work, raised the scissors to his right ear and swiveled them a few times, the others laughed as if at a joke, from his corner Lică giggled and said: Were you flying? Yes, I was flying, and they laughed again, ha, ha, ha! look at Leu soaring above the city, way up high, wheeling in ever larger circles, hovering like a hawk, like an eagle, oho! like a lion with big white wings, like a swan's, up above . . .

(*România Literară*, no. 11, March 1970)

On the Curb of the Sidewalk

Story reprinted from Cold (1967)

Icarus

Story reprinted from Excercises (1966)

Through the Keyhole

HE WAS LATE AGAIN. The hallway was deserted; he crossed it taking long strides, dragging the soles of his dusty shoes over the cherry-red carpet. He paused for a few seconds: from an adjacent room came the clacking of a typewriter, from another room, laughter, tittering, he was more than a quarter of an hour late, there was no point in hurrying. There were only a few more paces to the door of his office: grey, squat, different from the other one, a door that opened every day, and which would open again now, too. Before pressing the door handle, he was tempted for a moment to look through the keyhole, but he refrained, it was pointless. Petrache will have come in, of course he had come in, he was never absent, or only very seldom, for example that time when his father died after being hit by a bus. He had telephoned from the hospital, his voice had been calm, perhaps a little hoarse, and he had informed that that he would not be coming in, without any further explanation, and it was only later that they found out what had happened. He had come in the same as usual, he had entered their office to check on who was late. He's not a bad man—Magda was busy filing her nails, speaking through pursed lips—but he can't abide sloppiness, unpunctuality. It's just the way he is . . . He won't say anything to him this time either, he won't reprimand him, he'll merely fix him with a stare; it's hard to bear up under the gaze of those watery blue eyes, which clash with his dry, stern face; and he'll get all flustered this time too, he will hesitantly approach, mumble an excuse, about his clock, the trolleybus, an accident on the way there, Petrache will continue to stare at him without saying a word, then he will suddenly direct his gaze elsewhere, at the window, at the roofs of the houses opposite, small houses soon to be demolished. They're building a new apartment block.

He pushed open the door and entered. First, he saw Magda, her ruddy knees, her eyes, her mouth, even her nose, then Valentin, he muttered a good morning, Mr. Petrache answered him in a metallic voice and looked at the clock. Better he tell them the truth, which is to say, everything that had happened to him that nightmarish night, tell them how the swords had gleamed in the plant pots on the terrace and the winged lion or griffin or whatever it was . . . He had been in torment the whole night, he was utterly drained.

He sat down at his desk, Magda said something, holding her palms to her cheeks, Valentin laughed, Mr. Petrache looked out of the window at the wooden shutters of the houses across the road. The sky was covered in thin, silvery clouds.

He was late again! He attempted a smile, thereby to gain his clemency or at least to soften the harsh lines of his face, the deep furrows between his eyebrows. He did not succeed. Petrache turned his head back to the window.

He pulled out a drawer, searched for something, didn't find it, gave up. He picked up a pencil and started twisting it between finger and thumb. He gave a few slight coughs. I live a long way away, he said, and the trolleybuses are really crowded, you know. There isn't a bus route through my district. He fell silent. He gave another cough. As usual, Magda took his side: Those trolleybuses are awful! She always tried to stick up for him. He looked at her and thanked her with a smile, with a blink of the eyelids: she was looking at her long red nails in delight. She had a round face, a snub nose, an ordinary but pleasant face.

Mr. Petrache cleared his throat, but said nothing. Or couldn't he hear him? For he saw him move his lips, he was obviously talking, he was reprimanding him for being late, but his ears were blocked, he couldn't hear a thing, it was as if he were underwater, but the water was so clear that he could see the others, their faces, their habitual motions: Valentin was sharpening a pencil with serious, almost solemn mien, Magda was looking at her nails, then she started waving her hands, nodding her head, talking, talking . . . But he couldn't hear anything. He quickly pressed his palms to his ears a few times . . . don't let it happen again. Magda gave him a triumphant look, it meant he had been forgiven; he half rose from his chair to thank her and the next day he was late again.

He didn't have anything to do, he was bored sitting around the house, so he went to the cinema to pass the time. A stupid film was showing, or at least so it seemed at first: a character who was in love with the daughter of his landlord, living in a house with lots of rooms, most of them rented out to lowly clerks and people of no fixed occupation. He'd wangled a tiny room crammed full of all kinds of old junk; it had a single window, thick with dust and three-quarters obscured by crates of chipped jars and bottles, which looked out onto the bathroom. From the window he could watch a girl of seventeen or eighteen getting undressed, washing, letting herself be caressed, embraced and more by the young lad she brought with her to the bathroom, her younger cousin, who couldn't have been more than fourteen. What a brat! The girl's father collected postage stamps and was probably shacked up with the vendor from a porcelain shop who lived up in the mansard. There was an oppressive atmosphere in that house full of hallways, passages, and all kinds of hidden corners, which when they were deserted looked downright spooky; the doors, once white, were now peeling, dirty, and the handles were carved in the shapes of animal heads. The tenants maintained very odd relations among themselves, they hated each other, spied on each other, were in thrall to all kinds of manias that made them even more bizarre, and the whole film had something murky and mysterious about it, it was almost a silent film, with only a spoken line or two or three words at long intervals, rather a boring film as a whole, although it kept you on the edge of your seat, it forced you to be on the alert without any end result (but what does that mean, end result?), nothing happened as such! . . . After a while, the reel snapped and I didn't have the patience to wait and see the rest, I left the cinema, scowling at the usherette, who smiled at me inanely, and went out to wander the streets.

You're fibbing, said Magda, taking a satisfied sip of coffee. What did you say the film was called?

He made no reply, went back to his desk. No, he wasn't annoyed, but there was no fun in him telling her about it if she didn't believe him. Yes, a cinema at the edge of town, near that old railroad station, I don't know where exactly. I was passing and went inside, I didn't have anything to do that evening, I was bored to death. But no, it's simply not done! Like when those cattle being taken to the slaughterhouse suddenly charged at a tram. Have you ever seen cattle being taken to the slaughterhouse?

Yes, of course I have, when I was little.

Then what didn't she believe? That they charged at the tram, that they overturned it, that the police drew their pistols and started firing? . . . The chaos was unbelievable, the poor animals had gone completely out of their minds, they were stampeding at the overturned tram, people were screaming, a few women had fainted, somebody shouted that lions and tigers had escaped from the zoo and were swarming down another street. Which wasn't true.

All right, let's assume I believe you . . .

Let's assume? What does that mean? Do you or don't you believe me? It's not as if you're doing me a favor, I'm the one who's a sucker for wasting my time telling you the story!

Valentin was splitting his sides, but he'll laugh at anything. You'd laugh even if I showed you a finger, that's how daft you are, yes, I am, and he laughed and he laughed, clutching his belly. Then Magda burst out laughing to, it was infectious.

I don't know whether that film really existed, but when I was little I used to look through the keyhole of my aunt's room: she was as fat as a whale, her husband was too, they were both really funny. It's true! And she started to laugh again.

I would have liked Mr. Petrache to come in, I'd stopped laughing, I would have liked him to come in, to have seen the state of them: Magda was laughing her head off, leaning back in her chair, her skirt hitched up, baring her thick, tanned thighs.

Valentin has banging a pencil on the table, with tears in his eyes. I went to the door that gave onto the adjacent room to look through a hole that had been made specially. Don't worry, the boss is in a meeting . . . It was true, he wasn't in his office. A pity!

Tell us about another film, pleaded Magda and went over to his desk, swaying her hips. A film about knights and castles, about verdant meadows on which life-and-death battles are fought . . .

About the knight who turns into a wolf and eats his mother, said Valentin, delighted at his own sarcasm.

I didn't want to. There was no point and, to tell the truth, I didn't feel much like chattering. I had work to do. Better I bury my head in some documents and work. Or pretend to work and try to remember the street where that house was. After I left the cinema, that is . . .

What film was it you say you saw?

I don't answer. I left, the usherette looked at me, smiling inanely, and then in amazement that I was scowling, what did she expect? I left and set off completely at random downhill, along a street with broken cobbles, and then along another, I was walking in a daze, not thinking about anything. I think that's the best way: to walk without thinking about anything, not to be looking for anything, to have no aim, or to forget you have any aim. So, down a little street to the left (but going where?), then another, I have no idea how far I walked, but it couldn't have been very far from the cinema. I didn't walk all that long, but I'm not sure, it's very easy to be wrong in such cases.

Magda wrapped her soft arms around his neck, he hadn't even noticed when she crept up behind him. Go on, tell me! He sat perfectly still, silent. He hadn't gone far when all of a sudden, a house with large iron gates appeared, it had a white gravel drive and plant pots with swords.

Are you angry?

He told her he wasn't, barely moving his lips, she unwrapped her arms from around his neck and walked away with that swaying gait of hers that showed off her broad hips. Valentin smiled: that goofy smile of his which he thought ironical. Magda sat down at her desk and looked at her nails. She frowned. What a strange man! Even though she'd hinted countless times that she'd like to go to the cinema or the theatre with him, he'd never invited her, he'd even turned her down, claiming that he had to visit some sick uncle or other, after she'd queued for an hour to buy tickets one day. Nor did he want to visit her at home. After work, he shot off to take the trolleybus, although he wasn't married, he lived alone, at the edge of town somewhere. Nobody had been to his house.

Where do you see all those films? asked Magda, lifting her chubby arms above her head in comic exasperation. Valentin immediately started laughing, but he frowned, he broke off telling the story and buried his head in his thick files.

Come on, tell me the rest, she pleaded. What happened after that?

. . . in the end she ran off with a man with a moustache, who had a long red car, a tall man with the face of a fraudster. The girl's father had been a colonel and he was a great stamp collector: he had a stamp from some English colony or other in Africa, which showed a lion at which a native was hurling a spear, a very unusual three-cornered stamp, like an equilateral triangle. After the girl ran away, every evening the colonel got drunk on whiskey and gazed for hours at a time at that stamp, which seemed to come to life and the lion would start to run with the spear poking from it like the pinion of a wing. And at night the boy would enter the room of the woman from the porcelain shop, who also had other visitors. They would fearfully climb the stairs, constantly stopping to look right and left. In the evening or at night, their paths would cross in the hallways, they would pass each other like ghosts. It was the same during the day: they all spied on each other. They would ascend and descend the stairs that connected the four floors of the house, they would stalk each other, their faces solemn and at the same time ridiculous.

And then what?

And then, well, the young man, who was a clerk at a bank, went out for a walk one evening and entered a cinema, where he didn't have the patience to watch till the end of the film: it was rather a boring film in which the images repeated themselves obsessively, a kind of assemblage of gestures, or I don't know what to call it . . . He loses patience, he gets up and leaves. As he leaves, he has a little contretemps with the usherette, who tries to talk to him (there was something vulgar and repulsive about her, although she wasn't ugly) and he brushes her off. He walks out of the cinema, wanders the streets, all kinds of dark back alleys, and all of a sudden, he finds himself standing in front of a large iron gate, behind which glints the peculiarly white gravel of a drive, and on the terrace of the house, or rather the villa, since it was very large and was built lavishly, almost wastefully . . .

He broke off. Mr. Petrache entered the office, frowning as usual. He resumed his leafing through the documents in the file on his desk. Valentin coughed, only Magda seemed not to care: she took a sandwich from a drawer and started eating it in a leisurely fashion.

There was no longer any point in his hurrying. He would be late anyway. He looked down at his dusty shoes and as he walked he tried to wipe at least the toes on the cherry-red carpet, made threadbare over the years by the footfalls of so many clerks who had trodden it before him. From the typists' room could be heard the clacking of typewriters and muffled titters. The same sounds every morning, the same morning every day, the same day . . . He looked behind him, the corridor was long and empty. He was late, of that he was certain, but he couldn't tell how late: half an hour, an hour, maybe longer . . . He didn't pause in front of the door, he pressed the handle and went inside. Petrache was there: he was standing in front of the window, tall, thin, his arms folded over his chest. Magda was filing her nails. Valentin was busy writing in a thick ledger with green covers; he put down his fountain pen and stared at him. He probably looked awful: unshaven, sleepless, bloodshot eyes, his unknotted necktie draped around the collar of his jacket. Magda gave him a scolding but worried look, shook her head, he couldn't bear her looking at him, he whispered good morning and crept to his desk, from where he looked sidelong at Petrache, who had not budged from in front of the window. He took a file out of his desk, then another, he put a file back and took out yet another, he closed the drawer, making too loud a bang. Valentin gave a start and looked at him for a few seconds. Petrache remained silent. He was guilty, he had no more excuses, the clock, the tram, the traffic, it would have been ridiculous.

Best would be to tell them, to recount every single detail, or at least to describe the house, the gloomy, forbidding house, a real villa, with that huge terrace, where swords glinted in the rays of the mon, and the white gravel drive, and the black iron gate, and his running away, his fear, he didn't even dare to turn on the light, to look in the mirror. He had to tell them, and quickly too, to speak up before they did, not to wait for Mr. Petrache to speak, since then he wouldn't be able to interrupt him, and it was obvious that the boss was about to hold forth, to give a little speech, look at him chewing his thin pallid lips and rocking back and forth on the balls of his feet, with his hands thrust in his pockets. Let him be the first to speak! but how could he tell them, how could he tell them about the lion that for the last few nights had been flying above the town and about the swords sprouting from the plant pots? There was but a single solution: let me tell them I had a dream—and in fact didn't he dream it? to say that it was a dream, a nightmare, I couldn't sleep a wink all night, I haven't slept for so many nights, which was perfectly true, look at the dark rings under his eyes, at his bloodshot, sleepless eyes, at his unsteady, hesitant gait when he walks down the endless, deserted corridors those white corridors, with statues at intervals, also white, the corridors that gave onto dozens of whitewashed rooms with white curtains and white marble floors, and the light that came from long tubes embedded in the walls, and from above and from below . . .

What's wrong? said the woman leaning her elbows on his desk, tenderly, what's wrong?

He was sitting with his eyes closed, maybe he was asleep, maybe he was dreaming, the warm voice murmured in his ear: Tell me, aren't you feeling well? His eyelids were heavy and wouldn't obey him, they were leaden, tired of opening and closing all the time, and to see what? To see Petrache haughtily standing in front of the window, to see Valentin busy writing, poking out the tip of his tongue and glancing at the boss from the corner of his eye . . . Next to him was Magda, her velvety voice that pulled him away from the interminable, labyrinthine white corridors, brought him outside, back to reality back to what everybody, including him, called reality. Through half-closed eyes he saw Petrache twist half around, away from the window, his brows grimly knitted, and look at him. They were all looking at him. They were waiting. He had to tell them, he cleared his throat, he felt a lump rise in his throat, a bluish veil came down over his eyes, and there he was again, endlessly walking down empty corridors, with their marble floor and the light that wasn't neon, although still white, a tiring, milky white.

Tell me, are you ill?

Yes, that was it, he was ill, and Petrache asked him why he didn't go to the doctor to get medical leave, there was nothing he could do for him, nor could this situation be tolerated indefinitely. He said indefinitely while vigorously moving his perfectly outstretched arm, as if doing a gymnastic exercise, from left to right and back again, and it can't go on, let this be clear to everyone, you can't keep coming to work whenever it suits you, there has to be discipline, there's a timetable, nobody does just as he pleases.

Was he ill? In the pots grow steel swords instead of plants, swords shining in the light of the moon, and a lion, as if taken from a coat of arms or maybe a postage stamp, a lion wheels above the house. It was a sign of which he had to take heed.

I've no idea how I got there, I'd been to the cinema and found the film boring, a monotonous film, with the same scenes repeated over and over again, as if in a nightmare, I got annoyed at it and left, the usherette seemed amazed, she shrugged, then gave me a knowing smile, and she had a large mouth, rouged lips. I went out of the cinema and wandered the streets. I walked aimlessly. And it was nice, it was a warm, quiet night, there were scents on the air, it smelled of lilies and flowering tobacco. The lion was flying high above the houses, it was like a star, a guiding star. Then I saw the gate of black wrought iron, twisted in all sorts of arabesques, and I stopped. I had never seen a gate so tall and yet so enticing somehow, it was so lacy, it drew you to look inside, at the garden, where there was not a single flower, where not a single blade of grass sprouted, there was nothing but paths of white gravel, glinting around blocks of grey stone, yes, like tombstones, except somewhat taller. Without crosses.

Only after that did he see the swords, only after he entered. He heard the gravel crunching under his feet and he was not afraid; he was excited, naturally, but he was not afraid.

. . . nobody does just as he pleases in our country, I thought that that at least was clear to everybody. Petrache's arm sliced the air back and forth, first horizontally, from left to right, never the other way around, then vertically, and then his words became more staccato, his voice harsher, louder.

. . . you will take medical leave, a week, two weeks, if necessary you will admit yourself to hospital. If you are ill, that is, and it is plain to see that you are tired at the very least, that is plain to see, although it is strange for somebody your age to tire so easily. Valenin had risen to his feet and was respectfully watching the boss's arm, which was outstretched like a sword.

He really is very tired.

My legs in particular are aching, after so many nights running or standing and waiting, like an idiot, not even I know what I'm waiting for. Then I set off again: I go up and down stairs, I go up again, up that spiral stair with hundreds and hundreds of steps that get narrower and narrower, so many steps . . . And the corridors that in fact lead nowhere; but that's of no importance, of absolutely no importance, and in any event you can't be sure, sometimes it seems to you that everything has a purpose, and the endless stairs, and the empty white corridors, the terrifyingly white corridors, so long that it took you a long time to reach their end (what end?), to reach that huge white door at the end of a little corridor that you reach or imagine you have reached after going up and down hundreds and hundreds of steps, panting, sweating, hoping that it will all come to an end, although at intervals you realize that what you would like to call the end is nothing but a pause, a parenthesis: instead of the white, ghostly corridors, there is this other corridor, with its cherry-red carpet, over which you drag the soles of your dusty shoes, and you stop for a few seconds to listen to the clacking of the typewriters, the laughter, the titters of the typists, and you know you are late, there are still a few paces before you reach the door—this one will open, of course!—before you press the door handle for a second you are tempted to look through the keyhole here too, although it's both pointless and ridiculous. Petrache is inside, sitting, there can be no doubt as to that, with his arms folded across his chest, in front of the window. Valentin is writing diligently, Magda is filing or admiring her long, varnished nails, and she will come to your defense, the trolleybus is crowded, it's awful . . . And then Petrache leaves the room, sometimes after giving a short speech: . . . nobody does just as he pleases in our country, I thought at least that was clear to everybody!

And Magda's voice grew shriller, although it was still friendly. Are you ill? Why are you playing dumb, why don't you say something? What's wrong? Tell me, what's wrong?

He twisted the pencil between finger and thumb, with his head bowed, acknowledging his guilt before them all, therefore before her too, who had always stuck up for him in front of the boss, she was talking, worrying like a fool, and he sat in silence, without saying a single word, without apologizing, without even trying to give an explanation, no matter how improbable. All he's capable of doing is recounting those weird films that only he ever watches, probably in his dreams, he's good for nothing else.

He twisted the pencil between finger and thumb and his eyes were bloodshot, his eyelids puffy, he was ill, of course he was, but there was no way he could explain it to Petrache, he wouldn't have understood or, even worse, he would have accused him of lying. To roam the streets like a lunatic every night, to enter people's gardens, their houses, like a burglar, like a sleepwalker . . . He couldn't sleep (why didn't he take a sleeping pill?), and if he slept, it was still those places that he dreamed: the iron gate, the gravel, the swords, and then the white, empty corridors, sometimes he would reach an even more brightly lit landing, whence he would turn right down a short corridor, shorter than the others, with marble walls, at the end of which stood the door that he couldn't open.

God, how I begged it, how I pounded on it with my fists, kicked it, beat my forehead against it, but in vain! The door remained closed. Nothing could be heard from the other side, apart from a faint hum, a soft, prolonged drone, which might just have been in my ears, after straining for so long in my futile wait. The door remained closed.

You've waited for hours, days, years, in fact, if you think about it, you've done nothing but this your whole life: you've waited for the door at the end of the corridor to open (or else not quite the end!), that door in the attic. On the other side, probably, on the other side there is nothing but a void, a vast white emptiness. At least that's what it looked like, more often than not, when you kneeled there looking through the keyhole, with your forehead pressed to the golden, glossy wood. A vast white emptiness . . . Nothing, in other words! And only at intervals, a blue strip, blue above and slightly green underneath, a greenish ribbon that swiftly vanishes, then the white once more, and you wait, you wait, Valentin's voice rings out, sharply, then Magda's: Are you ill, what's wrong?

How to explain to them (they were on the other side of the door), how to tell them? Every time, every morning, dragging his shoes over the cherry-red carpet, he was determined to tell them, if not everything and all at once, then at least partially, gradually. It would be easier to tell them, his colleagues, in a roundabout way, taking it slowly, perhaps in the end they would believe him, which is to say, understand him. He didn't need them to believe him. In any case, he had even tried: Magda leaning her elbows on his desk, allowing him to see her breasts through the top of her blouse, Valentin chewing the end of a pencil, both of them listening attentively.

What about after that? What happened next?

Magda could intuit it, she instinctively sensed that he needed to recount those films that he had or hadn't seen, to describe those imaginary scenes (whether he or somebody else imagined

them, it was the same thing!), which blurred together in his mind
and finally, no matter how hard they tried, in their minds too.
Tell us the rest, from where you left off! They would smile incred-
ulously, but they liked him and they listened to him attentively,
curiously until they tired of it, until they got bored or Petrache
entered the office.

. . . he saw the swords, after he entered the garden. He heard
the gravel crunching underfoot and he was not afraid; he was
excited, but he was not afraid.

But why did you enter? asked Magda sternly. Who made
you enter, who? I don't know, he whispered and he looked at
Valentin, who was leaning the back of his neck on the cupboard
behind his desk. I don't know, the gravel gleamed enticingly, the
lion was hovering above the house, and then, it was probably
then that he felt he had to, he was required to enter. Required by
whom? Magda was now sitting on his desk, on top of his files.
Valentin laughed: What do you mean by whom, by the director,
and he gave a low laugh, as low as he could make it, a false laugh,
in other words, he was far too satisfied at his own joke and was
trying to draw the others' attention to it. Magda took no notice
of him, didn't even look at him. She was now lying on one elbow,
stretched out across the whole desktop. The gate was unlocked,
he didn't even need to push it open or press a handle. I don't
even know how he ended up inside, in the garden, the gravel
was crunching underfoot, but he wasn't afraid. It was as if he felt
lighter . . . After which he saw the swords. They were gleaming
in the moonlight, cold, merciless. The lion or griffin or whatever
it was must still have been up above, but he could no longer see
it. He walked past the grey stone slabs and climbed the short
flight of steps to the entrance. There were two entrances, he
went inside through the larger one, the main entrance. Maybe
here he made a mistake, maybe the two entrances didn't communicate. He was in a hurry to enter the villa because he had
begun (only now!) to be afraid. Behind him, the iron door had
presumably closed, he couldn't go back, he had nowhere to go,
he had nowhere to return to. It was too late.

From the hall—at the back he glimpsed two or three statues

of a shadowy white, the light was dim there—led a white marble stair, very broad at the base, which twisted in a spiral and
grew narrower the higher he climbed, while the steps became
(or seemed to become?) taller. He climbed for a long time before
he reached a landing. The stair continued, but it was perilously
narrow, it no longer had a bannister, and the void that yawned
on the left and right terrified him, so he stopped. True, he was
slightly disoriented. He looked around, everything was a milky
white. He saw a corridor branching off and he set off along it,
taking short, hesitant steps, at the end he saw the statue of a lion
embracing a swan. He went closer, fearfully, but he didn't touch
it, it seemed to be made of plaster and was cracked here and
there, but the plinth was white marble, with barely visible bluish
veins, the same as the walls of the corridor.

Then there is a door with a white enamel knob, before which
I hesitate for a long time till I decide to turn it, first from right to
left, the wrong way, then from left to right, the door gives way,
another push and I entered a room not very large, empty, white,
in which I walked round and round, disoriented, I groped like
a blindman in the milky murk till finally I found another door
that gave onto another room where there was a statue of a griffin
that stood in the very middle, on the floor of white marble with
bluish veins, the same as the plinth of the statue, of all the statues
(be they lions, griffins, birds) in all the blindingly white rooms,
where everything was frozen, motionless, apart from the sheer
curtain, which you moved aside to look out of the windows, but
on the other side of the panes were other rooms or corridors just
as white, or the cheap plaster head of some lion.

Reaching another corridor, after climbing a narrower stair
with even higher steps, I entered a room, then another, I came
out onto a corridor, there was a plaster griffin or a lion embracing
a swan, to the left another corridor, an enameled doorknob, I
turned it, entered, went out, a corridor, another, a room, another
corridor, I'm walking faster and faster, I go up and down stairs, I
enter dozens and dozens of rooms, corridors, hallways, the same
or different, hundreds of steps, and here is the more brightly
lit landing (or does it only seem that way?), I turn right down

a corridor narrower than the others (or does it only seem that way?), I run, the corridor is empty, there are no statues, and at the end is a tall door, all white, of course, with a knob in the form of a lion with a gaping maw. I grasp the lion's head with both hands and turn with all my might, from left to right and from right to left, the door won't open, I try again, harder, I throw my whole weight at it, grit my teeth, in vain, I pound my fists on the door, kick it, the door won't open, it doesn't even quiver beneath my blows, and I grasp the lion's head and I twist it, wrestle with it, it's stronger than I, the door won't open, I hit it with my palms, my fists, my knees, I kick it, I beat my brow against it in desperation, I am sweating from the exertion, from running down the endless corridors, and the door won't open, it is unbudging, solemn, merciless.

I let myself drop, I slump to the floor, sliding down the door, to my knees, I stay like that for a long time, with my arms hanging from the lion's head, till I discover the keyhole, that hole shaped like an elongated skull, from which the key is missing, and I peer through it, I press my eye to it and (what was I expecting?) all I see is white, a dense, milky white, probably another room, which is locked for some reason. There is nothing else to do, I get up and go down the empty corridors at random, in places there are plaster statues of always the same animals, in different postures, I walk blindly (forward? back?) and because my eyes are aching from all that white, I try to walk with my eyes closed, sometimes I lose my balance and feel the cold wall of white-washed brick or even marble, I lean my palms against it, my forehead, and I stand motionless for a while. Then I set off again.

After a time, instead of white slabs I see cherry-red carpet underfoot and then I realize that I'm late; I pause to listen to the clacking of the typewriters, the typists' laughter, another ten paces, I press the door handle and the door opens.

But it is nothing but a pause, a parenthesis or, how can I put it? perhaps it is actually a dream in which colors and human faces appear to me, a dream that swiftly passes because it is made up of scenes just as monotonous as the others, scenes that are always the same, and evening comes and I get bored and I am afraid,

I leave the house looking for a film to watch, which is to say, scenes, in black and white or color, old or new; the usherette is always amazed at the expression on my face, then she feels sorry for me, or she understands me more than the others and gives me a knowing smile with those vulgar red lips of hers; and I enter and leave the cinema, I wander the streets, I'd like them always to be different, likewise the houses and the gardens of the houses that I enter without the slightest embarrassment; some have flowerbeds, petunias, flowering tobacco, irises, and I throw myself down among the flowers hoping that the night will pass more quickly or, if possible, that I will fall asleep; although I know I have no escape: the iron gate, majestic, black, looms before me and it's enough for me to stop for only a second to find myself on the gravel paths once more, among the grey slabs, around which I walk gripped by senseless fear; the swords glint in the moon-light, and then I enter, I step inside the hall and, even though the movements have become mechanical by now, I hesitantly climb the white marble stair, I cast a furtive glance at the statues in the more shadowy corners of the hall, I climb, I sense the stair grow-ing narrower, the steps taller, and here is the landing, sometimes I don't stop, but it's all the same because I still have to come back down in the end, the stair grows narrower and narrower, darker and darker, and it comes to a sudden end in the darkness, my head bumps against something hard, the ceiling? I turn back, dizzied by the white emptiness that yawns all around the stair, I reach the landing, I take the first corridor (is it the same one?), then another, I enter a room, another room, a corridor, a room, another, another corridor, and finally the door that I recognize by the lion's head that serves as a knob.

A vast, white emptiness . . . Nevertheless, from time to time, there is a blue strip, a glossy ribbon of blueness and another of greenness underneath reward my eye exhausted by so much white. And I kneel and I wait, I have been waiting for so long, even if in the meantime my feet hurry over a cherry-red carpet, toward a room with human faces and gestures of tenderness or rejection, where sometimes I speak, which is to say, I lie, I recount films I haven't seen. I wait. Not for the door to open—I now know that it won't open, I have grown more modest—I now patiently wait to glimpse those blue strips and the green ribbons, the sky and the plain beyond, which gleam only for an instant and only for those who kneel with their foreheads pressed to the cold white of the final door.

From the Nightmares of My Childhood

I. Fragment

THERE WERE CORRIDORS long and narrow dark and naturally damp here and there a small barred window through which could be seen yet more walls as dark and as dank a bluish-grey light seeping as if from under the walls and gravel that crunched underfoot by now nobody was shoving me from behind any more but it was so frightening and so cold!

Somewhere in the distance wings struck up against the walls.

Then the children passed two by two they trampled the crunching gravel wearing long raw-silk shirts shaved bald their round heads emanated a thin bluish light they strode solemnly confidently they had been walking like that since who knows when traversing corridor after corridor with the same short firm steps with the same elongated chlorotic faces in perfect file leaving behind them a pleasant scent of soap and cleanliness their arms were lopped above the elbow the stumps swathed in huge bandages of dazzling white.

It started to rain.

A warm slightly perfumed rain wetted my tensed body I held out my cupped hands to rinse my face I no longer felt so cold and gradually I managed to move my legs farther then behind me once more I heard the sound of claws and again I felt the pitchfork tines prodding my hips I moved in a daze unable to stop I dragged myself limply down yet more corridors dark and narrow the gravel screeched beneath my staggering feet in places the corridor unexpectedly opened onto vast blue vaults they amplified the crunching footfalls creatures with gorilla bodies and long vulpine faces were hacking with cleavers at flesh laid on stumps flesh red with congealing blood lean flesh mangled by cleaver blades shapeless heaps of flesh I crossed those bloodied halls at a run and once more I felt the menace of the pitchforks and the noise of stalking claws behind me.

Somewhere in the distance wings striking up against walls.

And again the children passed files of white shirts a procession of dazzlingly bandaged stumps small firm steps without sadness their heads shaven bald emanated a bluish light.

There were corridors long and narrow dark galleries strangulated by walls walls walls and beyond them yet more yet more walls walls walls.

II. The Corridor

BEFORE ME STOOD a massive throne, as tall as a choir stall, its high back ornamented with arabesques embedded in the hard, glossy wood, probably oak. Behind me I feel the edge of a table and, when I slide my foot underneath it, a large chest in the Braşov style: flowery lid, padlocks, corners clad in iron. I'm on my knees, I push the throne with both hands, bracing my back against the quite narrow and increasingly painful edge of the table, although I know I'm not going to be able to budge it so much as an inch. I push desperately, my muscles tensed to bursting, the veins in my neck, on my temples fit to explode, but in vain: the throne does not budge. Pressed up against it is a yellowish desk and on top of it, upside down, a table with spindly legs, a kind of gueridon, and then another table, a heavy, oval table, also with its legs in the air, then yellow chairs and stools, piled on top of each other between the legs of the table, and behind them a glossy black cupboard, resting at a tilt on the desk and a few other pieces of furniture which, from where I am, are hard to make out in the semi-darkness. And cupboards upon cupboards, commodes, wardrobes, tables, armchairs, sideboards with mirrors or sliding panes, dressing tables, chairs large and small stacked higgledy-piggledy, most of them lacquered black, but a few of them yellow or red, and mirrors as far as the eye can see, silvery-green eyes.

It is a long corridor, crammed with furniture, dozens, hundreds of pieces of furniture. There are narrow spaces in between, but they do not communicate with each other; even if I decided to scale the furniture like an alpine crag, it wouldn't get me very far: the barriers rise almost to the ceiling, which is in any event not very high, pyramids of chairs and tables, so many precariously balanced obstacles. It will be a long time before I dare to clamber up all this wooden tracery; particularly toward the top, the chairs with the long thin legs, some of them curved, in the dim light, the pallid green light that I suspect comes from a widow at the very end of the corridor, the legs of the chairs and the tables, the sides of the tall cupboards, all of which is multiplied by the reflections in the mirrors and up above, next to the ceiling, the branches of the chandeliers, which have no bulbs, they are nothing but claws and crystal pendants, all of it forms a bizarre terrain, a frozen, terrifying vegetation—I don't have the courage . . .

Behind me there is even less light. Long black or brown tables, padlocked chests beneath, dressing tables above, commodes and armchairs, all of which nonetheless allow a glimpse of a tall white door, as if made from plaster, so dim in the green semi-darkness. A little to the right of the door there is a dark, narrow corridor, where I can't make anything out; there is probably furniture barring the way, cupboards, tables, armchairs, all kinds of furniture, hidden in the darkness.

I push with all my might, desperately, although I know that I won't be able to budge the throne, and I push it forward, not even to a side where there is a sliver of space. When I tire, I look at the intricate arabesques of the throne, I run my hand over the red griffins carved on the chest beside it, the lions with gaping maws, the mermaid caryatids of a gueridon, and I thrill with horror at the glint of the mirror hidden behind the back of a chair. I have to get out of here, once and for all, I have to brave the obstacles, to scale the heights like a doughty mountaineer, and, no matter how long it takes, to reach the end of the corridor, from where the green light shines through a window, sometimes bright, sometimes watery. I try to take heart, telling myself that the first barrier, which is tall and almost as broad as the corridor, will be hard to pass, but then, once I've gained some experience and I can see the window in front of me, the climb will be easier. Maybe there won't be so many obstacles after that: a few tables, chairs, filing cabinets, the usual office furniture of a public building, albeit untidier, dustier, with chairs piled on top of tables as if in readiness so they can clean the floor, and with unemptied wastepaper baskets and tables thick with dust. But even so, so far as I can tell, clambering up onto the table behind me, beyond the first wall of furniture there are other walls, maybe not so high, but just as dangerous. The whole corridor is obstructed with wave upon wave of furniture and the more closely I look,

in the intervals when the light grows brighter, the more my hope
diminishes. It's not at all easy to clamber up onto the lookout
post behind: first I rise slowly to my feet, my head bowed, as if
in guilt, hunched in fear of hitting myself on the corner of the
cupboard propped on a slant against the commode on top of the
table, I place one knee on the narrow strip unoccupied by the
commode, one hand gripping the handle of a drawer and, finally,
I manage to lift my other leg up and, my temple wedged against
one side of the cupboard, I peer in the direction of the window. I
remain in this position for a long time, waiting for the moment
when the light will grow brighter, but the few moments in which
it does grow brighter pass so quickly that I only have time to
glimpse one or two pieces of furniture somewhat farther away:
hideous, merciless monsters of wood; I pick out an upside-down
cupboard or sideboard, its doors hanging like crippled limbs, the
thin legs of chairs, the bars of chair backs; I see all these through
the bars of yet other chair and table legs, occluded in places by
the menacing bulk of a cupboard; sudden, terrifying glints, and
from up on the ceiling, the arms and claws of the chandeliers.
Nowhere is there any room to pass. And what silence! I can hear
my heartbeats, that familiar whining and rushing sound in the
ears when there is complete silence. I start to feel afraid: such
silence, such motionlessness. I am unable to overcome my fear
and when I clamber up onto the commode, I bang the cupboard
with my fist a few times, but the noise is faint, muffled, as if
the cupboard were crammed full of meat, leaving not a single
inch of space within; on thinking about it, it is as if I can smell
the meat, the blood in my nostrils: creatures, warm bodies, but
hacked to pieces, crushed, chopped by cleavers, by long, sharp
knives, mounds of flesh, there in the cupboards, commodes,
sideboards, wardrobes all around me, behind all those closed
doors, in the locked drawers, which I feel the need to kick, to
pound with my fists.

    And again I shove desperately, clenching my jaws, I force
myself to look neither left nor right, but only at the dark brown,
almost black, chairback in front of me. There is no symmetry
in the arabesques carved there, there is no sense to the straight

and curving lines, the absurd, abstract convolutions, the dust,
the reek of mold. I close my eyes, stop pushing, absently finger
the ancient back of the throne, I run my fingers over the smooth
runnels of the carving, and the smell of dust, mold, carpenter's
glue soothes me a little. I no longer push. With my eyes closed,
I await the window, that is, first the stair, the sound of my footfalls, those of a child running home after school, taking two,
three stairs at a time. I didn't stop when I got to the bottom; the
heavy door, the thick windowpanes and the iron (the cold iron
bars!) then the street, the people in a hurry, with large, veiny
hands, briefcases, hats and caps pulled down low; I didn't stop,
I would carry on down the narrow stair, darker in the cellar, the
passageway with its smell of mold from the cellar, and the little
window in the corner that gave onto the garden. A little window,
patched with cardboard in one corner, dirty, dusty, but on the
other side of it, the tall, green grass, the leafless trees with their
little pink flowers or red, orange, glossy fruits, and those boys,
tall, lithe, with bows over their shoulders. I didn't know how
to reach that garden, the space beyond the window, so green,
airless, endless, with no left, no right, I had to content myself
with hanging from the window ledge to look through the dirty,
dusty windowpane, which I always had to wipe with my sleeve.
I would see the white stallion pass by, with its flowing, lion's
mane, which hung to down to the grass in long locks, the magnificent, immaculate stallion, and the boys: how tall they were!
they lowered their heads, their bows to the ground; birds with
long, multicolored tail feathers and small, darting heads adorned
with green and blue tufts landed in the trees. Then I would flee
from the window, for I was afraid of the archers' eyes, their long
arms bending their bows, their sharp, lethal arrows aimed at the
birds, and I would run back down the dark, dirty passageway,
illumined only by the green of the window, I would run up the
stairs lest I see the window red with blood. It was dark outside,
I glimpsed the yellow headlights of passing motorcars and the
blue and red lights of the endlessly flickering advertising hoard-
ings. My eyes ached. I didn't know what to do. I went back
downstairs to the passageway in the cellar. I fearfully went to the

window. The archers had not released their arrows and the birds were waiting motionless in the trees. the ivory stallion with the lion's mane passed once again and the boys lowered their heads and their bows.

With closed eyes I wait by the window, the stair that leads down to the cellar, the little window patched with carboard and the archers, the stallion, the master of the garden and the birds with lyre-shaped tail feathers; I wait with my forehead resting against the furrowed back of the throne, let me run down the stairs whooping and, in fear, but also enchantment, let me go down the passageway that smells of mold. But the image does not coalesce; the grass has no blades, it is like a slime and in it there are halves, quarters of bodies, a bow on a shoulder, an out-stretched arm, and nothing more; there is no stallion, but only the head of an abstract horse, only a head, like a chess piece, and I have to will it to be white, I have to will the green grass and the multicolored birds; dreary snatches of what once was, fragments, what torture it is to piece them to together, and my eyes ache, my forehead, pressed against the throne, hurts. Only the smell of mold remains and, at intervals, the smell of blood.

And with all my might I push the throne, with both arms I push it forward, not even to the side, toward the gueridon with the red griffins and the lions with gaping maws, where there is a little space. I push stubbornly, desperately, and at the same time, I wonder whether my efforts are in vain, whether they are stu-pid. For I very much want to reach the window finally; to hang from the sill (I have grown since then, I would easily be able to look out of it while resting my elbows on the sill) and to see once more, even if only for a few moments, the tall green grass, the lithe archers, the birds: so many colors, so many wonderful colors in that still, gentle, green light; I want to be afraid of the stretched bows and then I want the ivory stallion to appear, the majestic master of the garden, and I want the archers to lower their heads and their bows.

I kneel and push the throne, which is made of solid oak and is probably glossy. I feel the sharp edge of the table in the small of my back. My back aches and my arms ache, my veins are swollen to bursting and it is silent, I hear the uneven beats of my heart. I keep pushing with all my might, even though I know that I won't be able to budge the throne. I look to the right of the throne, shielding my eyes from the door of a cupboard, hanging like a crippled wing, a cupboard that has toppled over a table and a number of chairs that must be resting on another table, and a little way away I glimpse a snatch of mirror in which is reflected, like an evil omen, the bulging black handle of a chest. I'm tired.

Nonetheless, I have nothing but this corridor crammed with furniture, dusty, upside-down tables and chairs, cupboards and chests and armchairs and the smell of mold and blood. Perhaps at the edges there are doors or hatches hidden in the wall, masked by the furniture, but they are locked and on the other side, even if they are not locked, on the other side, the same as in the drawers of the cupboards, the commodes, the nightstands, there is crammed meat hacked by cleavers, or maybe there is nothing, a void. O, God, it is the same corridor and the same window with the good, green light, but the corridor is now a labyrinth and the window is so far away. And I have grown, I am tall, when I stand up I bow my head as if in guilt, like a man flinching from a blow, so much fear! I am tall, I am strong, perhaps not tall and strong enough to smash all the furniture, all the obstacles, all the walls.

Waiting

It's raining, for days on end it's been raining, a steady drizzle, without surcease, and there is no sign that the rain is going to stop, the clouds are still closely packed, neither very high, nor very low, it's as if there were a single cloud, a gigantic whitish-grey belly, it's raining, and the oak to the right of the storeroom is sodden, waterlogged, its leaves hang motionless, as heavy as lead, the goods train that passed at dawn seemed barely to make headway through the liquefied air, the engine driver gave a vague wave of his hand: "It's a second Flood!" and attempted a smile, he made no response to that smile, you couldn't tell for sure whether it expressed sympathy or, quite the contrary, sarcasm, or perhaps both the one and the other, he made no response to the smile and stood shivering inside his waterproof cape, his left hand holding the dripping flag, his other hand in his pocket, he made no greeting, but merely raised the flag, that red rain-soaked scrap of cloth, and signaled departure half a minute earlier, not that it was of any importance. Manolache came out to stand on the threshold of the storeroom, or rather the former storeroom, with an old overcoat over his shoulders—the old man was cold and probably he was feeling unwell again—the train set in motion, creaking from every joint, and the rain continued to fall, at the same rate as it's falling now, he looked out of the window, it seemed to have grown a little lighter outside.

He got up from the chair, picked up his red cap, which was placed on top of the birdcage, and crammed it on his head, he opened the creaking door and began to descend the stairs. The previous evening, Lică had been willing to bet his life that the rain would stop. The three of them were playing cards, the same as every evening, and Lică was in high spirits, he was winning. "That's what you think," said Manolache grumpily and the stationmaster said, "Come on, play the game, in any event, it's not up to us." "Nothing is up to us," muttered Lică, "Nothing is," said Manolache with satisfaction, slapping his final card on the table, "Sorry lads, but this round's mine."

He entered Lică's office and seated himself on a rather rickety chair, one leg was coming unglued and wobbled, as did the chairback. Lică was dozing with his head on the table. He gave a start. He turned to the mustached man with the red, almost cherry-red, cap and started prattling away, quickly saying everything he had to say: "No train until lunchtime, then a goods train that's in a hurry, won't be stopping, the express will pass through at the usual time, nothing else has been announced. Mind you don't fall off that chair, it's busted real bad," he added, changing his tone. The stationmaster got up and went to the chair on which Lică was sitting, there were no other chairs in the dirty, dusty, unswept room. Lică made to stand up. "Sit down, don't worry. The slow train's probably late," added the stationmaster. I don't know, they still haven't announced anything. For a space both were silent, probably thinking the same thing, in any event, when the stationmaster asked, for the umpteenth time, "What the hell were they thinking of, cancelling the service?" the other man made no reply, but merely shrugged. To tell the truth, the question required no answer. They'd been asking each other the question for the last six months or more, first of all in genuine bewilderment, as it was the only passenger service that stopped at their station, and then in increasing resignation: they'd exhausted every hypothesis, every explanation. At first, when they found out about the cancellation of the service, they'd furiously set about writing a memorandum that stretched to quite a number of pages; they'd worked on it a whole week. They ended up quarrelling because of that damned memorandum; Lică insisted on expressions that were trenchant, even violent in places: "we regard it as a flagrant abuse that . . ." and "it is a mockery, an act of dastardliness . . ." and "why not rip up the railway line while you are about it . . ." "What do you mean, rip it up?" laughed the stationmaster. "Exactly what I said, abolish it . . ." The stationmaster stood up from the table and started pacing up and down the room. He couldn't send a memorandum like the one that young signalman wanted to write; he was barely out of school. And then again, he had to admit, they hadn't cancelled the service just for the sake of it. There'd been that accident . . . "What has the one thing got to do with the other?" asked Lică, losing his cool, "the goods train was derailed because of the snow, and the passenger service wasn't due for another three hours. What, haven't there been other accidents on the line?" "There was another one, a long time ago," said the stationmaster. "I was the signalman at another station."

The stationmaster said nothing more, he turned on his heel and went to the window. Lică joined him. It was still raining, the forest could be glimpsed, dark, lifeless. "Where can it have got to, in this rain?" The stationmaster asked the question in a whisper, his lips almost touching the windowpane, which misted slightly. Lică bowed his head. With the steel toecap of one boot he was scraping a floorboard. "Is it in the forest? Can it have found shelter in the forest?" The signalman went back to the table on which stood the telegraph transmitter and started clacking away.

They'd had a blazing row; Lică had wanted to leave, to hand in his resignation. And he'd been wrong. He'd lost his temper and had unable to reason straight. "You tell him, Mr Manolache!" The old man would shrug or hunch up, wringing his hands, what power did he have . . . And in the end, the truth is that nobody alighted at their station any more, not since it became possible to reach the sanatorium more easily from the other side; on this side, the road was completely broken and all kinds of wild beasts roamed around. Yes, that's right, you only ever got a hunter or some nutcase who didn't even hang around in the station long enough to ask directions or what the state of the road was like before quickly setting off through the forest with a rucksack on his back. Lică went out, slamming the door behind him. "That's no way to carry on," said Manolache, shaking his head. For three

days, the signalman and the stationmaster hadn't spoken a word
to each other apart from the bare necessities connected to the
train timetable. After which they made their peace, the three of
them got roaring drunk, they sang and stamped their feet, oho,
the things they did! When a train was announced, the stationmaster puffed and sighed, buttoned up his blue tunic, took the
flag from the neck of the bottle of rum they'd drained earlier, and
went out onto the platform. "Look at him tottering," said Lică
gleefully, looking out of the window, "you'd think he's hanging
onto the flag to stop himself falling." Manolache knocked back
his drink and hiccoughed: "A good job this train flashes by,
nobody will see him, nobody will be looking at him." Then the
stationmaster returned.

Manolache came inside too, the water streaming off his old,
ragged overcoat. "You can hear the wolves howling like it's winter," he said and sat down on the rickety chair that leaned against
the wall. Nobody said a word. Lică was running the palm of his
hand over a lever, the stationmaster was busy twirling his moustache, all three of them were pensive. It was still raining outside.

In the end, they hadn't sent the memorandum. It would have
been pointless: maybe nobody would have even bothered to read
it, or else it would have taken it so long for it to come to the attention of some dyspeptic bureaucrat and then to be passed higher up,
that nobody would have paid any attention to it. Even Lică was
agreed on that. From the mechanic on a goods train, they bought
a pack of Hungarian playing cards, almost new—theirs were in
tatters—and they played from dawn till dusk. "You shouldn't have
let it go," said Manolache, shuffling the cards, "mark my words,
you shouldn't have done it. You made a big mistake . . ." The
stationmaster made no reply and then Lică spoke, albeit without
much conviction: "It had grown," he said, "where could you have
kept it? It didn't fit inside the cage any more." "Come on, play,"
muttered the stationmaster and it wasn't till two or three days later
that he said: "We had to release it, it had grown . . ." "Mark my
words," said Manolache, stubbornly, "you shouldn't have."

"What time is the express due?" asked the burly man with the
moustache. Lică made no reply and the other man didn't push

it. Probably nothing had been announced yet, and Manolache said: "Are we playing?" But it was obvious from a mile off that he wasn't in the mood. "I've got a pain here," he said, pointing at the left lapel of his overcoat. "Why don't you take that wet overcoat off?" said the stationmaster. "I had a dream last night," the old man went on. "Don't anybody ask him what he dreamed," said the stationmaster, getting up and going over to the window. The clouds seemed to have thinned out. Manolache sighed. He had dreamed he was at the circus and he'd taken his undervest off after rehearsals. Only two spotlights were on, by the stands to the left. From that same direction appeared the lion, grinning like a man, approaching him without haste. It was looking at him intently, with its yellowish, perfectly round eyes. Only the two of them remained in the ring. He looked up above and the big top was no longer there, the starry sky was visible, far, far away, very far above, or very far below, and he grew dizzy, the ring somehow started spinning around and he felt himself sliding (no, he didn't take flight!), falling as if down a well after leaning too far over the side and the lion was falling too, or perhaps the lion was flying, it slid softly down his body which was tumbling into the sky as if into water . . .

It was true, the clouds had thinned out; they were no longer so densely packed. A faintly rosy light had started to glow over a section of the forest. He gripped the window sneck with his fist and waited. In the room all that could be heard was the drizzle, that monotonous, exasperating patter, and the breathing of the other two men. Manolache's breathing was labored, he was almost panting for breath, bent double on his chair; Lică had twisted around, away from the table, and was looking at the window, trying to peer over the stationmaster's broad shoulders: the sky seemed to be growing lighter. "Come over here a moment," the stationmaster told them. Manolache gave a start, as if awakened from sleep. Lică stood up and went to the window; the old man followed after a long moment. The stationmaster grasped the signalman's arm: "Look," he said, "there, above the forest." "Yes," murmured Lică, "it means it's going to take flight. I don't think it's raining over there any more either . . ."

That morning, it started to snow again. Wearing just a grey pullover, with his pointy sheepskin cap pulled down over his ears, Manolache was shoveling the snow off the platform and from next to the track, throwing it on the other side of the line, where, over the last few days, he'd built a rampart of snow taller than your chest. The stationmaster appeared at the window of his room on the upper floor, one cheek covered in shaving foam. "Good morning, Mr. Manolache!" he called and waved his arm, the hand in which he was holding the razor. Manolache turned his head toward the window, his sheepskin cap had fallen down over his eyes, he tried to push it back, he tripped over a rail or even his shovel, which slid past his legs, and he fell on his back in the snow. At the window, the stationmaster laughed heartily, he was in just his shirtsleeves, but he didn't care about the cold, what cold! Above the forest the sun had emerged from among the clouds. What a wonderful morning! And all of a sudden, here's Lică, he comes out of his office and shouts something. Manolache had still not picked himself up out of the snow, it was comfortable there, the stationmaster was laughing his head off, "What's that you say? I can't hear you," after which he started laughing again. Propping himself up with the shovel, the old man had picked himself up at last. "The 4233 has been derailed," boomed Lică's voice, "the express is going to stop here, until further instructions." "Derailed? How? Wait there, I'm coming down," shouted the stationmaster. "Just let me get my coat," and he wiped the foam of his still unshaven cheek, Manolache had planted the shovel in the mound of snow and gone inside the Traffic Control office, after Lică. Lică was busy with the telegraph transmitter, which was clacking and whistling at a great rate. "What's it say, what happened?" The stationmaster came in, with a solemn, comical face, it was plain to see that one cheek was unshaven, and there was still a bit of foam under one ear. He came in and slammed the door. On his head he wore the red cap, his tunic was unbuttoned.

"I'll bet you that by tomorrow the sun will come out," said Lică, dealing the cards. Neither of them answered him. "Don't you think?" he said and paused still holding the rest of the cards, he looked at the other two, in amazement or interrogatively, and repeated: "By tomorrow the sun will come out." "Deal the cards and spare us your theories," said the stationmaster, and Manolache muttered something about his rheumatism, which foretold nothing good. "Your rheumatism is wrong this time. Or maybe not, maybe it isn't wrong. The weather is changing, that's what! It's going to be nice, the sun will come out, that's why you're aching. Come on, play," said the stationmaster, "since it's not up to us." "Nothing is up to us," grumbled Lică, which cheered up old man Manolache somewhat, "Nothing is," he said, with obvious satisfaction, tossing a card on the pile in the middle of the table, "nothing."

And now, in front of the window, Lică might have said: "Look, I was right, it's not raining over the forest any more and it's going to stop raining here, either." The stationmaster grasped him by the arm, he was excited, the same as every other time: "Look over there, above the forest." The sky had taken on a rosy hue, as if it were reflecting a small fire or a pyre built in the forest. It was the signal. "Of course it's not raining any more," whispered the man with the moustache and then clasped the young man's arm in a claw-like grip. The sky grew even redder and from among the trees of the forest a silver-grey eagle took flight, it rose in a dizzying spiral, like the thread of a screw, rending the rosiness, the redness of the sky. "How big it's grown!" marveled Manolache, holding his hand to his mouth. "It keeps, growing, yes, it's growing," said the man with the moustache from between clenched teeth. The eagle looked smaller and smaller, wheeling higher and higher into the sky, looking down at the forested hills and the railroad that snaked among them. "It hasn't flown for a long time. Or else it flew and we didn't see it. Maybe it flew at night . . ." "At night? It can't fly at night." "Why can't it fly at night?" "It just can't. It's too dark, it's not a bat . . ." The stationmaster fell silent. The other two men's chatter was starting to get on his nerves; he turned away from the window, took a few steps around the room, and went out. It was no longer raining outside.

He hadn't been in a town since Maria's funeral. She hadn't wanted to be cremated at the sanatorium or buried in the nearby village. They'd had to carry her to the other station, on the other side of the forest, where they put the body on the train. But that had been possible only after the autopsy, which had been unavoidable; the people at the hospital had been dead set on it: "It's in the interests of science," they said, "and it's no skin off your nose anyway." In the end, he had agreed to it, they'd placed her on a bench in the clearing in front of the hospital and he'd waited for science to be advanced a little. Old man Manolache had come with him to help, Lică had remained at the station, on his own. After that, things had gone more quickly, the other station wasn't far, and from there to the first town was less than an hour by train. The funeral was over with the greatest of speed: there were just the two of them, the priest, and the gravediggers. They were back by the same evening, bringing with them a crate of rum and a pack of playing cards.

Winter was beginning. The rains had swiftly turned to sleet and snow, and within a short time, the snow covered everything. It snowed almost every day. On two occasions, special crews arrived to clear the line of snow; the snowplows of the locomotives often couldn't cope. It was around then that the accident happened. It wasn't a catastrophe to be reported in the newspapers: only two people died, and a few others suffered injuries of varying severity. And nobody was to blame. The train was derailed on a bend where the wind had piled up the snow, it was snowing large flakes and all that the engine driver could see was white before his eyes. He wasn't going very fast, but the rails were probably crusted with ice on the bend. It would have been terrible if they hadn't been able to halt the express coming behind the goods train; it had left the final station before their stop and was racing along, despite the snow, at an insane speed, as it was late. The engine driver saw the signal and came to a stop exactly in the station, where the three men, headed by the tall man with the moustache, were standing to attention, in a state of great excitement. At the windows of the carriages appeared the faces of the passengers, more cheerful than surprised. It was snowing so beautifully! And when they found out what was happening— some said that they might have to wait until that evening—most of them got off the train. Never had there been so many people on the platform! The stationmaster bustled back and forth, not knowing what to do in such a situation. Lică was chatting to the conductor, and Manolache vanished, in fact, no, there he is, in front of the storeroom, looking attentively and, obviously, over-awed, at all the elegant strangers thronging the platform; some of them entered the station office, where they found nobody, they came back out, saw the stationmaster, who was walking up and down the platform pointlessly, his cherry-red cap crammed down over his head, they went up to him and asked him for something to drink. "Manolache!" cried the stationmaster, and then the last bottles of rum were put up for grabs. On finding out that the train would be staying there for at least a few more hours, others set off toward the forest, chattering in delight about how beautiful the view was. A few of them even had skis, Manolache pointed them in the direction of a path, down which the young-est and boldest ventured, advancing a few hundred meters into the forest, on the road to the sanatorium. Only the beautiful lady who spoke neither Romanian nor French (she was Swedish, Lică later claimed, in the long discussions the three of them had), the tall woman with long blond hair, wearing a white pullover and blue trousers, only she, at first, refused to get off the train, preferring to sit in her compartment; in the overhead rack there was a birdcage which later the stationmaster was barely able to lift, lugging it down the narrow corridor of the sleeper car. She lay on the lower bunk, with her hands beneath her head, calm, waiting. Once or twice she got up and went to the window in the corridor, the stationmaster was just passing, then she went back inside the compartment, she looked for a few moments at the eagle chick, which was tapping its beak against the bars of the cage, and then she lay back down on the bunk, assuming the same position. Outside, the other travelers were walking up and down or talking among themselves in little motley groups. the train naturally had a dining car, but at lunchtime, they all were seized by a terrible hunger and there was no room for them in the carriage, the food had to be taken to the station building, to the former waiting room, and even to the bedrooms of the

three railroad men, who made no objections, showing themselves to be very hospitable. The snow continued to fall in large,
fluffy flakes. Ultimately, the good cheer was not much in keeping
with the reasons for that unexpected stop, but nobody seemed
to think about that. It was also at lunchtime that the tall blond
lady appeared on the platform; she climbed down from the train
without hesitation (being Swedish, as Lică explained the next
day, she was accustomed to far heavier snowfall than that) and
went straight up to the stationmaster, who stood out from all
the others thanks to his red cap and athletic frame. The words
she spoke could hardly be understood by that burly man who,
not knowing what to do—he had suddenly found himself face
to face with her—twisted his moustache nervously. Nor were
they able to understand each other by means of sign language:
slightly flexing her knees, she spread her long arms and flapped
them like wings, before abruptly moving them in front of her
and using her hands to indicate some object very small in size,
whereupon she spread her arms once more and waved them up
and down a few times. "She's a loony," the stationmaster said to
himself, and gently stroked his chin. "Maybe you're hungry," he
said, raising two fingers to his lips, and then placed his hand over
his stomach, but she continued to flap her arms and, at intervals,
leaned toward him and indicated some kind of small object with
her hands: a cup, or a snake, or a parrot, he couldn't tell what.
She then took him by the hand and pulled him toward the train.
As they climbed the steps of the carriage he admired her legs and
her haunches, clad in tight blue trousers, he followed her down
the corridor, they entered a compartment, she turned to him
and smiled.

He walked a few paces toward the forest and then came to
a stop. The ground was sodden from so much rain, in places
his boots stank into the mud higher than the laces. The cries of
the birds were strident, minatory; cries short and long pierced
the even rustle of the waves of leaves, a strange panting sound
came from beneath the earth. In the distance could be heard
groans mingled with murmuring and grunting, a uniform scraping, a persistent scratching and, above it all, the rat-a-tat of the

woodpeckers and the shriek of the owl, the hoarse howling of the wolf, and then a moment or two of silence, with nothing but the soft rustle of the leaves and yet again the previous din and small wings fluttering in fright. Better he go back. Almost the whole night he had sat at Manolache's bedside and now his head was aching. "The old man's dying," he said to himself, "he hasn't got much longer," and that instant, a loud fluttering was heard above the forest and a shadow fell over the trees. "How big it's grown," murmured the stationmaster, and now all that could be heard was the rustle of the leaves, the eagle had probably descended to the clearing next to the sanatorium, where Lică insisted they take the old man. "But how do we get there, the path's impassable, and do you know what, Lică?"—and he moved closer to the signal-man, his eyes glistening with excitement or perhaps fear—"I don't think they're taking people at the sanatorium, what I mean is that you know it's in need of repair, it was decrepit . . ." "Nonsense!" said Lică and looked at the old man, who was groaning softly, the palm of his hand pressed to his chest, "the truth is you're afraid." The stationmaster said nothing, it was only later, after the express had passed through and it started drizzling again, a steady downpour that could be heard pattering on the tin roof of the storeroom, it was only much later that he took Lică aside and begged him to take the first train and fetch a doctor. "It's pointless our telephoning, you have to go there yourself. You're a clever lad, you'll manage. Please go. We can't carry him given the state he's in, and then we'll see . . ." He was surprised by the readiness, even the haste, with which Lică agreed to go and fetch a doctor. There followed a night of agony, the old man tossed and turned in a delirium, he groaned in his sleep, woke up and talked incoherently; but even so, there were snatches that made sense, to do with his youth, when he had been an acrobat in the circus: he kept saying something about a trapeze suspended high up in the big top, about a lion that swooped down or fell on top of him, about them both sliding down a well full of stars. The old man's face was contorted in his effort to speak, to tell him something . . . But he couldn't help him.

He turned on his heel and headed back to the station, trying to sink into the mud as little as possible. Again he heard the sounds of the forest, now seemingly louder: the shrill cries of the birds and the muffled writhing of bodies creeping, running, crouching among the tree trunks. He could not help himself and suddenly turned his head. There was nobody behind him, there was nothing untoward to be seen.

"There in the corner," groaned the old man, "look, there he is," and he pointed his withered arm at a being visible only to him. The man at his bedside mopped the beads of sweat from his brow, he took the glass from the table and holding the back of his neck, helped him to drink. "No, I'm not afraid, really I'm not." "Why should you be afraid," said the other man, "you need to be patient, you have to wait." And outside it rained continuously, a dense drizzle; the rain came down tenaciously on the roof and the leaves of the oak tree, on the tracks along which no train had passed for twelve hours. Toward morning, the old man finally fell asleep, with one hand resting on his chest, the other clutching the edge of the bed. The rain had stopped; it could no longer be heard. Day was breaking. He went into the telegraph room, pressed a lever, then another, he turned a knob, then another. Nothing. The telegraph transmitter had fallen silent. He rested his head on his arms and sat like that for a long time, without thinking, feeling himself sinking into a damp darkness or, quite the opposite, floating up, like the body of a drowned man rising to the surface.

It wasn't easy to carry the birdcage along the narrow corridor of the sleeping car, even though the train carriage was empty, everybody had alighted and now they were walking around on the platform or behind the station—the more adventurous ones had set off down the path that led through the forest, carrying their skis—or else they had sat down to eat in the waiting room or in Lică's room, since there were no seats in the restaurant car. The birdcage banged against the walls of the corridor, and taking fright, the bird was trying to spread its wings, jabbing its beak against the bars or through them, at the man's thigh, which luckily was encased in the thick blue cloth of his railway uniform. The woman brought up the rear and whenever the man turned his head, an enigmatic smile appeared on her face, the same smile as before, in the compartment, when he had grown all flustered and tried to embrace her, before realizing how ridiculous he was; her smile was mechanical, as if at the push of a button a little pink bulb lit up behind her forehead, illumining her face and her blue eyes. She pointed at the birdcage and gave him an order in that harsh language of hers. He looked at the cage, then at her, and nodded his head obediently. He felt guilty about his stupid gesture of earlier and she grabbed the sleeve of his coat and lifted his arm and he understood or thought he understood this time, he stood on tiptoes, grasped the cage by its golden bars (were they really made of gold?) and took it out into the corridor. The woman smiled at him. He took the cage up to his room, beneath the puzzled eyes of Lică and the old man, then he went back out to fetch water and meat, the eagle was thirsty, it almost broke the cup, lunging at it with its hooked beak.

It was raining outside, for so many days it had been raining constantly, a steady drizzle, the clouds remained clumped, neither high nor low, it was as if there were a single cloud, a huge grey belly; it was raining, and the oak by the storeroom was sodden, swollen, the leaves were motionless, leaden; not one train passed through, for so long a time not a single train had passed through, and Lică hadn't returned. There was no way he could . . . From time to time he went out onto the platform, shivering in his waterproof cape, holding that dishcloth of a flag, which he took with him without even realizing it, probably out of habit, and he stood motionless in the rain for a long time, gazing vacantly down the railroad track. He was waiting. The old man had died, his eyes fixed on one corner of the room, he had lifted his head with a final effort, trying to stretch out his arm, but he didn't have the strength, his head fell back on the pillow, one hand clasped the fabric of his shirt, remained frozen in a claw, the stationmaster placed the other hand next to it and finally closed his eyelids, opened the window: outside it seemed to have grown lighter.

He went inside Lică's office and sat down on a chair in front of the table on which rested all the complicated telegraph equipment, now covered in dust. He pressed a lever, turned a knob, then gave up. Back then, when they found out about cancellation of the service, they'd furiously set about writing a memorandum that stretched to quite a few pages and they ended up falling out over it. They had a serious quarrel. Lică had threatened to leave, to hand in his resignation. He'd blown his top, he no longer even knew what he was saying and he was wrong, which is what Manolache thought too: he was wrong. The proof being that in the end they didn't send any memorandum, it would have been pointless, maybe it wouldn't have been read, and even if it had been, "You tell me, what do you imagine could have been done about it, once it's been decided, that's the way it stays. It's not up to us." And Lică muttered, "Nothing is up to us." "Nothing," said old man Manolache merrily. In the room, all that could be heard were the tiny raindrops, that monotonous, exasperating patter. But even so, the clouds seemed to have thinned out and they weren't so dense any more. A slightly rosy light had started to glow over the forest. He clasped the window sneck with his fist and waited.

Outside it was snowing. After a while the rains turned to sleet and snow. Soon the snow blanketed everything. It snowed almost every day, the same as in the winter of the accident. It hadn't been a disaster reported in the papers; and nobody was to blame. The train had been derailed on a bend, Lică was shouting at the top of his voice, and the stationmaster, up there, at the window, although he had heard, he cupped his hand to his ear and leaned out across the windowsill. "A goods train has been derailed," Lică shouted again, "the express has to stop here until further instructions." Manolache picked himself up and planted the shovel in the mound of snow. The engine driver saw the signal and, even though he was going at an insane speed—the train was late—he managed to brake exactly in the station, where all three were standing to attention, excited as could be. It was snowing large flakes and it was so beautiful that all the passengers alighted on the platform. She was the only one who didn't get off the train, at first, she preferred to stay in her compartment, maybe she didn't know what was happening, she didn't understand what anybody was saying; she had a manner of speech that was harsh and melodious at the same time and he shrugged, maybe she was hungry, he lifted his hand to his mouth, then his stomach, "Are you hungry?" Slightly flexing her knees, she spread her long arms and flapped them like wings, she flapped them a number of times. Then she leaned toward him and indicated some kind of small object with her hands, a snake or a bird, an eagle chick with moist round eyes, which she kept in a cage with golden bars, there on the overhead rack. He tried to embrace her, but he quickly realized that he had wrongly interpreted that mysterious smile which had lit up her face like a bulb when you flick the switch. It wasn't easy to carry the birdcage along the narrow corridor of the sleeping car, even though the train carriage was empty, everybody had alighted. The birdcage banged against the doors, it was heavy, and the bird was trying to spread its wings, jabbing its beak against the bars or through them, at the man's thigh, encased in the thick blue cloth of his railway uniform. The woman brought up the rear and he stopped to wait for her.

She was Swedish, claimed Lică, dealing the cards: blonde, tall, white sweater. She couldn't be anything other than Swedish. So she must be accustomed to snow a lot more terrible than . . . That was why she was in no hurry to get off the train, and when she did decide to get off, she did so casually, without looking around her. "I'll bet she was Swedish." Nobody answered him "Don't you think?" he said and paused, still holding the remaining cards, he looked at them in amazement said, stressing each syllable: "She was Swe-dish!" "Come on, deal the cards and spare us your theories," said the man with the moustache, casting a glance at the cage, and Manolache, who had caught that glance, muttered that it had been a mistake to release the eagle, he shouldn't have done it, "Mark my words." Then he rushed to the window. He never made mistakes. "Come here," he said and grasped Lică by the arm: "Look!" Above the forest the sky had turned dark red and after a short while the eagle burst into the air, as big as an airplane, and began to glide in broad circles, broader and broader, which also passed above the station. "Has it grown?" asked Lică and it was plain that he was a little afraid, not of the eagle that was growing so unnaturally (maybe it was some giant species from Sweden) so much as of the solemnity and barely restrained joy with which the stationmaster watched the bird's increasingly frequent flights. After that, Manolache took to his bed and the other two took turns keeping vigil at his bedside.

He walked a few steps toward the forest and came to a stop. The ground was sodden after so much rain. He had buried Manolache there, behind the station: he had dug a deep grave, fearful lest the wolves, scenting the corpse, come and dig it up with their claws. One whole morning he stood and dug in the rain. From the forest could be heard the shrill cries of the birds piercing through the rustle of the leaves and the even, monotonous patter of the rain; from afar came groans mingled with muttering and grunting and small wings fluttering in fright. It was as if a strange panting were coming from underground. There was a whole industry down there, factories and workshops working secretly, doggedly, day and night, without pause. He continued on his way, strolling peacefully; he had nothing left to do, no duties, he was free from morning to evening. He took a few deep breaths. For an instant he thought of going to the sanitorium—he would get there in three hours if he lengthened his stride—so that he could telephone, explain the situation, the old man dying, Lică running away, the telegraph transmitter breaking down, there were so many things to report; too many, even, all at once like that! And why didn't you report earlier? What could he have said? He was ill too, he'd probably caught a cold the day he buried the old man, he'd dug a very deep grave . . . And why were no more trains passing through the station? Now it was his turn to ask the questions, and he would speak in a deeper voice and even give a stern cough. They had closed down the station, and they had abandoned him there, in that wilderness, although to be honest, the thought didn't frighten him, on the contrary, from the very depths of his being he felt rising to his conscious mind a joy for which he could find no natural justification. He realized he was happier than he had been for a long time, perhaps happier than he had ever been. What was the point of going all the way to the sanatorium? Who knows?

Maybe there had been nobody there for a long time. Maybe he would find empty buildings, part of the roof would have been torn off by the wind, birds would be nesting among the exposed beams; beasts of the forest would have got inside, they would be prowling around the wards, among the beds, in the operating theatre; the last of the patients would have given up the ghost under the hot breath of the beasts licking their withered legs and arms. And even if it wasn't like that, even if the sanatorium had been repaired in the meantime, even if cutting-edge equipment had brought from abroad, even if the patients were lying on the terrace in multicolored chaises longues attended by tall, blond women in white uniforms, even if the sanatorium was thriving, even if the countless motorcars parked on the meadow in front lent an extra touch of modernity, there still would have been no point in him going. He had to remain at the station, he couldn't abandon his post, even though the telegraph transmitter was broken and the trains no longer passed through—or maybe during the days and nights when he had lain sick or when he had been sleeping to recover his strength, maybe lots of trains had passed through, one after the other, as many trains as passed in a week, in a month . . . In any event, he had to remain there and wait with his flag at the ready, the flat of his hand raised to the peak of his cap, always standing to attention, motionless.

Outside it was snowing. Manolache, with his pointy sheepskin cap pulled down over his ears, was shoveling the snow. The stationmaster was laughing up there in his room and calling out to him, "Good morning, old man Manolache," over the forest the sun had started to emerge from among the clouds. After that, the accident had happened and the express had been forced to stop in the station. Almost all the passengers had got off the train, they were as happy as little children. It was snowing beautifully, with large, fluffy flakes. Later on, the blond woman came, who started flapping her arms like wings, and then she pulled him behind her to her compartment, where he tried to kiss her. She didn't even try to fend him off, but from her smile he realized how ridiculous he was being. He saw the birdcage and even then, even in that moment, he still didn't understand. That came only much later, after the express had left, and after many nights: the old man had died, and Lică, the talkative signalman, had disappeared, he had run away. Only much later.

It's raining outside, who knows for how long it's been raining uninterruptedly, a steady drizzle; but soon the clouds will no longer be so dense as to make you imagine it is a single cloud, a huge, whitish-grey belly; it is raining and the oak tree by the storeroom is sodden; its leaves hang motionless, leaden. For a long time not one train has passed through, in vain does the stationmaster stand on the platform in his waterproof cape, holding his sopping wet flag in his left hand, his other hand ready to make the salute. Not one train passes through the station now, weeds and grass have sprouted among the ties, and the rails have started to rust.

But nonetheless he waits. He carefully shaves every day, he puts on his new clothes and waits. He sits on a bench on the platform and listens to the rustle of the forest, the noise the rain makes as it hits the leaves. From time to time, distant groans and screams. He sits and gazes for a long time at the forested hills that surround the station. Sometimes the rain stops for a short while, a swathe of sky starts to turn red, somewhere over the forest, and all the little sounds are drowned out by the flutter of huge wings. He then rises from the bench and standing to attention he watches, his throat dry with excitement, as the eagle flies in circles or a spiral. His face lights up as if in ecstasy, his fingers clench the handle of the flag or the blue frieze of his uniform. It won't be long. He will wait patiently, ready at any moment. The rain will then stop, the clouds will crumble and the wind will scatter them, the sky will clear. He will rise at the break of day and his eyes will glitter with joy. In the mirror he will smile as enigmatically and intensely as the woman in the train. He will shave, put on cologne, take great care brushing his clothes, which are like new, although lately he has been wearing them every day, from off the cage he will take the red cap that is almost a shade of burgundy and he will go down to the platform. He will enter Lică's office, look at the dusty telegraph, and then go to the window and look at the sky as it turns slightly pink above a spot known only to him. He will go outside, take a few steps in the direction of the forest, listen to the leaves rustling in waves and the cries of the birds, he will hear all the groans and grunts and far-off shrieks rising as if from underground or rather from the depths of the woods. He will turn around, gaze out at the other hill, the one in front of the station, he will look at the rusting railway tracks, overrun with grass and weeds; he will seat himself on the bench on the platform, and he will wait, carefully scanning the sky.

There, above the forest, the sky will continue to change color: it will gradually turn from pink to red, and then a brighter, stronger red, crimson, an imperial red! And then all the sounds of the forest will fall silent, the only thing to be heard will be the flapping of the gigantic eagle's silver wings, as it bursts from the tree canopy, growing vast, darkening the hills and woods with its shadow, and it will fly higher, ever higher, gleaming silver against the crimson silk of the sky, it will wheel, once, twice, countless time, first soaring, then swooping, and it will wheel ever more slowly, above the railway station, above your head, your face transfigured with excitement, your eyes moist with joy, your throat dry, your muscles aching as you crane your neck to watch the ever broader, ever lower circles that the eagle traces in the sky, and finally, a shadow will darken all, you will start to unbutton your uniform, your shirt, as the eagle flies nearer and nearer, lower and lower, as its wings thrum, rocking the sky, as the branches of the trees toss, as the oak bends to the ground, as the station roof is torn off in the gust, shadow and cold, the silver wings ever closer, ever closer: you no longer see the sky, the eagle is now your sky and you strain your chest, your whole body making a final effort.

But until then it is raining outside, it is raining constantly, a dense drizzle, uninterrupt. . .

(*România Literară*, no. 43, October 1970)

Shorter unpublished texts

I Drowned in the Sky

To Leonid Dimov

I WAS SITTING on the shore and watching the giddy oscillation of the green seaweed, among which slipped long, panic-stricken ivory-white fish. Or maybe they were just dreamy little cloud-lets, languid, puffy monsters visible through the limpid water of the sky. Striped, bulbous backs sank lower and lower, into the depths. And oh, the frightened wheeling of the fishes!

Then, from somewhere very low, the RED HORSE loomed huger and huger. It froze against the backdrop of the sky, seated on its hind legs, its mane bristling, flaming. I prostrated myself before the red horse, moving to within just two steps of the colorless chasm. And I lowered my forehead and my eyes wearied by so much light.

A strange, shrill voice rasped my eardrums. I turned my head and beside me, undulating like a flame, there was a blue figure waving its arms threateningly. Its thin voice, like a needle raking my eardrums, sternly questioned me about my past, about my intentions.

I slowly turned my head with obvious scorn and gazed upon the motionless red horse once more. Splinters of light leapt from its mane. All the other moving things had left its vicinity. The bluish thin circled me a few times and then vanished as abruptly as it had arrived. The silence that had been disturbed by its squeaks once more enveloped all.

I don't know how much time elapsed. The horse shone as brightly as a sun beneath the cupola of curdled milk, and the light docilely trickled or else splashed, crushed by the glowing massiveness of the sun horse. Maybe not much time elapsed. When I looked back, over my shoulder, there were now two of them, creeping up to me, silently. And both of them rushed up and shoved me, without a word, into the translucent chasm of the sky.

Since then I have been falling and cannot stop.

14 August 1959

In a Tavern

IT WAS A SLUM TAVERN, dirty, evil-smelling. Tables of scuffed wood, tablecloths stained with gravy, wine, ash, rickety chairs, and smoke, thick smoke everywhere. Two dusty, spherical light-shades strained to shine through the fog. Anguished, booze-flushed faces loomed and vanished through the clouds of smoke. A hoarse voice called out for somebody to open the door, to let some air in. The tavern-keeper dozing at the counter clomped to the door and half opened it. Along with the cold night air, a little man slipped inside, with jaunty gait and his hands in his pockets. He looked around cheerfully, then walked over to a table at the back of the tavern, where he sat down uninvited next to a giant of a man who was sitting in silence, leaning on his elbows, raising his glass to his mouth to drain it at intervals.

"How's it going? How's it going?" At which he slapped the massive shoulder with his scrawny yellow hand.

The giant shifted in his seat, the chair beneath him creaked, but he made no reply. He grasped his glass and knocked it back, glugging. An enormous, ugly face, with wrinkled skin around the inexpressive eyes, which were perhaps blue, perhaps grey. The large nose, planted in the middle of the face, resembled a potato; it was the only part that had escaped the invasion of ginger bristles. The red hair, cropped as short as a brush, left only a very little room for the corrugated forehead. He was hideous, matchlessly repulsive. The collar of his shirt was frayed, grubby, his clothes were in tatters, hung from him in rags.

The newcomer ordered himself a drink. And since he was bored, he began to go from one table to another, eager to strike up a conversation with somebody. Without much effort, he managed to find a few blokes to chat with, whom he ushered to his table, holding his hands on their backs.

"Here he is," he gesticulated, "this is my friend. He's as strong as the lot of you put together." And he gave a snort of laughter.

The giant remained silent, bowing his head. He was picking at a dry stain on the tablecloth.

"He's my friend," repeated the little man.

Without looking up, the friend leaned to one side and spat. The others smiled in embarrassment and didn't dare to sit down.

"Come on! Sit down . . ."

When the jug was empty, there was no need to make any signal for the barefoot little boy to come any fill it: his sole purpose in life seemed to be to watch for empty glasses and bottles.

The little man still seemed as cheerful as could be, he was chattering away, and after a while, he winked and said to the giant: "Go on, tell them where God is . . ."

The response was a mutter. Not even now did he look up.

"He's shy!"

They laughed and clinked glasses.

In the meantime, the tavernkeeper had fallen fast asleep, slumped over the counter, snoring. The unwashed, barefoot boy came to pour the drinks from time to time, the soles of his feet smacking against the floor. There were bits of straw in his tousled hair, his eyes were sticky with sleep, and he gave off a sour smell of sweat. The fog had thickened once more now that the door was closed.

"Show them God! Go on, you son of a bitch!"

But the giant was silent, holding his head between his hands.

"Show us God!" another of them pleaded in a reedy voice. "Go on, show us Him!"

Then he stood up, as big as a mountain, and roared; he gave a long, despairing roar, like a spitted cow.

"Show us Him! Show us Him!" they all roared.

And silence suddenly fell. The giant wept, with his head between his hands.

All the noise had woken the tavernkeeper. Sleepily, he wiped down the tables abandoned by almost all the customers. He went and opened the door wide, he made a sign to the boy squatting in one corner, and went into the room at the back of the tavern.

They were the only ones left in the tavern. The glasses had emptied. The boy didn't come to fill them.

"He's my friend? Do you hear?"

He was slurring. Between his thin, purple lips dangled a cigarette end. He nodded his head and spread his long narrow fingers as he spoke. The others sang or rather squealed like pigs, banging their glasses on the table and stamping their feet.

Viewed from outside, from the silent street, frozen in the pale light of the streetlamps, the raucous, smoke-enveloped group looked blurry, faint. One of the little men had climbed up on a chair and was waving his short, thin arms. Then all of them stood up and walked hesitantly to the open door. They were tottering, stumbling into chairs and tables, singing, hiccoughing. The ox was swaying, waving his arms, trying to keep his balance.

"He's my friend, you know! But he's a pig . . ."

And the giant tripped over the threshold, fell onto the sidewalk, tried to pick himself up, fell again. In the door of the tavern, the little men were cackling as if demented. Some of them were jumping up and down on one leg, pointing their fingers, others were clutching their sides; and the reedy voice cheerfully explained that he was a pig, a wonderful pig.

After crawling on his hands and knees a few yards, he got up, clutching a telegraph pole, and started to howl, raising one arm to the sky.

"He's furious there aren't any stars," explained the little man. And they all laughed shrilly, stridently. "He's a pig!" The little man went up to him and nudged him with his foot.

"On all fours! Do you hear!"

"Faster! Faster!" Yelled the little men behind him. And they tittered, tottering, leaning against each other.

"He's my best friend . . ."

The giant advanced on all fours, breathing heavily, stopping at each streetlamp, which he hugged, weeping. In their merriment, they were all stumbling, falling over, picking themselves up, swearing, but laughing all the while. "He's a pig!" They slapped their sides and sniggered in satisfaction.

And all of a sudden, the giant got up. He grew uninterruptedly, bigger and bigger in the yellow light of the electric bulbs, and from his lips, agape in terror, dripped repulsive spittle. With slow but precise movements, he took off his tattered clothes, which fell to the ground like peelings, his eyes bulged in horror at his enormous body, down which streamed sweat and the brighter and brighter, yellower and yellower light of the streetlamp. Around him, the little men stood frozen, dumbstruck.

August 1959

In the Salon

ONE EVENING, WHEN Manuel entered the salon, he found a large company religiously listening to the high and sedate song of a voluminous but stately woman. At the piano, Manuel's mother accompanied her, caressing the keys with her slender fingers. Everybody seemed captivated by Esmeralda's song. His aunt in particular: with parted lips, she tensely watched the singer's every movement.

Manuel crawled under the piano unobserved, where he began to count the guests' feet. Esmeralda's thighs were huge, ruddy hams. Leaning against a wall, the gentleman with the long face was smiling vacantly. They all clapped and cried: Bravo! Encore! His aunt wanted a more cheerful song. Wherefore she even strove to climb down from her high-backed chair and approached the piano. She whispered something in Manuel's mother's ear and softly tittered in great amusement. At the door appeared a short man in black clothes that were too large for his tiny body—a strange and at the same time comical little creature. You would have thought he was kneeling, so short were his legs. The singer began another song, a cheerful, jaunty one this time. The listeners tapped out the rhythm with the toes of their shoes, louder and louder, and finally they even clapped their hands in time. His aunt bobbed up and down on the high-backed chair, her eyes shining in pleasure. The little man, motionless at first, suddenly turned around and started dancing around the room with small, rapid steps. He nimbly raised his arms, as if they were on

271

strings, he threw his head back, and then he came to a stop on one leg, leaned forward and span. A larger, heavier step, and one thin arm, sliding through his coat sleeve, grew fantastically long, until it reached the ceiling; the other arm, pointing downward, touched the floor.

In that position, he received the admiring and frightened applause of everybody in the salon.

1959 (?)

The Obstacle

THE OTHER DAY, as I was going to work, a strange, obdurate, aggressive man planted himself in front of me. He didn't say anything, didn't give any explanation: he just stood there, with his arms and legs spread apart, in the middle of the sidewalk, and wouldn't let me past. In vain did I ask him to step aside or else I would be late for work and because of that, my boss would make a big scene yet again and might even dock my wages. In vain. He stood without budging and stared at me with his bulging, expressionless, fish-like eyes. That frozen stare, which seemed to be focused on a spot in front of me, was somehow familiar. The rest of his appearance wasn't unknown to me either. That disheveled, haystack-like hair, although it was darker than hay, that big, slightly hooked nose, protruding from the middle of a face that was childlike, but weary and betimes clenched—I had definitely seen those features somewhere before. And then the repulsive wart on his lower lip . . .

Amused by the ridiculous improbability of the situation, my initial annoyance had passed.

"Perhaps you want to stab me or something?" I said, barely restraining my laughter. The wind was ruffling his hair, covering his prematurely wrinkled brow. He did not budge. Not one facial muscle twitched. I realized that he couldn't actually be dangerous. But I had to get past him one way or another; I could hardly stand there looking at his ludicrous mug for the rest of my life. I quickly got down on all fours and tried to crawl between his outspread legs (as if through a triumphal arch!). But just as quickly, he closed his legs, catching my neck between his thighs. I struggled furiously trying to stand up or at least to pull my head free—I felt like I was choking—but without success. He was stronger than me and, without weakening his grip, he nonetheless managed to keep his balance. I strained with all my might to topple him, but despite my best efforts, I couldn't budge him so much as an inch. A real athlete! Then I decided to resort to different methods. I started yelling for help at the top of my voice. I was hoping that in the end somebody would come and, out of pity or at least a sense of civic duty, rescue me from the humiliating situation in which I found myself. There were plenty of passersby at that hour. I could see their legs as they hurried to get as far away as possible from the place of my ordeal. The men's legs walked away more calmly, taking long, undaunted strides, but the women sometimes stumbled in their high heels, while the children's legs ran in terror. When I heard the whistle of a traffic policeman, I plucked up courage and let out a long, desperate roar. After that, other legs passed, untroubled, heedless of my groans. Curious children's legs then surrounded us.

Finally, realizing that I could expect no help on the part of the passersby, I began to beg forgiveness in a strangled voice. Although I wasn't guilty of anything. I could hardly be held guilty for so legitimate a desire as to walk down the street minding my own business, nor did it matter where I had been going: to work, to the pub, what did he care! What right did he have to stop me and torture me in this cruel and ridiculous fashion!

1960 (?)

Pantolin in Love

ONE COULDN'T SAY that Pantolin is handsome, but nor could one say he is ugly. After all, his green hair is so glossy and green, like the leaves of a palm tree!

When he walked down the street, intrepid, raucous sparrows hopped before him, and he had to jump over them lest he crush them. He was also loved by the pigeons, which wheeled around him, enveloping him in a cloud of feathers and down. It was the first time he realized he could not fly. At first, he couldn't believe it; imitating the birds around him, he lifted his arms and flapped them like wings. He did not budge from the pavement. That bond with the ground depressed him, humiliated him, even. He yearningly watched the easy flight of the pigeons and envied even the sparrows that preferred to hop . . . stupid birds!

Then suddenly she emerged from next to a tall building. Pantolin did not know whether he had ever seen a giraffe before. The giraffe quietly strode along on her long thin legs. Probably she did not even see him, so lofty was her head. Her velvety skin resembled his new suit. When the giraffe passed him, Pantolin pressed himself up against a garden gate to make room for her. Startled, the pigeons rose into the air, and the frightened sparrows flew onto the fence. The giraffe looked neither left nor right, and Pantolin was left feeling so small . . . He gazed at her sadly as she moved into the distance, making the same long, deliberate strides. As she was about to cross the road—she was probably heading for the park—Pantolin could no longer restrain himself and ran after her. Out of breath, he caught up with her just as she majestically reached the entrance of the park. Aha, now she'll have to bow her head, beneath the boughs. And maybe she'll catch a glimpse of him . . .

The giraffe did not stop, she did not enter the park. Pantolin followed her for a few more streets and then gave up.

On the days that followed, Pantolin roamed the streets in search of her. The sparrows and pigeons now accompanied him only rarely. Pantolin had become grumpy, he no longer hopped to avoid the sparrows, and sometimes he even waved away the pigeons in annoyance when they came too close to his thatch of green hair. It was true: Pantolin was in love. The longer he went without seeing her, the more his love grew. There was no doubt about it, he could not forget the giraffe's long neck and her graceful gait. Sometimes he hated her and that wholly unfamiliar feeling disturbed him greatly. He dreamed that one day he would find her and she would look down and come to a stop. And then, as he sometimes told himself, he would climb the highest tree, from where he would look deep into her eyes. He would summon the pigeons to flutter gently above them, keeping vigil over their love.

One day, wandering the streets, Pantolin came to a circus. In the foreground of the enormous poster at the entrance could be seen the long, supple neck of the giraffe. Drawn by the noise and the roars, Pantolin sneaked inside the circus, around the back of the ring. There, on the sand, a fat, red-faced man holding a whip walked menacingly up to the giraffe, who was cowering in the corner. She had lowered her long neck and huddled on the ground. The whip whistled and cracked. The curtain parted and three other giraffes demurely stepped through, each carrying a fat, ruddy-faced man on her back.

This cured Pantolin of his first love.

22 March 1961

On a Bench

(*Two muscular men in striped t-shirts are carrying what looks like a park bench. The carefully place it next to three sunflowers and walk away. The sky is covered with a sheer grey curtain. The sweet, even light gradually fades. A bench next to three sunflowers and nothing more. The bench is green and has short iron legs.*)

The old man walked, taking precisely measured steps, his head tilted slightly to one side. Under his arm he held a thick hardbacked book. A little dog came behind him. How comical was the dog! Its long, pointy nose, its crooked paws, its floppy ears. Its slick, glossy pelt, like a cat's. Never had I seen a little dog like it! The old man saw the bench and hurried toward it. He leaned forward and wiped the dust off it with a handkerchief. Then he called the dog. The dog leapt up onto the bench with ease. It wagged its tail, looking up at the old man. It was obvious it was waiting for a treat. The old man rummaged in one of his pockets and took out a sugar cube. Behind them, the sunflowers swayed. The old man folded his hands in his lap, resting them on the thick tome, and stretched out his legs. Ah! he sighed. And he smiled. The light caressed his veiny, weather-beaten hands. Next to him sat the little dog with floppy ears and warm eyes, as serious as could be.

It started to rain. It was raining hard, round, little drops. Struck by the beads of rain on its head and muzzle, the little dog opened and closed its eyes, slightly puzzled. There was puzzlement and sadness in its dark eyes.

It kept raining and raining. The sunflowers' petals drooped. They clenched their leaves to their wet stems. The little dog snorted, sneezed. The old man opened the thick tome and placed it over the dog like a tent. The rain started falling more heavily. Only the little dog's eyes could be seen, like glossy buttons. The old man hunched his shoulders together and leaned back on the bench. Locks of wet hair were plastered to his forehead. The rain enameled his face and his smile.

(*Two sturdy men in sailor's shirts appear from behind. A smile of satisfaction on their faces. They nudge each other, pointing at the old man, and walk away.*

The rain drops its countless thin, sonorous curtains.)

22 March 1962

The Lake

AN IMMENSE MIRROR, larger that the mirror of a telescope. Above
the mirror, the moon hangs somewhere high above. It is round, it
has no points, its cheek is aged. A few pale, paper lily pads. Long,
green and orange fish, stretched over the gleam of the mirror,
await the wind. On one side, a little way away, a few weeping
willows, with small, thin, motionless leaves. Then I arrived and,
squatting down, I started to blow. I filled my cheeks, let the
veins in my neck burst! Nothing budged. I was afraid to tread
on the mirror in my boots, to shatter it. And once again I blew
with all my might. I rested my heels of my hands on the toes of
my boots, with the tips of my fingers I could feel the cold steel
caps. Before me, the enormous mirror with long green, orange
fish. I blew with all my might. I was unable to budge so much
as the tail of a fish. The crinkled cheek of the moon was by now
even yellower. What a huge mirror, bigger than all the mirrors
in the world! the moon hung above the mirror as if in mockery.
Rigid, powerless, the fish languish awaiting the wind. I then
went in search of people. I went first to my neighbors. I begged
them to come with me. Some were too fat, others were bored,
but in the end, they agreed. They all came. I walked hurriedly
in front of them. They could barely keep up with me. Some had
goiters, some were obese, some were lame, some one-eyed, some
blind, some had crooked, drooling mouths, some had bulging
eyes, some had beady eyes sunk in their sockets, some had squa-
mous hands, some were bandy-legged, some tottered unsteadily

behind me. The women were elderly, with pustuled or withered faces, stupid or cunning faces, but they strode panting behind me. They walked in silence, I could hear their labored breathing, the smacking of their toothless mouths that dared not ask the question. They formed a procession, with the sturdier men who were fleeter of foot at the front, then the women, the children, the old folks, and trailing behind, the lame, the obese, and finally the blind, holding each other by the hand.

The huge mirror, as big as a lake, reflected the sour face of the moon. The crêpe-paper willows hung frozen in the yellowish light. The fish, the beautiful green and orange fish, were just as motionless, inert. Beached on the mirror's silver, they awaited the wind. We all came to a stop at the edge of the lake, we kneeled or crouched, and we started to blow. We blew so furiously that the roofs of our mouths dried up. In their zeal, some spat, some choked, some cursed and swore in frustration: grotesque mirrored faces, puffing cheeks, bulging veins, eyes popping from their sockets. We blew and pushing each other, we left the shore, we slipped and slid, falling on top of each other, an avalanche of exhausted bodies, shouts, clenched hands, panting breath, screams of fear. The blind were the last to drown.

July 1962

The Parade

THE VILLAGE MAYOR was right in the middle, in a viewing stand that was all gold and velvet. Above, the country's emblem shone in the sun. Before the parade began, the mayor stood up and slowly moved his hand from right to left and from top to bottom, by way of a greeting. All those below burst into applause. When he sat back down, he gave the signal. First of all, those in the blue shirts passed, tall, with stony oval heads. They marched in time with the brass band. Then came those in the green shirts, triangular, determined. Daggers glinted at their belts, their thorny moustaches bristled at every step. Then the big fat women come rolling along, like beer barrels, trundled by pale little men holding submachineguns. Rumbling behind them came trams, like enormous yellow mole crickets. The mayor mopped his brow with his handkerchief and smiled. He was so pallid . . . The parade picked up its pace. Angels with white and pink aprons sped past, and functionaries on horseback with gauntlets and pencils as long as lances. Behind them raced monkeys with blue hair and multicolored turbans. Then came gigantic furnaces pushed by muscular arms, footballers with their shirts pulled up over their heads, pairs of frantically copulating dogs, skinny old women on all fours as if about to puke, champagne bottles disgorging foam almost as high as the official viewing stand, heads then passed, hundreds of thousands of bare heads, old heads and [. . .]

1959-62

Rivalry

BENEATH A PINK SKY rise the castle walls and polished spires. A sky forever pink, without night, without stars. Although sometimes a yellow, squashed moon appears. At the foot of the thick walls stretches a lawn of stunted, prickly grass—translucent antennae of lunar insects. There is but one tree in the whole picture: a slender poplar thrusting at the moon like a lance.

At the castle's breast the coat of arms grows ceaselessly like a mushroom. The heads and claws of the lions become ever fiercer in their petrified wait. Maybe they will finally descend, cumbersome, trampling the steel blades of the grass, and the battle will recommence.

1959-62

How I Met Pantolin

To Leonid Dimov

I WAS SITTING with my back to the door, on a chair, in front of the desk, writing. And he probably had stood at the door for a long time before deciding to enter. Particularly since I didn't hear his first timid knocks. I was sitting with my temple and ear resting on one hand and writing. To the right was the gleaming black piano, its maw agape. A little farther away, the curtained window through which the light of afternoon was barely able to pierce. I sooner sensed him when he tiptoed into the room, I sensed the presence of somebody behind me, and it was then I turned my head. He was embarrassed, he was swinging his long thin arms as he made ridiculous bows, arching his legs without bending his knees. Then he did a pirouette, fluttering his arms like wings. And the way he was dressed! His legs seemed improbably long in his black silk stockings, and his thin, childlike arms and frail, skinny chest were covered in a kind of very baggy long-sleeved shirt, also made of some silky material, with large yellow and black checks. Yet another, even lower bow. I asked him no question; he introduced himself to me: Pantolin! And I nodded my head: I thought I had seen that sad smile, those misty, almond-shaped eyes, somewhere before. He had a long, immobile face, a prominent, albeit thin, and slightly arched nose. With a gesture—his hand suddenly poked out of the baggy sleeve—he asked me to have patience and, nimbly, albeit stiffly, because of his too long and too straight legs, he reached the door and three quarters of him vanished: a leg encased in black silk remained inside the room and it was then that I noticed he was wearing some kind of slippers that had pointy, curled toes with pompons on the end. He bent down to pick something up, very carefully, from outside the door. He straightened up and came back cradling at his chest something that later I was to identify as a duck. But a very unusual duck. Its predominant color was pastel pink, darkening to violet at the tail, and the wings were speckled with green and mauve, likewise the head and neck. He carefully placed it on the gleaming piano and, turning toward me, gave a shrug, not knowing what to say. I thanked him wordlessly and invited him to sit. He didn't want to sit down. To tell the truth, I felt a little embarrassed too; although I realized that Pantolin liked me. With rather awkward abruptness, I tried to persuade him to sit down and, wrapping my fingers around his arm, I discovered how thin he was. And I felt how he flinched. From the piano, the duck gazed at us fixedly, as if made of porcelain. It held its broad, bright red beak cocked slightly to the side. The light from the window glazed its head and back. Pantolin was looking at it too. Then, suddenly, he wheeled one of his arms, did a pirouette, gave a bow, with his legs forming a parenthesis, and slipped out of the half-open door without touching it. He closed the door behind him, softly, soundlessly. I ran my fingers through my hair and took a few steps around the room. I sat back down at the desk. To the right was the piano, too bulky, too black. Through the window, the light was ever dimmer, ever greyer. The duck floated silently in the gleaming waters of the piano.

1963

The Curious One

HE SLOWLY OPENS the door, crosses the threshold, a furtive glance, the thick carpet muffles his steps; he leans for a few moments on the armchair, resting his chin on the upholstered back, then opens another door, looking over his shoulder— nobody there, they're all asleep—and enters the living room. There it is! On the oval table of solid walnut, in the black fruit bowl with the rusty yellow leaves—a bird: as red as coral, it is sleeping peacefully beneath the heavy, bronze-red rays of dusk; as big as a blackbird, perhaps a little bigger, with a sharp, gleaming, violet beak; the feathers near the tail have orange tints, perhaps also because of the crepuscular light filtering through the curtains. The child gazes somewhat in astonishment: by the opposite wall with the cherry-red velvet sofa, there is another bird on the sideboard, also red, but smaller. The chairs around the table have short legs, but very tall backs, like knights in shakos, armor and horse blankets. He places his foot as if on a step—the horse is perhaps under the table, in any event it is white—and from the chair, lifts himself by his hands noiselessly up onto the table. The bird sleeps on, peacefully, it feels, it senses nothing. The child's knees are scraped and slightly green. He moves his arms, bends them, his elbows clenched to his chest, he hesitates, looks at the vitrine: a ray of sunlight gilds the stemmed glasses on the top shelf. Then suddenly, with both hands, he grasps the bird below its belly, he lifts it from the fruit bowl, raises it to his mouth, it is dear to him, it has a small head, ridiculously small, and look, now it has opened its round, gleaming eye; the bird trembles, its body is warm, frightened; the child is touched, he puts it back in the fruit bowl, almost dropping it; the bird takes fright, puffs out its feathers, stretches its wings, it has crooked black legs with dry wrinkled skin; it takes flight. It hits the lightshade with one wing, amber tassels clatter against each other. It flies around the room, he watches it open-mouthed, he likes it, but he is also afraid. Outside the light has faded, it is heavier, it is viscous, it is molten brass. Like a blaze, the bird flies around the lightshade.

April 1965

Simple Melody

I SWAM FOR A LONG TIME in the calm waters of the sky, here and there were plump, curly clouds like perfumed wigs and nicely drawn suns with long slender rays. I wasn't tired, sometimes I would come to a stop, resting the soles of my feet on the back of an endless passing whale, and I would have to hop up and down to stay in the same place. Then I would go into freefall and be forced to swim or fly, I couldn't really tell which: I would move my arms and from time to time also my conjoined legs, which I flicked like a dolphin. After a while, I saw an island, that one-legged table, like a mushroom. I sped in that direction and grabbed onto the edge of the highly polished wood, which smelled of vanilla. Huge violet ferns blocked my view. I pulled myself up onto the table. I crawled on my hands and knees through the thickets of blue and violet plants until I reached the back of a cupboard, whence I was able to view the rest of the island. She was there . . . With long, thin legs, breasts, wings, cradling that little creature without paws, with its rabbit ears and pike-like muzzle. She clutched the animal to her chest and her face was tender, her eyes were closed. She loved it. A short distance away there was a bird with a long, needle-sharp beak. It was pecking from a jug. I advanced a little and realized that the cupboard was in fact a grandfather clock with a perfectly round face, and instead of a pendulum, it had a small, perfumed hand. I stood up, bowed, the hand stretched toward me and I gripped it in my own brine-blanched, wave-beaten hand. I kissed it. In

that instant I sensed somebody looking at me insistently, menacingly. I turned around: clinging to the edge of the table was one
of those winged lions, but with the stupid face of a barber, a sub-
urban coxcomb, with wavy hair and a moustache. I greeted him.
He made no reply. He continued to stare at me threateningly. I
moved back and sank to one knee, holding my arms around the
grandfather clock. This only infuriated the lion all the more. He
beat his wings, rose into the air, and glided over the island. Was
he jealous? The woman opened her eyes and looked at the lion
that was swooping through the air like a madman. She started to
laugh. She raised one arm and waved to him, probably for him to
descend. The lion did not obey. It was only then that the woman
set eyes on me: I was naked there, behind the grandfather clock.
I was pressed up against it, craning my neck to watch the lion's
desperate flight. The woman lazily came over to me, her wings
rustling. I got to my feet. She was beautiful, she had the long,
blond hair of an angel, her wings were pink and orange. She wore
a short dress, but with a train, and her legs were long and white,
likewise her arms, like velvety plants that coil around your body
and dizzy you with their perfume and softness.

The lion now clung to the edge of the table with its claws, its
tail hung down like the tassel of a curtain, and its stupid barber's
head, with its wavy hair and moustache, turned to look at Gala.
The girl had climbed up onto the table among the flowers that
sprouted from the hard, glossy wood, growing almost as high as
the perfumed wigs of the clouds, and she stood there next to the
grandfather clock, cradling that little creature. She adamantly
refused, in vain did the barber implore her, moving his leonine
head and wings in every direction, his wings that were those of
a fallen angel. It started to rain.

The door opened and the stationmaster came in. He coughed
in embarrassment. The barber turned around and saw him. He
invited him to take a seat. The guillotine was in perfect working
order. Gala smiled, the stationmaster's head rolled down the steps
of the swimming pool into the water. Carnivorous fish rushed at
it and the barber once more started imploring Gala. She laid the
animal in the grandfather clock and with a deft movement took

off her wings. She then unscrewed her breasts and one leg. She took off her wig. She remained standing like that, on one leg, the drops of rain struck her ivory head making a harmonious sound.

The barber took down his guitar from the peg and started to play, using his strong paws with their long, hooked claws. Evening fell, a warm breeze swayed the flowers.

1970

Sketch

AFTER REACHING THE ZENITH, the sun suddenly stopped. It was a yellow, shiny button sewn on the sky. The people didn't even notice. In a hurry, sweating, dusty, wearing grey glasses, none of them raised their eyes higher than the traffic lights at the intersections. It was the middle of a working day. On a side street, a strange animal appeared, as tall as a man, but with a fox's snout and large, pricked-up ears. In its arms it clasped a small body with sad eyes and a slobbering muzzle. It took a long, stealthy stride, flexing its knees; it looked all around in fright, ready to make a run for it. By the time it reached a square, its eyes were red, bulging in fear. It almost got run over by a car. Terrified, it ran in a zigzag, bumping into passersby. A less busy street loomed in front: salvation. It dashed down the middle of the street, letting out squeals incongruous with its appearance. But even so, nobody was the least bit disturbed. Sweating, dusty, wearing grey glasses, the people were looking at the ground or, from time to time, at the clock.

Little by little, a bluish light, which was not the light of evening, settled over the town. And as if at a signal, the taller buildings soundlessly began to collapse.

One Winter Morning

I GOT UP from the piano and sat down at the window, leaning my elbows on the sill and pressing my forehead against the cold pane.

It was a gloomy winter afternoon.

The snow creaked under the shuffling steps of an old couple walking arm in arm, leaning against each other. After they turned the corner, all there was to see was the frozen park flooded with snowy whiteness and the petrified, deserted street. The smoke from the chimneys rose to the grey sky in almost straight lines. After a while it started snowing again, with large, sparse flakes. My arms had gone numb and my forehead felt icy.

Then, all of a sudden, from up the street a knot of frightened people came running, shouting for help. As they passed the window, I noticed that a black bird bigger than a raven clung with strong claws to the shoulder of each of them. They were shouting in desperation. The birds' faience beaks were poking around in the people's ears. The black wings were flapping against their tense faces. They stretched their impotent hands to the sky, they writhed in the blood-flecked snow.

I somehow pitied them . . . I even thought about opening the window, but I decided it would have been pointless.

They had now reached the park, where the fierce struggle continued. They were crazily bumping into tree trunks, rolling around in the snow, picking themselves up, vainly waving their too-short arms, begging for help that was not forthcoming.

The snow fell solemnly, passionlessly, little by little covering people and birds.

The door of the room opened with a bang. I gave a start, turned my head. Shivering in his threadbare overcoat, a small man with a red, rumpled face stood in the doorway. He quickly came up to me and grabbed me by the hem of my jacket.

"I am afraid, sir! I am very afraid!"

He clung to my legs, trembling. He stood pressed up against me like that, his face buried in my clothes, for a long time. At intervals, I patted his wet hair. Outside it was snowing with large, sparse flakes.

A Spring Day

FROM THE CRACK of an old wall poked the whiskered head of a rat. It sniffed all around, crouched back a little, and then took a running leap into the stunted grass by the wall. It scurried a little to the left, then hid behind a log. The tip of its tails swished agitatedly among the blades of grass. It sat up on its hind legs and stroked its whiskers with its forepaws. It was a rat in the prime of life, well-proportioned. It had a rendezvous there with another rat, and here it came: cumbersome, its body like a zucchini, creeping along the bottom of the wall.

"You're rather late, my dear fellow!" the first rat upbraided him.

The other rat blinked in dismay. Probably the too harsh light of that spring day bothered him. He twisted a paw and scratched behind his ear. They both suddenly raised their snouts. There was a sharp smell of smoke and another familiar, intolerable reek. The sky was like misted blue glass. They twitched their whiskers, wrinkled their snouts. The fat rat leaned over to the other:

"Smells like smoke."

"Yes, like spring. It's not cold any more."

The other rat's whiskers drooped. In the distance loomed the pales of the fence and beyond them the street.

"It's not cold any more. There's the sun, look!"

"It's like a . . . I don't know what."

"Like a piece of raw meat. It's getting redder and redder . . ."

It made your eyes ache to look at it like that. A file of hurried,

293

disciplined ants was ascending the log. From beneath it poked
the antennae of a beetle.

"It's a bit stupid."

"What is?"

"I don't know."

Behind them was an outside toilet, made of planks, and next
to it crates of garbage.

"Spring again, and then summer, autumn . . . an endless
round . . ."

The sun was sinking, bloodier and bloodier. Footfalls slapped
dully over the damp soil. First, the rats huddled closer to the
log. They tucked their tails beneath themselves and gripping
the wood with their claws, they waited. Then one of them said:

"Sometimes I feel like going wild. Come what may!"

The log smelled of cow dung and melted snow, of freshly
turned earth.

"That sun up there . . . Do you reckon it's big?"

"It's big . . ."

"Bigger than a cat?"

"A lot bigger . . ."

The fat rat turned around, wagging his comically thin tail, as
thin as a shoelace. The beetle came out of hiding: it was black
and glossy. It took two steps toward them, but changed its mind.

"It's stupid . . ."

And it didn't only smell of spring. In the outside toilet, they
knew, there was an enormous hole and inside it something viscous and strange-smelling. It smelled like the footsteps of those
creatures as tall as the sky. The wall smelled like that, too. And
next to the toilet outhouse, the crates of garbage, potato peelings, slops, rancid cabbage, something fluffy and blood-soaked,
and that smell. And the spoor left by the footsteps of those huge
creatures smelled the same. It smelled like that everywhere. And
now it is spring again and the soil is wet, long reddish rays of
light fall on the log, the sun is like a piece of bloody meat. Maybe
the sun smells like that too . . .

"You think the sun does too?"

"The sun does too, and the fence, and the slops in the crates.

They all smell like that. Even we are going to end up smelling like that too. It's awful!" They twitched their whiskers I disgust. Then, with hurried steps they swept across the stunted grass as far as the wall. The more agile of the two leapt into the hole and half-twisted around.

"The smell!"

The fat one crept along the bottom of the wall without looking back.

On the Street

I WAS ON MY WAY BACK from a friend's where I'd played a few games of chess. I was walking slowly, counting my steps, thereby calculating the distance between lampposts; sometimes I would discover that it wasn't the same and I would be surprised, even annoyed, since at the same time I thought I was to blame for not having taken equal steps and then I would start all over again. I would have liked there to be strictly equidistant lampposts, although I realized that then there would have been no point in continuing to count my steps. There weren't many people around, but even so, caught up in my toponometric calculations, I sometimes bumped into people and some of them displayed quite violent disapproval. I therefore moved to the curb, so as not to get in anybody's way. I hopped, holding my arms out to keep my balance and forbade myself any contact whatever with the sidewalk. On the curb alone. My isolation was ostentatious, some people noticed me, but in the end, it was my own business: they shrugged and hurried past. At intersections, I crossed at a run, eager to reach the other sidewalk as quickly as I could. The other curb.

But in the end, I still haven't solved the problem. I don't know whether the length of my paces is to blame or whether the distance between lampposts really isn't equal. Around me, all the people are passing by in a great hurry.

Excavations

THEN THEY MOVED on to the next street. It was hot, their picks and shovels weighed heavier and heavier. The air was heavy, too, oppressive, it carried it on their shoulders and the tops of their heads along with the sun and their pickaxes. One of them came to a stop and struck the pavement with his shovel, leaning on it like a walking stick. This was where they were going to dig. Across the road was a hairdresser's, whose doors were open, the hairdressers drowsy in the torrid heat. A little farther away, there was a greengrocer's. It was as if the sight of the vegetables made you feel cooler.

They started to dig. Stripped to the waist, their bodies glistened with sweat, their muscles tensed painfully but still rhythmically. The picks grimly struck the heat-softened asphalt. Chunk after chunk of road came away and the pickaxe blows resounded louder and louder. Drawn by the noise, a fat barber came outside, tapping his fingers with a metal comb. He looked in puzzlement and shrugged. Behind him appeared another two barbers. A few kids with catapults went up to the diggers. Below the asphalt, the soil was sandy, the diggers no longer needed picks. They straightened their backs they grasped their shovels with a fierce determination that was incomprehensible to the barbers over the road. By the time Ilinca arrived, the hole was already quite large. Two of the diggers had jumped down inside. Only the one that remained at the top saw the girl, but he didn't pay any attention to her. With her basket full of vegetables, she came to a stop on the pavement next to them and was looking at them curiously. That morning she had gone to buy milk and seen them on a different street striking the earth just as furiously. Later, she had seen them again, but she hadn't stopped, they were digging in a different place, their faces tense to the point of grimacing. They were tall, strong, the sweat trickled in rivulets down their broad sunburnt backs. Behind them they left deep holes in which the children played: the holes were casemates, the children found worms there, too. Ilinca stared in puzzlement, her head cocked to one side. She moved the basket from one hand to the other. She couldn't really understand. The mound of earth was now growing seemingly higher than the others. The diggers said not a word to each other, they didn't pause for a single second. In the hole, all that could be seen now were the tops of their heads. Why all this digging?

The barbers went back inside. The children left too, intending to come back that evening. This hole would be bigger than all the others, they told each other. Maybe inside it they would find the dragon, the serpent beneath the city . . . They looked at each other with a pleasant shudder. Ilinca was still standing there. She gazed at the broad back, the hairy arms leaning on the spade and the heat wrapped her in a soporific blouse. She ought to leave so as not to get into an argument at home. She no longer felt the weight of the basket. Her arms were leaden and her whole being was slowly melting. The men in the hole were no longer visible. The man at the top gave her a stern glance from beneath his bushy eyebrows, then briskly turning around, he signaled to the men at the bottom. He squatted and, leaning over the hole, shouted something to them. Ilinca couldn't make out the words, it was as if they were in a different language; nor could she understand the men's answer. By now, the sun had climbed to right above the street. The man rummaged in a chest and produced a rope; to the rope he tied a mud-caked bucket and he lowered it carefully into the hole. He pulled it back up full of miry earth that smelled nasty. He emptied it and once more he lowered it into the gaping hole. The sun had grown larger and it was as if it were rotating. Right above the street, above the hole, Ilinca could feel it on the top of her head, like a basket full of corncobs. Motionless, she gazed vacantly at the broad glistening back of the digger. There was nobody passing on the street . . .

Exotic Painting

NOT A BREATH OF WIND in those climes. The small island floated solitarily, surrounded by the unbounded ocean waves. Up above, a sky of honey with bluish tints, and the sun that seeped through it perfumed the yellowish sand of the beach, the large, fleshy leaves of the trees. The shoreline was smooth, bathed in little waves whose heated water was heavy with seaweed. And in the distance, the heat released a steamy veil that dissolved the horizon. The large, idle women lolling on the beach occasionally shifted, as sluggish as huge worms. Above them, the multicolored wings of butterflies cooled the sultry heat of their flesh. The naked bodies gleamed, enameled in the sun, they crawled to the ocean and immersed themselves in the warm green water. With their arms bent behind the backs of their necks, they floated among the seaweed that caressed their breasts and bellies. Having returned to the sandy beach, lying motionless as toppled amphorae, they stared placidly into space.

And perhaps evening never fell.

As if by miracle, a breeze sometimes began to blow. A wafting breeze fluttered over the island. The petrified leaves started to rattle. The wind became stronger and the women's long hair swayed in time with the waves, which now seemed to be leaping more gaily.

A ship now appeared on the horizon. It approached quite swiftly, unhesitatingly, its sails stretched taut. It soon hit land and the musketeers nimbly disembarked. An entire company of them. With tall boots and jingling swords. With long, care-fully twisted moustaches. With broad-brimmed hats and ostrich feathers. The king's musketeers! They were tall and sturdy, ruddy, mustached. The captain, taller than the rest, saluted the women's bodies. They raised themselves on one elbow. They were smiling. Suddenly, the captain turned to his men. A curt order. With swords raised, moustaches bristling, the troop made the honor-ary salute. One, two! One, two! Their tall red boots kneaded the yellow sand of the beach. They creaked. One, two! One, two!

In fright, the enormous butterflies zigzagged into the upper air. The musketeers marched around the beach. Another curt order. The boots came to a halt in the sand. And the brown, mustached musketeers bowed low to the women's bodies. The wind then stopped blowing. The shiny ocean froze beneath the sky of honey with bluish tints. The wave of heat settled once more. Since evening never fell on the island.

DUMITRU TSEPENEAG is one of the most innovative Romanian writers of the second half of the twentieth century. He is the author of *Vain Art of the Fugue*, *Pisgeon Post*, and T*he Necessary Marriage*. He lives in France.

ALISTAIR IAN BLYTH (b. 1970) has translated numerous works of fiction and philosophy from the Romanian, most recently the novels *The Bulgarian Truck* by Dumitru Tsepeneag and *The Encounter* by Gabriela Adamesteanu for Dalkey Archive Press.

MICHAL AJVAZ, *The Golden Age.*
The Other City.

PIERRE ALBERT-BIROT, *Grabinoulor.*

YUZ ALESHKOVSKY, *Kangaroo.*

FELIPE ALFAU, *Chromos.*
Locos.

JOE AMATO, *Samuel Taylor's Last Night.*

IVAN ÂNGELO, *The Celebration.*
The Tower of Glass.

ANTÓNIO LOBO ANTUNES, *Knowledge of Hell.*
The Splendor of Portugal.

ALAIN ARIAS-MISSON, *Theatre of Incest.*

JOHN ASHBERY & JAMES SCHUYLER, *A Nest of Ninnies.*

ROBERT ASHLEY, *Perfect Lives.*

GABRIELA AVIGUR-ROTEM, *Heatwave and Crazy Birds.*

DJUNA BARNES, *Ladies Almanack.*
Ryder.

JOHN BARTH, *Letters.*
Sabbatical.

DONALD BARTHELME, *The King.*
Paradise.

SVETISLAV BASARA, *Chinese Letter.*

MIQUEL BAUÇÀ, *The Siege in the Room.*

RENÉ BELLETTO, *Dying.*

MAREK BIENCZYK, *Transparency.*

ANDREI BITOV, *Pushkin House.*

ANDREJ BLATNIK, *You Do Understand.*
Law of Desire.

LOUIS PAUL BOON, *Chapel Road.*
My Little War.
Summer in Termuren.

ROGER BOYLAN, *Killoyle.*

IGNÁCIO DE LOYOLA BRANDÃO, *Anonymous Celebrity.*
Zero.

BONNIE BREMSER, *Troia: Mexican Memoirs.*

CHRISTINE BROOKE-ROSE, *Amalgamemnon.*

BRIGID BROPHY, *In Transit.*
The Prancing Novelist.

GERALD L. BRUNS, *Modern Poetry and the Idea of Language.*

GABRIELLE BURTON, *Heartbreak Hotel.*

MICHEL BUTOR, *Degrees.*
Mobile.

G. CABRERA INFANTE, *Infante's Inferno.*
Three Trapped Tigers.

JULIETA CAMPOS, *The Fear of Losing Eurydice.*

ANNE CARSON, *Eros the Bittersweet.*

ORLY CASTEL-BLOOM, *Dolly City.*

LOUIS-FERDINAND CÉLINE, *North.*
Conversations with Professor Y.
London Bridge.

MARIE CHAIX, *The Laurels of Lake Constance.*

HUGO CHARTERIS, *The Tide Is Right.*

ERIC CHEVILLARD, *Demolishing Nisard.*
The Author and Me.

MARC CHOLODENKO, *Mordechai Schamz.*

JOSHUA COHEN, *Witz.*

EMILY HOLMES COLEMAN, *The Shutter of Snow.*

ERIC CHEVILLARD, *The Author and Me.*

ROBERT COOVER, *A Night at the Movies.*

STANLEY CRAWFORD, *Log of the S.S.*
The Mrs Unguentine.
Some Instructions to My Wife.

RENÉ CREVEL, *Putting My Foot in It.*

RALPH CUSACK, *Cadenza.*

NICHOLAS DELBANCO, *Sherbrookes.*
The Count of Concord.

NIGEL DENNIS, *Cards of Identity.*

PETER DIMOCK, *A Short Rhetoric for Leaving the Family.*

ARIEL DORFMAN, *Konfidenz.*

COLEMAN DOWELL, *Island People.*
Too Much Flesh and Jabez.

ARKADII DRAGOMOSHCHENKO, *Dust.*

RIKKI DUCORNET, *Phosphor in Dreamland.*
The Complete Butcher's Tales.

RIKKI DUCORNET (cont.), *The Jade Cabinet.*
The Fountains of Neptune.
WILLIAM EASTLAKE, *The Bamboo Bed.*
Castle Keep.
Lyric of the Circle Heart.
JEAN ECHENOZ, *Chopin's Move.*
STANLEY ELKIN, *A Bad Man.*
Criers and Kibitzers, Kibitzers and Criers.
The Dick Gibson Show.
The Franchiser.
The Living End.
Mrs. Ted Bliss.
FRANÇOIS EMMANUEL, *Invitation to a Voyage.*
PAUL EMOND, *The Dance of a Sham.*
SALVADOR ESPRIU, *Ariadne in the Grotesque Labyrinth.*
LESLIE A. FIEDLER, *Love and Death in the American Novel.*
JUAN FILLOY, *Op Oloop.*
ANDY FITCH, *Pop Poetics.*
GUSTAVE FLAUBERT, *Bouvard and Pécuchet.*
KASS FLEISHER, *Talking out of School.*
JON FOSSE, *Aliss at the Fire.*
Melancholy.
FORD MADOX FORD, *The March of Literature.*
MAX FRISCH, *I'm Not Stiller.*
Man in the Holocene.
CARLOS FUENTES, *Christopher Unborn.*
Distant Relations.
Terra Nostra.
Where the Air Is Clear.
TAKEHIKO FUKUNAGA, *Flowers of Grass.*
WILLIAM GADDIS, JR., *The Recognitions.*
JANICE GALLOWAY, *Foreign Parts.*
The Trick Is to Keep Breathing.
WILLIAM H. GASS, *Life Sentences.*
The Tunnel.
The World Within the Word.
Willie Masters' Lonesome Wife.
GÉRARD GAVARRY, *Hoppla! 1 2 3.*

ETIENNE GILSON, *The Arts of the Beautiful.*
Forms and Substances in the Arts.
C. S. GISCOMBE, *Giscome Road.*
Here.
DOUGLAS GLOVER, *Bad News of the Heart.*
WITOLD GOMBROWICZ, *A Kind of Testament.*
PAULO EMÍLIO SALES GOMES, *P's Three Women.*
GEORGI GOSPODINOV, *Natural Novel.*
JUAN GOYTISOLO, *Count Julian.*
Juan the Landless.
Makbara.
Marks of Identity.
HENRY GREEN, *Blindness.*
Concluding.
Doting.
Nothing.
JACK GREEN, *Fire the Bastards!*
JIŘÍ GRUŠA, *The Questionnaire.*
MELA HARTWIG, *Am I a Redundant Human Being?*
JOHN HAWKES, *The Passion Artist.*
Whistlejacket.
ELIZABETH HEIGHWAY, ED., *Contemporary Georgian Fiction.*
AIDAN HIGGINS, *Balcony of Europe.*
Blind Man's Bluff.
Bornholm Night-Ferry.
Langrishe, Go Down.
Scenes from a Receding Past.
KEIZO HINO, *Isle of Dreams.*
KAZUSHI HOSAKA, *Plainsong.*
ALDOUS HUXLEY, *Antic Hay.*
Point Counter Point.
Those Barren Leaves.
Time Must Have a Stop.
NAOYUKI II, *The Shadow of a Blue Cat.*
DRAGO JANČAR, *The Tree with No Name.*
MIKHEIL JAVAKHISHVILI, *Kvachi.*
GERT JONKE, *The Distant Sound.*
Homage to Czerny.
The System of Vienna.

FOR A FULL LIST OF PUBLICATIONS, VISIT: www.dalkeyarchive.com